THE INEAN DEBACLE

HENRY EATON

ALSO BY HENRY EATON

Siege of Ardon

Coming December 2025

Eye of the Storm

For
Lori, Samantha, Heather & Matthew

This book is a work of fiction. Names, characters, places, and incidents either are products of the author's imagination or are used fictitiously. Any resemblance to actual events or locales or persons, living or dead, is entirely coincidental.

Www.HenryEatonBooks.com

ISBN: 978-0-9852617-7-1

Manufactured in the United States of America

ONE

NEBRASKA, August 2221

A young girl raced through a cornfield, squealing as she looked over her shoulder. She spied her younger brother and older sister, catching up to her dozens of rows behind. She dove behind a pile of dried corn stalks tied with baling twine. She took her laser pistol, made from a few sticks tied together with string, from her pocket and shot back at them. She jumped up and aimed at her siblings as they got closer. "Pew, pew, pew!" she yelled. She dove back down and panted while waiting for them to catch up. They were playing a game called *Space Rangers*, a hit Halo-Vid program they watched each week. Even though she was only nine years old and the middle child, she took charge of playtime while they were outside. To her, it felt like a role she was comfortable in.

She glanced over the pile as a blinding flash of light threw her backward to the ground with a thud, knocking the air from her lungs. Her fake laser flew from her hand. The gold cross she wore around her neck fell off into the dirt. She tried to scream but could not. She was pinned down by some force and could not break free.

In the white light, a creature took form. It was hideous, and it bared its rotten teeth at her. The beast snarled as spit flew from its mouth. Its stubby horns protruded from its head above its fiery red eyes. She tried to scream but could not. She did, however, wet her shorts. The creature pulled back and held a blonde-haired woman by the throat with one hairy, ugly paw. Her feet dangled as the woman tried to hit the beast. It was useless. He was too strong and too large. She was tall for a human but vastly smaller than the beast that held her. She wore a uniform unfamiliar to the young Tamora, but it certainly looked military.

Tamora was also tall for her age. She was the same height as her older sister and the tallest child in her school class. She watched as the beast tossed the woman against a lofty glass wall. She slammed into the glass wall overlooking an unfamiliar city. The glass shook and rippled from the impact, and the woman slid into a heap on the floor. Tamora wanted to cry. She knew the woman was dead or at least badly hurt. Either way, she knew it was her on some far-off day. She knew this beast was coming for her. She knew it.

The flash disappeared, and she was left bug-eyed, lying in the dirt. Tears streaked from her eyes as her brother and sister rounded the corner. They both shot her with their fake lasers. She struggled to her feet, and they noticed she was shaken. Her shorts were wet. The tears rolled from her eyes, and she raced towards the house, screaming for her mother.

Her mother ran out of the house with a shotgun in her hands. She checked the cartridges in the double-barreled weapon and clicked it shut. She saw Tamora running at full speed, a cloud of dust kicked up from her feet as she emerged from behind the dilapidated barn with her brother and sister trailing and falling behind.

The thirty-five-year-old Reverend Barbara Benson ran down the steps and caught her daughter, who nearly knocked her over. Tamora clung to her mother's neck and cried. Barbara stared at Tamora's brother and sister, who arrived a moment later. Both were just as dumbfounded as she was. After several minutes, she quieted, and Barbara was able to hold the girl at arm's length.

"What happened, Tee?" her mother asked.

"I saw, um, I saw…" she cried again.

After a moment. "You saw what, dear?"

"I saw the big, scary monster kill her."

"Wh-what?" her mother stumbled with a glance toward Melanie and Robert. They both shrugged.

"I saw this animal kill a woman."

"Oh, dear. That didn't happen. Your brother and sister didn't see it, Tee," she said while looking at the other two, who shook their heads. "It's just your imagination playing with your mind." Barbara got up. "Come, I made fresh chocolate chip cookies, your favorite."

"No, it wasn't. I saw it, really."

"Okay, okay. Let's all go inside where it is safe."

Tamora sniffed as her mother placed her hand on her shoulder. The girl trembled as they walked into their home, with her mother guiding her into the kitchen. The others followed. It was no fun playing *Space Rangers* without their sister.

A few days later, Tamora played outside while her mother worked in the cornfields. Barbara Benson struggled with the sprinkler system as it spat and sputtered. Rusty water dribbled from the sprinkler heads amid bursts of air.

Behind her was a flash she barely noticed, and Tamora was thrown to the ground again by the blinding light. A similar hideous alien was choking the woman again. This time, she lay across a black leather sofa. The room she was in held shelves of old, dusty books, and on the opposite wall were shelves with large jars. In the jars floated the heads of aliens and people she did not know. She wanted to scream again, but could not. She felt her head was destined for one of those jars. He choked her until she stopped fighting. Her arms went limp and dropped to her side. The enormous alien removed his hairy paw from around her neck.

The scene changed to the bridge of a spaceship she had never seen before. The ship was being attacked as laser beam after laser beam carving its way into the ship's hull. Smoke and flames filled her view. There was the same woman with a man roughly her age.

She was at the forward controls trying to guide the ship away. He was barking orders. Her head was bloody as she fought with the controls. The vision vanished just as quickly as it had appeared. She got up and ran for the house, screaming again.

Her mother came out from the cornfield to get her while her brother and sister came in from a different direction. As she consoled her daughter, a military transport landed. A man got out with a duffel bag and slung it over his shoulder. The transport took off, and the man limped towards the gathering near the front porch. Melanie and Robert ran to him and tackled him. Tamora looked and slowly pulled away from her mother, then ran to him.

Their father was home from the Navy. They all hugged and went into the house. He studied the home as he walked up to it. The paint had been blasted away in spots by the wind and the sand. A few of the windows were cracked and needed to be replaced. The roof was missing shingles. It was still a solid home, but in serious need of repairs.

Money was short. A navy pension and farming were not enough to cover the basics of life. Forget about Barbara being a pastor of a Church. Very few people attended church anymore, and the few that did never put anything into the offering plate.

A few days later, Barbara woke in a fright. Her heart was pounding, and she was sweating. A bad dream about a woman on a ship that was being ripped apart: she now knew the visions her daughter experienced were true. Barbara also knew that the woman was her daughter, Tamora, in the future. She tossed the blankets aside, went downstairs, and got a drink of water. After a few minutes, she walked upstairs and peeked into Tamora's room. She was not there.

Barbara knew where Tamora was. She pulled on her work boots and a light jacket, grabbed her shotgun and a flashlight, and headed outside. The front door creaked on its rusted hinges as it opened. Walking down the front steps, Barbara passed the barn and took in the sounds of wild animals in the distance. The hooting, and screams made her pay close attention to the predators roaming about. Mountain Lions, Coyotes, and Hawks to name a few. She headed past the old tractor she used to work the cornfields and found Tamora lying on top of a round, concrete well cover. The girl had been staring at the sky, taking in all the stars. Her tablet held hundreds of star maps, and her laser pistol, made of sticks and strings, was clutched in her hands. She could name all of the visible constellations with ease. She had fallen asleep on the hard concrete cover.

Barbara scooped her up and carried her back into the house. She placed her back in the bed as she stirred.

"Mom?" she said with a yawn and stretched her arms.

"Yes, honey."

"I'm cold."

Barbara covered her in a blanket, and the girl pulled the blanket tight against her. "What's the matter?" she asked.

"I had one of your scary dreams."

Tamora sat up like she had been electrocuted.

"What? Really?"

"Yes, dear. I believe you."

Tamora hugged her mom. "Can we stop them from happening? I don't want to die."

"I think so, dear. Now get some sleep."

"Okay." She clutched her gold cross, which she had found in the dirt.

They separated, and Tamora crawled back under the warm blanket. Her mother left her room, pausing at the door momentarily to look at her child. She was afraid for her.

There would be many more visions for the young Tamora as she grew up, each more frightening than the previous.

The twenty-third century was a hard time for the people of Earth. Wars and a collapsing environment from those wars had plagued the planet. Families did not have much, and what they had was old and worn out. The children were dressed in old, soiled clothes, which were not much better than rags. Food was scarce when it grew at all. The Bensons hoped for a good corn crop so they could eat themselves. It made the Great Depression of the 1930s seem like a walk in the park. The children knew no better. To them, it was how it was. Most resources were allocated to the space fleet, which was searching for a new home for the human race before the Earth could no longer sustain the 2.5 billion who remained.

TWO

SEPTEMBER 17, 2246: 25 years later.

Orbiting high above the Earth, the nerve center of the Alliance space fleet floated halfway between the Earth and the moon. The station was enormous and featured a giant wheel, two miles in diameter, that rotated around a central hub. It was a design popularized back in the twentieth century. Ships of all sizes buzzed about like an angry beehive while inside, a lone starship was docked at the central hub of the port.

The U.A.S. *Saratoga* was an older starship. It showed many battle scars from its frequent skirmishes with beings that would wipe humans from the galaxy if they could.

Inside the central column, Captain Shawn Hackett stood at attention with his hands folded behind his back, watching the activity surrounding his ship through the tall windows. He studied the patchwork repairs to the hull from their previous battles. He also observed several space trucks hauling supply modules to the ship, which he assumed were supplies for a long journey.

As he watched the activity, he noticed the reflection of a man approaching from behind. He turned and saw Admiral Hodges walk up.

The Admiral had put on some weight in recent years, and his wife constantly got after him to lose thirty pounds or have a heart attack due to the stress of his job. He didn't listen.

"Captain," the admiral stated.

Hackett turned and snapped to attention while saluting. "Admiral."

"At ease," he said dryly while extending his hand, which held an envelope. "I have your orders."

Hackett was surprised to receive handwritten orders. Everything in this time period was done electronically. It would pop up on his tablet or wristwatch, and he could read them there. Something about handwritten notes held a level of secrecy and untraceability. He took the envelope and opened it. He pulled out several pieces of paper and studied them. One piece was folded twice and sealed. He slipped this one into his pocket. The others he read.

Hackett's eyes went big as he read on. "Another trip to Inea-four! We barely got out of there alive. Most of us, anyway." Hackett huffed as he thought back to Sasha Young. "A diplomatic mission at that. Is it even possible to use diplomacy with those savages?"

"Calm down, captain."

"Calm down? With all due respect, Admiral, unless you are sending the whole fleet with us, this is suicide. There is no reasoning with those animals. They want the Earth, and they want us all dead. And the way they kill is so savage. The Raping and torture is like a game to them."

"Captain, Shawn, walk with me." The admiral turned away, and he studied a few people lurking nearby. They saw him looking at them, and they scurried away.

Hackett nodded and walked with the admiral.

Hodges stared ahead as he walked. "Captain, the head of the fleet is concerned about what the Ineans are planning. Also, they are concerned about your mental state after losing people on the previous mission."

"Very good people at that."

"Yes, very good people," the admiral acknowledged. "The head of the fleet is also concerned that you are being pushed too quickly back into command after what the Ineans did to you. I told them you were ready. Don't let me down."

"Aye, sir."

"Besides, you have the toughest ship and the toughest crew we have. Other names have been suggested and quickly dismissed as options. You will get this done and get out of there in one piece."

"Yes, Admiral." Hackett stopped to look at him. "Be advised; we failed our last mission."

"The decision is final, Captain!" Hodges showed a rare flash of anger.

"Understood." Hackett knew it was pointless to argue.

"You have some new people joining your crew today. Keep an eye on them," he leaned towards Hackett and whispered. "Some of them I don't know and could be loyal to the opposition."

"Spies. I'll flush them out." Hackett whispered.

"I know you will."

"Thank you, Admiral. It's time for me to get on board and check on progress. It looks like the ship is almost ready." Hackett knew it was time to get away from Hodges before the snoops got suspicious. For all he knew, there might be a hidden microphone nearby.

Hodges stared out the window beside Hackett. "Tough old ship," he said with a grin.

"Old?" Hackett exclaimed.

Hodges laughed and patted Hackett on the shoulder. "You'll be fine." They saluted each other. Hodges turned to walk away, stopped, and turned back. "Captain?"

"Sir?" Hackett replied, turning back to the Admiral.

"The Angowains will have a delegation there as well as the Kosuan. You will have your hands full on this mission," Hodges added.

"Understood, sir. Nothing like an easy mission to make us soft," Hackett said with a nervous laugh and a slight shake of his head.

An easy mission, it would not be. The Ineans and Kosuan were locked in a fierce and nasty war that devastated many planets in their region. Many feared it would soon spill over to include the Angowains and the Alliance. Hackett's underlying job was to make sure that didn't happen. He knew deep down that it was impossible. It was no secret that the Ineans had desires for Earth. They had publicly stated it. He knew the Alliance would have to fight them at some point despite the appeasements by the Global Council. Appeasements that only the government knew about. The population would revolt if they knew the slightest of details. He didn't want to be the one to start the war. The war the Alliance could not win. A war the Alliance could not avoid.

"I need to go," the Admiral stated, observing a few people loitering in the corner watching him and the captain talk. Spies? They had returned and seemed to be everywhere. Most likely working for the wrong side, according to the Admiral.

Hodges was frequently outspoken in his displeasure with many of the vice admiral's dealings and decisions. This drew much scorn from his peers, who, as military people, knew the rules about questioning orders from a superior officer. This also made Hackett a target as well. He, like Hodges, did not support Vice Admiral Griffin and more privately questioned many of his decisions. Hackett found himself defending Hodges to other captains, who provided the vice admiral with ample criticism of both.

Hackett saluted the Admiral again, and they parted ways. He knew Hodges was on the 'watch' list. He knew he was as well. There were people in power siding with the enemy, and Hodges was fighting them. How long before he took a bullet? How long before they got Hackett?

Hodges continued to walk towards the elevators in the central column. Hackett watched the Admiral fade away and said to himself, *I can't let him down. He put a lot on the line for me, and I need to do this perfectly to prove him right and the others wrong.* As Hodges was about to enter the elevator, a woman stepped out and spoke briefly with him. She was a tall, thin, blonde-haired woman. Hackett's first thought was that she was a courier. Then, the doors closed after Hodges entered the elevator, and she started walking towards Hackett. He studied her for a moment as she approached and he turned his gaze back out the window toward the *Saratoga*.

She approached with a confident gait, came up beside him, and saluted. Hackett returned her salute and faced her. "Lieutenant Commander Tamora Benson reporting for duty, Captain," she snapped with the firmness of a well-trained officer.

"At ease, Lieutenant Commander," Hackett replied with no emotion as he looked at her briefly and spied the pilots wings on the left side of her jacket. Below the wings were several ribbons arranged in 3 rows above the pocket. On the right was a basic black name badge with her last name.

She remained at attention. "Here are my transfer papers, sir."

Hackett had to look up slightly to meet her light blue eyes. She's tall, he thought, but too skinny to be the kind of officer for a mission like this. Most races they came across would snap her in half instantly, especially the Ineans. The Ineans would also do far worse before killing her. Hackett was average in height at about 5 feet 10 inches, and this woman had him beat by an inch at least. Her long blonde hair was pulled back and braided into a single ponytail that hung past her shoulders. She was slim, too slim, and he thought she appeared too young for her reported age. He quickly noticed she already wore a U.A.S. *Saratoga* cap. The standard fleet issue was that she wasn't officially a member of the crew yet, but she had already been issued one. He wasn't sure why this bothered him, but it did. He also found her to be very attractive. He instantly decided she was the one to watch.

Hackett looked at her for a moment and opened her folder. *More papers.* He thought. This led him to believe there were more secrets. He flipped through some pages and stopped at a few key points. "Lieutenant Commander, you have piloting skills, tactical skills, and quite an impressive resume, including high marks for self-defense and hand-to-hand combat."

Hackett flipped through her file some more. Then he looked up. "Lieutenant Commander, don't take this the wrong way. When I look at you, I don't see what this folder says. Is this correct? I've only been the captain of this ship for six months, and we already have a reputation for taking on missions no one else wants. The one we are beginning today has a high potential of failure, including the fact that we may not come out of it alive." She went to speak until Hackett held up his hand to stop her. He needed to make it clear with this woman because he was concerned she wasn't ready for such missions yet, and he continued. "Why in the world would you want to transfer to our ship? It's older than what you are used to." Hackett stopped to allow her to answer.

"Captain, if I may speak, sir?" she asked. Hackett nodded yes. "I know what people think when they look at me, and I know many people feel that this is a dumb move to make, but let me tell you what I am made of." She waited for Hackett to give her permission, and he did so by nodding. "As far as my looks go, I don't consider myself any different from anybody else. I don't "cry" at the slightest bump or bruise, and my fingernails are short, so I won't be fussing over breaking any of those, either. I have worked hard to get where I am today, and quite frankly, I am bored with the missions I have been on. I long to be on the edge. I want action and adventure. I want to be in the thick of history as it's being made. If I die up there doing those things, then fine, so be it. I have no desire to be sitting behind a pretty console out of harm's way. That is pathetic." She was quite firm and voiced her opinion well.

Hackett looked at her for a moment. He suddenly liked this woman. She was tough and spoke her mind. She wasn't likely going to be a pushover after all, and she knew what she wanted. He did pick up on her constant usage of "I." It bothered him, and he knew she was career-minded. The first thing that came to his mind was a lecture by his first captain stating there was no "I" in the team. The team concept stuck with him, and he knew he would have to instill it in her. "Miss Benson, you won't have any problems on this ship. Just remember one thing: this is a team you are joining. That is all." With that, he signed her transfer orders with a pen she provided and saluted his new officer. "Welcome aboard, Lieutenant Commander." He noticed the pen stated U.A.S. *Saratoga* on the side of it.

She saluted back and picked up her duffel bag. "Sir, may I go stow my gear and get acquainted with the ship and crew?" she asked.

"Yes, please do, and I want you to pilot us out of space dock. We haven't received a new navigator yet, and we are shorthanded there. So I want you on the bridge for departure," Hackett replied and went back to looking out the window as his voice trailed off.

His thoughts were quickly replaced by the horrible memory of their previous navigator, another woman slightly older than Benson, who was also as attractive. She was built tougher and trained constantly. That toughness and training didn't help her, though, as the Inean soldiers that guided them from the meeting to their transport overpowered Hackett and his crew with ease and ripped the woman away. They dragged her into a crowd while Hackett struggled to his feet. Other Ineans were blocking him, and he could not help her. The woman was quickly subdued by the soldiers beating her. The last thing he remembered before he was knocked unconscious was her screaming as he saw the torn top of her uniform flying over his head. He knew what they did to her, and there was nothing he could do to prevent it. The thing that concerned him was that his party never recovered the body. She was most likely dead by now, probably that very day, but something told him otherwise. It would have been better if she had died then. Life as an Inean slave was a horrifying prospect. There was no proof of either case; it ate away at him.

Benson turned towards the window and stared out towards the activity surrounding the *Saratoga*. Then she looked at Hackett and said, "Will do, sir." She turned and walked towards the escalator that would bring her to the long glass walkway and toward the ship. Hackett watched her walk away. He thought she sounded like quite a woman, but then he remembered fleet rules about fraternization, and there was no way they could get involved. The fleet had strict rules regarding dating, which were consistent with those of many branches of the military. He flipped open her folder again and looked at the comments pages from each of her previous captains. Neither had written anything regarding her personal life, particularly with respect to her dating life. A look at her academy days revealed that she dated a fellow cadet early on, but there has been nothing since. Hackett concluded that she was career-minded only and had no need for anyone in her life. Too bad, he thought to himself. For the first time in a long time, he had an interest in a woman, and she was hands-off. He shrugged and went back to watching the activity around his ship. He thought back to Sasha sitting at the nav-con joking with Carol Davies, the ship's helmsman. Many on the ship looked forward to her pranks and off-color jokes. He recalled how she lit up the bridge with that devious grin. He needed to find a way to prevent another woman from going to that planet. Find a way to eliminate the gruesome fate that Sasha Young could not escape.

Benson walked towards the escalator and glanced over her shoulder towards Hackett. He seemed familiar for some reason. She knew him. She wasn't sure from where, though. He was looking out the windows again at his ship. Benson was attracted to him the same way he was to her; however, she also remembered the fleet's rules. She watched him for a moment and realized he was married, married to that ship. She saw it in his eyes. That ship meant everything right now to him. She shook her head and continued walking. For the first time since Cadet Harrison during the academy, she had an interest in someone. Sadness overwhelmed her for a moment as she thought back to Harrison. Just a week before their wedding, the base commander had knocked on the door of her dorm room at Annapolis. She knew as soon as she opened the door why he was there. She remembered it like it was yesterday, the pain of that day still fresh. The commander handed her an envelope that she opened with shaky hands. In it, she read the letter from the fleet about how Harrison died that morning on a training mission. No other details; those would come later. She crumpled the paper into a tight ball and threw it at the commander. He pulled her to him, and she broke down and cried on his shoulder.

She glanced back at Hackett again as she was about to step on the escalator. There was something nagging at her about him. Something familiar about him: something that was luring her in, and deep down, she was tempted to explore that urge that had been absent for nearly ten years. Unfortunately, she knew she couldn't even attempt it. She was being watched like a hawk and was expected to fail because of her looks. To get involved with a captain while under his command would mean a certain court-martial, and she'd be kicked out of the fleet.

She reached the long, glass-covered tube that would bring her to the *Saratoga*. She stopped and looked around at all the people scurrying about their various tasks. She stepped into the tube and onto a magnetic-levitation floating platform about four feet in length. She dropped her duffel bag at her feet and grasped the handlebars on either side of her. The front and back were open, allowing passengers to walk on and off. She held on and squeezed the button on the left handlebar, and the small cart zipped off toward the ship several hundred feet down the tube. She held the control right up until the end. The platform had sensors that detected when it was closing in on another object, and it slowed automatically and stopped against the platform in front of it. She released the handle, and the brake applied. She stepped forward onto the next one and so on until she made it to the hatch. A total of five platforms had stacked up at the opening.

THREE

BENSON PAUSED and studied the hull around the hatch. The armor plating was thick beneath the gel coating, which collected microscopic particles before they sandblasted the hull. The hatch was constructed of layers of various metals and armor-plated, making it virtually blast-proof. It was a rugged ship despite its age. A moment later, she ducked through the main hatch and paused. She studied the activity before her: crew members hurrying about to make the ship ready to leave port, technicians scrambling to get their tasks completed and get off the ship. She marveled at how crowded the ship was. She walked towards the center, turned a corner, and proceeded down a corridor, only to be immediately lost. She had never been on a Class II starship before. The newer ships had maps and touch pads along the walls that provided guidance. The codes above each hatch didn't make sense to her, although she vaguely remembered them from the academy. Unfortunately, none of the ships she had served aboard used the obsolete codes. The newer starships had dropped the naval codes for decks, compartments, and relative positions to the ship's centerline. However, this ship still used them. This ship is old. She said to herself as she glanced back towards the hatch she had just passed through to get a reference point before proceeding further. What the ship lacked in conveniences, it more than made up for with its rugged hull and tough-as-nails crew. It would take time to adjust and relearn what she had forgotten. She held a hand up to block a crewman from passing, "Excuse me!" she said firmly, and the crewman stopped as he tried to hurry by. "How do I get to deck five from here?" she asked him.

He looked her up and down, shook his head, and told her how to get there. She thanked him and began walking. She wondered what his problem was. Probably the same one everyone else had when they looked at her. Most people assumed she had advanced in rank due to her appearance. No one considered that she might deserve it or didn't have to pay special favors for the bars on her shoulders. In some ways, she accepted it. In other ways, it made her furious the way fellow officers and subordinates treated her.

The corridors on this ship were narrow. She was not accustomed to the structural ribs protruding into the walkway every 30 feet. It wasn't as cramped as an old submarine, but very close to it. She tripped on a few of the ribbed supports and nearly fell. This drew snickers from passersby until they noticed her rank and hurried away. Benson bumped several people with her duffel bag as she pushed her way through the mass of people, apologizing to each one. Yet, several still gave her an annoyed look if they bothered to look at her.

She looked down one corridor and checked the code above. She turned the corner into another without looking and flattened an enlisted crewman with her duffel bag. This sent his box of small glass tubes with small corks in each one spilling all over the floor. She apologized and went to help him. They bumped heads while bending over to pick up the test tubes, which were filled with water and air samples from throughout the ship. When the last of the tubes had been retrieved, they both stood; he saluted her, and she returned the salute. She then turned, tripped over her duffel bag, and fell flat on her face. She heard a man laughing and bolted up quickly, her face red from embarrassment. She noticed his rank and promptly snapped to attention, saluting him. He was still laughing when he saluted back.

Benson was a perfectionist. She strove to be the best, which irritated her when she failed. Embarrassment at her mistakes, especially when people were watching, drove her crazy. Now, everyone in the corridor was watching as she pushed herself from the floor. The pain in her forehead was mild compared to the pain of her humiliation.

"Lieutenant Commander Benson, I presume?" asked the man with three gold bars on his shoulders.

"Yes, I am, um, sorry, sir. I ah… I'm not used to these narrow corridors," she stammered, cursing herself for acting like a fool.

"Yes, I can see that. I'm the ship's XO, Commander Bill Morris. May I help you with anything?" he asked with a more reasonable tone.

Benson was embarrassed and mad at herself for the first few minutes on board. She was also frustrated with not being able to find her quarters. "Well, I am trying to find my quarters. I'm in room five-dash-twenty-one 'B' dash thirty-four, but I can't find it."

"Let me help you. I'm sorry for laughing. It's so easy to spot the "noobs" on the ship because they all make the same mistakes. Follow me," he said. They both reached for her duffel bag. He got there first. He picked it up and threw it over his shoulder. They began walking along the corridor and had to step sideways through some partially closed blast doors and around another corner to the outer ring of the forward hull. He stopped in front of her door and punched a code on the pad, and the doors slid open.

"The code is the last six digits of your fleet ID number. Mine also works for these doors because my rank is high enough to allow it," he stated as he backed up to let her pass. She turned to accept her bag back, and while her back was turned, the doors slid shut. She turned and abruptly stopped as she walked into the closed door with a thunk! She huffed, threw her bag down, punched in her code, and they opened again.

Morris was trying his best not to laugh. She saw the smirk on his face and didn't find it amusing. "Let me show you a trick. There are only a few automatic doors on this ship, so you will be doing a lot of that in the first week. If you drop your bag in the doorway, the sensors will keep it open indefinitely."

"Thank you for your help, Commander. Now, how do I get to the bridge?" she asked, hoping he would tell her and not guide her like a lost little girl.

"Go to the end of this corridor and take a left," he pointed. "The elevator is on the right, about two hundred feet in. Take it to deck zero-zero. That is the bridge. Also, if you go to the ship's schematics on your terminal, it will show you the places every newbie needs to know about." He was having some fun with his slight digs at this new person on board.

"Thank you, Commander." She saluted and waited for him to respond. When he did, she stepped into her room. She grabbed her duffel bag and allowed the door to close behind her. These quarters were small compared to what she left on the *Challenger*. The walls were bare and a dingy battleship gray color. The lighting appeared to be set low. She cleared her throat. "Lights up!" she commanded. Nothing happened. "Computer lights up," she commanded again, still nothing. She looked around the room and spied the switch on the wall next to the door she had just entered. She huffed, went to it, and turned the control. The lights got brighter. "Manual lighting, how archaic," she mumbled. She continued the tour of her new quarters. The bed was located on the left, positioned under a small rectangular porthole, and a dresser was situated on the right. There was a short partition between the dresser and her desk. The desk had an older 3D computer terminal on it with a pull-out keyboard just below the polished desktop. Opposite her desk was the closet for her belongings, and between the bed and the closet was a doorway. Curious, she approached the door and pressed the button, and it opened. A man was standing there with his back to her, naked and drying off.

"Oh, crap! Excuse me," she said as she turned around.

"You're new," he said as he rolled his eyes. It wasn't the first time it had happened to him, and his response was more matter-of-fact than Benson could understand. He grabbed another towel and wrapped it around himself, and put his hand out to shake Benson's. "Hi, I'm Lieutenant Commander Dan Giovanella. I'm the head communications officer of the *Saratoga*."

Benson kept her back to him and said, "Pleased to meet you. I'm Lieutenant Commander Tamora Benson. I ah, um… I am sorry. I didn't know where that door went," she fumbled for the words.

Giovanella checked the towel around his waist before replying. "It's okay. You can turn around."

She first turned her head, peeked carefully, and noticed he wrapped a towel around his waist. He was reaching for her hand. She grasped his hand firmly and apologized once again as she shook it.

He laughed. "Don't worry about it. You'll learn to knock first. This is an old ship and lacks many of the conveniences found in newer ones. You know, like private bathrooms, automatic doors, and so on. This is a shared room, and my quarters are through that door there." He pointed to the door and looked back at Benson. Her face was still red, and she was trying not to look at him. "Let me close the door so I can finish dressing."

Benson stumbled again. "Oh, uh, yes, of course." She turned away, and the door closed behind her. "Damn it, Tamora! What the hell are you doing?" she huffed in frustration as she grabbed her duffel bag and tossed it onto her bed. She walked over, dumped it out, and began putting her belongings away. After several minutes, she returned to the bathroom door and knocked. There was no answer. She pressed the button, and the door slid open. She peeked around the corner. *Good, nobody here*, she said to herself. She reached down, picked up a box of her personal items, turned around, and walked into the door as it slid shut with a smack. "Son of a bitch" she cursed out loud. She shook her head in wonder at what else could go wrong. She hit the button and walked in. She took some time to clean up and splash some water on her face, hoping it would make a difference.

It had been a long journey from her previous ship back to Earth. It began ten days before when the *Challenger* left her behind at the

Vega outpost, and she had to wait for transport back to 61 Cygni, where she had to wait again for transport back to Earth. Although the trip was uneventful, she still craved a hot shower.

After her shower, she changed into a fresh uniform and finished putting her belongings away. She opened her top dresser drawer, put away her personal items, and paused at a small black box. She opened it and lifted out a gold cross, which hung on a delicate gold chain. She looked at the cross for a moment and placed it back in the box. She had had the cross since she was six years old and wore it every day until Harrison died. Her faith also died that day, and she had not worn it since. Yet, she could not part with it. It was a link to her childhood, a link to her mother and father, who had given it to her. She placed the box in her drawer and returned to unpacking.

FOUR

ON THE BRIDGE, Commander Morris tapped Hackett on the shoulder to get his attention. Hackett followed Morris back to his station behind Hackett's chair. "Sir, have you met our new navigator?" Morris whispered.

"Yes, I did. Is there a problem, Commander?" Hackett asked, not knowing whether he was referring to her appearance or the fact that she was a woman navigator, given what had happened to Sasha Young.

"Ah… No, sir, just thought I would ask, that's all," he said, thinking twice about what he was going to say.

"Yes, I noticed her qualifications, Commander, quite impressive. I think you should review her folder. That should answer all of your questions. The bridge is yours, Commander."

"Aye, sir."

Hackett grinned slightly and walked toward the elevator. Morris remained at his station, shook his head, and chuckled softly, assuming Hackett thought the same about her.

Morris remained at his station behind where the Captain sat. From here, he could monitor everything that transpired across the ship, including all major systems. Morris punched up the day's duty roster and watched it scroll across his monitor. He noticed that Captain Hackett had modified it. He read on and discovered that he had placed Benson at the navigator's console for departure. Hmm, perfect, he said to himself, and he closed the file. He began his pre-flight checklist and paged climate systems to send theirs in. He proceeded to study each report in preparation for the ship's departure.

As was his custom before leaving port, Hackett began his usual walk around the ship. It gave him a sense of the vessel's condition and its crew's readiness before a mission began. He regarded people he passed and stopped to talk to a few who were new to the ship to see how they were acclimating to their surroundings. They all seemed to be finding their way okay and had no questions. He was also trying to find out who the spies were. None of the people he met appeared to be the ones to watch. He made a mental note to check them off "his list."

Hackett pulled open a hatch in the wall near the elevators and stepped into a small, dimly lit service tunnel. He reached down to the deck, turned a round handle, and lifted the hatch. He looked down momentarily and stepped onto the silver rung of the ladder. He continued down while the wall opening swung closed with a hiss and a click behind him. He pulled the hatch shut over his head with a solid click. He progressed downward to deck five. Hackett never took the same route twice as he wandered about his ship. He was amazed at what he found hidden in the dark, secluded corners. Besides, he was impatient with the elevators and seldom used them, preferring ladders and stairs instead. It seemed he was always rushing to get around the ship and couldn't waste time waiting for an elevator. He began his walk around the deck when he noticed an ensign wrestling with several conduits. He was trying to stuff them back into an overhead compartment where they belonged. He walked up to assist the ensign, who wasn't sure how to get them back in.

As they discussed their options, Benson rounded the corner

while looking around and nearly ran them both over. She stopped short and saluted the Captain. He saluted back and pulled her aside. "Miss Benson, it isn't necessary to salute me every time we meet in a hallway or anywhere on the ship. I am more lax in that area than most captains."

"Yes, sir, sorry, sir, I won't let it happen again, sir," she said nervously.

Hackett shook his head. "That's okay. Please do me a favor?"

"What is it, sir?" she asked.

Hackett looked at her for a second. "Lighten up."

Nervously, she stammered, "Yes, sir." She cursed herself, knowing she was overreacting.

Hackett and Ensign Wolaski returned to their conversation, ignoring Benson, who stood behind them. She listened for a minute, feeling awkward and unable to think of a way to excuse herself. Then she spoke up. "Captain, sir?"

"Yes, Lieutenant Commander?" Hackett replied without turning to look at her.

"I couldn't help overhearing. I might be able to fix that for you." She hoped to start atoning for her clumsiness by helping them fix the problem.

Hackett stepped back and put his hand out to bring Ensign Wolaski with him. "Please, Miss Benson." He motioned to her to step forward and try.

Benson stepped up a couple of rungs on the short ladder and reached into the cramped overhead compartment. She poked around in the compartment, studying the cables and rearranging them to get a better view of what was there. She found a large blue conduit and knew if she unplugged it, the other cables would slide around it, and then she could reconnect it. She thought that blue meant low priority, which it did on the newer ships, so the worst thing that would happen was they would get a warning and reroute message. She unplugged it. Alarms went off. Quickly, the lights went out and were replaced by the red emergency lights. Morris was on the PA, instantly wanting to know what happened. Benson hurried, stuffed everything back in, and reconnected the cable, bringing everything back to normal. She jumped back, scared stiff.

"Well, Lieutenant Commander, that's a unique way of solving that problem. Please, in the future, do not disconnect the energizer relay control cable," Hackett said, studying her. He knew what she was thinking, and it was something he would have done six months before.

"I'm sorry, Captain, I thought blue meant low priority! I'm really sorry, sir."

"Ensign, you can put that together now."

"Aye, sir," Ensign Wolaski replied.

Hackett turned to Benson. "Come," he said firmly. He knew she was getting frustrated. The look of discouragement on her face was unmistakable.

She uncharacteristically slumped her shoulders from his tone and knew she was in deep trouble or worse. What could be worse? She wondered. Getting kicked off the ship after only being there for less than an hour would be worse. It would make her the laughingstock of the fleet if that happened.

"Lieutenant Commander, I know what you are going through. I would have done the same thing six months ago. You will need to review the technical manuals for this ship before unplugging any components. Yes, blue means low priority on a new ship. On this ship, it means energizer. Please don't touch anything violet, yet," he finished with a glance her way. She was upset. "Also, I know you're frustrated. The first week is the toughest. So stick with it, and everything will fall into place. Okay?"

She looked at him. "Yes, sir, thank you. I thought it was me. I just seem so out of place here." Then she bit her lip, wondering if that was too much information.

"That's fine. Where are you heading?" Hackett asked.

"Bridge, sir. I wanted to go over the nav-con before we ship out. That way, I can eliminate another surprise."

Hackett glanced up at her. "Well, you can't get there from here. Come this way," he said as he turned a corner, "and watch out for…"

Crack! He was too late. She stumbled forward and cursed, dropping an uncharacteristic f-bomb as she grabbed her head, looking back at the pipe she nearly embedded in her forehead.

"…The pipe that is hanging down," he continued.

"Thanks!"

He glanced over his shoulder at her, and she forced a smile back at him. "So, it takes about a week to get used to this ship?" she said as she rubbed her forehead.

"No, it takes a week to figure out where the big hazards are. I still walk into things myself. I'm not going to tell you how many times that damn pipe got me." Hackett smiled back and took her to the elevator area. "Take this to deck zero-zero, and you'll be on the bridge."

She held out her hand to Hackett. "Thank you, sir."

Hackett took her hand and shook it. It was warm and soft, he thought. He quickly forced the thought from his mind and said, "No problem. I have to finish my walk around before we get underway." He nodded and walked off, glad to be away from her before he did something stupid. He was afraid he would start acting like a schoolboy when the girl touched his hand for the first time, causing him to act like an idiot.

Benson stood and watched him until he disappeared around the corner. She thought about how nice he was and wondered if he... No, never mind, Tamora. Don't even think that way about the Captain. Hackett was only a few years older, and her mind kept wandering.

Once the elevator doors opened, she turned and nearly flattened a person trying to get off. She excused herself and waited. When the coast was clear, she stepped in. The elevator went up briskly. To her, it seemed rickety as it rattled and groaned its way to the bridge. She leaned against the wall and let out a sigh of relief that she didn't get busted back down to lieutenant for nearly blowing the ship up, especially in port. The Captain was treating her well, she thought, and she wanted to know if it was just her or if everyone got treated that way. She was brought back harshly as the elevator stopped quickly at the top, sending her stumbling to the side. The doors opened, and she pulled herself up and looked. Good, nobody saw that. She said to herself. She straightened the top of her snug-fitting uniform and proceeded onto the bridge.

The bridge was much smaller than the *Challenger*. However, it seemed cozy to her. She walked around briefly, looked at each station, and introduced herself to a few of the people there. She also made mental notes as to how the bridge was arranged. This ship was completely different from the *Challenger*. She walked over to the navigation console, which was not occupied. She slid the chair back until it clicked and locked into position. She dropped into the seat and pulled the short armrest down, activating the heads-up display (HUD). The HUD displayed numerous details and settings. She leaned forward and began to study the controls.

Commander Morris walked over and knelt beside her. He instructed her to become familiar with the controls and demonstrated how to activate the control panel in demo mode and how to deactivate it.

"Thank you, Commander," she said.

He went back to his station to continue preparing the ship for departure. Benson spent nearly an hour running the test simulations and felt confident for the first time since arriving.

"Commander Morris?" Benson asked.

"Yes, Lieutenant Commander?" He acknowledged with a casual glance towards her, wondering what her question was.

"When is the ship leaving port, sir, and when should I report back?" she asked.

Morris looked at his panel for the answers and replied, "In six hours, Miss Benson. However, I want you back in five. Any particular reason you want to leave the bridge?" he asked.

"I am familiar with this console, and I wanted to get familiar with the rest of the ship, sir." It was the truth. There was nothing more annoying to her than someone who didn't know where anything was on a starship. Least of all, she didn't want to be that person.

He looked back down at his console and displayed her simulation scores, and he was impressed: Hundreds across the board. She learned that fast, he thought. "Very well, Lieutenant Commander. Good idea, you may go." He went back to his reports.

"Thank you, sir." She raised the armrest and lifted herself out of the chair that slid back towards the console while she headed for the elevator. This time, she held on.

Lieutenant Daniella Larson walked over to Morris. "How did she do, sir? Is she as good as they say?" Morris glanced at her and displayed Benson's scores on his monitor. Larson leaned close to him, "Damn, how'd we get her. Those are perfect scores. Has anyone done that before?" Larson asked while glancing up at him with her dark eyes. Larson was known to wear a little makeup to enhance her look. She enjoyed making herself look good, especially when Morris was around, even though he never responded to her subtle advances. Today, as with most days, her hair was pulled back into a short, single-braided ponytail. Her shirt and jacket hugged her body perfectly. She left the top two buttons of both undone, displaying enough cleavage to get Morris's attention, and it did. Unfortunately for her, he didn't take the next step, which continually left her frustrated.

Morris closed the file. "Not to my knowledge. I had a chance to review her file, and you're right. She is good, and she wants your job," he said, smirking.

Larson wasn't sure how to take that, so she glared at him for a brief moment. She thanked him and went back to her station. She continued to stare at Morris out of the corner of her eye. She was studying him to see if he was joking or not.

Lieutenant Commander Dan Giovanella looked up from his communications console and turned toward Morris. "Commander, the ambassadors are ready to come aboard, sir. These are the last of the people we are expecting."

Morris glanced toward Giovanella. "Thank you, Lieutenant Commander. Contact the Captain and have him meet me at the main docking hatch." Morris secured his station. "Larson, you have the bridge."

"Aye, sir," she replied. Larson was frequently handed the responsibility of being the officer of the watch, and she enjoyed being in charge. It was a responsibility handed down through generations on American naval ships and now starships.

Giovanella paged Hackett. "Yes, sir. Out, sir." He punched off the comm. "The captain will meet you there, Commander."

"Thank you, on my way," Morris replied, and he proceeded toward the elevator.

FIVE

MORRIS WAS ALREADY WAITING by the hatch when Hackett arrived. Both exchanged nods and faced the open hatch, through which the ambassadors would be coming at any moment.

Morris looked at Hackett. "Benson is unique, isn't she?"

"Yes, Commander. I take it you checked out her file?" Hackett asked with a wink.

"Well, yes, I did. She came to the bridge and took the nav-con tests and aced them in good time," Morris stated with a tone indicating that he was impressed.

Hackett looked forward while speaking to Morris. "I would hope so because she strikes me as being a klutz. I hope she isn't a liability on this mission because we don't need any screw-ups."

Both men stood silently waiting as Morris digested what Hackett said. He had a knack for saying what was on his mind. Sometimes, he was blunt, and everyone involved knew where he stood on a subject. People listened to Hackett because he was usually right, not because his comments were polished. This bluntness frequently got him into trouble with the Vice Admiral and the President of the NAU.

The ambassadors entered the ship wearing their traditional blue suits, and both officers snapped to attention and saluted. They relaxed when the ambassadors grunted while ducking to enter the starship. Hackett was the first to speak. “Welcome aboard, gentlemen. Hope your stay on our ship will be satisfactory.”

Morris just nodded.

The first man spoke, instantly turning up his nose at the thought of taking this ship to Inea. "I am Ambassador Wilcox, and this is my assistant, Ambassador Channing, Captain. We are taking this ship because no newer ones are available, and your crew has experience with the Ineans. Please remember that when you ask how our stay was when this is over," he stated condescendingly.

The other man spoke up. "Thank you, Captain, for your hospitality. I appreciate the opportunity to take this ship, which symbolizes our strength and the quality of our workmanship."

Wilcox looked at his associate with a disgusted look and then at Hackett. “Please show us to our rooms, Captain. I, for one, would like to skip the ship's tour. Unlike others, I have important work to do.” The Ambassador looked down at his baggage and then at Hackett and Morris. He was waiting for one of them to carry his bags. Channing wasn’t quite as bad and carried his own luggage. Morris picked up Wilcox’s baggage, and Hackett led the way, accompanied by two security guards who cleared the corridors along the route.

Wilcox spoke up while walking. “Captain, when is dinner served on this antiquated rust bucket?” He was under orders from the head of the fleet to irritate Hackett to see if he would crack, but so far, nothing.

Hackett had to bite his tongue and thought for a moment about his response. “Dinner is any time you are ready, Ambassador Wilcox. The guards here will show you where the galley is when you are ready.”

“You have food prepared and waiting every day, Captain?” Wilcox asked.

"No, sir, this is an older ship, as you so eloquently pointed out. Everyone on this ship prepares their own food and does their own dishes afterward. The stock of food is considerable. However, we discourage waste for obvious reasons," Hackett said, finally getting a shot in.

"I am not cooking my own meals, and I don't do dishes, Captain!" Wilcox was fuming.

"Well, sir, then you will go hungry," Hackett said bluntly. "Everyone on this ship is self-sufficient, and that includes laundry as well. We don't have a cook, we don't have people working in our laundry room, and we don't have an official dishwasher. We do not have the room to staff those positions, and everyone contributes." Hackett was on a roll as he had been briefed in a secret memo from Admiral Hodges on Wilcox's quirky personality.

Channing saw that Wilcox was about to go on one of his tirades, so he stepped in as quickly as possible. "Captain, we are delighted to see that your crew accepts responsibility towards the ship as a whole and would be honored to do our part while on board. I must admit that it has been a while since I've been in the kitchen."

Hackett grinned to himself, "Thank you, Ambassador." He held out his hand as they reached the doorway. "Here are your rooms, gentlemen." Hackett winked at Morris, who shook his head slightly at the Captain's fib. The ship had an entire staff in the kitchen and laundry. However, Wilcox obviously had not done his homework on their transportation. Hackett filed the Ambassador's lack of preparation away to use later. He was also curious as to why he had not prepared.

Wilcox walked into his room and yelled his displeasure about the rooms. "Captain, these are a disgrace! These are puny. I can't live, let alone work, in this shoe box!" He continued to rant, and Hackett checked with Channing.

"These are small, Captain. I assume this is the best you have. They will have to do," Channing said, trying to be polite. His expression said otherwise.

"You are correct. These are the best we have," Hackett replied. He returned to Wilcox's room while he was still ranting.

"Mr. Wilcox," Hackett said firmly. "This is the best we have. My quarters are not this good, or I would give them to you. I do not appreciate the continued criticism of my ship. You said yourself this is the best you will have for this mission, so complaining to me will get you nowhere, sir." Hackett made a giant leap talking down to the Ambassador. Wilcox answered directly to the head of the fleet, and Hackett was already in hot water with him. Vice Admiral Griffin was looking for any excuse to be rid of Hackett.

Wilcox was shocked. No one had talked to him like that in years. Most people feared the ambassadors because they reported directly to the vice admiral. Hackett knew this, of course. Hackett needed to rein this guy in fast, or this would be an extremely long mission.

"Captain, I am offended and outraged at your tone! I will report this incident to the President himself. I will also be referred to as 'Ambassador' when I am addressed. Do you understand?" Wilcox threatened.

"I would expect as much, and when you do, 'Ambassador,' please ask him how we can improve this to your liking and then let me know." Hackett stood at attention and saluted Wilcox. Then added, "I will be on the bridge filing my own report, sir. These guards are at your disposal. Please, do not abuse them." With that said, Hackett turned and walked away, mumbling to himself. Morris followed and caught up to him.

"Captain, you've got balls. Did you see the look on his face?" Morris was destined for his own command after this next mission. However, Hackett knew Morris was intimidated by authorities like Vice Admiral Griffin and the Ambassador, which could cloud his thinking in a crisis. Hackett believed you need to think on your feet out in space, or you die, and you can't be worrying about what certain people may think.

"Commander, we are in trouble if headquarters really believes that guy can get the Ineans to sign a peace agreement. We'll be at war before the week is out," Hackett blurted. He realized afterward that he should have kept that thought to himself.

"Aye, sir," Morris agreed, at least on the outside, and both men walked back to the bridge without saying another word.

. . .

On the bridge, the crew was preparing for departure when Giovanella said there was a message for the Captain from Admiral Hodges. Hackett turned towards Morris. “That didn’t take long.” He turned towards his communications officer. “Well, let’s see it, Mr. Giovanella.”

“Yes, sir,” he replied.

The image of Admiral Hodges erased the view of the spaceport on the main viewport at the front of the bridge.

The Admiral spoke first. "Captain, is everything all right over there?"

Hackett looked at the screen. “Why, yes, Admiral, why would you ask?” Hackett knew why. Wilcox had sent a message back to headquarters, and here comes the inquiry.

“The fleet admiral just contacted me and wanted assurance that your guests are settled in and comfortable, Captain. I also called to wish you luck.” Hodges had that look that said, You poor bastard. Better you than me.

“Well, Admiral, they are as comfortable as they will ever be on this ship, and I assure you, we gave them the best accommodations we had,” Hackett replied.

Hodges nodded, knowing what he said was true. “I understand, Captain, and thank you for that report. Command out.” The image on the forward viewport returned to that of the inside of the space dock.

Morris reported from his station. “Time to departure, two hours.”

SIX

IN THE CENTRAL part of the *Saratoga*, crews rushed to secure all of the cargo they would need for this mission in the lower decks. This mission was expected to last just over a month, putting the ship nearly 16 light years away from the nearest Alliance outpost. So, everything they needed had to go along with them. As the last cargo ship docked to the underside of the *Saratoga*, the crews working in the hold had difficulty finding space for it all.

Two of the people working on the detail, Ensign Lisa Woods and Lieutenant Bob Perry, had been on the ship for some time and spent considerable time together. They knew every nook and cranny, patch, and repair the ship ever had. They struggled to find a place for everything and crawled out of the hold after placing a plain container on a pallet at the opening. Woods thought this was odd. However, Perry was insistent on this container being accessible. They hoped no one wanted anything from deeper in the hold.

They secured the hatch and locked it. Woods, an average-height woman roughly five feet and a half tall, wore her dark hair loose and flowing above the shoulders of her average body. Bob Perry was the same, just an average human male with no extraordinary physical qualities. Despite the fleet's policy, they had a close relationship and spent many nights together. It was hard to keep their relationship a secret, considering the amount of time spent rendezvousing in many unique places on the ship. They had discovered areas on this ship that were not even depicted on the schematics, including passageways between the primary and secondary hulls that had been created during the ship's previous retrofitting.

Woods and Perry finished with the cargo and began walking forward. Perry whispered in her ear, and she looked up, nodding yes. They walked briskly forward toward the secondary energizer. Perry leaned against the wall, opened the hatch, and proceeded into the vertical tunnel that led down to the laser cannons at the bottom of the forward hull. Woods looked around to ensure no one saw them, followed him down, and closed the hatch. They proceeded down another couple of decks and through one more hatch that opened to a broader section of the tunnel. When Woods turned around after closing the hatch, Bob Perry already had the picnic basket open and was spreading out the blanket. Lisa Woods came over and started removing food from the basket. She inflated a pair of air pillows and made herself as comfortable as possible. Perry joined her with his plate of food. They sat and looked out the oddly placed porthole at the activity going on in the spaceport. They ate their dinner. When finished, Perry took out another blanket and pulled it over them. Woods reached up and disabled the light. Neither of them would be seen for several hours.

Benson walked through the elevator doors precisely one hour before departure time. She walked to the right and towards the navigation console, lifted the chair's armrest, and it slid back. Benson settled into the seat, and it slid forward with a solid click of the lock. The HUD display flickered and began displaying information. She promptly began entering the course information for their trip to Inea. The rest of the bridge crew filed in and followed suit. The mood of the crew had turned from happy to solemn as word spread about the destination of their mission. Tactical officer Lieutenant

Daniella Larson stood at her station beside Commander Morris, which was behind the Captain. Both had their chairs swung out of the way for now. Helmsman, Ensign Carol Davies, sat in the chair to the left of Benson and directly in front of the Captain's chair. The helm and navigation consoles were shared directly forward of the Captain's chair, along with the communications console. Between the helm and navigation consoles was a small control panel with a large bubble in the center, reminiscent of an old-style compass. The bubble controls were connected directly to the ship's gyro and nav-con controls. It served as a manual navigation and helm control. This panel was responsible for manually directing positioning if the main systems failed. It was a device that the newer ships did not use. You could dial in your course and heading with this control, and off you go with the simple press of a button. Benson had not seen this device since the academy.

Carol Davies leaned across the control panel and towards Benson to introduce herself. Benson gave a slight nod as she watched Davies dial in their course with ease, and she reached down to remove the manual, reviewing the controls in case she needed to use the device.

The communications officer, Lieutenant Commander Dan Giovanella, was already at his station to the left of the helm occupied by Davies. Climate controls were against the wall to the Captain's left, and also on the left, next to the elevator entrance, were the particle accelerator and energizer controls. To the Captain's right were the sensor controls, which were staffed by Lieutenant Stephan Bowers, and the particle deflector controls were behind him. Each station around the perimeter of the bridge was in its own pocket in the wall. Each station, except for the three in front of the Captain and the two directly behind him, had a small porthole to the outside. The main display at the front of the bridge featured a large panel in the center, with smaller displays on either side. The smaller displays showed an overview of several ships' systems, including a plot of their intended course with any obstacles labeled. The main screen showed the activity outside the ship.

Chief engineer Commander Vincent O'Toole was next to

arrive. He surveyed the bridge and sat at the engineering console, positioned against the rear wall of the bridge, between the science stations and the security console. All four resided between the two elevators. The two senior science officers on the *Saratoga* had completed their preflight checklists and waited with their arms folded, facing forward. Everyone on the bridge went about their business quietly and methodically, like they had done daily since joining the service.

Hackett entered the bridge, followed by Wilcox, Channing, and two well-armed security officers who carried electromagnetic chairs for the ambassadors to sit in during departure. The guards secured the chairs to the floor between the Captain's chair and the sensors console. Then the officers retreated to their posts at the entrance to each elevator. They stood at attention, each with a hand on their laser rifles.

The security officers wore thick, bulletproof, and laser-proof vests. Each wore a helmet with slightly darkened visors to protect their eyes from lasers. Both guards wore thin armored gloves and carried type-one pulse rifles that were strong enough to kill a person but not enough to punch a hole through the hull. Their clothing was dark gray, almost black, with simple Alliance insignia on their collars. Each man was the size of a football linebacker, and that was no accident. Security on a starship needed to be impassable, and there was no excuse for a ship being taken over by a hostile race or terrorist group. There were plenty of terrorist groups eager to steal a starship, and the damage they could do was frightening to the people of Earth. A single starship had the firepower to destroy dozens of cities and bring the fragile Global Union to its knees. The officers were trained in various forms of self-defense and received ongoing training. Their size ensured no one short of an Inean would make it on the bridge alive.

Benson looked around the bridge and made a mental note of all the people she would be working with for the next several months. She noticed just how small this bridge was. Not much room for anything else up here. *Definitely a no-frills ship*, she thought. Benson turned, glanced right at the ambassadors, and quickly looked forward again. She snapped back again as her eyes widened in horror when she realized Ambassador Wilcox was on board. They made eye contact, and he started to say something. She looked back at her console quickly. "Dang!" she cursed softly to herself before he could speak.

Wilcox went to speak and thought the better of it for now. Hackett, however, noticed the exchange and became concerned. It was obvious she knew him from before and didn't want anything to do with him now. Former lover? Hackett had no idea. However, he needed to know for the sake of the mission.

Indeed, Benson did know the Ambassador, lovers they were not. On a previous mission several months prior, when she served on the *Challenger*, the Ambassador took a liking to her, as most visitors did, and requested that they meet for dinner. She went along thinking it would mean a part for her on the mission they were on. She hoped to add to her list, justifying another promotion. The Ambassador made several advances toward her that she refused. He offered her a cushy job as his personal assistant, which she also refused. She knew what he truly wanted. If she took the job, she would be discarded like many of his previous assistants or wind up dead. Captain Jefferson made it a point to inform her about Wilcox's reputation with women, which was not flattering. She had no trouble telling him she wasn't interested. She logged the incident and notified her Captain. However, Wilcox, having connections and wanting revenge, reported the incident to his superiors, including Vice Admiral Griffin, who oversees all Alliance dealings. Unfortunately, his report was contrary to hers, and the fleet admiral ordered Benson arrested based on pressure from Wilcox. If it weren't for Captain Lawrence Jefferson having read the report Benson filed and reviewed written interviews with several crew members who had been present in the dining hall at the time, she would have been arrested and thrown in the brig. Instead, Jefferson filed a scathing report of the Ambassador with Alliance Command that turned the tables on the Ambassador, and he grudgingly dropped his case against Benson. Jefferson pursued the case against Benson's wishes. However, it cost Wilcox dearly. He would have been relieved if he were not so skilled at interacting with alien cultures. Besides, he had the head of the fleet in his back pocket, ensuring he escaped prison. The Ambassador never forgave Benson for saying no. Here he was again, on a diplomatic mission, and she was sitting less than five feet away.

When Benson put in for a transfer, it was a dream come true for the fleet admiral. He quickly sent her to the *Saratoga*, where he secretly sent people he considered a problem, hoping the ship would never return. That was his hope for this mission to Inea. He would be rid of Benson, who had become a liability in his mind, and Hackett, who was often critical of Vice Admiral Griffin. He would also be rid of Ambassador Wilcox, whose arrogance was casting a negative impression of Admiral Griffin and President Wakefield.

Ambassador Channing also saw Benson's expression, and he looked at Wilcox. He knew there would be trouble, and he wouldn't have to wait long for it to boil over. He glanced over at Hackett, and he saw Hackett studying the two of them.

Channing couldn't let it happen again. He knew Benson was a good officer, and Wilcox, however arrogant and self-righteous he was, was the best negotiator the fleet had. He excused himself from Wilcox and made a motion to Hackett to follow.

Hackett caught the signal and turned the bridge over to Morris. He followed Channing to the elevator. Once both men were out of sight, Wilcox cleared his throat and moved towards Benson.

"Is it Ensign Benson?" he asked her with sarcasm.

She didn't look up and answered bluntly, "It's Lieutenant Commander Tamora Benson… Sir."

"Oh, I see. I stand corrected, Ensign. We should meet later and discuss your role in the upcoming mission, yes?" he pressed on.

Benson shook her head in disgust and thought, What a shameless jerk. He wasn't ashamed of the past. She knew he blamed her for his trouble.

Benson was beginning to have doubts about transferring to this ship. She knew Wilcox wouldn't let up, not on this trip, certainly not on such a small ship. There was no place for her to go to stay away from him. She thought back to the last time they had words. She knew he would make good on his threat to destroy her. It would be easy for him to do so now, only a few feet away.

“Ensign Benson?” he asked, putting his face in front of hers.

"No! Sir. It is not acceptable that we meet," she replied harshly. Her face was getting red now. In her mind, she was willing him to go away. Unfortunately, it didn't work. He stood, facing her, leaning towards her face, trying to intimidate her. So far, she hadn't budged. She didn't cross the line; he dared her to step over. She knew better than to tell him off or say something he could use against her. It would mean leverage to get what he truly wanted from her. She bit her lower lip and didn't take the bait.

Morris was watching the conversation with interest. The hostility between the two was glaringly obvious.

“I want to go over the upcoming mission, and you would be a perfect addition to our team. What do you say, Commander Benson?” he said, toying with her now.

Morris went to step in, but Benson handled it for him. "Sir! If the Captain orders me on the mission, then I will perform my duties to the best of my ability. However, this station needs to be programmed and secured for departure, Sir!" Benson stated with her head down, emphasizing "sir" each time. She had removed the manual again from its holder on the side of the manual navigation computer by her knee, attempting to look busy until the ship was ready to leave.

Hackett guided the elevator down a few decks and then stopped between decks. He looked at the Ambassador, who appeared concerned. "You have something to say, Ambassador?" Hackett asked with his military firmness, which made Channing tense.

"Yes, Captain, it affects this mission," he said, fidgeting slightly from Hackett's harsh commanding tone.

Hackett folded his arms and looked at him, wondering what the issue was. “Go ahead, Ambassador, I’m listening,” he said with modest irritation.

"Several months ago, we were on a mission to Altair-three. We used the *Challenger*, and 'that' woman was there. Wilcox made several advances toward her that she refused. No woman had ever refused him before and gotten away with it. He lied to the fleet admiral and eventually was court-martialled, but only after the Captain," he thought for a second. "Jefferson corroborated her story with other crew members. He got off with a slap on the wrist. It left a permanent blemish on his record. The board of inquiry investigated and found that Wilcox not only lied but was trying to coax her into his bed with promises of promotions and cushy jobs."

"Interesting," Hackett said, and he pressed the button, and the elevator moved up towards the bridge. He stopped it again when Channing continued.

"Wait, it gets worse. Wilcox vowed to destroy her career if she wouldn't 'come around.' Her presence here could derail this mission before we leave port, Captain." Channing placed his hands on his hips and stared at the Captain, hoping to drive home his point.

"Thank you, Ambassador, for the information. I will make every effort to keep them separated as best I can," Hackett replied.

"It won't be that easy, Captain. He will use his authority with Vice Admiral Griffin to assign her as his assistant to Inea. He'll then set her up to cost us the mission that will destroy her career," Channing replied.

Hackett reflected on their previous navigator and quickly replied, "We are going to Inea. It will cost her more than her job if she goes there. It will cost her her life. I plan on making sure that doesn't happen, Ambassador. Thank you. We need to be on the bridge." Hackett reached for the controls and sent the elevator chattering towards the bridge again. Hackett was deep in thought when they walked onto the bridge, and he failed to notice Morris trying to get his attention. Hackett was going to make sure Benson was never alone or near the Ambassador for the rest of the trip, which was no easy task on such a small, crowded ship.

Morris walked up to the Captain and gestured to talk at the rear of the bridge. Hackett longed for a bridge with a situation room to avoid the elevator conferences. He sprang from his chair mere seconds after sitting and walked back with Morris, who whispered, “Sir, we have a problem.”

“I know, Commander, we’ll both talk to her,” Hackett said, pointing over his shoulder with his thumb in Benson’s direction, “and we need to find out her story. In the meantime, print up any reports on them and have them ready.”

“We should do it the first chance we get, sir,” Morris said.

Hackett nodded, “Agreed.” Both men went back to their stations.

“Time to departure?” Hackett asked.

“Fourteen minutes, sir,” replied Morris.

“Commander Morris. Close all air locks and secure all hatches,” Hackett said.

“Yes, sir,” he replied. Morris called down to security and requested that they close all hatches.

“Mr. O’Toole, bring the primary energizer online,” Hackett said.

O’Toole replied, “Primary energizer powering up, Captain. It will take a couple of minutes to stabilize.”

After a few minutes, O’Toole turned from his station to tell the Captain what he already knew. Hackett could feel the energizer’s vibration through the floor. “Captain, the energizer is running and stable.”

“Thank you, Mr. O’Toole. Miss Davies, please clear all moorings and release all docking clamps,” Hackett said, glancing at his mini terminal, which was integrated into the left armrest of his chair.

Davies pressed several buttons, and the ship shifted slightly. Benson fired the thrusters to hold the ship’s position. “Captain, all moorings cleared. We are running on internal power.”

“Very good. Mr. Giovanella, contact the dock master and tell them we are ready.”

“Aye, sir.” After a pause, Giovanella continued. “Dockmaster says the port is clear, and we are free to depart, sir.”

"Thank you. Miss Benson, take us out, please," Hackett said.

It was time for Benson to put a disastrous day behind her. She had already embarrassed herself in front of much of the crew and herself, and now HE was sitting behind her. All she had right now was her ability to pilot the ship out of spacedock. It was her time to impress her shipmates.

"Firing port thrusters to move us away from spacedock," she stated.

The ship moved sideways away from the dock. "Reverse thrusters firing, one-quarter power." The ship began to move backward. Benson manually dialed the course and aimed directly for the center of the opening to space. "Captain, may I try a different maneuver once we clear the doors?"

Hackett looked at her. "Yes, as long as it is within fleet regulations."

She nodded and programmed what she had planned. The ship exited the space dock in full reverse power.

An image of Cadet Harrison lying in his coffin popped into her mind. He was bleeding from his hands. His mouth was moving. She couldn't hear what he was saying. He was talking to her. However, she didn't understand. As suddenly as the vision appeared, it was gone. She shook it off and pressed a few buttons as the ship rolled sideways 180 degrees on its 'Y' axis, while simultaneously rolling on its 'Z' axis to -31 degrees. The rear thrusters fired to full power, pressing everyone into their seats. Once the ship stabilized, Benson activated the quantum drive as bright blue beams shot from the Quantum nacelles to a point in front of the ship, tearing a hole in space. Space and stars in front of the starship twisted around a central point and lit up in bright colors as they flew into the middle of the disturbance. She slid the throttle control forward a few inches on the touch panel, pressing everyone back into their seats further. The ship accelerated to quantum speed in mere seconds. Everyone on the bridge was impressed with her piloting. The image on the main viewer was of a spiraling tunnel directly in front of them.

Hackett was the first to speak. "That was interesting, Miss Benson."

"Thank you, Sir. This ship is impressive. The *Challenger* handles like a slug compared to this ship," Benson stated. She was beginning to like this old tub, as some referred to it.

"Well, I am ready to vomit. There will be no more of these reckless indulgences, Captain," Wilcox growled. He groaned as he lifted his slightly overweight body from his chair and motioned to Channing to follow him as he stomped off the bridge. The two guards came forward, disengaged the chairs, and took them off the bridge.

SEVEN

HACKETT LOOKED AT BENSON. It was time. "Miss Benson, please secure your station and come with us."

She looked up, "Yes, sir," and secured her terminal. *Crap! Did he see me hesitate?*

"Larson, the bridge is yours," Hackett stated firmly.

Benson pushed away from the nav-con and followed Hackett and Morris to the elevator. All three of them stood silently as the lift went down. The doors hissed as they slid open onto deck five. Hackett walked out first, followed by Benson and then Morris. They walked forward over a hundred feet, turned left at the galley, and then right several feet up and into Conference Room One. Hackett sat at the head of the table. Morris sat beside him, and they had Benson sit across from them.

Once they were all seated, Benson spoke first. "Captain, I can explain."

Hackett waved her off and began talking. "Miss Benson. We have concerns regarding your previous relationship with Ambassador Wilcox. I need you to explain the situation between you two in case it interferes with the mission."

She sat up straight and looked at Hackett. She was shocked at the question. "Oh. That." She wished he were reprimanding her for the maneuver she just pulled. She sat nervously for a moment, fiddling with her hands. She glanced at Morris, who was watching her. She folded her hands on the table, exhaled, and looked back toward Hackett. "There is nothing between us," she began. "There never was. He came onto me while I was on the *Challenger.* I refused, of course. That wasn't the end of it, however." She looked up toward the light on the wall, hoping a bolt of electricity struck her dead instead of answering this question. She looked back toward Hackett and continued. "I immediately reported the incident to Captain Jefferson. He pursued the case with the Vice Admiral, and now Wilcox has been after me for several months, looking for revenge." She finished and sat back, folding her arms against her chest in anger.

"That's what we figured by reading the reports filed. I just wanted to hear it from you," Hackett said firmly with no emotion. "Commander Morris contacted command to pull the file on the Ambassador regarding that incident. I will make sure he stays away from you on this mission. We will talk to him ourselves."

“Thank you, sir, but I can handle him.”

“By the looks of the report, I would agree.” He paused a moment. “We don’t need trouble on this mission, so we’ll talk to him,” Hackett said. “That will be all, Miss Benson.”

"Thank you, sir," she replied, and got up quickly, exiting the room and returning to the bridge.

Hackett looked at Morris, who was rummaging in a folder. He eventually removed a couple of pieces of paper to show the Captain. "Captain, here is the report filed by Captain Jefferson, and this is the final fleet ruling on the matter." Hackett took the papers from Morris and scanned them for several minutes. He was interested in one clause in the final ruling that he circled and showed to Morris.

Morris looked at the paper and rubbed his chin with his hand. "Huh, that's interesting, Captain. The Ambassador is ignoring a fleet resolution that he must stay away from her and never contact her."

"Very interesting, he's violated two major parts of that clause; that means he can do time in the brig," Hackett emphasized. "It's time to talk to the Ambassador. Please page him here, Commander."

"Yes, sir." Morris got up, walked to the comm pad on the wall, and pressed an unlabeled and well-worn button on the keypad. It beeped, and Morris called for Wilcox to reply. He did. However, his tone told Morris that he wasn't pleased with the interruption. After several minutes of arguing, Wilcox finally agreed to come forward.

He arrived late, and Hackett knew it was intentional. After everyone was seated, Hackett told the Ambassador why he was called in. "Sir, I want it made known that I am aware of the incident between you and Lieutenant Commander Benson on the *Challenger* several months ago. I have here the official fleet ruling on the matter, along with Benson's report and that of Captain Jefferson."

The Ambassador was quick to respond. "That's all rubbish, Captain. The girl made a pass at me, which I refused, and it got blown out of proportion. When I said no, she threatened to run to her Captain, who was having an affair with her. It was sick, really. She threatened to have me thrown in jail, which Jefferson nearly succeeded in doing."

Hackett looked at the papers and looked into Wilcox's eyes. "That isn't what these three reports say, Ambassador." Wilcox tried to respond, but Hackett wouldn't let him. "I also have the report from my first officer about your interaction with Lieutenant Commander Benson a short time ago on the bridge."

The Ambassador just smiled at Hackett. "That poor girl is still hooked on me. That is so pathetic. I tried to be nice to her, but she wouldn't even look at me, Captain. I hope you will see the severity of having her on the bridge for this mission and remove her from your bridge for this mission."

Hackett knew that would play into the Ambassador's hands, so he couldn't do that. He had an alternate plan for Wilcox. "I need her on the bridge, so let's do this. I will make sure she makes every attempt to stay clear of you as long as you do not include her in any part of your mission. Let's say not as a personal assistant. Does that work for you?"

"Well, Captain, this is a small ship, and the odds of us running into one another are great. Here's my proposal. I will contact the fleet and inform them that I would like her to be my transport pilot. Then I'll say I need her to act as my personal assistant, and you know what, Captain?" Wilcox said smugly.

Hackett looked at Wilcox. “No, what?” Sarcastically.

Wilcox leaned across the table. "They will order you to make her comply, and you will do it because you are not a fool, Captain. Don't waste your time protecting her. Unless you have a thing for her? She has a way with authority figures. Just ask her previous Captain." Wilcox leaned back and grinned at Hackett.

Hackett sat back in his chair. Morris was watching as the conversation deteriorated. "I see, Ambassador. I look forward to receiving those orders. I will also file a report with my superiors, letting them know about how you've treated her so far on this mission. Also, as you may or may not know about what happened to our last navigator, I will be very reluctant to send another woman down to that planet." The Ambassador went to speak and stopped as Hackett continued. "That will be all, Ambassador.”

Hackett got up and motioned for Morris to follow. Both men walked into the corridor. Morris spoke first as the door closed. “Sir, what are you going to do?”

“I'm going to wait and see how much weight that report holds before I get into a pissing contest with that guy,” Hackett said.

“Yeah. Do you think he'll call your bluff?” Morris asked.

Hackett looked at Morris and froze him in his tracks. "Who's bluffing? We are being watched on this mission, and this might be part of the test. Just keep your nose clean and eyes open, Commander." Hackett walked away towards the elevator to return to the bridge. "Besides, Wilcox and Benson will not cost us this mission or our lives when we deal with the Ineans. I won't allow it."

“Yes, Captain, I agree. However, I do have a question,” Morris said.

“Go ahead.”

"Why didn't you reply when he mentioned a connection between Benson and Captain Jefferson? He's now trying to implicate you," Morris said.

"We both know it's crap, and I'm in no mood to argue his idiotic accusations, Commander. Besides, I know Jefferson personally, and he would never get involved with a member of his crew," Hackett stated. "He is right about wanting to protect her. It has to do with what happened to Sasha Young. You had a front-row seat to what the Ineans did to her. If I can avoid sending another woman to such a brutal death, then I will."

"Yes, Captain, I understand. That is one incident I will never forget. I still wake up in the middle of the night from it." Morris replied as both men continued on to the bridge. It was still to be a busy day.

"Sasha!" Morris yelled as an Inean soldier punched him in the face. "Sasha!" He yelled again, blood starting to trickle from the corner of his mouth. The Inean soldiers pulled the woman from his grasp and proceeded to beat her. Morris pushed forward as the torn top of her uniform flew past his head, and he saw the Inean guards tearing at her. She was screaming, but he was powerless to help. He glanced over toward Hackett, who was being beaten by several Ineans. There was nothing he could do either. He glanced back toward the woman navigator. She was bloodied now, still screaming as the Ineans continued to toss her around and hit her. The group of Ineans grew to well over twenty, and they all laughed and cheered their comrades on.

Morris shook off the thoughts as he entered the elevator behind Hackett.

EIGHT

ENSIGN WOODS and Lieutenant Perry sat back and watched the ship roll and go to star speed. They lay back in each other's arms and watched the stars spiral by.

Woods leaned toward him. "You do know we are going back to Inea, don't you?"

"Yeah, I heard. They'll keep sending us to that hellhole until we don't come back," he said while rubbing her shoulder.

"Don't say that," she said as she turned away.

"It's true, you know. The admiral has it in for us, and it's because of the Captain's attitude towards the vice admiral and the president of the NAU. I just don't think we're coming back from this one."

"I know. I have that gut feeling as well. Let's prove it wrong. Okay?" Woods said as she ran her fingers through his hair.

"Okay," he said, and they kissed.

"Should we transfer to another ship before Hackett gets us killed?" Perry asked.

"I thought about that. I heard there are a couple of openings on the *Draco*. I also heard Morris was going to be the Captain," she said.

Perry looked at her while continuing to rub her shoulders. “Let’s put in for it then. It’ll have to be safer than here. Deal?”

"Deal," she replied. She picked up her watch from the floor and looked at it. "Time to get back to work." They sat up, cleaned up their picnic, and pulled on their clothes. They proceeded up to their living quarters and stowed their picnic basket away. No one knew about their hiding places, and they wanted to keep it that way.

NINE

CHANNING FLINCHED as Wilcox swore at him. He tried not to. It was a habit he could not break. When Wilcox yelled, it rattled through his body. The force of his yelling jolted most people. Although Channing had to take it, he was still the assistant to the Alliance's best negotiator. He was proud of that fact, even though he despised Wilcox, the arrogant, rude, and self-righteous bastard that he was. He had heard it all before. Besides, he knew the true story, and he wouldn't be dragged into it again.

Wilcox stormed for the door and pushed it sideways when it didn't open fast enough. "Damn rust bucket!" he yelled. Channing followed Wilcox back to his room. Wilcox opened his suitcase, removed a portable computer and quantum transceiver, and placed them on the desk. He plugged it into the communications port on the wall and powered up the portable computer. He proceeded to establish a video connection with Vice Admiral Griffin.

The image of Max Griffin, the head of the fleet, flashed onto the screen. "Ambassador, why are you contacting me so soon?"

"Admiral, there is a problem," Wilcox said, facing the screen.

Maxwell Griffin wasn't one easily ruffled, but this Ambassador was the one person who irritated him quickly. Griffin was harsh with his response. "What is it now, Wilcox?"

“Sir, ‘THAT’ woman is on this ship. The one that could have caused a lot of trouble for us before,” Wilcox yelled.

“Still blaming her for your mistake, Wilcox. What do you want me to do?” Griffin said harshly.

“I want you to order Captain Hackett to make her my pilot and my assistant for the mission. She is perfect for the job, especially on Inea.” Wilcox was adamant about his request.

“And if I don’t?” Griffin asked.

“Then this mission is compromised already, sir!”

Griffin slammed his pen to his desk in apparent anger at being manipulated this way, and he yelled at Wilcox. "How is that, Wilcox? And don't forget what those animals did to my niece!" he yelled, slamming his fist to the table.

"Simple, Sir. You put us on this old, rusty, bucket-of-bolts of a ship that probably won't make it, and the Captain is too wrapped up in protecting his crew. Make it happen, Admiral, and the mission will go fine," Wilcox said.

"I will think about it, Ambassador. I won't promise anything. Remember what I told you about what those animals did to my niece and Hackett's navigator! They went to Inea under a flag of truce, and those animals ripped the poor girl to pieces! I don't like Hackett. That is a fact. However, I do admire him for protecting his crew. Command out." The Admiral forcefully switched off the connection, leaving Wilcox staring at a blank screen.

Wilcox slammed the lid down and swore, then yelled at Channing and told him to get out. Channing had had enough of this jerk. He stormed out of the room and went to the bridge. He stormed off the elevator and approached the Captain.

"Captain, we need to talk!" he said. His face was red, and sweat was beading on his forehead.

"Let's go then," Hackett replied as he studied Channing. He turned toward Morris. "Mr. Morris, please come with us."

Channing grabbed Hackett's arm. Bad idea. Hackett instinctively pulled back hard and nearly knocked Channing to the floor.

"I don't care who you are! Never grab me!" he said with a brief flashback to Inea. The Ineans had grabbed him and slammed him face-first and hard onto a table. They had held him down as one of the guards opened a jar containing a large, furry spider with a body that would fill a man's hand. It was black and gnashed its pointed teeth at him as it leaped from the jar and ran across the table toward him.

Hackett quickly dispelled the image with a glance toward Morris. Morris overlooked the lapse. Everyone on the bridge turned to see what was going on. The two guards posted at the elevator entrances stepped forward and stopped when Channing spoke.

Channing was briefly shaken. "I apologize, Captain. Bring her instead!" he said, pointing to Benson.

Hackett stopped and looked at him, then Benson, and then Morris. Then back to Benson. "Miss Benson. Come with us. Mr. Morris, the bridge is yours." Hackett was growing tired of the controversy surrounding his new navigator, and the aggravation was evident in his voice.

The three of them filed into the elevator and returned to deck five. Benson glanced over to Hackett and saw his expression. He was definitely angry and wouldn't return her stare. She could see his face becoming redder, and he was tense. She was now convinced she had made a huge mistake coming to this ship. While he was a lenient captain, he allowed no room for controversy or trouble, she was told. No one spoke while they proceeded back to the same conference room. After they were all seated at the table, Hackett motioned for Channing to speak first.

"Captain, Lieutenant Commander," he regarded them both. "I want to tell you, Captain, that my colleague is not well. I think he expects this mission to fail and is using her as his excuse, Sir. Actually, I think he is insane."

Channing thought about what he had said. There was no turning back now. He had raised doubts about Wilcox and, in doing so, put his own job on the line.

Hackett leaned forward. "How so?"

"He is putting pressure on the head of the fleet to put her in the hot seat so when the mission fails, she takes the fall. I've seen him do this before," Channing continued.

"If this mission fails, we probably all die, including Wilcox. Has he thought of that?" Hackett said, with an edge to his voice.

"He's a survivor, Captain. He'll find a way and leave us for dead if he can. Wilcox is all about Wilcox and what young woman he can screw next," Channing replied.

Benson watched the conversation with interest. It was the first time she had been on a mission where the possibility of dying was so strong. She began to think that she had made a very big mistake.

'Take, eat. This is my body, which is given to you for everlasting life.' The image of her mother giving communion ran through her mind. What was that? It's been a long time since I've heard those words. She instinctively glanced up toward the ceiling. She couldn't help thinking that someone was trying to tell her something. Yes, someone was. Someone was telling her she was about to die and needed to atone for her life.

"Why did you need Lieutenant Commander Benson here to tell me this?" Hackett asked.

"Because, Captain, she is not at fault. She is a victim of sexual abuse at the hands of the Ambassador, and I wanted to let you know that in front of her, so you would understand that she is tough and has done the right thing. She didn't ask for him to come on to her. She has handled herself quite well." He sat back.

Hackett wanted to know more. He didn't quite know how to ask or why he wanted to know, so he struggled to form the proper words. "Miss Benson, is this true?"

She nodded yes. Hackett looked at her. "What do you want me to do? Do you want to sit this mission out?" he asked her.

Benson cleared her throat, sat up straight, and folded her hands on the table. She looked at Channing and then Hackett. "Sir, I transferred to this vessel for one reason and one reason only, and that was because I wanted a tough assignment. Well, Captain, I guess this is it. I don't want to sit this out. I can handle this with no compromise in my ability. I know you don't know me yet. Just give me a chance to prove myself. The Ambassador is low-class scum, and I can hold my own against him; if not, I'll just kill him." She sat back, cracked her knuckles, and just smiled.

Channing looked at her for a second. He was unaccustomed to a woman cracking her knuckles.

Hackett looked at her and admired her for her firmness. "Hmm, I don't think that will be necessary, and I appreciate your willingness to go on this mission. However, if you need to talk to anybody, feel free to pull me aside. If you don't want to talk to a man, then I can have one of our nurses speak with you."

"That won't be necessary, Captain. Thank you, though. Mr. Channing, thank you for coming forward with the information," she replied.

"Okay, let's put this behind us once and for all and concentrate on this mission. Thank you, Ambassador and Lieutenant Commander." Hackett got up and started for the door. He was followed by Channing and Benson.

Later, Benson strolled the dimly lit corridor toward her quarters. She read the signs next to each door and noted the bulkhead numbers. She finally saw the pattern in the overhead compartment numbers. It was now 2200 hours, and she had completed her third four-hour split shift of the day.

The work on a starship was grueling, which required the crew to work short shifts separated by long breaks. Much of the crew took advantage of these breaks to work out in the gym or relax in one of the several lounges. While the ship was small compared to the new ships, it had several sports centers: two racquetball courts, a basketball court, a tennis court, and a full gymnasium with weights, treadmills, and bicycles.

She continued her way down to her quarters on deck five after finding one of the racquetball courts. She would check this out in the next day or two. She was an excellent player and won most of her matches easily. Some would argue that she is the best in the fleet. It was her "win-at-all-cost" attitude that made her this way. She also rode herself hard when she made a mistake, which was a carryover from her daily work ethic. Because of her attitude and skill, many of her crewmates from the *Challenger* avoided her when she took the court.

After some time, she turned a corner and entered her quarters. She sat at her desk, pressed a few buttons on the computer, and waited for her messages to arrive. While she waited, she kicked off her shoes and socks, untied her hair, and undid her uniform top. She pulled off her uniform jacket and placed it over the back of chair. She relaxed and composed a letter home.

Benson was the farm girl from Nebraska. She had an older sister and a younger brother. Her father was a former Navy man who had served on several vessels, including some older submarines. He had retired many years ago and was now in his seventies. He was also in poor health, and Tamora worried she wouldn't see him much anymore. Her sister had gone into medicine, and her brother was in the fleet academy as an engineer. Her mother was healthy but unable to manage the farm on her own and was trying to sell it. It upset Tamora to think about not calling the farm home anymore or losing her father while she was hundreds of light-years from Earth.

She dictated a message home and read it over to ensure it was correct. When satisfied, she pressed the send button and shut down her computer as the screen displayed "New Message Received." She didn't see the prompt as the lid clicked shut. She grabbed her towel and knocked on the door to the bathroom. No one answered, so she pressed the open button, and as the door slid open, she peeked around the corner. *Good, nobody here.* She stripped, set the water temperature and spray, and stepped into the shower. The frosted glass door slid shut with a hiss and click. In the shower, she stood with the hot water hitting her face and thought about her life and the jerk of an ambassador chasing her. She also reflected on the day and burst out laughing at the comedy of the mistakes she made. Once out of the shower, she toweled off and brushed her teeth and hair. She instinctively wrapped a towel around herself and went back into her room. She pulled the towel off, folded it, and placed it on the chair by her desk. She turned, pulled the blankets out slightly, and crawled into the bed. "Lights off!" she commanded. Nothing happened. She flipped the blankets off with a huff and went to the switch on the wall as she mumbled about the old ship. The room went dark, and she fumbled her way to the bed.

Hackett remained on the bridge until midnight and monitored the shift change, which happened without incident. He finalized his reports for the day and found they were unusually full of notes for the first day of a mission. He excused himself from the bridge and handed it over to the night-shift Commander, Lieutenant Commander Lou Dobson. Dobson sat in the Captain's chair after Hackett left.

Hackett did not need or get a lot of sleep. What he lacked were proper eating habits. He would go nearly an entire day without food because it was inconvenient to take the time. This day would be no exception. Since breakfast, he had eaten nothing and was too tired to stop now. He went to his quarters and filed his personal log, including his own thoughts on Benson and the mission.

Hackett was starting his seventh month in command of this ship and had been in the fleet for several years. He was also the youngest to command a starship. He had a couple of brothers and a sister, but he was the only one to reach space. He was the middle child, and his parents had retired years before. His rank of Captain was the highest achieved by anyone in his family for any branch of the military. He was a lenient captain, but he expected big things from his crew, and they knew it.

"Captain's personal log: We left port today for our mission to Inea. I'm sure this is a test to see if I break down because of the incident just a few months ago with those hideous Inean poison spiders. I feel okay so far, and I think this mission will go according to plan. However, we did have an incident today involving a new member of the crew, Lieutenant Commander Tamora Benson.

Apparently, Ambassador Wilcox had a thing for her, and she turned him down on a previous mission while on the *Challenger.* Unfortunately, he wasn't ready to call it quits and started after her on the bridge. I have talked with both of them. At this point, I'm inclined to believe Benson's story. I reviewed the logs and reports from the previous incident involving the *Challenger*. I also have first-hand information from Commander Morris and Ambassador Channing from today's episode to back her up. I already filed my report with command, and it should be on the Admiral's desk in the morning."

Hackett paused for a drink of water and then continued. "This Benson woman seems to know her stuff. Unfortunately, she needs to be brought up to speed on these older systems. She piloted out of spacedock perfectly and did a good job of impressing me with a few trick maneuvers before we went to star speed. She is a very attractive woman, and I even did a double-take when she first came on board. However, I feel that she may be part of this test I was warned about, so I'll be keeping an eye on her as well.

"The rest of the ship seems to be functioning properly, and there are no other incidents to report. End log," he said, and he closed his computer and went to bed.

TEN

THE NEXT DAY was an early start for Hackett. Having gone to bed just a few hours before, his alarm reminded him that it was 0500 hours. He groaned while slowly dragging himself from the bed. He turned off his alarm, stretched, and headed towards the shower for his morning wake-up of hot, steamy water. He shaved, brushed his teeth, and pulled on a fresh uniform. Hackett heard his stomach growl, and for once, there was no immediate crisis to prevent him from eating.

He straightened his collar and heard something metallic hit the floor. He looked down and spied a gold bar that was once on his shoulder. He bent down, picked it up, and studied it. He straightened and looked in the mirror. The sight of the missing Captain's bar gave him an ominous feeling in the pit of his stomach, and he wondered if it was an omen. After a few seconds, he shook away the thought and reattached the gold bar to his shoulder. He checked the rest of his uniform to ensure it was perfectly fitted and wrinkle-free. He plucked a few pieces of lint from the front of his jacket. When satisfied with his appearance, he turned and headed out the door.

The galley was full at this early hour, and standing room only as usual. Hackett walked up to the line, grabbed a tray, and proceeded through, gathering quite an assortment of food. However, he couldn't pass the coffee urn without topping off his cup. He stood along the far wall of the galley and placed his tray on the narrow wire shelf. On the wall were a few large monitors displaying news feeds from Earth. He added sugar and cream to his coffee and peppered his eggs and home fries. He began to eat when he noticed Benson enter the room through the hatch a few feet away. She looked around and turned to leave. He caught her eye and called her over.

He looked her up and down, mentally noting how thin she was. "Miss Benson, you should eat something. It's a long day to go without food," Hackett said after quickly swallowing.

"I know, but there is no place to eat," she said as she studied the room.

"Oh, don't worry about that. People come and go quickly in here. Go grab a tray, and I'll make room for you," he replied.

"Thank you, Captain." She smiled and turned toward the growing food line.

After a few minutes, she returned with a mountain of food that would choke a horse. She had a little of everything on the plate. How it all fit without tumbling off was a testament to her engineering skills. It was also a sad reminder that her eating habits were as bad as Hackett's.

Hackett stopped and stared at the heap of food. "Hope you're hungry."

She nodded, having taken a mouthful of food. "This is probably it for today," she replied after swallowing.

Hackett grunted while nodding in agreement that he knew what she was talking about. They stood and ate their breakfast, conversing about various subjects, ranging from sports to their childhoods, career challenges, and families. Hackett was curious about her in more ways than one. He was trying to discover her true intentions on this mission and why she was really here. He didn't trust her, and nothing she said put his concerns at ease or gave him any indication either way. Second, he was attracted to her. He knew that was dangerous, or was this the fleet's plan? Send a woman like this to deceive him or manipulate him. *Bastards!* he thought.

Hackett liked to know who his crew was and enjoyed talking with them. He frequently found hidden talents and sometimes found people in the wrong position. He wanted to know who his crew was. With her, though, it was more personal. He was fighting a battle to control his desires for this woman and hoped to find something in her character that would send him running in the opposite direction, but so far, nothing had.

On the other hand, Benson didn't mind talking to the Captain about her life, and she didn't mind asking about his. It seemed to many in the room who thought that they had been friends for years. Benson was also curious about Hackett, with each question becoming increasingly personal. It was the first time in many years that she was interested in someone, and she wanted to know more. They were both aware of regulations, and neither had any intention of violating the rules. For them, at least for now, it was mere curiosity.

Time passed quickly, and it was five minutes before the shift changed. Both of them had to be on the bridge. They discarded their trays, stepped into the corridor, and walked together, still talking as they came across Commander Morris, who was also heading toward the elevator. The three of them continued up to the bridge. Morris noticed that their conversation changed when he arrived, and he looked at both of them for a sign of anything that could be trouble.

When the elevator reached the bridge, Benson exited, and Morris asked Hackett to remain. He closed the door and didn't go anywhere.

Morris looked at Hackett. “Sir, may I ask you something?”

Hackett returned the look and then turned toward the doors. "Sure, what is it, Commander?"

"Sir, I couldn't help noticing that you seemed to be in a deep conversation with the lieutenant commander when I arrived, and it changed right after. I need not remind you of the implications, Sir," Morris said.

Hackett was shocked by the question and then thought for a moment. "I suppose it could have looked that way, Commander. The mess hall was crowded, and she took a standing spot next to me, and we struck up an innocent conversation that carried on into the hall. I'm not aware that we stopped when you arrived. I can assure you that there is nothing there. I am aware of the regs, Commander. Besides, I think she was planted here by Command to test me, so I won't be getting involved."

"I'm sorry, Captain, I had to ask. Besides, if it were me, I would find a way," he said with a wink. Hackett let it go and opened the doors, and they took their stations. Hackett knew there had been something between Morris and their previous navigator, Sasha Young. He had chosen to never make an issue out of it. Morris seemed, at least on the surface, to be dealing with her horrific death.

Benson lay in the course and was going over her terminal for the morning. Like all the others on the bridge, she checked the logs from the previous shift. Benson was more interested in the subtle course changes over the night, and she recalculated the time it would take to reach Inea. Hackett took his seat and began his review.

“Status, Commander Morris,” Hackett asked.

"Sir, all the ship's functions are normal. However, we are in the vicinity of Agasi-23, which is a recently discovered rogue planet passing through this part of space. Long-range scans from one of our outposts have yielded interesting results for mineral scans. Command would like more detailed, close-up scans to confirm."

“Understood, Commander. Miss Benson, lay in an intercept course and calculate how much time we can stay and still make Inea on time,” Hackett stated. He got up from his chair and moved toward the science stations at the rear of the bridge.

“Aye, sir.” She ran her fingers over the buttons and waited for the information to display. When it did, she turned towards Hackett. “Captain, we can stay for 17 hours and 20 minutes. We would have to travel at quantum six-point-two for the rest of the trip.”

“Very well, lay in an orbital trajectory,” Hackett said while watching the data scroll past on the large monitors around the science stations.

The image of the frozen planet began to fill the middle display as the ship closed in.

“Mr. Herndon, what can you tell us about this planet?” Hackett asked.

"Sir, it is slightly larger than Earth. It has a large quantity of water ice on the surface, which could have been oceans at one time. The atmosphere is thin with most of the gases now frozen solid on the surface as well."

“Where did it come from?”

“A rough guess so far would be a star system about twenty-five light years away. Given its current trajectory and speed, it could have been ejected about fifteen thousand years ago.”

“Could it have been a habitable planet back then?”

"Good possibility, given the readings I am receiving. Look at these mineral readings and the geographic lines under the ice. Could have been a civilization here at one time," Herndon said excitedly.

"Where is this planet heading?" Hackett asked. In a way, he hoped it would become part of another solar system someday. But his hopes were dashed when Herndon displayed a chart on one of the smaller monitors.

"Looks like it will remain in the void of space for thousands of years still. I would like to land a few probes on the surface to gather samples and data on any previous inhabitants."

"Go ahead, launch your probes. We only have a few hours, so we may need to leave them here until our return," Hackett stated while he watched the data on the monitors. He was joined by Morris, who was also intrigued by the possibility of an alien civilization that may have had to move away from its dying planet, much like the prospect of what the people of Earth may face in the near future.

Herndon performed several calculations and programmed the sensor packs for specific items he sought. He glanced at Hackett, who nodded, and he launched four probes toward the planet. "Probes are away, sir."

"Time until they land?" Morris asked with an eye on the clock above the display.

"About thirty minutes for the first one."

"Understood. Captain, the ambassadors should be apprised of this diversion," Morris stated as the elevator doors slid open to their right.

Ambassador Wilcox stepped onto the bridge and stopped. He looked at the dim, frozen planet which filled the main display at the front of the bridge and huffed. He then turned toward Hackett. "Captain Hackett! I object to this frivolous delay in our mission. You will stop this activity at once and continue to Inea!" the Ambassador growled.

Hackett turned towards Wilcox and went nose-to-nose with him while Morris stepped back. "Sir, I need not remind you of our primary mission, which is to seek a new home for our people because our planet is dying," Hackett stated firmly.

Wilcox did not back off. "Captain, as *you* may know, the Ineans have technology that can save our planet. That is why we are going there, to negotiate a deal for the plans to build these devices. Besides, what can this lifeless rock provide us with? We will leave at once, or I will take Command of this vessel under the guidelines of Article Seven, which states that-"

"Do not quote regulations to me, Sir. I am well aware of what Article Seven states, and it does not apply here. Besides, we will leave in a few hours and have you to Inea with plenty of time to spare. Now get off my bridge," Hackett interrupted.

Morris watched the Captain's interaction with the Ambassador, and Hackett remained calm and firm in his stand against Wilcox. There was no sign of him backing off or snapping under pressure, which Admiral Hodges feared.

"You cannot talk to me that way, Captain. The admiral will hear about this. Now, get this ship underway to Inea!" the Ambassador commanded.

"We will get underway when we are done investigating this

planet, and I look forward to hearing from the admiral. Now, get off my bridge."

Wilcox looked around the bridge at all the faces staring at him, wondering who would blink first, and it would be Wilcox, this time. He huffed. "This is not the end of this, Captain!" He stomped off the bridge.

Everyone turned away and went back to their tasks.

ELEVEN

BENSON WAS SITTING in her quarters, staring at the computer screen. On it were the case files from her previous encounter with Ambassador Wilcox. She thought back to the dinner she had with him on the *Challenger*. He sat across from her, holding her hand and smiling as he described her role in the upcoming mission. It would mean an advancement in her rank, he told her. It would also place her at his side while he negotiated their people's future in the galaxy. All of this intrigued her, but in the back of her mind was the warning from Captain Jefferson about what it meant.

She thought back to a meeting she had with Captain Jefferson. She was in his office, sitting across from him. *"Miss Benson, I need not remind you about Wilcox's reputation with women."*

"I understand, Captain. I just-"

"Just nothing, Lieutenant Commander. You will die after you are brutalized by him and with whom he is negotiating."

"But, Captain-"

"Tamora! Women are just a tool for him to use to get his way. He does not care about women and thinks nothing of what happens. Get your head around this. He is an animal. Just say no."

"Yes, sir."

She opened a different file, and the picture of a woman appeared in the left-hand corner. To the right side was some biographical data. She was a lieutenant and had been in the fleet for 15 years. As she scrolled down, she paused on one sentence: "Killed on assignment under the direction of Ambassador Wilcox."

She closed that file and opened another. It was similar. Another attractive young officer in the prime of her life and career. She scrolled down and stopped and read one sentence that was highlighted: "Killed on assignment under the direction of Ambassador Wilcox."

She opened another and another, and the results were the same. All had been brutalized by Wilcox and then butchered by the opposing counsel. All were mauled to their death.

She closed all the files and opened the fleet mission agenda for Inea. She scanned the file for her name. The first instance was what she knew. She was to get close to Hackett to see if he could be compromised. She looked on and found a sentence that made her stomach lurch: "Assign to Wilcox for Inea landing to satisfy Inean demands."

She wanted to vomit.

She closed the files on the computer and went to the head. She looked in the mirror and splashed water on her face. Her mind was spinning with the implications: she was being sent to her death, a horrible death, and she needed a way out. There was only one person who could help her: Hackett.

She would have to come clean with him about her assignment and hope he would help her. He had a reputation for protecting his crew, and she would have to show her loyalty to him to be worthy of it.

She toweled off her face and went in search of Hackett.

TWELVE

HACKETT STOOD toward the back of the science labs, monitoring the data upload from the remote probes. There was quite a buzz at the discovery of cities frozen beneath nearly a mile of ice. There were roads, forests, farms, and many other features, including minerals that had been frozen for thousands of years. However, any civilization that had been here was long gone. No power signals or heat were coming from below the ice, and the science team hoped the inhabitants had escaped to another planet.

Herndon turned to his team, "Whatever happened to this planet when it was ejected from its solar system happened quickly to preserve their culture for perhaps an eternity."

"I want to send a team down there with a habitat module and explore a city," one of the female officers said excitedly.

"I can requisition one today and have it dropped by the end of the week," Herndon replied.

"I want to be the first to volunteer!" another piped up.

Hackett stepped forward, "We need to gather as much information as we can with one more hour remaining and forward our findings to the Alliance Geo-Sciences division. They will dispatch the necessary people and equipment as they see fit."

“But Captain, time is not in our favor,” Herndon stated.

“Judging by your calculations, we have six years to investigate before the planet drifts out of range,” Hackett replied with a wince of pain.

"But, sir?" the woman officer replied.

“You have your orders. I will request that the *Saratoga* be the lead investigating ship when the time comes," Hackett said with a turn towards the hatch. "I suggest you wrap this up so we can get underway with our primary mission."

“Yes, sir,” each member of the room replied.

Hackett slipped into the corridor and leaned against the wall as the sharp pain in his head was joined by a crunching noise in his mind. He knew instantly what it was. He spied the elevator to take him to the ship's medical ward. He composed himself as best as possible and made his way toward the elevator.

He made it to the elevator doors, and they slid open. Lieutenant Commander Benson stepped out. "Captain, I need to speak with you for a moment," she said, her voice urgent.

“Not now, Miss Benson.”

He pushed past her and into the elevator as the crunching got worse. She saw he was in pain and went to say something as he closed the door. He slumped against the wall while resisting the pain. He thought back to the torture he endured at the hands of the Ineans just a few short months ago. His body had healed from the ordeal; his mind was a different story. He managed to hide many of the effects of the torture. Many believed he would never command again. Plus, he had an ally in Admiral Hodges, who leaned on the three-star Admiral, Maxwell Griffin, to reinstate him as soon as possible, even though he was probably not ready.

The doors slid open, and he stumbled towards the hatch to the medical facility. He staggered in with one hand to his head, sweat beading and running down his face, his body shaking as the pain in his head was like a knife being twisted in his brain.

A nurse rushed towards him and guided him to an examination table, where he was asked to sit at the end. She quickly checked his vitals as the lead doctor walked over with his clipboard.

"Lie back, Captain," Dr. Alice Williams stated.

"NO, just give me the new pills to fight this," Hackett insisted.

"What new pills?" she asked.

"Don't play games with me. The Admiral slipped up and told me there was a new treatment for the Inean spiders. Give me some."

"I can't just do that, Captain. There are pro-"

"I don't care about procedures. Just do it, now!"

She huffed and retreated to her office, and returned a few minutes later with a tan bottle with dozens of silver pills inside. "I just want it on the record that I do not agree with this."

"Yes, yes, noted," he replied quickly.

She handed him two oblong, silver pills, and the nurse provided a small cup of water. He downed them quickly and looked up at the doctor, who was obviously not pleased with being bossed around by her patient. "Now, lie back and let us monitor you," she said, placing her hands on his shoulders.

Hackett did as he was told, for once, and soon began to feel lightheaded and drowsy. He slowly drifted off to sleep.

His mind wandered back two months to Inea. His captors held him face up on a cold stone table and stripped him of his clothes. They pulled his arms harshly over his head and tied his ankles and wrists with leather straps to the stone. The large Ineans then whipped him several times.

"What is the status of your fleet, Captain?" the large Inean asked in his deep, rough voice.

"We are here to negotiate a treaty between our two peoples. Now release me at once," he demanded.

The Inean laughed, "I will release you when you tell me what I want to know."

"Never!"

"We'll see about that." He turned to one of his equally large assistants, "Bring in the Tarechque."

"Yes, at once," the large assistant said. He bowed and backed out of the room. The remaining Ineans whipped Hackett many more times until the assistant returned with a container about the size of a shoe box. He opened the box while the others stood back, and he peeked in and grinned, showing his pointed teeth. He glanced at the leader of their group, who turned towards Hackett.

"Tell me, Captain, what is the status of your fleet?"

"Go-to-hell!"

"I thought you would say that. Let me introduce you to a little friend of mine." The assistant stepped forward and lowered the box to Hackett's stomach. He tilted the box slightly, and a large, fuzzy spider larger than the palm of a human hand crawled out onto Hackett's bare flesh. He glanced at the beast with its inch-long fangs dripping with venom. He knew that if he showed any fear, it would come back to haunt him. He put his head down and tried to be calm. It did not last long as he tensed when the creature moved, and it sank its fangs into his skin, releasing its poison. Hackett flinched again, and the critter began biting him all over his body. Soon his skin began to burn. Large, red welts began rising over his body where he had been bitten. His blood started to burn in his veins, and he felt the burning creep up his neck. Soon, each time the animal bit him, he heard a crunching sound, and his head began to pound. His body convulsed, and he vomited all over himself, which drove the fuzzy spider crazier.

The assistant returned with another box and let several more spiders loose on Hackett. There was no part of his body spared from the assault. His vision blurred, and he could no longer hold his bowels. He began to scream from the pain as the lead Inean leaned close to his ear. "What is the status of your fleet, Captain?"

"I...I...Argh!"

Hackett began shaking his head side to side from the pain while the assistant retrieved the spiders to be used another day. He urinated on one of the Ineans while his wounds were whipped repeatedly, inflicting as much pain as possible. Hackett refused to answer.

After several hours, the Ineans unstrapped him from the cold stone and dragged his bloodied, shaking body to a holding cell. They tossed him in, and he landed with a puff of dirt, his body convulsing as he bled into the dirt floor. He remained in the cell for three days. Each day, the Ineans tortured him while his crew negotiated for his release.

Hackett woke up a few minutes later in the medical facility, where the doctor watched the screen above the bed for any signs of trouble. He sat up, and the pain in his head was subsiding quickly. Unfortunately, all his strength was gone now.

"May I go now?" he asked.

"You are the most stubborn person I have ever met," the doctor huffed. She brushed her brunette hair back over her left ear and adjusted her glasses to study Hackett for a moment. "Promise me that you will check in daily, or if there are any problems."

"Alice, I can-"

"You will do as I say, or I will relieve you of command," she said firmly.

"You wouldn't!"

"I would, and I will if there are any more episodes or if you miss checking in," she glared at him as he met her stare.

"Fine," he replied as he slid off the exam table. He fixed his uniform as he watched the doctor scribble some notes on her tablet.

She held the bottle up in front of her face so he could see it. "Take one every other day, with breakfast. And lay off the coffee for a few days. The caffeine may react with it."

She held the bottle out for him to take. She retracted it when he reached for it, "Understood, Captain?"

"Perfectly, Alice."

He took the bottle from her and walked out of the exam room.

Dr. Williams returned to her office, removed her white lab coat, and draped it over the back of her chair. She sat and pressed the comm button by the monitor. "Page Commander Morris."

A moment later, Morris responded, "Go ahead."

"Commander, Dr. Williams here."

"Yes, Doc," his voice sounded distant over the small speaker on her computer terminal.

“I just treated the captain for complications from the Inean spiders.”

“Is he all right?”

"He thinks he is. I did not remove him from command at this time. I did give him strict instructions to keep me informed of any more problems," she said while twirling the stylus from her tablet in her fingers.

"We are talking about Captain Hackett here." his tone was unmistakably laced with concern.

“Yes, Commander. What choice do we have? Do you want to take the lead on this mission?”

“Hell, no! I see your point. I’ll watch him. Morris out.”

She hit the off button and went back to her notes.

THIRTEEN

A FEW HOURS LATER, the science teams finished collecting their equipment from the rogue planet and one of its two lumpy moons. Now began the slow process of studying the data. The rest of the crew prepared the old ship for departure on its primary mission to Inea.

Hackett sat in his chair at the center of the bridge, reviewing the preflight reports and the summary Ensign Herndon had prepared to submit to the Geo-Sciences division of the Alliance. Hackett added his own recommendation that the planet warranted further investigation, based on the level of culture found and the possibility that whoever had lived there may have escaped alive before their world froze solid.

Hackett glanced at the clock above the main screen and saw it had counted down to under five minutes. "Commander Morris, all stations ready to leave orbit?"

"Aye, sir, all stations are ready."

"Navigator set course for Inea-Four. Set speed to quantum six-point-three when we are clear."

"Aye, sir," Benson replied. "Course is set and ready, Captain."

"Helm, take us out."

The ship shuddered slightly as the rear thrusters went to full power, pushing the ship away from the planet. Soon, they were past the outermost moon, which was no more than a lumpy, captured asteroid that tumbled around the rogue planet. The field coils in the nacelles began to glow as they charged with plasma created by the collision of matter and antimatter in the ship's main engine. Bright beams of energy blasted from the nacelles and began tearing a hole in space, and the ship moved towards the disturbance.

On the bridge, Commander Vincent O'Toole, the *Saratoga*'s senior engineer, observed the engine readings carefully on his terminals at the rear of the bridge. Everything was perfectly normal, and he was pleased as the ship was about to enter the wormhole. Suddenly, red lights began flashing on the starboard nacelle readings. "Emergency Shutdown!" he yelled. It was too late as the ship lurched violently to port, tossing everyone on the bridge to the floor. The red warning lights began flashing along with the fire alarms.

Hackett looked up to see the wormhole collapse with a violent flash. The ship began to tumble. The image on the main display spun. "Status!" he yelled.

O'Toole pulled himself up to his console and studied the readings on the large monitor in his station. The readings flickered. "Sir, we've had an explosion in our starboard nacelle near the antimatter containment vessels. So far, containment is holding. Crap! Fire suppression is not responding."

"What caused the explosion?" Hackett asked as he stumbled to the rear of the bridge. "Helm, steady the ship! Comm, apprise Command of our situation."

"Aye, sir," each responded while the crew returned to their stations.

O'Toole glanced at Hackett when he arrived to see much of the engineer's panel flashing red data. "Captain, I don't know yet what caused the explosion. All I can say is that everything was perfectly normal and then instantly went to hell. As far as I can tell, there is nothing in that area of the nacelle to cause such an explosion."

“What are you implying, Commander?” Hackett asked.

“Sabotage, sir.”

Everyone on the bridge turned and looked at the engineer once he said it.

Hackett turned to the security chief, who was seated next to the engineer, "I want this ship locked down immediately."

The head of security, Lieutenant Malcolm Desai, began paging his security teams without looking at Hackett. Desai was in his mid-fifties and had been the lead security officer on the *Saratoga* for 10 years. There had never been a successful terrorist attack on his watch. Rage filled him at the prospect that someone had gotten past his ironclad security. "All security teams are locking down the ship, sir," he stated angrily.

Alliance marines scrambled to their positions throughout the ship, and within minutes, every section of the ship had been secured. Armed guards in bulletproof vests, black helmets with tinted visors, black jackets with minimal insignia, black padded gloves, and steel-toed boots with aggressive tread were armed with Glock 30, 45-caliber pistols on their hips with spare magazines secured to their belts. A sharp knife was strapped to their thigh, and securely in their hands was the newly designed MiL246 laser assault rifle.

Entrances to sensitive areas were guarded by two marines on either side of each hatch, and no one entered or exited without proper clearance. A few minutes later, four marines entered the bridge and relieved the regular security personnel who patrolled the corridors. They took their positions on either side of the two hatches and stood at attention, waiting for something to happen.

Ensign Davies turned toward Hackett, "Captain, engines are not responding. We are still tumbling."

Lieutenant Bowers turned around. "Sir, we have not escaped the planet's gravity well. We do not have sufficient velocity to get away."

"Meaning?" Hackett asked, already knowing the answer.

"We are already slowing and arcing back towards the planet. I am still calculating how much time we have left." Bowers stated.

"O'Toole, get that fire out and get the mains back online,"

Hackett said as he looked at the rogue planet spiraling back into view on the main screen.

"Yes, Sir. I will need to go to the engine room and coordinate from there."

"Go!"

Hackett looked around the bridge as Ambassador Wilcox stumbled onto the bridge.

"This is your disaster, Captain! Your lack of security on this sensitive mission will kill us all!" Wilcox screamed while Channing struggled to restrain him.

The two closest marines switched on their laser rifles and took a few steps toward Wilcox as he went face-to-face with Hackett. They stopped when Hackett held up his hand.

"Ambassador, now is not the time! We need to put the fire out in the starboard nacelle and get the engines back online, or we will crash into that planet very soon," Hackett stated while pointing to the planet, which rotated into view every few seconds on the main screen.

Channing was becoming nauseous and had to turn his gaze from the spinning stars and planet on the main screen.

"Now IS the time, Captain! Your incompetence has ruined this mission. Your incompetence will be responsible for millions of deaths on Earth if we do not get the scrubber technology from the Ineans!"

"Get off the bridge, Ambassador, and let my people do their jobs," Hackett stated angrily as his nose touched the Ambassador's nose. He was doing his best to not strangle the Ambassador. The two marines inched closer.

"The Admiral and the president will hear about this. This is your last Command, Hackett. You should never have been placed back in Command so soon after the Inean torture, if at all."

"For the last time, Ambassador, get off the bridge and file whatever reports you feel you need to file. Now I have work to do." Hackett turned his back on Wilcox.

Wilcox stepped forward, forcefully grabbed Hackett's arm, and tried to turn him. "Don't turn your back on me, Captain."

Hackett turned quickly, ripping his arm from Wilcox's grip. Wilcox raised his fist to punch Hackett when the armor-clad marine leveled his laser rifle toward Wilcox's head.

"The Captain said to leave the bridge," the marine stated firmly. His laser rifle emitted a soft, high-pitched whine and stopped after a few seconds. It was charged and ready to fire. Wilcox knew it and unclenched his fist.

"Escort the Ambassador to his quarters," Hackett stated, and he turned back to view the helm controls in front of Ensign Davies.

The marine responded, "Aye, Captain. Ambassador, come with me."

"We are not finished, Captain!"

Hackett ignored Wilcox.

Mr. Giovanella, "send a message to command outlining our situation. Apprise any ships in the area that we may need assistance."

"Aye, sir."

Bowers cleared his throat, "Sir, fire is spreading in the nacelle. It is getting closer to the antimatter containment. I am picking up fluctuations in the magnetic containment field. If we can't stabilize it soon, we will lose containment."

"How much time do we have?"

"Less than thirty minutes. That's the best I can do."

FOURTEEN

DOZENS of light years away on the steamy, hot planet of Inea, numerous Inean warriors spilled out of an interplanetary transport as the dust settled around the landed craft. They roared and bellowed with anticipation as one of their comrades walked down the runway from the ship with a rusty iron chain in his hand. Several feet behind him, a woman emerged with the chain clipped to a collar wrapped around her neck. It was tight and cutting into her flesh. She grabbed at it with her hands, but it was no use. Blood slowly oozed out from around the collar. She was followed by another person and then another. The chain gang of human men and women seemed endless, their clothes torn and dirty, barely clinging to their bodies. Many cried. Many uselessly fought their captors. The Ineans were so much larger.

The Ineans guided the prisoners through a gate and up the brick path to the Emperor's tower. There, the Emperor could view the latest slaves stolen from various Earth colonies and outposts. Once the Emperor gave his approval by nodding, the slaves would be sold off and the proceeds used to fund the growing war with the Kosuan, which was a bloody war that was stalled, neither side winning, both sides losing.

The transport blasted off toward space with a deafening roar.

The Emperor nodded, and the gathering crowd cheered. The humans were then taken into a nearby market where they were stripped and sprayed with hot water and soap.

A soldier, probably a clerk, walked along the line of future slaves with a paint pen and wrote Inean numbers on their stomachs and backs. They would soon be sold as slaves to the highest bidder, a fate several knew would result in death.

The soldiers unhooked the chains from the posts, and everyone slumped to the ground. The ones whose feet never touched the ground while the chain was hung collapsed completely, fainting from lack of air. The soldiers guided them through the market, dragging some. They stopped by a platform that had been hastily constructed. The platform stood about 3 feet high and 12 feet square. It was surrounded by dozens of Ineans cheering and hollering, working themselves into a frenzy. The soldiers wrapped the platform twice and dropped the chain. Kicking up dust. The people dropped to the ground and stared, frightened at the angry mob.

The soldiers laughed at them and took their seats in the front row. Soon they would be bidding for their prizes.

An older Inean male made his way to the platform, followed by two others, and the crowd immediately quieted, focusing their attention on him.

He faced the crowd and bellowed like an announcer at a wrestling match. "Fellow Ineans, it is a glorious day!" He paused for the crowd to roar in agreement as he turned to face the Ineans behind him. All that was missing was the old-style microphone hanging from the rafters. He didn't need one. His voice was loud enough to be heard outside. "We have before us the finest selection of human slaves your hard-earned de'nars can buy!" Again, the crowd roared.

The two large-built guards who followed the older Inean stepped down and unhooked the chain around the first slave's neck, a woman, her neck raw from the tight fitting collar. Her body was slightly blistered from the scalding water sprayed on her earlier in a rushed attempt to clean her. Her long brunette hair got tangled in the chain as they yanked her away. She screamed as the chain fell to the ground, and the guards laughed. She fought them as best as she could. However, she was too small, and the guards laughed at her feeble struggle. To them, she was a toy, an amusement. They dragged her, one with each arm, up onto the platform. They spread her arms out tight until she cried out, and they laughed again with their deep, roaring laugh. They turned her to the crowd to show off the first slave to be sold.

She stood trembling as she looked out at the fierce crowd before her. What mattered now was somehow staying alive. She had heard about these auctions and knew her role. She also knew she most likely would not survive the day. She held onto hope anyway.

Only 48 hours before, she sat on her front porch with her husband and two children on one of the few Earth colonies to survive. The children played at their feet while she and her husband swung on the porch swing, discussing the day. Then it happened. It got quiet, very quiet. The birds stopped chirping, and the crickets on this planet stopped. Then there was a loud whoosh. Suddenly, the children looked up as four lizard-like beings slithered to the porch with great speed and grabbed the woman from her husband's grip. Those beings were poachers, paid handsomely by the Ineans to abduct human men and women and bring them back to Inea undetected. Her abduction had gone wrong, however. The local Alliance monitoring station detected their craft and now converged on their home. They grabbed her away while the children screamed, and her husband punched one of the poachers. He swung as hard as he could, but couldn't hurt the leather-clad lizards. They dragged his wife away while he tried to grab her back, and then there was a loud snap! She watched in horror as her husband's head erupted into flame and exploded. The rest of his body hung for what seemed like an eternity, but it was only a few seconds before his headless body fell to the ground. The children screamed hysterically, and the lizard with the gun turned toward them to shoot. Still, his companions grabbed him at the last second, and they slithered back to their ship without shooting the children.

They tossed the woman in the back with others who had been knocked out. They started the engines, and their ship took off while Alliance fighters closed in. The pilot used a few trick moves, flew his ship to the bottom of a lake, and waited for the Alliance ships to give up.

Here she stood. In front of a roaring crowd of hostile aliens, knowing her husband was dead. Her children? What of her children? They were only five and seven years old! No relatives lived nearby. The government must have them, she feared. They would be better off on their own.

Everyone looked up as another transport set down on the tarmac, another load of slaves to sell. Even though the Ineans signed an agreement with the Alliance a few months ago to stop the slave trade, they not only didn't stop, they stepped up their efforts, now importing hundreds a day. Many days topped a thousand. The Alliance was powerless to stop the poachers. Their small ships were fast, and they hid well when chased, sometimes hiding for days before rocketing to space and away from Earth and its colonies. The women were like catnip, a drug. The Ineans couldn't get enough of them. The men were sent to the dangerous mines on Inean outposts, where they worked until they dropped from exhaustion. Most died within days.

The crowd roared at the sight of another ship, and more Ineans poured into the arena.

The woman looked down at the others chained beneath her. Many looked at her with fright in their eyes. She noticed none of them were old. The oldest, she guessed, was about forty.

The Inean on the podium yelled, "Thanks be to the Great God Marduk for allowing Inea to find Earth!" The crowd, already in a frenzy, jumped up and down, screaming and yelling. They pounded on each other. The woman, of course, didn't understand him. He spoke in the Inean language. It all sounded like gibberish to them, a loud and forceful gibberish. "I will start the bidding at two hundred de'nars for the human bitch," he said while turning to see the whole crowd. The guards turned the woman in unison, so everyone could see.

Two hundred de'nars were a week's wage for the average Inean. Many of the slaves sold today would bring in 10 times that amount. Many buyers would prefer to go without food for days or even weeks just to add a human to their collection. It would be looked at as a status symbol among their peers. The human men would bring less. The main bidders were mine owners seeking cheap labor to perform the hazardous work that no one on Inea wanted to do.

The clerk had returned and stood by the steps to the podium. He was writing down the bids and tracking what type of human fetched the most money.

Many in the crowd yelled out as the auctioneer tracked the bids, which were going higher and higher. After several minutes, the bidding subsided, and the auctioneer declared the winner, who immediately pushed his way down to the platform. He reached into his pocket and handed the clerk his money. The clerk wrote down the information and quickly pocketed the cash. He looked at the first winner and handed him a slip to show ownership.

He growled and showed the guards his slip. They tossed the woman off the platform onto the ground at his feet like discarded trash. She landed with a thud as a cloud of dirt and dust billowed around her. She noticed the dirt was stained with blood, fresh human blood. She caught her breath, jumped to her feet, and was two steps into a run when the Inean who bought her clenched his hand tightly around her neck, stopping her suddenly. Her feet, still in run mode, came out from under her and dangled as he held up his prize. The Inean males were much larger than their human counterparts. She was too weak and too small. She gave up and prepared to die. Her arms and legs dangled as he held her up to the crowd by her neck. Blood oozed between his rough, hairy fingers. It dripped from her mouth and nose as he held her up. The crowd cheered. He threw her to the ground as the crowd cheered again. She was barely conscious as her head spun around. She coughed up blood while trying to get air into her lungs. The Inean grabbed her by a leg and dragged her across the dirt. Her head dragged in the dirt, leaving a blood-streaked path toward a side entrance. When the Inean reached the door, he held her up in the air by her leg and faced the crowd. They all cheered. He tossed her over his shoulder and walked out of the Coliseum.

The others to be sold watched, screaming in horror as the first slave to be auctioned off was brutally handled. She didn't die, though, not yet. She was tough and needed to live long enough to find her children wherever they were now.

FIFTEEN

HACKETT LEANED over Giovanella's shoulder and pressed a button. "O'Toole, containment is weakening. We have less than half an hour."

"I see it, Captain. We can't blow the bulkhead to put the fire out," O'Toole said. "Nothing in the nacelle is responding to commands."

Benson turned towards Hackett. "Send out a couple of technicians with explosive charges to blow the hull plate."

"It would take too long," O'Toole said over the speaker.

"What other plan do we have?" Hackett asked.

There was silence for a few seconds. "O'Toole?"

"I don't have anything yet," O'Toole replied.

"Do Benson's plan."

"Sir, but-"

"Do it! We are wasting time."

"Yes, Sir. O'Toole out."

Everyone on the bridge, including Benson, knew by O'Toole's tone that he was not pleased with the plan. This brought back painful memories of a similar situation during her first week on the *Challenger*. On that first mission, she had proposed a plan that was contrary to what the first officer had proposed for dealing with the Kosuan. Captain Jefferson liked her proposal, and from that day forward, the first officer was always on her back. Every little detail was critiqued. This had gone on for months until he was transferred to another ship. Those months were hell and made her reluctant to speak up for many months after his departure.

She remembered a conversation before he left. He had her pinned against the wall, not physically, but by his presence. His hands were placed against the wall on either side of her head while he stared at her, inches from her face. He said that women who looked like her only got ahead because of their looks, not their brains. He had questioned if she had been doing favors for the Captain. She said nothing. There was nothing she could say that would change his mind. It was the last conversation they had. One-sided as it was. They all were, and it hurt. She knew she worked hard and deserved every promotion she received. Unfortunately, he wasn't the only one who thought she had used her looks. She had heard many people say the same thing behind her back and to her face. Over time, it got a little better. Now she was making waves with the head of engineering. Not good to place someone with a higher rank on her bad side, but the damage was done. She thought maybe, just maybe, if she talked to him as soon as possible, it would eliminate a repeat performance. She was snapped back to the present when a warning light started flashing on her panel. The light was a reminder to change the ship's course before colliding with the rogue planet. She couldn't until the engines began responding to commands again.

Hackett sat thinking. He was concerned that his only option came from a new officer who had just joined the crew the previous day. He knew little about her other than what was in her record. He was also concerned about the safety of the ship and crew. This would be a hazardous procedure and could potentially destroy the ship, jeopardizing their primary mission.

Their primary mission, "mission impossible," it had been called, and rightfully so by many of the crew: Go to the hostile planet Inea. The indisputable hell hole of the universe, if there ever was one. A hell hole that left some of his crew dead, his navigator brutalized, and hopefully for her, dead.

He had become a mental wreck on the verge of suicide one moment and in complete control the next. All because of the poisonous spiders used by the Ineans to torture their enemy, and Hackett and his people *were* the enemy.

Their mission: to secure peace, ha! What a joke! Hackett said to himself. Secure peace, and then, out of their good nature, they will give us the technology to save the Earth from utter destruction by its own sun. It was a stalling tactic. If nothing else. He just wasn't sure which side was stalling or why. That 'why' would take some time to answer, and the answer could be the death of them all.

Two technicians secured their helmets and stepped into the airlock carrying a rectangular case with handles on the long ends. Once inside, the hatch closed. The bomb technicians checked their spacesuit environment packs and gave the thumbs up to the airlock operator. Air was blown out of the airlock, and a minute later, the hatch above the support pylon to the starboard nacelle opened.

The technicians activated their magnetic boots and exited the airlock. Walking in magnetic boots was difficult and slow, and time was not on their side. Bowers' best estimate before the antimatter containment breach was less than ten minutes. These techs would barely have enough time to set the charges, leaving no time remaining to escape the blast.

They trudged along at a snail's pace along the pylon, and the tip of the nacelle came into view. Small debris floated around the stricken field coils, which continued to glow from the plasma charge stored for the wormhole initiator canon.

One of the techs spoke up while walking, "Turning on thermal imaging." he pressed a button on the side of his helmet. He began recording the temperature of the nacelle. The top of the helmet housed four different cameras: normal optical view, thermal imaging, bioimaging, and infrared imaging.

On the bridge, the view on the main screen split into a thermal view on the left and a live visual on the right from the other technician's camera. The sensors showed the heat was dangerously close to the antimatter containment. It also showed Hackett that the nacelle was buckled slightly. He stood and stared at the view on the screen, concerned that if they managed to put out the fire, how would they get home? The ship needed energy focused from both nacelles to tear open a wormhole, but one would not do it, and now Earth would be decades away instead of a day.

"Captain, the temperature on the containment vessel is reaching 500 degrees Celsius. Magnetic bonds holding the antimatter are beginning to deteriorate. We need to put that fire out now!" Bowers stated with an edge to his voice.

"Lieutenant Daniels, how much time do you need?" Hackett asked.

"We need a few more minutes to get there, and then we need to set the charges, Captain," his voice hissed over the overhead speaker.

"We may not have enough time," Hackett stated.

"Sir! They don't have enough time," Bowers exclaimed. "Magnetic containment is collapsing."

"Rizzo, set the charge," Daniels said as the two techs moved as fast as they could along the nacelle to the point where the charges should be placed.

"Magnetic mounts set. Arming charge," Rizzo stated.

"Captain, we are sending more power to the containment system. Might buy us a few minutes." O'Toole said over the speaker.

"Daniels, Rizzo, did you hear that?" Hackett asked.

"Yes, sir," Daniels replied.

A minute later, they arrived at their destination. They set the bomb on the hull and released their magnetic boots. They ignited their jet-packs and headed back towards the airlock. While on their way, Daniels looked over his shoulder at the distorted nacelle and hit the detonate button on the remote in his hand.

There was a blinding flash behind them as the airlock hatch slid open. Both men hit the inner hatch as the outside hatch closed.

On the bridge, Hackett and the rest of his bridge crew watched the bomb tear the weakened upper hull plate off the nacelle. Fire and debris followed the hull plate into space. The vacuum of space quickly snuffed out the blaze.

The engineering console at the rear of the bridge lit up once again with flashing red lights. Bowers raced over to see what was wrong. "Captain, the explosion forced antimatter into the mixing chamber. Chamber temp is past critical!"

"O'Toole! Evac the mix chamber!" Hackett yelled while he watched the temperature soar.

Antimatter flowed rapidly into the mix chamber from the overheated antimatter, causing the injectors to stick open. This caused the antimatter to react explosively with the chamber itself.

"Evacuating now!"

Suddenly, the ship shuddered and twisted violently away from the planet below. Flames and hull pieces blasted away from the upper side of the drive module. Excess plasma burst from the rear engine nozzles, and the ship lurched away from the planet, slamming everyone about the ship.

Now they had a new problem.

SIXTEEN

BENSON WALKED through the early morning fog and mist to the front doors of her mother's church in Crawford, Nebraska. She opened the double red doors and stepped in. Candles burned on the windowsills, illuminating the congregation. More candles burned at the altar.

Her mother stood in the pulpit giving one of her fiery sermons. In the pews were various people. All appeared dead! They were in different stages of death and decay. Some were burned, and some were just bones with rags for clothes. Some were partially decomposed. She ambled slowly forward to an empty seat at the front. She studied everyone who was there until she sat down. She froze. To the left of the vacant seat was Harrison Schmidt. He was not decomposed like the rest.

Schmidt looked up at her with concern. "You are not supposed to be here."

“What? Am I dead?” Benson gasped.

"This isn't supposed to be," he said. He looked forward again while repeating, "This isn't supposed to be."

Benson felt weak and sat while her stomach turned. “Am I dead? Where am I?”

"This isn't supposed to be," Schmidt repeated yet again.

She studied him for a long time. It had been ten years since he was killed on a training mission while they were both in the academy. They were to be married just days later. Now, in her mother's church, he was sitting next to her. He looked just as he did back then. If he were here, then she had to be dead. The ship must have exploded, killing everyone on board.

She looked forward as her mother's sermon shifted to talking about the dead.

Behind the altar, there was a bright light that grew brighter in intensity. The dead seated around her got up, entered the light, and vanished. Soon, the light disappeared, and she was sitting alone. She looked around and focused on a candle flickering by the pulpit.

She heard Harrison's voice yet again, trailing away, "This isn't supposed to be."

SEVENTEEN

THE BRIDGE of the *Challenger* was abuzz with news from Communications Officer Lieutenant Charlie Rogers, who had just informed Captain Jefferson that the *Saratoga* was in trouble. They were concerned for Lieutenant Commander Benson, who had transferred from their ship weeks before to take an assignment on the *Saratoga*.

Jefferson, who had been in engineering, stepped onto the bridge. "Status?"

Rogers turned to him. "Captain, the report from the *Saratoga* is that they had an explosion in their starboard nacelle. All attempts to extinguish the fire have failed, and containment is threatened. They are also without propulsion and are spiraling toward a rogue planet they were studying. That is all we know right now."

"Have you tried contacting the *Saratoga*?" Jefferson asked as he sat in the Captain's chair.

"I have been trying, but there has been no response."

"Navigator, do you have the coordinates?"

Lieutenant Adaline Huber quickly performed several calculations. "Yes, Captain. I have plotted the course, and it should take about six hours at maximum speed."

"Lay in the course and execute immediately," Jefferson stated.

"Aye, Sir. Course laid in. Hold on, full speed in three…two… one," she stated.

Adaline was from the northern German port city of Kiel. She spoke with a heavy accent that suggested she was more comfortable with her native German than with English.

The *Challenger* turned and sped off in the direction of the rogue planet.

Rogers turned back toward Jefferson. "Sir, I am receiving a message from command stating the *Saratoga* may have been hit by terrorists. All ships must lockdown immediately and perform security sweeps."

"Understood," Jefferson said as he read the report from command on his terminal. He turned towards his security officer, who was waiting for the order. "Security, put the ship in lockdown mode."

"Aye, sir," he replied. He quickly placed the security protocols in motion.

As this was happening, the first officer, Commander Randy Jordan, entered the bridge. "What is the situation, Captain?"

"We are en route to the last known location of the *Saratoga* to investigate what happened," Jefferson replied. "We have initiated a security lockdown per order of command under the assumption that terrorists may have attacked the *Saratoga*."

Jordan paused for a moment to digest what his Captain told him. "Any word?"

"None," Jefferson replied.

He knew Jordan was asking about Benson. Jordan had taken over for the previous first officer, who had made Benson's life hell the first few months she was on board. The two of them had grown close as friends in the short time he was there. He wished it were more. Benson, however, was more than happy to keep it friendly. Everywhere she went, men hit on her. Some did not take it well, while others were OK. Her refusal to get close to anyone earned her the nickname "Ice Queen." It was a label she hated, and it was a label that attracted all sorts of people who tried to get her in bed.

. . .

Hours passed when sensors officer Ensign Peter Leone, a tall, stocky man, spoke up. "Captain, I have the rogue planet on visual, and I am detecting debris above the planet."

“How much debris?” Jefferson asked as he walked towards the sensors station along with Commander Jordan.

"Small fragments and a few hull plates-s-s-s-s," he dragged out the last word as another object entered his sensors' view. "I found the *Saratoga*. It is tumbling out of control and away from the planet. Here are the coordinates.”

“The ship is intact?” Jordan asked.

“As far as I can tell from here, yes.”

“Anything else?”

"There is a lot of radiation in the area, which is blocking most of my scans. We will have to get closer. I must warn you that the radiation is coming from their quantum drive."

“Understood. Mr. Jordan, charge shields and prepare transports for rescue operations,” Jefferson stated.

“Aye, sir.”

Jefferson glanced toward his communications officer. "Comm, notify medical to prepare to receive injured and possible radiation exposure."

“Aye, sir.”

“Comm, any response from the *Saratoga*?”

“None, sir.”

“Sensors, any danger from that ship exploding?”

“Not at the moment, Captain. The fire in the nacelle appears to have blown out.”

"Navigator, catch up to that ship. Match course and heading. Then pull up alongside that ship and match rotation and speed," Jefferson said.

“Aye, sir,” replied the navigator.

The *Challenger* spun around, fired her thrusters to full power again, and caught up with the damaged ship after several minutes.

The fire in the nacelle had been extinguished, but the antimatter containment chamber was now exposed to space.

Jefferson's communications officer continued calling out to the *Saratoga*. There was still no contact with anyone on the ship. The *Saratoga* kept flying away out of control, as if it were on autopilot. The *Challenger* eased alongside the *Saratoga* and matched its speed and awkward rotation. The *Saratoga* was still spiraling out of control. Jefferson grabbed a few officers to follow him, and they left the bridge. "Mister Jordan, the bridge is yours."

Jefferson and his officers descended a few decks to the forward hangar bay and began distributing pressure suits. Once in their pressure suits, they entered a class one transport and exited the *Challenger*'s forward bay under the primary hull. The transport swooped down beside the *Saratoga*'s port side docking hatch on the primary hull.

The transport inched sideways and mated with the *Saratoga*'s hatch with a solid clunk. The light over the hatch changed from red to yellow and then to green in a matter of seconds. Jefferson spun the handle on the hatch and pulled the hatch open, exposing the *Saratoga*'s hatch. He reached forward and cleaned out the single square hole and the four smaller round holes around it. Another officer stepped forward and pressed a handle assembly into the door until it clicked into place. He then spun the handle until it stopped. Jefferson checked with his team to ensure their pressure suits were good. Everyone gave him the thumbs up, and with that, he pushed the hatch forward with a creak. The hatch swung open and banged against the inner bulkhead with a clang. Jefferson stepped into the darkened ship, followed by the rest of his crew members, who had their scanners open and were testing everything from air quality to radiation levels to the artificial gravity system.

They made their way slowly along the littered corridor, stepping over parts of beams and ceiling panels. The only lights flashing were emergency lights. Jefferson was the first to arrive at the elevators and discovered that they were not working. The panel was dark. He led his team up to the next deck and then up a crawl tube to the rear of the bridge. The bridge was filled with smoke and flames. The air was poor. They found several people and had them brought back to the *Challenger*. Jefferson found Benson. She was slumped over her console with blood running down the control panel from her head. It dripped on the floor, forming a small puddle. He checked for a pulse and barely found one. She was mumbling, and he leaned closer. She was saying, "This isn't supposed to be." Over and over.

He called the *Challenger* to have medics ready to receive her and the rest of the crew when the transport docked.

The bridge was cleared, and one of Jefferson's men sat at the nav-con and began firing thrusters blindly. There was no display to watch his progress, only the voice of the *Challenger*'s helmsman echoing instructions through the headset of his pressure suit. The ship slowed and finally came to a stop while Jefferson's team shut down every system and searched for more survivors. Several other crew members woke up from their ordeal and were evacuated to the *Challenger* when another transport came beside them.

A pair of engineers arrived with a portable power cell. They hurried toward the engine room to charge the field coils surrounding the antimatter containment. With no power supplied by the *Saratoga*'s engines, the reserve power cells would quickly run out, causing the ship to blow apart and destroy not only the *Saratoga* but the *Challenger* as well, which had now docked with it.

Once everyone had been evacuated and the ship was under control, Jefferson returned to his ship to check on the people they had just saved. He walked into the medical center, and it looked like a disaster relief operation. Check that. It was disaster relief. People everywhere were covered in soot and blood. A few broken bones but no fatalities. He pulled a nurse aside and asked for Captain Hackett. She pointed to the rear of the room where he was seated, talking to another nurse.

He walked over and introduced himself. "Captain Hackett, I'm Captain Jefferson. Pleased to meet you."

“Likewise,” said Hackett. “Did you get everyone off?”

“Yes, we did,” Jefferson replied. “How are you doing?”

"I'll be fine, just inhaled some smoke." Hackett excused himself from the nurse, who was finished. "How is my ship?" he eventually asked.

"I've seen better. It's in rough shape. Repairable, we think." Jefferson said as he was looking around the room.

Hackett saw him looking. He knew who he was looking for. "I think she's over here, Captain." They both walked to the other side of the sick bay near the doors and behind a short wall. She was sitting up in a bed with a bandage on her head. Dried blood still streaked down her cheeks and on the front of her uniform. Black soot now colored her hair. She was a mess, like everyone else from the *Saratoga*. She squinted to look at the two captains. She seemed in good spirits. She sat back and rested her head on the pillow, hoping to ease the pounding in her head. It didn't work.

"How are you, Miss Benson?" Hackett asked.

"I'm all right. The doctor says I have a mild concussion. I'd hate to know what a bad one feels like. My head is splitting. Other than that, I'm good. How about the rest of the crew? And how bad was the explosion?" she asked.

"I'm fine, and as far as I know, the rest of the crew is as well. The ship got roughed up, but it should be fixable," Hackett replied.

"Anytime you would like to come back, just say the word," Jefferson said.

"Sorry, Captain. I think I found my home. For the first time, I feel like I made a difference, and it feels good, Sir," she replied.

"I figured as much, Lieutenant Commander." He saluted her, patted her on the shoulder, and walked off.

Hackett held out his hand to shake hers and patted her on the shoulder. "Good job. See you on the bridge when you are ready."

"Aye, sir!" she said as she began to get up. A couple of nurses intercepted her and made her go back to bed. "I guess it will be a little while," she said, glancing toward the nurses with a laugh. Hackett just shook his head and walked towards Jefferson.

"How about a look around, Captain?" he asked. "It will be only a matter of time before the *Saratoga* is replaced, might even be today. It would be nice to see what these newer ships have to offer."

"Sure, come this way." Both men walked out of the medical bay and roamed the ship for a short time.

Hackett's communicator, which he wore on his wrist like a watch, beeped, and he pressed it to respond. "Hackett here."

"Sir, this is Commander Morris. We have restored our environmental systems, and gravity plating is now functioning. We are bringing the Energizer online. The rest of the crew can come back on board shortly."

"Excellent job, Commander. How is our quantum drive?" Hackett asked.

"Quantum drive is a mess. O'Toole says he can have it restored in a few hours. They burned up several relays. One of the plutonium injectors fried as well. He says it is repairable." Morris sounded excited.

"Excellent, and one last question, are we still on target for our original mission?" Hackett knew he was pushing it.

"We'll be about ten hours behind. Ambassador Wilcox has been in contact with the Ineans, and they will wait for us, but..." Morris trailed off.

Hackett wondered what had taken Wilcox so long. He figured he would have been in contact with Vice Admiral Griffin sooner. "But what, Commander?" Hackett knew something was up that Morris didn't want to say over an open comm.

"Well, you know. The Ambassador is his usual self. He's talking to the Vice Admiral about you. He wants you court-martialled for endangering him and his assistant. I don't think he'll get much sympathy. I thought you should know so you are prepared."

"Thank you, Commander. Let's get this mission done so we can be rid of him once and for all." Hackett said as Jefferson's look got his attention.

"Amen to that, Captain. Morris out."

Hackett was perturbed. "What is it, Captain Jefferson?"

"Nothing. It's just that when the ambassadors were here a few months ago, we said the same thing," Jefferson replied.

Hackett shook his head and laughed as well. He then excused himself and went to the hangar bay for the next transport back to the *Saratoga*. The *Challenger* had pulled away after life support and minimal power had been restored. No sense in taking any more risk than necessary.

He made it to the bridge. When the doors opened, he noticed the haze still lingering in the air, which still smelled like burned plastics and wiring. Many of the systems had already been replaced or repaired. The atmosphere leaks had been fixed, and the buckled hull plates had been reinforced. All they waited for was the quantum drive.

The rest of the crew trickled back on board. Benson had been released from medical and took a few moments to say hi to some old friends while waiting for the next transport back to the *Saratoga*. Once on the *Saratoga*, she took a brief look around and realized that it had been a close one. The ship still stank of burnt circuits and fried cables. Crews from both ships worked on the many problems. She made her way to the bridge. When the doors opened, she took her station and began to run diagnostics on the controls. A few told her it was a good call. She was uncomfortable with the praise and quietly went to her console. The one thing that made her feel good was that she was slowly being accepted into this crew.

Hackett couldn't resist. He went to the back of the bridge where Morris was and whispered, "Think she belongs on this ship now?"

Morris knew there was only one way to answer. "Yes, Captain, I have to agree with you there. Looks like my job is in trouble," he said, giving the Captain a look that said he was only half joking.

"Mine, too," Hackett said, and he walked over to the comm for orders from command. Giovanella was still in medical on the *Challenger*, having his burns tended to, so there was a replacement manning the station now. The ensign replied that there were no new orders. Hackett found that to be odd as he went back to his chair. Once he sat, he felt a vibration in the floor that could only be the quantum drive coming to life again. He looked around, and other people felt it too.

After another hour of repairs, the *Saratoga* left the scene and proceeded to Inea, only ten hours behind schedule. It was now 0300 hours, and Hackett ordered the long-overdue shift change, instructing his regulars not to report until midday.

Hackett, Benson, and Davies went down to deck five together in the elevator. Davies was the first to speak. "Lieutenant Commander, would you like a nightcap in the lounge before turning in? There are some people I would like you to meet."

Benson was inclined to say no, but when she looked at Hackett, he nodded that she should, so she agreed to join them. She looked at Hackett once again. "Are you coming as well, sir?"

He knew she would back out if he declined, so after some thought, he agreed. Davies looked at both of them and shook her head. They all exited and went to the forward lounge, where they ordered some drinks. Hackett sat on a stool by the bar, and Davies took Benson to a table to meet her friends. The person tending the bar approached the Captain and congratulated him on a job well done.

"It wasn't me. It was Benson there." He pointed to Benson, who was sitting at the table. The bartender looked at Benson and saw that she was still sizing up Hackett. Then he looked at Hackett, who was looking at Benson in the mirror.

“Something you want to tell me, Captain?” the bartender asked.

"No, why?" Hackett replied, wondering what now.

"No reason. Here, let me clean this for you," and he wiped the cloudy smoke off the mirror behind the bar. He then looked at Hackett.

Hackett knew he was caught. “All right, can you keep a secret?”

“Yes, Captain,” the bartender said.

"Ever since she came on board, I have been preoccupied with looking at her," Hackett said.

"Nooo, really," the bartender said sarcastically. Dragging out his reply.

"Not like that. I just feel attracted to her, and I think she feels the same way. It's too bad our difference in ranks won't allow us to find out. I also suspect she's a spy for the Admiral, so now I'm not sure what to think," Hackett said, trailing off as someone approached.

"Captain, everything happens for a reason. After her quick solution to our problem today, and based on what I've heard about her, how long do you think it will be before she is promoted? Besides, someone will have to take Morris's place in a few months. So, if I were you, I would write one hell of a recommendation for her file. Then, if she's promoted and you two still feel a certain way, you might get what you want. That's what I would do, and, of course, this conversation never took place."

"Interesting concept. I'll have to keep that in mind," Hackett replied, and the bartender walked away to wait on another person. Hackett drifted off deep into thought at what the bartender had proposed. At first, he didn't think it would work. However, the more he thought about it, he knew there was a way to pull it off. Several people on the ship already suspected the attraction between the two officers, and anything Hackett proposed would be scrutinized. It would be tricky, but he suspected it was not impossible to make this work. He made several mental notes for later when he could scour the regulation manual for any possible problems to overcome.

Hackett realized there was music playing in the background and noticed a few people had gotten up from their tables and began dancing in the middle of the room. He could feel the tension leave the room. Of course, a few brews had also helped in that cause. Several people had paired up at this late hour to unwind. Hackett noticed that Benson had shot down everyone who asked her to dance. She looked up at the Captain and made a gesture toward the floor with her eyes. He frowned and tapped his Captain's bars on his collar, and she frowned as well. Davies saw the exchange and whispered something to her.

Benson shook her head no. It was too late. Davies was already out of her chair and walking towards Hackett. "Sir, Miss Benson would like you to dance with her. Under article 144, a senior officer can engage in social behavior with a junior officer or crew member for the sake of social interaction as long as there is no intent on either side, Sir."

Benson had dropped her head to the table in embarrassment.

Hackett took a sip of his drink and turned to look at Benson sitting there. After a moment, he spoke. "It does say that, doesn't it?

Well, Miss Davies, tell your client I accept." He got up to follow her back to the table. The bartender gave him a nod as well and refilled his glass.

A new song began to play, and it was a slow song. Hackett walked up to Benson. "Miss Benson, would you like to dance?"

"I would be honored, sir." As she got up, she looked at Davies and whispered, "You are so dead."

Davies laughed, as did the rest of the people at the table.

Hackett and Benson walked out to the floor and, for a moment, had difficulty figuring out who would lead. Then Hackett held up a finger and started. He had his left arm behind her back. He connected his right hand with her left. They were very close, and, of course, Morris walked in.

Morris saw the two and was starting to walk to them when he was called back by the bartender. The bartender told him it was innocent and that Davies had orchestrated it under Article 144. The bartender told him how Hackett spoke to him and that nothing would happen to violate regulations. Morris accepted it and sat down, and ordered a drink. Morris ordered a double shot of bourbon, chugged it down in one gulp, and brought the glass down to the counter with a snap. He pushed the glass towards Linques, who refilled it. Morris retrieved the full shot glass and looked at Linques, "Leave the bottle, please."

Linques nodded and walked away. He knew Morris would down several shots before retiring for the evening. It was the only way he could sleep since Sasha Young was killed. In some ways, Morris was more of an emotional liability than Hackett. He would never admit to it. He downed the next glass and placed it back on the counter. He reached for the bottle and went to fill the glass again, but then decided to drink directly from the bottle. He turned to watch Hackett and Benson dance across the floor. Hackett was right; Morris could try for her, but he knew she would never go with Morris. Her mission was Hackett. He knew she was fixated on Hackett more so than her orders had required her to be. He knew she had crossed the line and gotten emotionally attached to the subject of her mission. He feared for her life on this mission and worried about Hackett, for he was growing attached to her, just as he had with Sasha. In his condition, it could kill him or her or both.

Benson and Hackett went around the room awkwardly and didn't say much until the song ended. When it did end, they bowed to each other; she returned to her table, and he walked back to the bar and sipped the drink, waiting for him.

“It’s not like you to have more than one, Captain,” Morris said.

"Well, it's been a tough day. I think I'm entitled to a small indulgence. Don't you, Commander?" Hackett said. "Or are you going to critique every single thing I do?"

"No, Captain. I'm sorry. With the promotion coming up, I've been a bit hard on everyone. I suppose I'm just getting ready for the move, Captain," he turned to face Hackett, "and I'm sorry about her as well. I know firsthand how it is. I, too, had a thing for a woman not so long ago and couldn't touch either."

"Thank you, Commander, and I know about Sasha."

Morris paused. "Just do us all a favor."

"And what would that be?" Hackett replied.

"Be careful, Captain, that's all. Just be careful. Even today, when I see the looks between you two, it makes me wonder, what if? And you know what?" Morris was spilling now.

“And what, Commander?” Hackett replied hesitantly, wondering where Morris was heading.

"Sometimes I think I made the wrong choice." He finished his drink and placed the bottle back down on the bar. "Good night, Captain." He got up and walked away.

"Good night, Commander," Hackett said as he watched his first officer walk out of the room.

Hackett turned towards the bartender, “Now there’s a story for you, Mr. Linques.”

Benson plopped on a stool beside the Captain. "Sir, can I ask you a question?"

"Go ahead," he replied without looking at her. He finally looked up in the mirror at the table she had just come from, and everyone was watching. *Uh oh,* he thought.

"Um, I was just curious, sir, and you don't have to answer if you don't want to, but I was wondering if-" Another slow song came on, and she changed her mind. "Would you like to dance one more time?"

"Of course, Miss Benson." They got up and danced to the second song. They were much closer this time as they danced while Hackett talked to Benson. "Miss Benson."

“My first name is Tamora, sir,” she replied.

"Yes, I know. As you are aware, this is dangerous for both of us. So it's officially Miss Benson."

She looked at him and nodded.

Hackett stared into her eyes, those luring blue eyes that seemed to draw him in. "Anyway, I want you to know that I'm putting in a commendation for what you did today."

“Thank you, Captain, but why would you tell me now?”

“I think you know.”

"I see," she said, staring into his eyes, and they both just looked at one another for the entire dance. She knew he felt the same as she did. After the dance was over, Hackett invited her to the bar for one last drink. She gladly went along.

Once seated, the bartender took their order and walked off. Hackett turned to her. "Miss Benson, I asked you over here because I sense that there is a dangerous attraction between us. I wanted to make sure about that."

She looked at him and wasn't sure what to say. He continued, "I think it would be prudent if we considered our careers first. Neither of us is ready to give up our careers for another person just yet, but there's no rule that says we can't be good friends. Do you understand where I am going with this?"

"Yes, Captain, I do. I feel the same way as you. So, how would we work this?" she asked.

"We would have to make it a point to stay clear of one another for the bulk of the day. There is nothing that says we can't meet socially. Anything more would open an inquiry. If you're unsure, just follow my lead or ask me."

Benson wasn't entirely sure what he was saying. She did feel he knew enough to keep them out of trouble, so she agreed. She nodded, and after a moment, she spoke up. "So, how would we handle tomorrow?"

Hackett thought for a moment and took a sip of his drink. "To put certain people at ease, we shouldn't eat breakfast or lunch together, and our conversations while on duty should remain professional. I would avoid eye contact and any suggestive gestures. If we meet for any reason, we should do it in public like this. If someone sees us sneaking around, then that would be a red flag."

“I understand, Captain. What if we get caught?” She asked.

"As I said, we are just friends, just like tonight. This is a friendly conversation, and no one can prevent that," he said while looking into her bright blue eyes.

"OK then, I can do this."

They said good night, and the Captain left the room before he got in trouble. Benson went back to her new friends for one more round. She wasn't much of a drinker, but she figured one more would be OK. Besides, Hackett pushed off all their shifts until noontime.

“So, Lieutenant Commander, what did the Captain want to talk to you about?” Davies pried.

Benson knew instantly that this was what he meant. "He just wanted to assure me that what we do is merely friendly, and there is nothing to it beyond that."

“It took you two that long to discuss that?” Davies pressed.

"Ensign, I don't answer to you. That is all we discussed. Neither of us wants to jeopardize our careers, so we will only be friends. That is all." Benson blasted Davies.

"Sorry, Lieutenant Commander. I won't ask again." Everyone at the table finished their drinks and ordered more, except for Benson. She excused herself and left the room. On her way back to her quarters, she roamed about the deck looking to see what was where. She found the Captain's quarters and continued without a second glance. She also noticed several people still hard at work wiping the smoke from the walls and ceilings of the corridors. It was the first time in years she was happy. It was also the first time in her career that she felt she belonged, now just to fix the situation with O'Toole.

She returned to her quarters, sat at her desk, and looked at her computer terminal. It was blinking one message received. She reached forward and touched her screen, and the message opened. It was a text-only message, and she read it. It was from Vice Admiral Griffin. He wanted to know if she had time to evaluate the Captain? He went on about ensuring her that it was vital for her to get close and find out if Hackett was all right. Her mood changed.

She stared at it briefly and now felt terrible about what she was doing. She was getting close to the Captain to see if he would violate orders. The fleet wanted to know if he was still in control. The problem was that she sincerely believed she was falling for him, which wasn't part of the plan.

"Computer, please take a message and direct it to Vice-Admiral Griffin." The computer beeped, indicating it was ready.

"Admiral Griffin, I received your message. I have successfully gained the Captain's confidence and attention. I will be moving in over the next couple of days to see if he falters. However, he strikes me as being tough, and I'm not sure if he'll crack. Additionally, Admiral, as I mentioned earlier when we met, I am uncomfortable with this. I think it is morally wrong to deceive in this manner. Lieutenant Commander Benson out." After a brief pause, "Computer, send the message." It beeped, and she closed the lid and went to bed.

EIGHTEEN

"TAMORA, WHAT ARE YOU DOING?" her mother asked as she walked up behind the child.

Tamora was sitting on the concrete cover of the shallow well behind the barn. Her eyes were closed as she faced the sky. She lowered her head and smiled at her mother with her 10-year-old grin. "I'm talking to God, Mom."

"Why on Earth are you doing that?" Her mother asked without thinking. She was shocked by her daughter's response, and now she was more shocked at her response, being a minister, after all.

"Because He talks to me," she replied.

"Oh, dear. Sweetie, He really doesn't talk to people anymore," her mother said, searching for a better response. "He hates us."

"But Mom, He does talk to me. He doesn't hate us, He..." she replied, and her mother quickly cut her off.

"We will not talk about this anymore, dear," she said. "Now, let's go have some cookies."

"Okay, Mom," the child replied, and she hopped down from the well.

. . .

The elder Benson had recently closed the church where she ministered. No one outside her family attended anymore, and the maintenance was too much in addition to the farm work. The church had become rundown. Shutters hung from the windows while others flapped in the breeze. Several windows were long since broken, and the glass littered the ground. The outside of the church was a mess: paint was flaking off in sheets, exposing the bare, rotting wood below. The old-style slate shingles on the roof revealed many gaps where several had broken and fallen to the ground, allowing what little rain that fell to leak into the church. The weather had played a role in the church's demise, with the extremes in violent weather, hail, high winds, and occasional sideways rainstorms, to name a few. It would eventually be lost to a wildfire. No one would notice it was gone.

They now traveled nearly 30 miles on Sundays to attend a church in Crawford. There, her family fit into a congregation of almost fifty people. They had not seen this many people on a Sunday in many years.

Benson opened her eyes and rolled over in her bed. She stared at her clock and groaned. It was only 6 am. She still had plenty of time to sleep. However, the memories from her childhood continued to play over and over in her mind. No matter how hard she tried, she could not block them out and fall back asleep.

She lay in bed, staring at the ceiling, when suddenly she was engulfed in a blinding white light. The visions from her childhood returned. It all came back to her, every detail which had been shown to her 25 years before, which she had forgotten until now. All of it returned, including the fear she experienced. She remembered how frightened she was. She saw the Ineans. She saw herself being punched and tossed around once again. Then she saw Hackett lying in the snow, frozen stiff, dead.

The light was gone, and she sat up, sweating and panting from the horror she saw. She collected herself and finally crawled out of bed. She groped her way to the head. She splashed water on her face and stared at her reflection in the mirror. The reflection changed to a man's face, one she had not seen in nearly ten years. Now he kept coming back.

"Harrison?" she gasped.

It was Harrison Schmidt, the cadet she was to marry back in the academy. He stared back at her, but he didn't appear to be happy. Suddenly, they were both back in the academy, both in their khaki cadets' uniforms, laughing arm in arm as they strolled along a brick path. It was a cool day in early spring, with a blue, cloudless sky overhead. They continued to walk towards a building on the campus at Annapolis. It was the chapel they went to every week. It was the chapel where they were to get married. A wedding scheduled in a few short weeks. A wedding that would never happen.

"I'll be back from our training mission in a week. We can go up to the Berkshires for the weekend. Kind of a pre honeymoon," he said with a grin.

"I'll miss you just the same. Hurry back," she replied.

They walked into the chapel and stopped before a statue of Christ on the cross. The statue started to speak to her, and suddenly she was back in the bathroom on the *Saratoga*, staring at herself in the mirror. A tear rolled down her cheek from seeing Harrison staring back at her. She stumbled back and sat on the closed toilet. She put her head in her hands and sobbed. It had been so long. The pain was still as strong as the day he was killed. She looked up at the ceiling, still sobbing, "What are you trying to tell me? Am I about to die?"

No response, just the hum of the ship as she stared at her reflection in the mirror.

Knock, knock, knock, "Lieutenant Commander Benson, are you all right?" Giovanella said through the door to his quarters.

"Yeah, I'm okay. I'll be done in a couple of minutes," she replied. She wiped her face with the towel.

"Take your time. I thought I heard crying," Giovanella said with concern.

"Oh, just an allergy. All the smoke and dust from yesterday," she said, hoping he would believe her. She walked back into her room in search of a uniform. The door slid shut behind her. She dressed as she thought about what she was seeing. She shook it off as just the stress of the mission.

NINETEEN

IT WAS NEARLY MIDDAY. Hackett and Morris were finishing their leisurely lunch when Hackett was paged by Ambassador Wilcox. The Ambassador was irate. Hackett was not surprised. He demanded that Hackett come to his quarters immediately. Hackett said he would be there soon, and he closed the connection and put his wristwatch communicator back in his shirt pocket.

Hackett looked at Morris, “So you want to be more like me, eh? Do you want to take this one?”

"No, thank you, sir. I will gladly ride shotgun, though," he replied with a slight laugh.

“Still don’t trust me?” Hackett asked.

“On the contrary, sir, I want to see how you handle this clown without killing him.”

They cleaned up the mess from their lunch and exited the mess hall. Hackett checked in with the bridge while heading to the Ambassador's quarters. Hackett knocked on the door, which promptly slid open, and he was greeted by Ambassador Channing. Channing had an apologetic look, so Hackett knew he didn't share Wilcox's sentiments.

Wilcox was hunched over his cramped desk in the corner, typing a message or something into his portable computer. He looked up at the Captain and the first officer and continued typing. He was banging on the keys viciously, and when he was done, he slammed the computer's lid down and jumped from his chair. He walked up to Hackett quickly and nearly bit his nose off.

“What gives you the right to do what you did, Captain?” he yelled.

Hackett stood his ground while Morris backed off a few steps towards Channing.

"It would help if I knew what you were talking about, Ambassador," Hackett said firmly and with a calm even Morris could not muster. Hackett was not easily drawn into someone's hostility.

"That woman! How could you tell the admiral what you told him? I need her for a special mission to the surface of Inea. You are jeopardizing this mission before we even get there!" he yelled. Their noses touched. Hackett made no effort to back off.

"Maybe if you would explain why it is so important for THAT woman to go on the mission and for what purpose, maybe I would allow it. I am not going to hand over a member of my crew who, technically, you abused on a previous mission. I see this as a continuation of the same obsession, Ambassador," Hackett replied, still calm, with a slight smirk starting to form on his face. So the admiral took his concerns to the vice admiral, and he sided with him so far. Hackett felt good about that. "In addition, Ambassador, I have seen what the Ineans do to women firsthand, and I won't allow it to happen again."

Wilcox backed off and threw his hands up in the air. “I can’t tell you. It is important for the mission!” he yelled.

“If you can’t explain, then she stays here, sir, and I obviously have the backing of command on this issue. So I consider this over,” Hackett said as he turned towards the door. Wilcox ran around him and blocked the door.

“All right, Captain, I need her because of her piloting skills.”

"Ambassador, there are over a hundred people on this ship capable of piloting a transport. Why HER?" Hackett returned the

Ambassador's stare, and Morris thought for a second that this would quickly get ugly.

"The pilot needs to be a woman, Captain." The Ambassador was still evading the real reason, and Hackett knew it.

"Well, Ambassador, that narrows it down to over 40 candidates. That still doesn't answer my question as to why HER. Sir." Hackett was irritating the Ambassador by emphasizing 'her' in every response.

Wilcox stomped around the room and returned to the Captain again. "Okay, okay, fine, have it your way," he huffed. "I want her on the mission because she is pretty. I want her to be my assistant so the Inean males see her and respect me for having her, Captain."

Hackett looked at him and felt he was finally getting a truthful answer. “Explain every aspect of what this assistant is expected to do.”

“Every detail?” he asked.

"Yes, every, LITTLE, detail, Ambassador," Hackett said, adding, "and I know bullcrap when I hear it, so keep it straight."

"Fine. Benson will pilot the transport to the planet's surface. She will wear a skimpy outfit that hides next to nothing and remain at my side the entire time we are on the planet. She will be required to act like we are together in every aspect, Captain," he said, with his arms folded.

Hackett thought for a moment, and he had his answer to that. "Ambassador, first of all, it is Lieutenant Commander Benson. I will not order anyone to be your personal slut. According to her folder, she has strong moral beliefs. She has a long list of refusing compromising duties in her record, and she would not accept this mission. However, I will allow her to pilot the transport in full uniform and represent the Alliance with you to the Ineans. She will perform her duties as a fleet officer to the fullest of her beliefs, which does not include being your slut." He paused for a moment to let it sink in. "That is what I will allow a member of my crew to do, sir." Hackett offered this, knowing full well the Ambassador would not accept it.

“But,” he tried to say.

"No buts, that is how it will be, Ambassador. Take it or leave it," Hackett said.

"Fine, Captain, have it your way. I can't believe people still follow those archaic moral beliefs!" Wilcox said, sounding defeated.

"Maybe if we did, our society wouldn't be in the predicament it finds itself today, Ambassador. You know, being on the brink of extinction," he added.

"One more thing, Captain. Why do you protect her so much?" Wilcox asked.

"I would protect any member of my crew the same way, Ambassador. I would die to protect them. That is why I'm the Captain of this ship. I'm not a hard captain, but my crew knows that if I get a hundred percent out of them, I will give them a hundred percent in return. Loyalty is a two-way street, and it works on this ship, and, like I said earlier, I know firsthand what those animals can and will do," Hackett said.

Morris took mental notes.

Wilcox was taken aback and genuinely considered what Hackett had said. Wilcox knew it would not work.

Hackett and Morris took the moment of silence from Wilcox as a chance to exit.

TWENTY

ON THE BRIDGE, the rest of the day shift had already arrived and taken their stations. Most of them had finished their logs and daily diagnostics of their equipment. Hackett merely walked around the bridge and checked in with each person there. He made it to the engineering console and noticed several warning indicators blinking. When satisfied with everything else, he left the bridge to Morris and went to the engine room.

Senior Engineer O'Toole was concerned about the primary plasma converter in the reaction chamber. The converter was made of gold-coated Hafnium platters enclosed in a carbon nanotube matrix. They had enough raw gold on board. What they lacked were the Hafnium Carbide platters, which measured three inches by 8 inches by just under an inch thick. Together, these components created the coupling that generated power from the plasma streaming in the chamber. This power flowed to the massive coils that created the quantum field in the nacelles. The remainder would be stored in batteries around the ship and would ultimately serve as the ship's primary power source. It appeared to him that several of the platters had been damaged during the explosion in the nacelle, which blew back into the quantum chamber and knocked them out of alignment. His problem was that the remaining platters were being forced to take up the slack and would burn out long before reaching Inea. He was reviewing a sample with his team, and none of them liked what they saw.

Hackett walked into the engineering compartment and saw the engineer and his staff huddled together. Hackett knew there was a problem. He walked up to them to listen in. When O'Toole saw him, he made room for him to join the discussion.

"Captain, we have a problem with our primary power converter matrix." He held up a charred, flaking Hafnium platter for the Captain to look at. "Most of our supply is burning up like this, and if we maintain our current speed, we won't make it to Inea, not even close." Hackett held it up to the light. A good Hafnium Carbide platter was bright gold in color after it had been coated. It had perfectly razor-sharp square edges. These platters were not. They had been burned by the tremendous heat to a dull gray color, and the material was melted and pitted, indicating that they had been subjected to heat exceeding 5000 degrees Celsius. The gold coating had long since been vaporized from them. It was obviously burned beyond any further use by the intense bombardment of heat and radiation. They were too far gone and could not be refinished.

Hackett continued to study the burned-up device and then turned to O'Toole. "What's causing it, Commander?"

"It must have been during yesterday's power surge from putting out the fire in the nacelle. The grid must have been knocked out of alignment enough to cause turbulence in the plasma stream, which overheated the grid. That is causing the rapid deterioration you see here."

"I see. What are our options?" Hackett asked.

"Not many, sir. Our best hope of obtaining the materials we need and of the necessary quality is from the refining facility on Verna-3. It is only seven light years off our course. Unfortunately, it is controlled by the Kosuan," O'Toole said.

. . .

The Kosuan and Ineans had been fighting a bloody war for years, and neither side wanted an Alliance ship lurking around. The Kosuan were especially concerned about the recent attempts by the Alliance to secure peace with the Ineans, and they feared the Alliance would assist them in their fight against the Kosuan.

Hackett knew he would have difficulty convincing the Kosuan to provide him with the materials his ship needed. He was afraid he might have to ask Ambassador Wilcox for help and knew what he would want in exchange. Hackett wasn't about to make Benson another victim of the Ambassador's desires, even if it meant the mission failed.

Hackett looked over the remains of the ceramic compound, which he had picked up again and held in his hand, as pieces flaked off onto the table. He realized everyone was looking at him, waiting for instructions. He handed it back to O'Toole and asked if that was their only option.

O'Toole took the old part from Hackett. "We could turn around and head home at minimal quantum speed and get what we need from our own people, sir, but nobody wants to abandon our mission. We've come this far and can't see spending the next two months limping home."

Hackett thought for a moment. “Very well, Commander, we will go to Verna-3 and purchase them, somehow, from the Kosuan. I will be on the bridge,” he said. He turned and exited the engine room.

On his way to the bridge, he pondered several plans to acquire the necessary materials without the Ambassador's help. He couldn't contact Alliance headquarters because they would order him to engage Ambassador Wilcox in the negotiations.

Hackett walked onto the bridge and looked around as he felt the hum of the ship's forward energizer through the floor. He looked over at Benson and wondered if he could protect her after all. "Miss Benson."

She turned to face him. “Yes, sir?”

"Change course for Verna-3, best speed, and let me know how long it will take to get there," he said.

Morris looked up from his terminal and looked at Hackett.

"Yes, sir, Verna-3, best speed." She retrieved the coordinates, programmed the route, and turned her head toward the Captain. "That will take us 48 hours from here, sir."

Very well, execute the course change, Miss Benson," he said while turning to Morris. "Mr. Morris, come with me. Miss Benson, the bridge is yours."

"Aye, sir," Benson stated. She paused in shock, and she locked her station.

Hackett turned and headed for the elevator. He stopped, turned, looked around the bridge, and paused briefly. Both men stepped into the rickety lift and went to conference room one.

Once the elevator doors closed, Benson ran her fingers over the controls on the armrest of the Captain's chair. It was the first time in her career that she had been given this opportunity. She was now in charge, and her mind wandered back in time to when she played *Space Rangers*. It was a dream come true for her. A few more of the visions she once had many years ago came back to her. A chill went up her spine as she realized Hackett was the man from those visions, and they were heading into the hell that frightened her as a child. More of it was coming back to her. Now she was scared for an entirely different reason. She gripped the arms of the chair tightly and didn't let go as more of the visions replayed in her mind.

Morris turned to the Captain once the doors closed. "Verna-3, sir? Isn't that controlled by the Kosuan?"

Hackett sat in the chair at the head of the table. "Yes, to both questions." Morris sat across from him, and Hackett continued. "Our power matrix was damaged yesterday from the explosion. At its current rate of degradation, we won't be able to make Inea. Verna-3, while under the control of the Kosuan, is our best bet to obtain the materials we need, but we have a few problems."

Morris looked at him and repeated, "Just a few, sir."

"We need a diplomatic solution to use without using the diplomats and one without getting shot at," Hackett added.

Morris thought for a moment. "You don't want to use Wilcox

because if he secures what we need, then he could use them as leverage against you and get Lieutenant Commander Benson to do his original plan."

"That pretty much sums it up, Commander. I don't think Wilcox will let us use Channing for this either," Hackett replied, rubbing the back of his neck. Morris noticed the level of stress Hackett was showing. He also knew it was uncharacteristic for him to display it openly, especially knowing full well Morris was watching for any flaw in his command ability so he could report back to the admiral.

"Then why don't we ask him, and if he refuses, then we know where he stands on the issue. We could also ask Benson how far she would allow this to go."

Hackett shook his head no. "After what those animals did to Sasha, no way in hell am I going to allow another woman down there, especially with what Wilcox has in mind, Commander."

"So, we are on our own then?"

"Yes, Commander. I need all of the information available on Verna-3, including who is in charge, what they have for armaments, and what we could use for bargaining power."

"Aye, sir."

"I'll need it in three hours."

"All right. I will get on it immediately." Morris said, and he was out of his seat, leaving the room.

Hackett remained pondering his options regarding Wilcox and command for a few minutes. He was treading thin ice, avoiding both on this issue. He knew command would force him to allow Wilcox to take charge of the Verna-3 landing, and then Wilcox would want something from Hackett. That something would be Benson. Hackett could not allow it to happen.

On the bridge, Benson was in the Captain's chair and enjoying every second of it. It was the first time she had been given this responsibility during a mission. She couldn't help wondering if she was there because Hackett liked her or because he felt she was qualified. Neither of her two previous captains would have allowed her to be in command.

She drifted back to when she was nine years old, running through the cornfields with her brother and sister, chasing her with their homemade laser guns made from sticks and string. Her sister called out, "Captain Benson, wait up!"

Tamora stopped, turned, lifted her own fake gun, and shot her brother and sister with it. They fell to the ground, overacting their death, which was part of the fun. She approached them, took their fake laser guns away, and knelt down. "You are now galactic prisoners of the Alliance."

Her brother opened his eyes, grabbed her, and tossed her to the ground. He retrieved his laser and ran off laughing. Her sister jumped on top of her and held her to the ground. "Now you're our prisoner..." Benson returned to the present once again, but now she pondered how simple her life had been.

Hackett returned to the bridge and asked Benson for a status report. She replied that everything was normal. It wasn't, of course. The detour they were heading into was by no means normal. They both knew that part. He took command for the final hour of her shift, and she left the bridge.

Benson went back to her quarters and showered. She checked her messages and noticed one new message from Admiral Griffin. She knew what it was and closed the computer's lid, pretending she hadn't seen it on her screen. She gathered a few things and left her room.

She walked down one corridor where technicians were still working at this late hour. It was dark and cold in this part of the ship. The technicians were busy repairing the main power cable and had much of the wall torn apart, exposing pipes, cables, and other components. They were searching for a break in the cable, but so far had no luck.

She was amazed at how cold it got just walking several feet down an open corridor from the last heat source. It was downright frigid. She folded her arms in front of her while white wisps of breath escaped from her mouth. She recalled the vision of her, Hackett, Morris, and Larson on some icy planet. She had realized who the people were only a short time ago. Surely it was not this mission. The report on Inea was hot, scorching hot. Definitely no snow or ice there. Verna-3 was a colder planet, but still, nothing to compare to her vision. She surmised that it was a future mission. One she wasn't looking forward to. She hated the cold. When she was young, she always found an excuse to stay indoors in the winter.

She arrived at the forward lounge at about 2230 and looked around. There was a lot of activity in the dimly lit room, and she decided to remain for a little while. She sat by the bar and ordered Kentucky bourbon over ice. It was her preferred poison when she wanted something strong. She sat back and watched as several people got up and performed their acts.

She sipped the drink and realized it wasn't any Earthly whiskey she was drinking. This was potent. She sipped it again and then chugged it down in one more gulp. The alcohol burned her throat, and she could feel the tension ease out of every joint in her body. She hadn't realized how tense she had been until now.

She held the empty glass up and waved it at the bartender when he glanced her way. He strode over, refilled her glass, and then hurried off to the next person waiting. She downed this one quickly and turned to watch the show.

A short time later, she looked up at the clock on the wall, pushed her drink away, and headed for the door. As the door opened for her to exit, Hackett was about to enter. He asked her to stay for a little while. He then mumbled something about Wilcox, but would not elaborate as he held out his hand to guide her back into the lounge. She was happy to see him, and they turned and reentered together. The room was packed now, standing room only. They found a spot by the far corner of the bar and squeezed onto the last two stools. Hackett ordered their drinks, and they sat and watched the show.

One by one, people got up on the stage, made of empty food storage crates, and sang, told jokes, or played instruments. Some were timid at first, and others had no problems being on stage. The judges were randomly picked and not serious about their scorekeeping, which was part of the fun. It was one of the few times a crewman could poke fun at an officer and get away with it.

Davies was on stage and telling off-color jokes that drew jeers from many in the room. It was her way of winding up a group. She gave way to another officer who sang an old song. Unfortunately for him, the crowd didn't care for his rendition, and they hooked him quickly. It was all fun, and no one felt bad about it. Many people screwed up their performances on purpose just to get the room going. Everyone had a good laugh and enjoyed the entertainment.

Hackett and Benson stayed together the entire time, chatting about family, careers, and other topics. He was testing her to find out her true mission. She was tough to crack and did not yield much information. She was testing him as she had been instructed. However, it had taken on a more personal touch. Hackett caught on to the shift in her questions and answers. He knew she was probing. He just didn't know what she was searching for.

Time went by quickly, and it was after midnight before the room began to clear. Towards the end of the evening, Hackett and Benson debated the best way to handle the Kosuan, and they both enjoyed each other's arguments. Neither of them noticed the room was clearing. Others had wondered about them being together until they heard the discussion.

"That will not work, Captain. The Kosuan are savages and need to be treated as such. You can't send a diplomat in to do this job: that is why all previous attempts to reason with them have failed. They think we are weaklings, and as soon as they are done fighting with the Ineans, we are next. The only way to deal with the Kosuan is to go in and be tough. They will respect that."

"I see. So what you are saying is to barge in and take what we want, and we end up like them," Hackett said with a grin.

"No, no, no, we must be aggressive so they respect us and work with us. The Kosuan eat diplomats for breakfast. If we are diplomatic tomorrow, then we are dead. It is best that Wilcox stays out of this one. You and Commander Morris have a much better chance of succeeding. Plus, there is no need for a bloody shootout if you play it properly."

Many people shook their heads as they walked by. Some were genuinely interested. The bartender watched and noticed that none of them thought the captain and lieutenant commander had crossed the line. Many considered Benson some sort of Alliance specialist regarding the Kosuan.

It was now just past 0100, and they finally looked around. It was just them and the bartender enjoying the two officers bantering.

"Well, Miss Benson, I enjoyed our, um, discussion," he stammered for a brief moment, "but it is time to check in for the night."

She looked at the clock and realized that this was the most fun she had had in a long time. She excused herself for the night and went to her quarters. While she was walking, she thought about the next time they would be together and how she couldn't wait.

On the other hand, Hackett spent a few minutes talking to the bartender, who said that some of the crew were jealous of them until they listened to some of the conversation.

"Mr. Linques, I think I know what attracts me to her, and it isn't the looks. It is that brain of hers. She has some unique ideas," Hackett said.

"I have to agree with you there, Captain. She has a good head on her shoulders, but you do need to be careful."

Harold Linques was in his early fifties and had spent several years serving on starships as a civilian. His primary function was to cook, but he enjoyed tending bar the most because it allowed him to interact with the crew. Many crew members would talk to him because everything discussed was kept secret. He never reported to the Captain or command about anything a crew member spoke about. That is the reason Hackett trusted him with his innermost secrets.

"Oh, I couldn't agree more, Harold. I will have to admit it will be difficult." Hackett finished his drink and handed over his glass. "Good night, sir."

"Good night, Captain," Linques replied.

Hackett left the dimly lit lounge and winced at the brightly lit corridor when the door opened. His eyes adjusted quickly, and he took his time returning to his quarters for a shower. He set his alarm and went to bed shortly after. He lay there for some time, staring at the ceiling, thinking about his new navigator, the Kosuan, the admiral and Vice Admiral Griffin, the Ambassador, and the Ineans. This was a challenging mission for Hackett, and he had too many variables to juggle. All of the missions this crew had been on were simple compared with this one.

His ship was also heavily damaged, and everyone knew they would end up in a fight before this mission was over. The only question now was whether it would be the Kosuan, the Ineans, or someone else?

Hackett knew Benson was there to spy on him. He didn't think she was there to trick him. He also didn't know her true feelings for him, and the battle playing out in her mind.

TWENTY-ONE

O'TOOLE WALKED towards the mess hall for breakfast. He had not slept much the past few days, and the pressure of holding the engines together was beginning to take its toll on him. Most of his time was spent in the engine room, trying his best to hold the matrix together with limited supplies.

He turned a corner and was joined by Benson. She greeted him, but he did not return the pleasantries. Instead, he grasped her arm to stop her, and he glared at her.

"I know everyone thinks you are some hero for putting out the fire. But let me tell you one thing, Benson, I have been up for two days straight, band-aiding the quantum drive from the mess you created. I do not care what the Captain thinks of you, you are more reckless than he is, and you get away with it by batting your blue eyes at people."

He gave her a shove and continued on toward the mess hall. Others walking by slowed to see what was happening and then kept moving.

Benson remained in the corridor briefly, back against the wall. She was in shock, and now anger was coming over her. She would get even with him for what he did. Even if he outranked her, she did not deserve that treatment.

She flashed back to one of her altercations with then-Commander Najas, who is now a one-star admiral under the leadership of Vice Admiral Griffin. He had done something similar, grasping her arm, pinning her against the wall when no one was looking. He had spoken to her the same way, accusing her of manipulating the Captain against him. She hated him for it and had nearly danced for joy when he got promoted off the *Challenger*.

She took a deep breath, tugged her uniform back to where it belonged, and continued to the mess hall. She could not shake the thoughts of Najas and others who had treated her poorly over the years. She walked in and glared at O'Toole, who was talking with other officers. She knew they were talking about her. She grabbed a tray and a plate and walked down the line, piling food aggressively onto the plate. She stood against the wall and quickly ate her breakfast. After a few minutes, she left without speaking to anyone.

TWENTY-TWO

MORRIS WAS COMPOSING his daily report to Admiral Hodges regarding the Captain's activities and mental condition on this mission. He sat at his desk, pondering what he should write. "Computer, open report to Admiral Hodges." His terminal beeped to indicate that it was ready. "Admiral Hodges, this is the first officer's special log entry. The ship sustained serious damage from what we believe to be a terrorist attack. The Captain acted properly during the ordeal with no hesitation or second-guessing himself. The mission continues, despite several setbacks. There was no indication of any influence from the Inean procedure performed on him two months ago. I took the liberty of confronting him on the subject, and he informed me that my bringing it up was the first he had thought of it all day. I don't see the Captain giving in to this fear of the Alliance doctors. On another note, the Captain has taken a slight interest in Lieutenant Commander Tamora Benson. I will continue to follow this development. Miss Benson has been doing her job of testing the Captain. He did, however, indicate that he is on to her. He assures me that there is nothing to worry about or anything that violates the Alliance code. I will continue to watch this unfold if it does. The last item that concerns me is the Captain's interaction with Ambassador Wilcox. They are at each other at every turn. It would be interesting to see if the Captain can maintain his ground with the Ambassador without compromising the mission. It is my professional opinion that Captain Shawn Hackett remains in charge. He is in control and has control. Commander Morris, out. Computer, please send."

On his terminal, the message "Message Sent" popped up. Morris closed his computer and left his quarters to check in with engineering regarding the Hafnium Carbide matrix.

TWENTY-THREE

LIEUTENANT PERRY ROAMED about the cargo hold to ensure nothing was damaged or out of place. He spied an open container and was about to investigate when Ensign Woods rounded the corner and started to block his path. "So, up for a late-night excursion to the observation deck above engineering?" she asked while standing in a way that drew attention to her breasts.

"I can't wait," he said while trying to look at the open container.

She glanced in the direction he was looking and saw the container with its lid askew. "Should we check it out?"

"No, it's all right for now," he said, trying not to look in that direction while she was there.

“I think we should look it over to see what is missing,” she said.

“I will check it later.” He turned to go in the other direction. “Come, help me grab a pallet of ale for the captain to bring to Verna-3.”

"Okay," she replied. She walked ahead of him, which he used as an opportunity to admire her rear end. She glanced over her shoulder at Perry and saw him checking her out. She was pleased. "So, what do you think of this diversion to Kosuan territory?"

"Hopefully, we won't get shot up too badly," he replied, knowing he got caught staring.

"I hear this Benson is going to the surface with the captain to get the Hafnium Carbide we need for the engines."

"That's what I heard as well. From what I can tell, the lieutenant commander definitely has the Captain's eye."

Woods walked up to a motorized pallet jack and stood on it. She gripped the controls and leaned towards Perry. "I saw you checking her out the other day. Just remember, mister, you keep that up, and I will burn your eyes out with a torch." She grinned at him while patting his cheek.

"I'll keep that in mind," he grinned while stepping away from the pallet jack. She squeezed the handle, and it began to roll forward. She navigated around the narrow pathways and found the crate she was looking for, and slid the forks into the notches in the bottom. She lifted the crate a few inches off the floor. She looked around, and Perry was gone.

Perry had walked back towards the open crate he had spied earlier and slightly slid the top to the side. He peeked in and noticed the packing foam balls had settled where something had been removed. He pulled out his PDA and scanned the barcode on the side of the crate. The PDA displayed what was supposed to be in the crate. However, he suspected that it was not accurate. He reached in and saw a black cylinder with magnetic locks on the side, a dimly lit keypad that got brighter when he touched it, and a few blinking lights. He stepped back. "Bombs!" he exclaimed to himself, and based on their size, up to four had been taken from the crate. He knew at least one had been exploded, so that meant two or three remained unaccounted for. He heard the beeping of the powered pallet jack coming his way, so he closed the lid back to the way it was. He ducked away so he would not be seen there.

Perry painted a slight grin on his face as he rounded a different corner and caught up to Lisa Woods.

"Where did you go?" she asked as she dropped the pallet by the entrance to the cargo hold.

"Had to check a few crates that had broken loose the other day to make sure they were secured and ready for what awaits us tomorrow."

"Oh, I see. Well, give me a hand with this. It has to be on the flight deck within the hour."

"As you wish," he replied.

TWENTY-FOUR

THE DINING HALL was only half full during the late afternoon. Benson sat by herself, sipping a cup of coffee. She was on a short break from the bridge and decided to catch up on some reading. She was reading a suspense novel by a British author named Josh Harding, who burst onto the scene a few years ago and was now at the Alliance Academy in Annapolis, Maryland.

A shadow passed by her slowly and paused a moment. Then a chair slid out, and Ambassador Wilcox sat across from her. She kept reading, waiting for him to start in on her. She didn't have to wait long.

He stared at her with his hands folded before him, tapping his index fingers together. "So Tamora, I would have expected you to be studying the Ineans for our landing in a few days if we ever make it."

She lowered the book just enough to make eye contact. “I was unaware that I had been assigned to go to the surface with you,” she stated. She started to bring the book up to continue reading.

“I have convinced the fleet admiral that you would be the perfect personal assistant for me on Inea.”

“I doubt that,” she huffed.

“Your captain is receiving the orders now.”

“What would be my job down there?” She already knew, but she wanted to actually hear him say it.

"You would pilot me to the planet and assist me while negotiating with the Ineans," he said, placing his hand on her book so she could not return to reading.

“That is all?” she asked, knowing it wasn’t.

“Oh, and there are a few other things you will be required to do while the Ineans watch,” he stated with a widening grin.

“I would rather the Ineans just kill me.”

She wanted to vomit at the thought of the Ineans or anyone else watching her intimately interact with Wilcox. Now, the urge to kill him crossed her mind. At least being thrown in the brig would be better than the fate that awaited her on Inea.

"Well, if you are lucky, perhaps." He groaned while pushing himself out of the chair. "Channing will provide you with ALL the details and what to wear. Or should I say what not to wear."

"You son of a bitch!" she sprung from her seat and started toward him.

“Lieutenant Commander Benson. Please come to the bridge. Lieutenant Commander Benson. Please come to the bridge.” Hackett’s voice broadcast over the speaker in the dining hall.

She picked up her book and glared at Wilcox while a fist formed in her other hand. “You will get no satisfaction from me!”

“I already have, Ensign,” he laughed and started towards the coffee pot.

She turned and stomped off towards the doors.

TWENTY-FIVE

MUCH LATER THAT day the forward lounge was dimly lit during the evening hours. Benson sat at a small table near the middle of the room, sipping on a glass of wine. She glanced over her notes for the Verna-3 landing while stewing over what Wilcox had planned for her. She was also angry over what O'Toole said. She waited for Captain Hackett to arrive and review the mission. At least, that was their excuse. What really was happening was dinner together.

She glanced up and watched several crewmen put together the stage for the evening. This evening's entertainment was being performed by about a dozen people. It would be a short play. Unlike the entertainment from the previous evenings, this would be a well-thought-out and practiced routine.

She watched Commander Morris arrive and found a small table on a dimly lit side of the room. The waitress took his drink order. Benson was sure it would be a beer. Sure enough, in a couple of minutes, he received a brown bottle of beer and a glass to pour it into. He was soon joined by Larson. She ordered a drink, and Benson guessed it would be something strong. She had watched many weapons officers over the years. She knew that weapons officers tended to fight hard and drink harder. Larson, it turned out, would be no different. Only Benson guessed it would be vodka. Instead, she received a small glass with ice and a half-full bottle of bourbon. She was still satisfied that Larson fit the profile.

Many of the actors arrived and had begun to warm up when Hackett finally arrived.

"Sorry, I'm late. Been here long?" he asked.

"A little while. I took the time to study a few members of the crew."

"That should have been very entertaining," he stated.

"You have no idea," she grinned back.

The waitress arrived, took Hackett's drink order, and hurried off. The room was nearly full and would be for several hours. Benson already knew what he drank on easy days, which, from his perspective, was a beer. On hard days, his choices went towards the hardest whiskey on the ship.

"So, Lieutenant Commander, what did you want to talk to me about?" Hackett asked.

"I was cornered earlier today by the Ambassador. He told me I was going to the surface of Inea as his assistant. Is this true?"

"Not that I am aware of. We had spoken about that a few days ago. That was when the fleet admiral sided with me, and that you would not be going down to that planet with him," Hackett replied.

"I see, so it was a lie."

"From Wilcox, most likely," Hackett said as he grabbed the bottle of beer. "Do me a favor."

She nodded.

"Stay away from him. Don't make eye contact. If he speaks to you, just leave and let me know."

"I'm not a fan of running away from a problem, Captain," she said as the waitress came around with the dinner menus.

"I know. Remember one thing. He is violating a directive to stay away from you. So I want any and all interactions documented."

"To be used against him later?" she asked while scanning the menu.

"Leverage. Out here, you need leverage."

"I'm learning quickly," she stated.

Benson glanced at the menu and put it back down on the table. She already knew what she wanted.

The waitress returned. "Would you like something to start off with?"

Hackett looked up. "Whatever the Lieutenant Commander wants. I'll eat just about anything."

The waitress looked down toward Benson. "That is true."

They all laughed.

Benson picked up the menu and glanced at it quickly. "Onion straws and stuffed mushrooms."

"Someone's hungry, Captain." The waitress said with a grin.

"That makes two of us."

The waitress grinned again and walked away after surveying their drinks. She made a mental note to bring back two fresh drinks.

Benson sipped the last of her white wine and put the glass down. She cleared her throat and looked Hackett in the eyes.

Hackett was momentarily concerned about what she was going to say. It was evident that she was uncomfortable with whatever it was.

"I, um, am in a situation, Captain, and I know you have every right to throw me off the ship."

"Oh?" he said. He leaned in for some reason. Not because it was noisy, which it was, but because he sensed some sort of secret coming.

"I am going to violate an order from the admiral."

"Be careful, Lieutenant Commander."

"I wish I could," she exhaled, which Hackett found uncharacteristic for her.

"I was ordered to get close to you and compromise you," she said. "I'm so sorry."

"What was the reason for that?"

"I'm not sure why, and that is why I told you. Also, I found the assignment morally wrong and can't do it any longer."

He patted her hand that was in front of her. The one holding the wine glass. "I know why you are here. I also know it was your hardest assignment because of your beliefs and your past."

"My past?"

"Yes. There is no record of you dating since Cadet Harrison. What was it, 10 years ago?"

"I don't want to talk about that," she said, longing for a drink that was slow in coming. She needed something for her hands to do, and holding a full wine glass was good enough. However, something stronger now was needed.

"I understand." He took a sip of beer. Really wasn't a sip. It was more like half the bottle, and it was empty.

The waitress returned with fresh drinks and the appetizers. "Are you ready to order?" she asked with a glance toward Benson.

"I'm not that hungry right now."

"Yes, you are. Let me order. Shall I?"

Benson nodded. She was intrigued by what else the Captain knew about her.

"The Lieutenant Commander Benson will ha-a-a-a-ve…" he dragged out the last word while studying her face, "the Chicken sauteed with vegetables over rice and a garden salad with oil and vinegar dressing."

"How did you know?" she asked with sincere curiosity.

He grinned. "Quite simple. I watched your eyes scan the menu and noticed they stopped about halfway down. That was when you put the menu down. I glanced at mine and saw what was there. Simple, really."

"Oh, let me try your order then."

"Go right ahead."

The waitress watched the exchange with interest and almost forgot to write down their order.

"The Captain will have a large streak. No, strike that. A filet mignon, medium rare with a baked potato, sour cream, and squash," she said. She folded her hands, grinned, and supported her chin in her hands.

"Wow, very good."

"Will there be anything else?" the waitress asked.

"I will have red wine from here on out," Hackett said.

"What kind?" the waitress asked.

"Californian," Benson added.

"Okay, I'll be back," the waitress scurried off.

TWENTY-SIX

IT WAS STILL early in the evening when Benson and Hackett parted, and she took the time to find the gymnasium. It was two decks below her quarters. She carried her duffel bag into the women's locker room and found an empty locker. She stripped and redressed in her workout clothes. Tight spandex shorts and an equally tight shirt. She didn't like tight clothes, except for working out. She closed her locker and walked out into the gym. A few people worked out, mainly with weights and treadmills. She continued looking for a punching bag. She had some frustration that needed to be vented. She found them in an adjacent room, four of them. She stretched and cleared her mind. She spied a roll of boxer's tape on a shelf and carefully wrapped her hands. Taking her time, still mentally preparing herself for the abuse she would dish out.

She was ready. She began to lightly punch the heavy sack hanging from the ceiling. It barely budged. She hit it harder and harder. Kicking now, she grunted with each brutal hit, and sweat quickly beaded on her forehead. She continued to pound the punching bag. She visualized the punching bag as Ambassador Wilcox, then O'Toole, then the crewman who first greeted her when she stepped on board. Lastly, she visualized the bag as Hackett. Why? She knew why. Her mission to trip him up was compromised. She liked him; she wasn't supposed to, but she did. He wasn't the enemy portrayed by Vice Admiral Griffin. Griffin had lied to her, telling her Hackett was secretly working with the Ineans to pillage the Earth. She was also told he was a madman, crazy, and not to be trusted. She was ordered to be fearful of Hackett and to find his secret plans, then report back. None of it was turning out to be true. Now it was Griffin whom she questioned. She now wanted to know what scared the vice admiral about Hackett. She had secretly changed her mission to find out what it was. She feared that the future of their race depended on finding out.

There was a hiss behind her. Someone had entered the room. She never heard it over her own grunts and groans of beating the round canvas sack. She kept pulverizing the poor, hapless punching bag harder and harder.

O'Toole stood behind her and watched as she beat the bag. His first thought was that she was angry, but then he realized she was good. He knew she could probably mop the floor with him, and he came to the realization that he was wrong about her. She wasn't there for her looks. She was there because she was qualified. She proved that by putting out the fire in the nacelle a few days before. She was proving right now that she could hold her own in a fight. He watched as his loathing changed to admiration.

She saw a shadow moving behind her. Her mind was still fixated on destroying the punching bag when she turned and swung at O'Toole. He ducked away and raised his taped hands to defend himself when she realized who it was. She raised her hands to stop. "Sorry, I get wrapped up in my exercises, and I saw a shadow behind me," she said, panting, slouching over with her hands on her knees. She straightened and placed them on her hips when she caught her breath.

O'Toole stared at her for a moment. Admiring her, but not like before, admiring her for her beauty. Those tight workout clothes didn't help, either. "I didn't mean to sneak up on you, sorry."

“That’s okay. I missed,” she replied, turning toward the smaller, firmer bag hanging from the ceiling.

“I’m sorry about the other day. I misjudged you,” O’Toole said.

"That's okay," she said while sizing up her next victim. She didn't look at him; she was unaccustomed to people apologizing to her.

“No, it isn’t. You belong here with this crew. I was wrong about you,” he continued.

"Oh, yeah, well, prove it. I'm tired of people looking at me and saying I can't do this because of my appearance. I feel I was cursed somehow," she blurted out as she turned toward him finally.

"You're not cursed. You have talent and skills. It's our society that is cursed, not you," he said as she started to go around him. He knew what she wanted and was prepared to give it to her. He sized her up at the same time while turning to keep his eyes on her. "You want to fight me, don't you?"

"Bring it on," She said, tapping her hands to his.

"Bring it on? That's it? Bring it on. Okay, fine, here it comes then." He swung and caught the side of her face. A glancing blow she partially blocked. She fired back, and they proceeded to box. He landed some good shots, forcing her to step back. She connected with a couple, and he fell back. She swung around with her foot and kicked him in the chest. He spun as she connected, taking all the force out of her kick. He came around and connected with his foot to the center of her back. She bent backward and grimaced as she stumbled forward and fell to her knees. He moved in to finish her off. She was waiting for him. He went to kick her in the head, and for an instant, he really wanted to hurt her. She rolled, caught his foot with both hands, and twisted. He flew over her and landed on the mat-covered floor with a thud. She pounced, grabbed one of his legs, and pulled it straight up while stuffing a knee into his chest. It was over. He put his hands up. She won.

She got up and extended her hand to him. He grabbed it, and she helped him to his feet. He smiled. "Feel better now?"

She looked back and grinned. A bruise was forming below her left eye. A trace of blood formed at the corner of her mouth.

O'Toole looked about the same. "Much better. Did I hurt you?" she asked.

"Only my pride. Let me buy you a drink," he said as he reached over and wiped the trickle of blood from her lower lip. He was beginning to like her.

"Okay, fine," she agreed.

They looked up, and they had quite the audience. Two security guards had been called in because no one knew what was happening. They quickly backed down when they saw the fighters end their battle. For all they knew, it was a sparring match to prepare for Verna-3.

They moved toward the door, and he placed his arm around her shoulders, drawing her to him as it hissed open. She elbowed him hard in the ribs, and he backed off. She grinned at him, and he laughed.

They went to their respective locker rooms, showered, and dressed. They met outside the gym and went to the forward lounge for a late drink.

Hackett excused himself and left the bridge to Bowers. He walked around the ship, mainly to see how repairs were going. All done for now. His mind shifted to Benson. What was he going to do about her? He thought about their conversation earlier in the evening and how she had probed into his personal life, not in a suspicious manner, but rather as someone who genuinely wanted to know for themselves. He didn't mind. It proved to him that she was confused about how she felt, which could prove useful when the time came.

He walked towards the forward lounge for coffee before turning in for the evening. He disliked slow days like this. To him, they were boring. He had grown accustomed to living on the edge, and today was too routine for his liking. He decided to visit the engineering department in the morning. He needed to quiz O'Toole on his thoughts about the mission.

The doors hissed open, and he walked into the lounge. He stopped and surveyed the room. He spied Benson and O'Toole together, enjoying drinks and each other from what he could see from here. *Good! Takes the heat off of me!* he said to himself, but part of him was disappointed. He did like her. He wished it could be more. However, that would give Vice Admiral Griffin the ammunition he needed to throw him in the brig. Then Morris's words returned to haunt him: *Sometimes I think I made the wrong choice.* How true it was. Now he understood Morris a little better.

He stopped staring and sat on a stool at the bar. He ordered a coffee, black this time, with no cream and no sugar. He sat with his back to Benson and O'Toole. He rethought about talking to O'Toole. He may be involved after all.

He flipped open his folder, looking, hoping to find something he had overlooked. Nothing. As it turned out, the information was vague about Verna-3 and the Kosuan. He finished his coffee and left to continue his walk around his ship.

Benson and O'Toole finished their nightcap and left the lounge. They walked about the ship. He pointed out many of the ship's unique features, and she showed genuine interest. They laughed and joked like old friends, even though they had only been friendly for a few hours. He walked beside her, closer now. She didn't back off this time. She liked him. They walked towards her quarters, and she typed in her code; the door slid open. She backed into the doorway and stopped. He was looking at her oddly. *Crap!* she thought. *He's going to try to kiss me now. Two hours ago, we tried to kill each other, and now the fool wants to kiss me!*

He leaned in and saw her expression. He backed off. He knew that one all too well. *Don't rush. Take your time.* He reached out his hand instead. "It's been a pleasure, Tamora. One I hope isn't the last." *Yeah, that's better.*

She sighed internally in relief. *That was close.* "I enjoyed our time together," she said as she grabbed his hand and shook it. "I look forward to the next." She smiled and turned quickly to enter her room. The door closed behind her. *Dang, that was too close.*

TWENTY-SEVEN

THE SHIP SLOWED during the overnight hours to conserve its remaining Hafnium platters, which delayed its orbital insertion by an hour to 1400 hours. Hackett looked around the mess hall and ordered his staff to their positions as soon as possible. Most people left the room and headed to their posts. Hackett and Morris followed some distance behind and finished their discussion.

Once on the bridge, everyone immediately became busy, performing diagnostics on all their systems before confronting the Kosuan. This new aspect of their mission carried a high degree of risk, and to succeed, they would have to be extremely careful. The Kosuan are well-armed and have a considerable amount of personnel on the planet ahead. Plus, recent friction between the two races would keep the tension level high, causing trouble for this crew with their damaged ship.

The ship still suffered many structural problems from the terrorist attack and previous encounters with the Ineans. Many of the hull plates and structural ribs remained damaged. The ship truly needed a month in space dock, but it wasn't going to happen on this trip. The best they could do was avoid a fight. Could they do it?

Hackett looked around the bridge at all the faces that depended on him to make the right decisions, keeping them alive. He felt the need to address the crew before they arrived at the planet. He walked to the front of the bridge and turned to face them. "Attention, everyone." He waited a moment for all eyes to look at him. "We are all tired, and our ship is in tough shape. However, the Kosuan are not interested in starting a war with the Alliance while they are fighting with the Ineans. We can use this to our advantage when approaching one of their planets in a few hours. I don't think we will have the assistance of Ambassador Wilcox or his assistant, so we are on our own to negotiate a deal for the supplies we need to complete our mission to Inea.

Nevertheless, it will still be challenging. I need everyone to be as sharp as they can be so we get out of here alive and with the materials we need. I want to avoid a firefight for obvious reasons. Thank you." Hackett returned to his seat, and his crew returned to their tasks.

In the engine room, Commander O'Toole was readying his department for what he hoped would be a refit of the composite gold/hafnium matrix for his engines. However, he couldn't help preparing his people for combat. The Kosuan are not the easiest beings to deal with, and O'Toole knew that the odds were not in their favor. Everyone in engineering was outfitted in pressure suits and had their helmets nearby in case they were needed. Technicians opened the emergency lockers, removed their equipment, and waited.

Ensign Lisa Woods and Lieutenant Robert Perry rushed to secure the cargo hold. They removed supplies to bring up to the kitchen. They needed to be done before the ship approached Verna-3. Woods looked at Perry. "Hey, did you see the captain talking with that lieutenant commander the other night?"

Perry looked up and took a breath. "Sure did. What's up with them anyway?"

Woods leaned forward on a cargo container and rested. "I don't know. They must be aware of the regulations. The Captain isn't stupid, but they are not even trying to hide it."

"I know. Something seems to be happening between them, or

maybe that's what we are to believe. This might be fun to watch," Perry said as he returned to work.

"Yeah, at least people stopped talking about us the last couple of days," Woods replied.

"That's a good thing. Come, help me load the cargo elevator so we can get out of here," Perry said as he carried a box forward.

"Okay. Let me just tie this down before I forget it," she replied. Woods tugged on a tie-down strap until it clicked into place. She then pulled one over the top and looped it through the latch, and yanked it down hard until it clicked into place. She tested it to ensure it was secure.

"Are you sure that is necessary?" Perry asked.

"We are going into orbit around a Kosuan-controlled planet. You know damn well that we will be shot at," she said while testing the strap again. "Here I come." She picked up a box and walked to the cargo elevator.

Back on the bridge, the viewer displayed a bright white dot growing as they approached. The mood on the bridge was cautiously optimistic.

Giovanella turned to Hackett, "Sir, we are being hailed from Verna-3."

"Here we go, people," Hackett said. "Put it on the viewer."

"Aye, sir," he said, and the image of a Kosuan male appeared on the screen. The Kosuan were very aggressive-looking and didn't like to be bothered, especially by humans. Kosuan, like the Ineans, were large-boned and larger and stronger than humans. Their appearance was quite intimidating, to put it mildly.

"Alliance ship, you are violating our territory. Turn around and leave, or we will destroy your puny little ship," the image growled sternly.

Hackett stood up to face the viewer. "I am Captain Shawn Hackett of the *Saratoga*. We come to your world to purchase any refined Hafnium Carbide plates you are willing to sell us."

"Argh! We do not sell our minerals to Earthers. Turn your ship around. We know you are going to Inea to help them against us, Captain." The Kosuan was getting agitated. More agitated than he already sounded.

"That is not correct. We are traveling to Inea to make arrangements for peace with them. We are not interested in your conflict with the Ineans," Hackett replied.

"How do I know you are telling the truth, Captain?" the Kosuan asked.

"You don't. What I say to you, I will swear on the honor of your family. We are in need of the elements so we can finish our mission to Inea in the hope of establishing peace," Hackett said, hoping to strike a chord with the Kosuan's solid beliefs and values. It appeared to work.

"I am sending two ships to escort you into orbit, Captain. One wrong move, and I will order them to blast you to bits," the Kosuan said.

Hackett looked at the screen for a second. "That will be acceptable. Excuse me for not catching your name."

"My name is not important. The fact that I can carry out my last statement is! I want you and your first officer to come to the surface so we can discuss your request. Here are my coordinates," he said harshly.

"May I bring one more person as an observer?" Hackett asked.

"Only one more, Mahoh, voh-nah!" he growled, and the viewer returned to the growing image of the rusty-looking planet.

As the *Saratoga* drew closer, the planet's details began to reveal themselves. It was a reddish planet with odd-looking, light blue oceans. The world was shrouded in a thick atmosphere, composed of many of the same gases as Earth's. The planet was slightly larger than Earth, so the gravity wouldn't interfere with humans who went to the surface. There were mountains, valleys, lakes, and green patches of vegetation near the planet's temperate zone. Thick, heavy ice and glaciers covered both polar regions. The overall temperature was slightly lower than Earth's as the planet was farther away from its average-sized star.

The landing site was on the equator of the planet. The Kosuan chose this spot for their mining because it had the most tolerable weather. They had difficulty adapting to the cold weather because their own world, Kosua Prime, was a hot, humid planet that orbited closer to its star than Earth. Kosua Prime was also the only known habitable binary planet. It shares its orbit around its star, Mu Arae, with an equal-sized planet. The pair danced around each other as they rotated around their star. Many thought Mu Arae was a variable star until Earth travelers went to the stars and discovered the bizarre nature of the system. The binary planets came together when Mu Arae pulled a gas giant from a neighboring system billions of years ago. The gas giant now orbits Mu Arae closely every 20 days. This led Earth astronomers to mistakenly call the star a variable. All this leads to a hellish environment for an intelligent race to evolve—a very rough and rugged one to contend with, one that Hackett and his crew will soon have to deal with.

Even though Verna-3 was a hostile environment in its own right, it was the complete opposite of Kosua Prime. It was cold. Frigid for the most part, except for the equatorial regions, where it was barely tolerable. The Kosuan had a difficult time keeping warm even here. They had to, of course. It was the only planet in their region of space where they could get the resources necessary for their race's survival. It was a planet they needed to be on.

Two Kosuan warships lifted off from the planet. They sped quickly toward the *Saratoga*. Overtaking it in a matter of minutes. The Kosuan took positions on either side of the *Saratoga* and flew towards the planet with their guns trained on the *Saratoga*, which was sandwiched between them. Hackett didn't raise the shields, hoping the Kosuan would see it as a sign of trust. So far, the mission was going according to plan.

Kosuan warships were blood red in color and painted with a fierce, wildcat-like creature on either side, pouncing its prey with long, powerful, and deeply clawed paws outstretched toward its victim, blood dripping from its fully exposed fangs, its eyes filled with fire and fixed forward. A fearful sight for someone who knew this race's reputation for conquering its opponents. The ship resembled a wedge-shaped horseshoe with its points facing forward, similar to the forward hull of the *Saratoga*. The forward tips were lined with several torpedo ports facing forward. The underside held the quantum cooling grids for the main engines.

The Kosuan ships were very Spartan in accommodations, definitely a "no-frills" ship. These ships held one purpose and one only: they were warships. Every inch of these ships was dedicated to military use. The most dangerous feature of these ships was their ability to rapidly fire weapons from several ports and fly circles around their enemies at sub-light speeds.

"Captain, we are entering orbit above the coordinates received," Davies said.

"Very well, Ensign. Miss Larson, you have the bridge. Miss Benson, you seem to know these people. You are with us," Hackett stated without looking at her.

"Yes, Captain," Benson replied, and she yielded her station to a replacement.

Hackett spread his orders around the bridge to make sure everyone was prepared. "Mr. Giovanella, I want you to keep a lock on us and to be ready to extract us if we get in trouble."

Hackett, Morris, and Benson headed for the elevator for their long trip to the aft hangar bay below the engine room. Several minutes later, they entered the hangar and were handed transmitters, laser pistols, and Alliance jackets that doubled as protective vests. They readied themselves for what promised to be a less-than-receptive visit. Hackett was the first to enter the transport, followed by Morris and then Benson. Hackett gave the order to begin. Sirens sounded, warning people to clear the flight deck due to decompression. Huge pumps started to roar, and a powerful rush of air swept across the deck as it was sucked out of the hangar. Several more minutes passed, and the large bay doors slid open, exposing the flight deck to the vacuum of space. Hackett was at the controls and piloted the transport out of the hangar and into space. The transport flew quickly towards the planet below. The flight was uneventful, and they landed in the center of the compound just a few minutes after leaving their ship.

Benson pulled on her snug-fitting black gloves, which matched her black jacket. She turned on her "AT"(alien translator) and slid it into a pocket inside her jacket. She then placed the earpiece in her ear and tucked the wire inside her jacket before buttoning it. She adjusted her cap and flipped down her sunglasses. Even though the star was not bright, the planet's atmosphere did little to block the dangerous radiation from the star above. Hackett and Morris did the same, and with a nod from Hackett, they exited the transport and stepped out on this cool planet. A slight breeze kicked up from the south. It was the first time humans had set foot on a Kosuan mining planet. Benson flipped up her collar against the chilly air and buttoned the rest of her jacket. She then opened her scanner and began taking readings of the atmosphere and surroundings. "Air quality is acceptable for the short term, Sir. We should make it a point to be off this rock in under six hours," she stated.

"Understood," Hackett replied. "I plan to be out of here in less than one."

"I am detecting several hundred Kosuan in the buildings around us. I am also detecting a considerable amount of diamonds underground in addition to the material we are after, Captain. Also, an unusually high amount of other rare minerals," she continued. "There is a large power complex about 10 clicks southwest of here. It appears to be the only power source driving the mining machines below the surface and powering the facility we see here."

They turned to face a recently built stone building. Several Kosuan spilled out of the building and surrounded them in a noisy rush designed to disorient an opponent. None of Hackett's crew raised a weapon. They were prepared for this. The Kosuan grabbed them and forced them into an older stone building, down a long, damp hallway that reeked of sweaty animals and other unpleasant odors, none of which they could identify or dare to guess what they were. At the end of the hall, the soldiers pushed them through a doorway and slammed it shut behind them.

The three of them turned to survey the room. Benson, scanner in hand, swept it around the room. "That's the only entrance to this room, Captain," she said.

"Understood." He lifted his arm, pressed the button on his wristwatch communicator, and contacted the ship. "*Saratoga,* come in, please?"

"*Saratoga,* here, Captain. What is your status?" Larson replied amongst the static.

"We are in a holding room of sorts. Keep this channel open, and we will check in soon. Hackett out," he said, and quickly put his hand down by his side as the door to the room opened, and the Kosuan with whom they spoke while approaching the planet walked in with two soldiers. They closed the door and walked up to Hackett and his people. Each picked an officer and proceeded to get extremely close to intimidate Hackett and his people. Thanks to Benson, Hackett knew this, and they stood their ground. Morris and Benson leaned back as hard as they could.

"I am Garook. I am the administrator of this snowball," he said with a tone suggesting he wasn't pleased with his assignment. Hackett picked up on this rather quickly and hoped he could use the Kosuan's situation to his advantage. Regardless, he was still dangerous and stood close to Hackett, towering over him by at least a foot. Hackett's nose would have touched the Kosuan's chest if he were closer.

"I am Captain Hackett. We would like to purchase several dozen Hafnium Carbide platters for our ship, Garook," Hackett said without hesitation or any indication that he was not pleased to have this being so close.

"I understand, Captain. I do have a question. What happens to you if we do not provide you with them?" Garook asked, hoping Hackett would reveal the ship's true condition, which the two escort ships had been unable to determine. If they only knew how bad off Hackett's ship really was, they would have pounced on it already, and Hackett and his two officers would have been dead by now. The Kosuan scanners were being jammed by O'Toole's leaking quantum field coils and could not give Garook what he needed to know. For now, he would play along.

"We would turn around and head back to our nearest outpost to receive them, Garook," Hackett said.

"So why come here then?"

Garook was probing to see if the ship was dangerously low on power, which would make for an easy kill for his ships.

"This was, for the most part, on our way. So, by stopping here, we can still proceed on our mission to Inea," Hackett said.

The two soldiers stepped back, and Benson nearly fell to the ground. They laughed at her as she stumbled to regain her footing. Garook pulled a knife and held it to Hackett's throat.

"My ships have their weapons pointing at yours, Captain," he said.

"I know that. You should be aware that my ship's laser cannons are manually locked onto your ships, and the personnel I have left in charge have orders to fire if they are fired upon or if your personnel attempt to board our ship. Plus, I have a channel open so they can listen in on our conversation. If you kill me, then your two ships will be next," Hackett said without yielding to the Kosuan.

Garook was silent. Hackett continued, "So, do we have a deal, Garook, or do you want to take a chance that I'm bluffing?"

Garook released Hackett and pushed him back. "You smell foul, Captain." Hackett felt the same about the Kosuan. His breath was the worst Hackett had ever smelled, and it took all he had to not show his disgust. Garook stared at him for a second. "However, your reputation precedes you."

Garook motioned for his bodyguards to follow him to the corner of the room. Hackett took the time to confer with his people. Benson told him to back off a little. "The Kosuan respect toughness. However, if you are too tough, they won't bargain," she said, while Hackett agreed, and the Kosuan returned.

"Captain Hackett, we will agree to sell you the raw material you need on one condition," Garook said, smiling at the three humans.

"What is your condition?" Hackett asked.

Garook laughed and walked up to Benson, who was sporting a mild shiner under her left eye from her workout with O'Toole, and with one hand, squeezed her face. "I want this female for my pleasure, Captain." Garook knew an Alliance captain wouldn't allow it, but he wasn't prepared for Hackett's response. Morris was just as shocked.

"Well, Garook, I would normally agree to your terms, but she is mine," Hackett said. Morris nearly broke his neck as he turned to look at him. Garook released his grip and stepped back. Hackett continued, "She is my mate, and it would be against both our cultures for you to have her."

Garook was shocked, which was unusual for a Kosuan, and he knew under his own laws, he could be killed for touching another male's mate like he did. "Prove it!"

Hackett walked up to Benson and pulled her head to his, kissed her on the lips, and pulled her closer with his other arm. She wrapped her arms around him and squeezed and kissed him in return. After a moment, they separated, keeping an arm around each other. Hackett looked at Morris, whose chin was nearly on the floor. "Satisfied, Garook, or should I kill you now for touching my mate?" Hackett pulled away from Benson and stepped up to Garook. He pulled his laser pistol from its holster and held it to Garook's head. "What will it be?"

Garook cleared his throat while listening to the laser pistol whining, indicating it was charged and ready to fire. "A thousand apologies, Captain. We will take some of your supplies instead. Let's say a few cases of your best ale and some food supplies?"

Hackett thought for a moment and looked back at Garook. He pushed him away and said, “Deal.”

“Mr. Morris, make the arrangements.” And he stepped back to be beside Benson.

“Ye-e-e-s-s-s-s, Captain.” Morris walked to the side of the room and contacted the ship. All the while, he kept an eye on Hackett and Benson.

Garook shuffled to Hackett and Benson and sniffed them both. He then made an approving gesture and sniffed Benson again. "You two are mated," he said in his most pleasant gruff voice. He turned to the other Kosuan, who began arguing among themselves, and ordered them to get the containers.

Morris, who had been utterly unprepared for how Hackett and

Benson proved their point, was also taken aback by the Kosuan's senses about their odor. Kosuan had a keen sense of such things and knew they were involved somehow. What would Morris put in his report? He knew Hackett was an excellent officer, and he didn't want him to get in trouble, even though his methods were, at best, unorthodox. He didn't know Benson well. He was learning just how good an officer she was, or did they plan this ahead of time? Morris knew what they had talked about the two nights before. *Oh, the Hell with it,* he said to himself.

"Captain Hackett. You are unlike any other humans we have encountered," Garook said.

“Out here, Garook, it takes a special type of warrior. A typical human wouldn’t last five minutes out here,” Hackett replied.

“You allow your females to fight?” Garook was confused as he studied Benson’s shiner.

"Yes, males of our culture tend to mate with females who closely match themselves. She is tough, and if I ordered her to do so, she could rip the heart out of your chest and eat it before it stopped beating. Something I'm sure you wouldn't want me to order."

Benson did her best to block the vision of such an act and hoped the Kosuan didn't take Hackett up on his comment.

The other two Kosuan showed up several minutes later with a composite container of shiny silver Hafnium plates. Hackett knew by looking at it that his engineer would not be pleased. The platters would have to be cut to the proper dimensions and then coated with gold, making them highly conductive. This would have to be done in the ship's parts printer.

Another transport brought the supplies requested down to the planet, and several Kosuan warriors carried them into the room with Hackett and company. The second transport quickly departed and headed back to the *Saratoga*. The guards opened the tops of the bottles, chugged down a few of the brews, and wiped their mouths on the backs of their hands.

"Ahhh, that is good, Captain. Join us for a couple," Garook said. Hackett hesitated briefly before accepting the offer. The beer was warm, but it still went down smoothly. They all had another round.

It was Benson who, this time, got into a chugging contest with Garook. She couldn't beat him either. After a couple more rounds, Morris was forced into the act. The six of them consumed an entire case in just a matter of minutes. More supplies were carried in, and Morris turned, picked up the cylinders, and started for the door.

Hackett, Morris, and Benson left the Kosuan to their alcohol and returned to the *Saratoga*. Once safely on board, Hackett turned to the two of them. “Miss Benson, thank you for allowing that on the planet below.”

"No problem, sir," she said, quite pleased with herself. Hackett sensed she didn't mind kissing. The prospect of what Ambassador Wilcox wanted to do repulsed her.

Hackett continued, “Go back to the bridge and prepare to get us out of here quickly.”

"Yes, sir," she replied, and she hurried out the door.

“Mr. Morris?” Hackett said.

“Yes, Captain,” Morris responded.

“What happened down there was staged. Don’t make anything more out of it than that for your report, Commander,” Hackett said.

"I won't, Captain. I'm just not sure where the staged part leaves off, and the real stuff begins," Morris replied.

“There is no real stuff!" Hackett growled. "Just report the truth, Commander. First, let's get these to O'Toole so he can begin printing new nozzles for the antimatter injectors," Hackett stated.

"Yes, sir," he replied, and they both rushed out of the hangar bay and headed to the central elevator for engineering.

In the engine room, O'Toole was less than impressed with the Kosuan material and showed the Captain how inferior it was. "See, Captain, how yellow this is?" He poured some into his hand and moved it around with his thumb. Hackett nodded that he could see the yellow tint. "There are a lot of impurities mixed into this. We won't get maximum power out of these at all, and we risk burning them out faster than normal, Sir."

“Do the best you can with them. It looks like they are the best we will get,” Hackett said.

“Yes, Captain, just don’t push the ship too hard because they will burn out no matter how I align them,” O’Toole said.

"I know, Commander. I can't promise you that," Hackett said firmly as he motioned for Morris to follow him out of engineering. He turned back to the engineer for an instant. "How long before you can have them printed and coated, Mr. O'Toole?"

“It will take a few hours, sir,” he replied.

“Very well, we may have to leave here before they get suspicious about why we are hanging around,” Hackett said.

"Yes, Captain, we can leave and install them away from here," he replied. Hackett and Morris left and went to the bridge. Hackett was feeling odd at the alcohol he consumed with the Kosuan and vowed to himself he wouldn't drink for a while. He also thought about kissing and holding Benson. He thought about how much he enjoyed it and, maybe, there was a chance with her. He looked at Benson when he entered the bridge. She didn't give him a look as he sat down. That was good. He could tell that the alcohol was having the same effect on her as well.

Lieutenant Stephen Bowers turned towards Hackett. "Sir, other Kosuan ships are approaching."

"Thank you, Lieutenant. Helm, time to break orbit, maximum sustainable speed," Hackett said as he made his way to his chair.

Ensign Carol Davies programmed the settings and took the ship out of orbit.

“Captain, the Kosuan are powering up their weapons, sir,” reported Bowers.

"Battle stations, charge shields!" Hackett ordered, but one of the Kosuan ships had fired and hit the aft shield. The ship shook from the assault as it began to leave orbit. The other ship was now firing and was hitting the shields surrounding the secondary hull. Both ships continued firing until the *Saratoga* disappeared in a flash of light that shook the Kosuan ships. Hackett immediately ordered the shields down to conserve what remained of their primary power couplings.

O'Toole contacted the bridge and told the Captain they had about 30 minutes of power remaining. The shields had drawn too much power from the quantum drive, which burned up another injector. The ship had only one left, and it was deteriorating relatively quickly. Hackett ordered the ship to maintain course and speed for another 15 minutes to ensure the Kosuan didn't follow them.

TWENTY-EIGHT

THE ELEVATOR DOORS SLID OPEN, and Ambassador Wilcox entered the bridge and walked up to Hackett. "Captain, have you secured the materials you needed from the Kosuan?" he asked.

"Yes, Ambassador, we did, and on behalf of the crew, I want to thank you for your help! Our engineer is checking to see if they are usable as we speak," Hackett replied sarcastically.

Wilcox heard the Captain's tone and let it go for now. It would sound much better in his report to the vice admiral. "Good, then we can finally get on our mission to Inea."

The Ambassador was up to something, and Hackett knew it. Wilcox began to walk away but stopped and turned to face Hackett. "Oh, by the way, Captain, Command wasn't very pleased with the report I sent them about you. I'm sure you'll be hearing from them soon. I wouldn't be surprised if they overrule you on your points of interest." After saying that, he looked at Benson and bumped her chair as he walked past.

Hackett knew what he meant and chose to ignore it for now. The Ambassador entered the elevator and left the bridge without saying another word.

Suddenly, the ship dropped out of the wormhole, and the lights throughout the ship dimmed to a minimum level. The yellow warning lights began to flash. The light on Hackett's comm pad began to blink on his chair.

"Hackett here," he said after he hit the open button.

"Sir, this is O'Toole. We just burned up our last platter. We will finish the shutdown process and begin fitting the ones provided by the Kosuan. Unfortunately, this is going to be a slow process, Sir," he said.

Everyone on the bridge heard the message and understood the stakes. If the *Saratoga* were attacked, they could not use shields or laser cannons for very long. Long-range scans showed ships in the area, including several Kosuan and Inean warships.

"How long do you need, Commander?" Hackett asked calmly.

"At least half a day, sir. These Kosuan platters, as you know, could be better and are crudely cut. We will have to rework these considerably for them to be useful, Sir," O'Toole said.

"Very well, Commander, use whatever you need to make them work. Even if you partially install a few of them so we can protect ourselves while you finish the rest," Hackett said.

"That will work, Captain. O'Toole out."

Hackett turned to Giovanella. "Mr. Giovanella, rig the ship for silent running, and Commander Morris, initiate energy conservation level five, please."

Both men went to work, informing the crew of the orders. Hackett turned to look at Bowers at the sensors console. "Mr. Bowers, keep me informed about the ships in the vicinity. I want to know the second anyone comes this way."

"Yes, Captain. We do have two Inean ships that will pass close to our position in about three-and-a-half hours," he replied as several lights dimmed. Several computers shut down to save what little power they had.

"Lieutenant Larson, manually load the torpedo tubes and set them for manual firing, just in case," Hackett said.

"Aye, sir," she replied. She locked her station and left the bridge.

Several minutes passed, and the elevator lift doors opened.

Ambassador Wilcox stomped onto the bridge. "What is the meaning of interrupting my communications with Alliance Command?" he demanded as he landed before Hackett.

"Ambassador, we just burned out our last crystal, and we are running silent until we regain full power again. There are plenty of Inean and Kosuan ships out there within close proximity to us that would love nothing more than to take a few pokes at us. So, until full power is restored, there will be no external communications of any type. Now, please get off my bridge." Hackett's demeanor was calm, but he remained firm with a slight twist of annoyance towards Wilcox.

Wilcox, on the other hand, wasn't ready to let it go. "Captain, I demand that you allow me to continue my communication with headquarters. If you do not, I will assume Command of this vessel under Article 139."

"That won't do you any good, Ambassador, because we are dead in the water right now. If we are attacked, we don't have shields and can only muster a few short bursts of laser power. Thus, if we are attacked by an Inean or Kosuan ship, we are dead for certain. Do you understand?" Hackett was becoming more agitated, and it was coming out in the tone of his voice.

"Restore communications right now, or you are relieved, Captain! This is a trick of yours to prevent the reception of the new orders from Command." Wilcox was becoming angrier, and his face was getting red. He leaned in on Hackett, which wasn't the best idea. "I know what you are up to, Hackett, and it won't work!"

"I cannot and will not. The safety of this crew comes first, Ambassador and your article 139 does not apply here, so leave the bridge, or I will have security escort you to your quarters again." Hackett's tone was beginning to show a noticeable edge, and he was determined to get under Wilcox's skin with his emphasizing "again," which he noticed got to Wilcox. Hackett had reached the end of his tolerance for the Ambassador. "Oh, and I have no need to avoid orders, Ambassador! The vice admiral already settled our previous discussion."

Wilcox stood in front of Hackett and reached into his pocket, removed a laser pistol, and pointed it at Hackett. "Captain Shawn Hackett, you are hereby relieved of command effective immediately," he said, pointing the gun at Hackett's head. Hackett could hear the whine of the laser building its charge to fire, so he knew it was a live one. Both security guards stepped forward with guns raised at Wilcox.

"If I don't, you will shoot me, Ambassador?" Hackett asked as he stood in front of the Ambassador with his arms folded. "Look around. You won't leave the bridge alive."

"If I have to, Captain, I will get off the bridge now." Wilcox was shaking and could accidentally shoot the Captain.

Hackett remained composed and sat back in the chair. "You are committing mutiny, Ambassador, which is a serious crime. I will not leave this chair, and the crew will not follow your orders. If you kill me, then there is no one to turn the command codes over to you."

"You have 30 seconds, Captain!" Wilcox said, hands shaking as he pointed the gun at the Captain.

“Mr. Morris, have additional security come to the bridge and remove the ambassador,” Hackett requested.

"Yes, Captain!" Morris replied.

Everyone on the bridge had turned to watch the showdown.

“Don’t you dare touch that button, Commander!” Wilcox yelled, but it was too late. Morris had already called for security.

Hackett pressed the comm button on his wristwatch. "Miss Larson, are the torpedo tubes loaded?"

"Yes, Captain," she replied over the tinny-sounding speaker.

"You! You get away from that console!" Wilcox stammered as he swung his laser from side to side, unsure of where to point it.

"Close the launch tube doors and set the torpedoes to detonate," he paused to look at Wilcox. Then he continued, "30 seconds," as Wilcox trained his laser back towards Hackett.

“Yes, sir,” Larson replied.

“I will pull the trigger, Captain. You have 10 seconds,” Wilcox said.

"All that means is I won't be here when the ship goes nova,

and if I don't stop the countdown soon, I won't be able to. YOU have 5 seconds to put that gun down, or you will die right after me."

Several seconds passed, and Hackett looked at Wilcox. "Shouldn't you have pulled the trigger by now? Why am I still alive?"

He did not answer, and two more security guards rushed onto the bridge and backed up the two who were already there. They took up positions by the doors and aimed their guns at Wilcox. Benson, Davies, and Giovanella evacuated their seats because they were in the line of fire should the guards have to shoot. The computer was counting down the seconds and made it under 10. Wilcox turned and looked at all the concerned and scared faces around the bridge. The last one he looked at was Benson, and he threw his gun down to the floor. Hackett immediately ordered Larson to cancel the self-destruct, and the guards overpowered the Ambassador and took him away.

A sigh of relief went up around the bridge as everyone was relieved that this latest episode was over. Hackett looked around the bridge and decided it was time to switch duty shifts. This would allow the regulars to unwind and grab a cup of coffee.

Once the change was complete, Hackett reviewed the tactical grid, which showed the ships in the area. He estimated they had two hours to get the quantum generators up and running and then bring the energizer back online. He left the bridge to Morris, who was working on his reports. Hackett went to the galley, got a coffee, and was about to walk back out the door when Benson came up behind him.

“Captain, may I have a word?” she requested.

Hackett turned to look at her, wondering what she wanted. He had to let her speak. "What's on your mind, Lieutenant Commander?"

She finished pouring her coffee and followed Hackett to a table in the middle of the room. “Would you have destroyed the ship over Wilcox?” she asked.

“Lieutenant Commander, what is the minimum time to manually program a torpedo to detonate?" he asked, staring into her blue eyes.

"One minute." And now she knew. "So you told Larson to program thirty seconds, which was a code."

"Yep, and that fool Wilcox took it, hook, line, and sinker."

"Were you not concerned that he would shoot you? He is nuts," she asked while holding her coffee mug with two hands and taking a sip.

"Actually, yes. He was shaking so much that I anticipated that he might get a shot off without wanting to. He didn't, though. He may be a fool, but he is a smart fool," Hackett replied with a slight grin.

"What happens now?" she hesitated.

"I will need to bring in Channing to discuss how we proceed, and then we will plan our mission. Regarding your role, I imagine you would keep your clothes." He said with a slight grin.

"That's reassuring."

"I would hope so."

Hackett could hear the crunching of the spiders biting him in his mind, and he was thinking, *not now.* He stared at Benson as she took a sip of her coffee, followed by licking her lips. He envisioned kissing those lips again, and the crunching subsided. He filed it away as a coincidence.

"Is there anything else?" he asked because he could sense that there was more coming.

"It's just that I am not accustomed to this seat-of-your-pants, make-it-up-as-you-go mentality. I think getting used to this will take some time," she said.

Hackett looked at her for a moment. "Well, Lieutenant Commander, this is life on the edge, this is where you wanted to be, and from my standpoint, you are adapting quite well." He paused a moment and looked into her eyes. "The rules out here are different, and 'we' are writing the book on how future generations interact with these cultures. Hang in there, and let's get back to work," Hackett said, and they both got up and went back into the corridor.

"Thank you, Captain," Benson replied once in the corridor. She was relieved, in a way, from what he said. *How did he know what I was feeling?* she wondered as she walked away. It was like he saw right through her, and now she was scared for a different reason. Hackett knew what she was thinking! Or was it just a coincidence? *It couldn't be*, she thought. It wasn't the first time he answered a question she had only thought to ask. He knew she was there for other reasons.

"Captain Hackett to the bridge," came Morris's nervous voice over the speaker on the ceiling. Hackett replied to the page that he was on his way.

Hackett entered the dimly lit bridge and spotted Morris at the sensor console, reviewing the information that had been handed to him. He looked up when Hackett arrived. "Captain, there are two Inean ships coming our way. They have changed course and speed to intercept us in just over an hour. O'Toole says it will be at least that long before we could be underway again."

"I see, Commander," Hackett said as he took a turn at the viewer. "Get down to the engine room and assist in any way you can. We need those engines and energizer back online before they get here."

"Yes, sir, on my way," Morris replied.

Morris walked into the engine room, paused briefly, and watched people scramble. The mood was frantic. Everyone knew they would come under attack very soon and had no shields to protect them from the Inean lasers and torpedoes. O'Toole was at a work-table with the empty power coupling lattice suspended from an overhead beam. He was cleaning the grid and removing bits of old crystals to make room for the new gold-coated Hafnium Carbide platters. At another station, two technicians used a precision-cutting laser to shape the Kosuan platters to fit the Alliance grid. This was a slow and tedious process, measured in thousandths of a millimeter. If he cut them incorrectly, they would be useless, and they had already wasted one. They could not afford to waste any more.

"Lieutenant Barrows, how are those platters coming?" O'Toole asked with a slight edge to his voice.

"I'll have a second one ready for you in a couple of minutes, sir," he replied without taking his eyes off the display.

"Let me have the first one then," he said to Barrows.

Barrows handed it to him, and O'Toole mounted it in a machine and coated the silver Hafnium with gold. After a minute, he removed the gold-plated Hafnium and cleaned it. He fumbled with it and nearly dropped it on the floor, which could have shattered into pieces. O'Toole cursed his clumsiness and tried again. After a few minutes, Barrows handed him another Hafnium platter to install, and he began the next one.

O'Toole struggled under the pressure to make them fit properly. The gold-coated platters had to be aligned precisely to produce the maximum power and prevent them from burning out, unlike the previous ones. They needed to be positioned in a way that allowed the hot plasma created in the mix chamber to flow smoothly over them, producing the enormous electrical charge required for the quantum field coils. If a jagged edge stood out or the grid was bent, causing turbulence in the plasma flow, not only would the Hafnium platters burn out, but it could also cause a burn-through in the casing and cause a catastrophic problem. He had two crewmen bring a laser-alignment fixture to the table and set it around the grid. The three of them worked on the grid and finally got the first one in position. O'Toole secured it into place and started on the second one.

Time ticked by rapidly, and Morris remained standing off to the side while O'Toole fought with the stubborn matrix. Morris said nothing while O'Toole was fitting the second platter. Barrows had placed another one on a foam pad on the table by O'Toole and went back to cut another.

Morris walked over and watched Barrows set up the jig to hold the crude, yellow Hafnium plates. It was a difficult task, and the pressure to hurry was taking its toll. Barrows fumbled the platter, but managed to catch it as he attempted to set it in the fixture. Morris jumped in and held it for him so he could secure it in the proper position.

Once secured, Barrows gave Morris a nod of thanks. Morris

then stepped back and observed as the master machinist programmed the settings and made the cutting lasers dance all around. He carved it to perfection in minutes when it would typically take nearly an hour for anyone else to do the same job.

Morris glanced at the clock on the wall and realized they needed more time. It was taking an average of 10 minutes to cut and place the gold-plated Hafnium in the grid. It turned out that they would need 10 minutes more than they had. The Inean ships would be here before they completed their task. He contacted the bridge. “Captain, this is Morris in engineering,” he said.

“Go ahead, Commander,” Hackett replied over the tinny speaker.

"Sir, we are wrapping up down here, but we need a few more minutes. It would be a good idea if we fired the plasma drive and ran the other way to buy us those few minutes," Morris said.

"Good idea, Commander, Mr. Roberts, lay in a reverse course and go to full reverse thrust," Hackett said, ending the comm-link to Morris.

With the Inean ships closing in on firing range, Hackett recalled his main bridge crew to take over. Once everyone was in place, he ordered Giovanella to contact the lead ship and ask about their intentions.

Giovanella tried and tried, but there was no reply.

It was now less than 10 minutes to go. Hackett was beginning to get nervous, and he called engineering. They were moving as fast as they could. However, they still needed more time. One last platter to install, and O'Toole had it in his hands. The Inean ships were nearly upon them when he got it fitted. He glued it into place and let it set for a few seconds. He released the alignment fixture and had the two crewmen hold the matrix while he unhooked it from the overhead beam. The fixture was heavy, and both men struggled with it. They began to walk back to the mix chamber when the ship shook violently. The men stumbled and nearly lost their grip on the grid. The red warning lights came on as they struggled and regained control at the last second, then proceeded to the chamber and installed the grid.

On the bridge, Benson moved the *Saratoga* away from an Inean torpedo that exploded close to the ship. The Inean ships continued to close in. Hackett turned to look at Larson, who was at her tactical station. "Larson, fire a full spread of torpedoes now!" he commanded.

"Aye, sir, firing," she said, and several red streaks immediately flew from the underside of the *Saratoga*. Some hit their targets, and a couple missed.

"Helm, turn us around and use our aft engines to give us more speed," Hackett ordered.

Benson and Davies spun the ship around and fired the thrusters in unison. However, one Inean ship was close enough to fire its lasers and hit the *Saratoga* in the hangar bay doors, causing one of the huge doors to buckle. Another blast carved a hole under the hangar bay close to the aft torpedo launchers. Larson looked at the red lights on her panel and the message displayed on her monitor: "No response -- aft torpedoes." She looked at Hackett, "Captain, we have lost contact with our aft torpedo launchers."

Hackett heard her and didn't acknowledge the message. Instead, he called down to engineering for the latest status report. He was told everything was in place, and they were starting the energizer now.

After a few seconds, the ship began to vibrate from the massive energizer coming to life. Larson reported that she had shields and was raising them. Before they came up completely, another Inean laser rocked the ship hard as it tore into the starboard-side nacelle that would prevent the ship from creating a wormhole and escaping.

"Shields holding, Captain, lasers almost charged," Larson reported.

Despite Benson's fancy moves, the Inean ships managed to slide up on either side of the *Saratoga*. They proceeded to fire at the ship's sides. Most of the Inean laser blasts were targeted at the engineering section. The Ineans needed to get the *Saratoga*'s shields down while the ship was still weak so they could finish the job. If they failed soon, the fight would be lost, forcing them to continue on a more critical mission.

“Captain, we have full power to our laser cannons!” Larson reported to Hackett.

“Fire port and starboard lasers at those ships until they move off, Lieutenant,” Hackett said.

Bright blue beams of light repeatedly fired from the laser cannons on the underside of the ship's primary hull. They struck the Inean vessels in their midsections. The constant barrage caused the sides of the Inean ships' hulls to begin glowing red from the energy they absorbed. The Inean commanders realized they had blown their opportunity and broke off the attack before their ships were destroyed. Both ships went at high speed towards the Kosuan outpost from which the *Saratoga* had just come to complete their mission.

“Damage reports?” Hackett ordered.

Larson was already on it and had a preliminary list. "Sir, we have damage to the aft torpedo launchers, hangar bay doors, and minor hull fractures, all in the secondary hull. The engine room reports an overload in the starboard nacelle, which should be resolved in approximately 20 minutes. There are no casualties or injuries to report."

"Thank you, Lieutenant," Hackett said, turning his attention forward. "Helm, all stop."

“All stop, aye, sir,” replied Davies as the ship came to a halt.

"Plot a course to Inea and have it ready," Hackett said.

Benson replied, “Yes, sir.”

TWENTY-NINE

HACKETT HIT his comm-pad button and paged Ambassador Channing to meet him and Commander Morris in Conference Room One in 30 minutes. The Ambassador replied that he would. Hackett informed Morris of the meeting and said to be there in 20 minutes. Hackett then turned the bridge over to Lieutenant Daniella Larson.

Hackett wandered into the conference room to gather his notes. Now that Wilcox had been arrested and was no longer in charge of the negotiations, Hackett had to persuade Channing to take over the negotiations. Hackett knew Channing had never led a negotiation and would be reluctant. Hackett felt Channing could be convinced if it was done correctly.

Morris entered the room, and Hackett had him sit beside him to review his notes before Channing arrived. After a few more minutes, the Ambassador entered the room. Hackett had him sit across from them.

Hackett started. "Ambassador Channing, are you prepared to take over for Ambassador Wilcox when we get to Inea?"

"I hope so, sir," Channing stated with some hesitation. "We really do need Wilcox on this mission."

Hackett stared, shocked for a moment. He wasn't really sure if Channing knew what transpired on the bridge.

Hackett sat back in his chair and continued to stare at Channing. "Ambassador, Wilcox is in the brig and faces serious charges. I question his mental state, which puts me in a position where I must consider the crew's safety and the success of this mission. You are the only one on board familiar with these talks, and you must take over."

Channing adjusted himself in his seat as he thought about his response. "The problem, Captain, is I have never been allowed to take the lead in any negotiations. My role has always been to support Wilcox and research everything he needed. I can't help you, Sir," he replied.

Hackett tossed his pen on the table in disgust and leaned back in his chair. "Ambassador, take a look at the success Wilcox has had. It was all your work. It is time you received the credit you deserve."

Channing looked up at Hackett and pondered what Hackett had said. It was not the first time someone had told him that. The last time was on the *Challenger*, and Captain Jefferson was adamant that Channing should go on his own and abandon Wilcox before he ended up dead or in a Kosuan prison colony.

Channing sat forward and stayed focused on Hackett. "Captain, I will help, but there are certain items we will need to straighten out, and I will need assistance. I can't do it alone."

Hackett was cautious, not really knowing where Channing was going with this. "What sort of help would you require?"

"Wilcox was correct in requesting Lieutenant Commander Benson to pilot and to be his assistant, so I would still want her on the mission. Also, Captain, I am aware of your previous visit there and would want you to go to the surface as well. I would want Lieutenant Larson as the fourth member of the landing party," Channing stated.

Hackett was quick to respond. "That would weaken our bridge staff, Ambassador. By removing our navigator, tactical officer, and the ship's Captain, you put us at great risk both in orbit and on the surface." He paused for a moment, "And why Larson? I am unwilling to send another woman to that planet without a good explanation, Ambassador."

Channing saw the Captain's concerns and tried to put them to rest. "Captain, they won't attack us while in orbit on a diplomatic mission."

"We were just attacked by two of their ships, who saw an opportunity and tried to take advantage of it," Hackett quickly reminded Channing of the attack.

"I know, Captain, they won't attack in orbit. I have their sworn statement that they won't," Channing pleaded.

"And what of the women? What do you request for attire?" Hackett wanted to know if he shared Wilcox's interests before committing to this.

"It would be better for the women to adhere to the local customs, but I understand Lieutenant Commander Benson's and your apprehension regarding that. So whatever you order them to do will have to work." Channing knew which way Hackett would go on that subject and moved on to the next topic, Larson. "Also, as for Lieutenant Larson, I want her on the mission because she is tough and can be of considerable value when dealing with an aggressive race like the Ineans."

Hackett looked towards Morris, who remained expressionless. "Mr. Morris, I want you to fill the posts vacated by Larson and Benson. Plus, I want you to take Command the entire time we are on the planet so we have a well-trained staff in charge," Hackett said.

"Aye, sir," Morris agreed and flipped through his duty roster to see who was available.

"Ambassador, if the Ineans so much as look at them the wrong way, I will personally hold you responsible. Do you understand?"

Channing leaned forward and looked the Captain in the eyes. "Yes, I will ensure their safety while on the planet, Captain. Or I will hold Wilcox accountable. It is his deal, after all."

"That will be acceptable. I will talk to the women, but I think we all know what the answers will be," Hackett stated.

"I understand, Captain, and I will plan on the original arrangements that were set up a few days ago, I believe," Channing said as he looked at his notes. "Also, I will need to contact Command for orders and inform Admiral Hodges of our changes, Captain."

"Once we get underway, I will lift the silent running command, and you can contact the Admiral. I will also be filing my report to include the incident with Wilcox and our discussions to this point, Sir," Hackett said in an attempt to remind Channing that he was in charge and retained the final say regarding the mission and his crew.

"Very well, Captain. Are we finished here?" Channing suddenly seemed upset with Hackett, who let it slide, for now, and the captain excused the Ambassador.

Hackett spoke with Morris for a few more minutes until the call came from the bridge. As they walked to the bridge, Morris had one more question. “Captain, now that Wilcox is out of the picture, do you think Benson and Larson will go along with the required attire?”

Hackett didn't say anything for a minute as he thought about the answer. "I don't know, Commander, I just don't know. We will speak with them both one more time before we arrive. My gut says no."

They entered the elevator and said nothing else until they reached the bridge. Hackett thought the whole time that this issue was behind him. Once on the bridge, both men took their stations. Lieutenant Larson informed the Captain and the first officer that the quantum drive had been restored.

Hackett turned to Larson for a moment, quickly shaking off what he was thinking, and thanked her for the information. He ordered Davies and Benson to set course and proceed finally to Inea.

The ship groaned and shuddered as it accelerated to star speed, but it was very sluggish. Benson's expression was disturbed as she looked at her display and pressed several buttons. Her expression got Hackett's attention, as well as the shudder through the ship as it picked up speed.

"Is there a problem, Lieutenant Commander?" he asked from his chair just a few feet behind her.

"Yes, Captain. The engines won't balance, and I can't get full power. I can barely squeeze Quantum Two out of them right now. An imbalance would explain the vibration," she said.

Hackett pressed the page button on his comm pad. "Engine room?"

"O'Toole here, Sir, we see it. Have nav-con throttle back to sublight speed while we make some adjustments down here," he replied over the speaker with a frustrated tone.

"Understood. Keep me posted, Commander. Hackett out." Hackett punched it off and leaned forward. "Miss Benson, reduce speed to point seven until further notice, and tell me how long before we reach Inea."

"Aye, sir, sublight point seven. Calculating new ETA … Roughly three days, Captain, at quantum four," she replied.

"Thank you," he replied.

Hackett ordered Benson and Larson to meet with him and Commander Morris at eighteen-thirty hours in conference room one. He had Giovanella contact Ambassador Channing to have him attend, and he ordered the lifting of the silent running mode. This would allow Hackett and Channing to contact Command about their respective issues.

The rest of the afternoon went by without incident, and everyone was thankful for that.

O'Toole was still in engineering, wrestling with his engines. The difficulty was keeping the Kosuan platters appropriately aligned. He thought it was no wonder the Kosuan had so much trouble with their star drives. He strolled to the terminal and ran several simulations to confirm his findings. He would have to take the ship out of star speed to fix the problem before these Kosuan platters burned up. He called over his assistant to review the data before he informed the Captain of the bad news.

Barrows walked over, reran the simulation, and tried some of his own data. The ultimate results confirmed what O'Toole already knew. The only thing that varied was when they would deteriorate. O'Toole had no choice. He informed Hackett.

“O’Toole to Captain,” was the frustrated sounding message over the PA speaker.

“Hackett here,” he replied with a flick of a button.

“Sir, can you come down here? You need to see this,” O’Toole said.

"On my way," he said, hitting the switch off. He finished making his last note and got up. "Mr. Morris?" Hackett waited for an acknowledgment. When Morris looked up from his terminal, Hackett finished. "The bridge is yours."

“Aye, sir,” he said.

Hackett proceeded to the elevator and down to the engine room. It was a trip he was getting tired of making. After a few minutes, he arrived and was greeted by O'Toole, who brought him over to the computer station, where he reran the simulation he had run previously. Hackett watched the simulation and saw how the gold-coated platters disintegrated the first time and how the new ones would now.

“Captain, it’s an easy procedure and should only take about 15 minutes to complete, but we need to drop out of star speed and let them cool down before we can fix the problem. I estimate about an hour total,” the engineer stated.

“Very well, Commander, do what you have to do. Contact the bridge and coordinate with Commander Morris,” Hackett said.

“Thank you, Captain. This should fix it once and for all,” the engineer said.

Hackett nodded but didn't think so. He left the engine room and walked towards the conference room for their meeting in just over an hour. He brought up the photograph of the woman in the skimpy outfit for the women to see, and he also looked up alternatives in the vast Alliance database. There were none. It sank in that they were, in fact, flying into Hell blind.

Information on the Inean culture was still scarce, and he paged Ambassador Channing to check with his people to see if they knew of any alternatives.

Hackett returned to his report to Admiral Hodges and completed it. He sent it to Command and returned to work, formulating his plan for the Inea landing. He worked on his notes for quite some time and was surprised to see Morris enter the room after the ship went to quantum speed again. Soon after Morris arrived, Ambassador Channing entered, followed by Larson and Benson. Everyone sat at the table, and Hackett opened the meeting.

"Thank you for being on time," Hackett said to get everyone's attention. "Due to circumstances that everyone in this room is aware of, Ambassador Channing is taking over for Ambassador Wilcox. Ambassador Channing made his request for assistance known to Commander Morris and I earlier, and everyone at this table will play an important role in the upcoming negotiations. However, an old issue pertaining to this mission doesn't seem to want to go away. With that, I will let the Ambassador take over the meeting."

"Thank you, Captain. I wanted to say that it is a privilege to work with all of you on this mission. I have been impressed with the crew's conduct in crisis after crisis, and their willingness to get involved and solve complex tasks, especially when dealing with Ambassador Wilcox. I wasn't allowed to speak previously, but now that I have taken over this mission and we have the backing of Command, we can now proceed." He stopped to take a drink of water.

Channing continued, "Lieutenant Commander Benson, you will be the pilot of the transport that brings us to and from the surface. You will also serve as my personal assistant during the proceedings, which means you will have access to confidential information on both sides. You will remain at my side the entire time we are there. The Captain has been assigned the second chair during the meetings, and Lieutenant Larson, you will be his assistant. Does everyone understand their roles so far?"

Channing paused to look around the room, and everyone nodded yes. "Good. Now the sticking points are as follows. We can do this without any physical contact, as previously proposed. However, the Inean culture regards women differently than we do. So, for a woman to be present at the meeting, they must adhere to certain rules. I verified this a short time ago, and unfortunately, I don't see any way around this. First, I want to say that I expect everyone who goes to the surface to act professionally. The Inean dress code for a woman is less than what I would expect either of you to be comfortable wearing. I've come up with a few discrete modifications that may satisfy everyone."

Channing placed his PDA on the central viewer, and the two-sided holographic monitor lit up with a picture of the old outfit they initially looked at. Channing then displayed his proposed changes for everyone to see beside them. The new one concealed more skin and offered a bit more modesty. However, it was still skimpy enough to make waves back home. Channing let everyone take a moment to digest the images before he continued.

"I have your local customs department working on a prototype. They said they could have something in about an hour." Channing said as he looked at his watch. "Now, Miss Benson, you rightfully refused to wear the outfit on the left, but what are your thoughts on the other one? Miss Larson, this is the first you've seen of either, and I would be interested in your thoughts."

Larson piped up quickly. “I have one question, Ambassador.”

Hackett knew by her tone that this would be a wise-ass comment. He could always rely on Larson to put an interesting twist on any subject, which would be no different. He knew it was her way of dealing with uncomfortable situations, and quite frankly, he looked forward to some of her less-than-socially correct comments. He liked Larson for her candidness and knew she spoke what was on her mind, not what people wanted to hear.

“Yes, Miss Larson?” Channing replied.

"What do the men wear?" she asked, raising her eyebrows.

“Being a military-based political system, the men wear their military uniforms as a sign of strength.”

"Some things never change," Mumbled Benson, not thinking anyone heard her. Everyone did.

"No, Miss Benson, you are right. Some things don't change," Channing replied.

“I don’t see the need to go down there in anything less than full dress uniform with a fully charged laser in my hand,” Benson replied as she studied it further. It hid what it was designed to hide and nothing else, which was still too little for her.

“I agree with Benson,” said Larson hesitantly. “I think the men should wear the other one.”

“I’ll second that,” said Benson.

Hackett looked at the women for a moment. "We'd get thrown out of there for sure then," he said, smiling at them. Everyone laughed for a moment and then returned to business.

“Are you sure you won’t compromise?” Channing asked.

“Compromise is for people who don’t believe strongly about their position,” Benson added.

"Okay, since that has been established, there are a few more things of importance that the women won't like. First, they can't speak unless spoken to in public, and that includes among ourselves. In private, it isn't an issue. And lastly, they must bow to the Inean men when they come and go from the room. Is everyone okay with that?"

Everyone nodded their acceptance of that. It was time for the Captain to have some fun. "I think it's about time we adopted those policies in our society," he said, looking at Larson and Benson. He waited a moment and continued, "What, no comment from the peanut gallery?" he laughed, as did Morris and Channing.

"Now, why must we go there to begin with if we are to be treated as such?" Larson was having difficulty understanding the culture.

"Because the Ineans always include females in their politics, many women of their species have done quite well, even adhering to old ways of thinking regarding certain traditions," Channing answered.

“But, the way they treat human women is well documented, especially the last time we were here. Who’s going to make sure we are safe? Let’s not forget what happened last time to Sasha,” Larson stated, trying her best to hold back.

“I have the full backing of the Inean government on that issue. No one will be touched.” Channing replied.

"We had that agreement last time, and they raped and killed

Sasha easily. I don't trust their word, and the government doesn't have much control over its military to promise us anything, Ambassador!" Larson was getting red-faced, her anger about her friend Sasha's demise all too apparent.

"All I can quote, Lieutenant, is what they assure me. It's all we have to go on right now," Channing replied more apologetically.

"Fine, if I die down there, I want it before they rape me," she said, kicking back in her chair in frustration, anger, and hurt. A lot of emotions for a woman called The Rock. Nothing fazed her. Nothing had ruffled her feathers until this. Hackett and Morris watched her and wondered to themselves if her attitude would surface on the planet. Would she seek revenge? Morris wanted revenge for what they did to Sasha, so didn't Hackett, and they both knew Larson would act on her emotions. She may be called The Rock, but she was also a loose cannon.

Hackett wanted revenge for that and for what the Ineans did to him. The thought of the spiders biting him entered his mind. The crunching sound of their fangs tearing into his flesh, the cool burning sensation of their venom under his skin, the face of the Inean soldier interrogating him, and the rancid smell of death and decay in the torture room.

Hackett was now transported back in time to that fateful day six months before. He saw himself strapped to a table, naked and cold, barely above zero in this torture chamber. A dozen, no, about 20 of the palm-sized fuzzy spiders crawling all over him, biting him everywhere. His screams were muffled by the rope through his mouth.

The spiders were in a frenzy as they attacked him, biting and inflicting their venom into his bloodstream. The poison would go to the brain and cause him to become a walking time bomb. A human time bomb that could explode at any moment. This was what scared the vice admiral. If Hackett snapped, he could destroy a planet with the ship he had. He could start an interstellar war at the push of a button. He could kill someone with his bare hands and not remember it afterward. This mission put him in a dangerous position. Unfortunately, he was still the most qualified for the job.

Hackett shook off the thoughts. He needed to. If he stayed

fixated on it, it would take over his mind, and disaster would follow. "Now, Ambassador, maybe you can fill us in with a timetable of sorts for how things should run on this mission. We've established roles, costumes, and some specific protocols, but how about the details of our agenda?" Hackett asked.

Channing went into great detail on the specifics of the mission with the people in the room, and the meeting went well into the night. Finally, Hackett found a breakpoint and seized a chance to end for the night.

"Now, for the second day," Channing began.

"How about if we break until tomorrow. I'm sure everyone would agree that this is a lot of information to digest," Hackett said, cutting Channing off from starting a new section.

Everyone agreed with the Captain. It was nearly midnight, and they had been at it quite a while. "Miss Benson, I owe you a drink, and quite frankly, I feel like one myself."

"Yes, you do, Captain, and that comes with interest," She said with a wink.

The wink got Morris's attention, so Hackett needed to find out what she meant. "And what is the interest?"

"Dinner, I'm starving," she said. Then Larson, Morris, and Channing spoke up, which gave Hackett a chance to dismiss any credibility to the rumors flying around the ship.

"Why don't we all go then? But let's change the subject of any conversation away from the landing," Hackett said, and everyone agreed. "You can leave your notes here for the night. I'll lock the hatch on our way out."

Everyone filed out, went to the officer's lounge, and sat at one of the tables in the middle of the room. Harold Linques came over, took everyone's drink order, and left a sheet of paper that was a simple attempt at a menu. Everyone passed it around, and when he returned with the drinks, he took their food orders. Because it was so late, everyone ordered light meals.

The chef made it a point to have theme nights; tonight, it was Chinese. He passed the order off to his assistant, who went off to prepare the dinners.

People were dancing to music in the center of the room. Benson made eyes at the Captain, and Larson just plain asked Morris to dance. The two couples got up, weaved their way to the floor, and danced to a few songs. The mood of the evening was light.

Benson felt bad for Channing and asked him to dance the next one. Then Larson got in the act and danced with the Captain and so on. Everyone loosened up quite a bit that evening and had a good time. The food was good. The conversation was limited, but just as well.

Hackett saw Morris taking mental notes, and he had to ask, "What's on your mind, Commander?"

“Just taking notes for when I take command of my own ship, Captain,” he said. “None of this is taught at the academy.”

"No, it isn't, Commander, and if an admiral were here, we'd probably wind up in the brig," Hackett commented.

Morris could only agree with him. Channing approached the Captain and the first officer, wishing them a good night. Morris decided to turn in as well and was followed by Larson. That left Hackett and Benson alone in the lounge.

Hackett looked at her and decided to test the waters. He came up beside her and held out his arm for her to loop hers through. “Walk you home, Miss Benson?” he asked.

"I would be delighted, Captain," she said with a smile, bringing her arm up and through his as they walked out the door together. Once outside, she removed her hand, fearing someone might get the wrong impression, or would it be right? She didn't know anymore.

They took the long way around deck five to her quarters. They talked about various things, and neither was in a rush to part company as they approached her quarters, so they continued walking. Hackett looked down; she was walking rather close, and he didn't mind at all. They made the loop around the deck and arrived at her quarters again. She punched in her code, backed into the doorway, and stopped to hold the doors open. She faced him, and he knew what she wanted, so he began to lean forward as a pair of ensigns walked by, so he pulled back and wished her a good night, and left. As he walked back to his quarters, he thought *that was too close*. He started falling for her, knowing he had to toughen up and restrain from that for now. He knew she was here to test him, but still, he thought she felt the same attraction he did.

Benson stepped inside her quarters and leaned against the wall. "Stupid Tamora, what are you doing?" she asked herself softly. She took a deep breath, walked over to her computer, and sat in front of it. "Computer, open a new message to Vice Admiral Griffin," she said, and she untied her hair while the computer prepared to take the letter.

"Vice Admiral Griffin, from Lieutenant Commander Benson, *U. A. S. Saratoga*. I have been close to the Captain for many days now. While I feel that he is interested in me, I don't see where he is weak. I would have to conclude so far that the Captain is fit and able to command. He also shows great restraint when it comes to me, and I don't see him compromising the crew or the mission when faced with our situation. I await your instructions on how to proceed. Benson out."

She let out a sigh. "God, I hate this job sometimes," she said aloud as she ran her fingers through her hair. She didn't see that the computer added the last things she said to the message. "Computer, send the message." The computer displayed a message that it had sent, and she went to take a shower. When she got out of the shower, she toweled off and lay across her bed, thinking about the past few days.

She looked up at her clock, and it was 0200. She had to be up again in three hours, so she got up, pulled the blankets down, and slid into the bed. Then she huffed and got up to shut the light off.

Morris, however, had taken one too many pages out of Hackett's book when he left the lounge. He took a left, as did Larson. Ambassador Channing went right. Morris hesitated long enough for Larson to catch up, which was only a few steps, but the pause was obvious. He walked with her around the deck, and they discussed the mission and whether he felt it would be successful. They also discussed Hackett and Benson; Larson was in favor of it if they got together.

“Commander,” she said, “You must notice the looks they give each other?”

“Well, actually, I get confused signals from the two of them,” he stated.

"I know what you mean. They are fighting this attraction they have for each other, but they're losing the battle, it seems," Larson said. "There must be a way we can help them," she added.

"I don't know what we can do or if we should do anything. They both know what's at stake here, and if we get involved, it could have a bearing on us as well," he said.

They didn't speak much the rest of the way while Morris thought about what the Captain was going through. Morris was having a tough time resisting the urge to get involved with Larson. At least to him, he was maintaining the status quo.

They parted ways and went to their respective quarters for the night. Morris stopped, watched her walk away, and waited for her to round the corner before he went to his quarters.

THIRTY

BEEP... Beep… Beep… Blared Hackett's alarm. He groaned as he rolled over to press the off button. He lay in bed for a moment, staring at the ceiling, watching the room lighten slowly until he felt something large and furry crawling up his leg. He flipped the blankets off and noticed an Inean spider in his bed, then another and another crept up over the side of the bed. Soon, he was covered in the black, fuzzy, red-spotted, palm-sized, silver-faced spiders, and they began to bite him with their venomous, inch-long, razor-like fangs. He screamed in fear as he batted them off. There were too many. Their fangs gnashed in his face as they kept biting. Blood splattered everywhere as the vicious arachnids tore into his flesh with an awful crunching sound. He screamed in agony as someone was saying, "Captain, Captain, wake up."

Hackett's eyes flew open, and Morris was inches from his face. He threw the blankets off and bolted from his bed, nearly knocking Morris over. He ran a few steps and stopped. Feeling for spiders, He patted himself down and slumped against the wall. His heart was pounding, his breathing was rapid and shallow, sweat beaded on his forehead, trickled down his cheeks, and soaked into his t-shirt. He continued to look around the room for the spiders.

“Captain, are you all right?” Morris asked.

He looked up at Morris. "Yeah, fine, never felt better. Why are you here?" Hackett replied, gasping for air.

“It’s 0630, sir. The duty shift started a half-hour ago,” Morris stated.

Hackett was shocked. He never once blew a shift in all his years in the academy and in the fleet. He straightened and pulled away from the wall. At that point, he noticed the security officer and doctor standing there as well. "You're kidding me?" he finally asked.

“No, sir, are you okay?” Morris pressed. “Was it the Inean spiders again?”

"Yes, on both accounts," he said as he stood up straight and faced them. "I'm okay. I haven't had one of those in weeks. I suppose it's all a part of the process, Commander." Hackett looked into their faces. Morris wasn't buying it. The security guard had no idea what was happening, and the doctor was sizing up the Captain's state of mind.

“Very well, Captain, I’ll see you on the bridge then?” Morris asked hesitantly.

“I’ll be there shortly, Commander. I’m going to take a shower and grab some coffee first,” Hackett said more calmly this time.

"I'll see you there," Morris said, guiding the others into the hallway. Hackett entered the head and stared at his reflection in the mirror, taking a moment to think about his nightmare. He mumbled curses to himself and proceeded to take a shower. The warm water felt good as it splashed over his body, calming his nerves. Several minutes passed before Hackett opened his eyes and turned the water off. He got out, and like a machine, he dried himself off, brushed his teeth, and shaved.

Hackett instinctively wrapped a towel around himself, went to the closet, and selected a uniform. He stood before the mirror, discarded his towel, and pulled on his pants, shirt, socks, and boots. He tugged his collar tight and fixed his shirt to remove the slightest hint of any wrinkle. He adjusted the bars on his collars and gave himself a satisfactory nod of approval. He made his bed to military specifications and left for the galley in search of coffee.

The galley was nearly empty as he poured his coffee and found a table in the middle of the room. Hackett sipped his coffee, still thinking about the nightmare he had had. It was unusual that he remembered the details so well. All he could hear in his mind was the crunching of them biting, which sent a shudder through his body. It was getting louder in his head, and he tried to shake it off, but it wouldn't go away. It kept getting louder and louder. His brain began to throb as he fought against the venom taking over. He grabbed his head with both hands and yelled in pain. He sprang from his chair, and two crewmen came to assist. Hackett threw them to the floor with ease. The pain was unbearable, and he collapsed to his knees. His eyes bulged from his head as he screamed from the pain.

The chef called the medics to the galley, and after a few moments, several guards ran in, followed by the medics. Each time they tried to grab Hackett, his flailing arms would knock them away. Finally, four of them subdued him long enough for a medic to give him a sedative.

The medics had the guards escort him to the medical facility. One medic remained behind to tend to the first two crew members who tried to help him. They were both shaken but okay.

In medical, the doctor had a bed ready, and the guards held him down long enough for her to tie the restraints. Hackett was groggy and didn't know what had happened. He kept moving his head from side to side, saying, "No, no, stop." His eyes were closed tightly from the pain in his head.

A nurse wheeled in a portable CT scanner and set it up. She struggled to hold him steady while the scanner swept across his head, attempting to take detailed images of his brain. Hackett, not being a big man, was extremely strong for his size. It was necessary to rerun the scanner to fill in the missing information that the first scan missed.

Hackett was coming back now. It was too late. The damage was done. The nurse finished her tests and wheeled the scanner back to her office to view the results. The doctor entered the room and approached Hackett.

"Sir, do you know where you are?" she asked.

"Yes," he whispered because of the pain.

"Where, Captain?" The doctor asked.

"Medi...cal," Hackett struggled.

"Do you know why you are here?" the doctor asked.

"Inean sp … ider … sss. I'm o … kay now. Let … me sit … up, doc," he said.

"What happened, Captain?" The doctor asked.

"I had a dream… about… the spiders. I couldn't… get them out of my… head, and… they took over. They're gone now. That was the… first time I couldn't… hold them back. It must have been something… I ate or drank last night," he said as his sentences came together better as he talked.

"What did you eat last evening and drink, sir?" the doctor pried.

"Chinese food and a couple… of mixed drinks," Hackett said.

"Okay, Captain, I'm going to remove the restraints and let you sit up. I want a blood and urine sample, nurse, and I want to perform a full spectrum on them. I want to include the DNA cross-check to ensure the Captain's DNA is okay," the doctor said as he untied the restraints.

"Yes, Doctor, I will take care of it now," the nurse said.

Hackett sat up and asked the nurse for something for his headache. She left and came back with a couple of pills and water. He downed them both. She took her samples and left the room. An armed guard stood by the door facing the Captain. Hackett knew he must have really lost it this time. He hoped it was the food he ate that triggered the episode.

The news was spreading around the ship that Hackett had finally snapped and beat up a couple of crewmen. It didn't take long for Morris to hear it as well. Morris left the bridge to Larson and went to medical to check the Captain's condition.

Morris walked in and saw him sitting on the bed, still in uniform. He asked the doctor if it was okay to talk to him, and the doctor replied that it was.

Morris ambled toward Hackett, sizing up his condition. "How are you, sir?"

"I'll be fine now. The doctor seems to think something added to the Chinese food we ate last night triggered the reaction to those damn spiders. The first screening of my blood indicates a potential poison." Hackett looked at him for a second.

"Everything is under control, sir. However, we are undecided about how to proceed with the mission at this point," Morris said.

"I'll be fine, Commander, really. We need to look into what was added to the food. I would like you to schedule the second meeting with the landing party and yourself for late this afternoon, so we can wrap it up and conduct a review tomorrow. I also want you there just in case I need to be replaced," Hackett said. He wanted to prove to Morris that he was back under control.

While Morris was there, the doctor returned and handed the Captain some pills and water. "Here, take these, Captain. This will negate the effects of the poison, allowing you to return to duty. I will also talk to the chef and find out what was in the Chinese food you ate."

"That's a negative, doc. I want security to look into it," Hackett stated.

"Why is that?" Morris asked.

"I know the chef. He knows what I can and cannot eat. This was no accident."

Morris nodded. "I will have security investigate, sir."

"Thank you," Hackett said, and he took the medication. Morris stepped back and allowed him to slide off the bed. He walked over to the mirror on the wall and fixed his uniform and hair. He turned to Morris. "Shall we go to the bridge now, Commander?" he asked, turning and going out the door. Morris followed closely and caught up to him.

"Are you sure you want to go to the bridge?"

"Yes, I'm fine now. Just have to learn how to control that better," Hackett said. "What time is it anyway?"

"It's 1000 hours, sir," Morris replied.

"Thank you. Well, this is the latest I've started a day in years."

They both entered the elevator, and Morris watched Hackett. He knew the Captain was stubborn and wouldn't step down easily.

They walked onto the bridge, and Lieutenant Larson was in command at the moment. Ambassador Channing was standing there waiting for them to arrive.

Channing studied Hackett as he entered the bridge. He was looking for anything to allow him to abandon this mission. "Captain, are you all right?" he asked.

"Yes, Ambassador, I will be fine. It's just a chemical reaction between something I ate last night and a previous imbalance. The doctor took care of it, which should be the end of it. Thank you for your concern," he replied without looking at him.

“This won’t affect our mission, will it?” Channing asked, still groping for something, anything he could use.

"Not in the least. As a matter of fact, Mr. Morris will be scheduling the next meeting for us for later today so we can wrap it up," Hackett said with a nod towards Morris, who was also keeping an eye on the Captain.

As Hackett turned towards her, Larson surrendered the Captain's chair, and she returned to her station. Hackett sat and asked for a status report. Larson turned and told him everything was functioning properly.

Channing spoke up before the Captain moved to his next subject. "Captain, I wanted to tell you before our next meeting that the Kosuan will also be there. This looks like a multi-sided peace agreement. I thought you would like to know. Possibly the same Kosuan you dealt with the other day."

“I understand, Ambassador, and yes, that may change a couple of things,” Hackett replied. “Time to Inea, navigator?”

Benson looked at her console and turned to the Captain. “About 72 hours at this speed, Captain.”

“Thank you,” he said and turned to talk to Morris. “What is the duty shift like today, Commander?”

"This shift is six on, two off, and four on. The shift ends at eighteen-hundred hours, sir," Morris replied.

"Set the meeting for eighteen-thirty, same as yesterday, Commander," Hackett said. He was feeling good again, and the pain in his head had subsided to a dull throbbing ache just above his eyes. He remained concerned, however, about his inability to control this thing. What if he ate something on Inea and had a spell during the negotiations? He would have to discreetly scan his food beforehand to ensure his safety.

He also thought about the Kosuan being at the meeting. If, in fact, the same Kosuan showed up, then he would have to pair up with Benson, and Larson would have to pair up with Channing. Pairing up with Benson appealed to him. However, he had to be careful about how he proposed it, and they would have to be cautious on the surface not to arouse suspicions that it was a setup. The Ineans and Kosuan had a keen sense when it came to the chemical changes in a person that occurred during emotional interaction. The Kosuan, a few days ago, could sense the chemical changes in either him or Benson on the surface when they kissed. The Ineans enjoyed sexual contact with the females of their species as well as humans. They would enjoy watching two humans go about it just before they killed them, of course.

There had been rumors that some Ineans had actually eaten humans they had tortured and killed, but it was only rumored. Of course, Hackett didn't discount these rumors based on how his people had been treated the last time they came here. For all he knew, Sasha might have been an entrée at some banquet. *Oh, Sasha,* he thought, *what could I have done differently?* He would definitely scan his food from now on.

Hackett looked at Benson for a minute, sitting in front of him at the nav-con. Her long blond hair was pulled back in a braided ponytail. He visualized kissing her neck and ears. Her uniform fit snugly, showcasing the shape of her body. He was getting aroused. He sat back up straight as he pulled himself out of his daydream. *Wow,* he thought, *time to get to work.*

"Mr. Morris, you have the bridge. I'm going to the engine room to see firsthand how the new matrix is holding together," Hackett said.

"Yes, Captain," Morris replied.

Hackett walked to the elevator, stopped, and looked around the bridge momentarily, taking in all the people who depended on him to make the right choices. He suddenly felt alone and detached from his crew and began to wonder if his bout with the spider's venom would cause his crew to question him should he give an awkward command. Would they genuinely follow him, or would they hesitate and question his orders? Life-and-death decisions hinged on split seconds out here. Any hesitation could mean death. The doors slid open, and he turned and stepped in. Once inside, he set the control to go down to deck six. He leaned against the side of the lift while it descended. He thought about Benson and how she had ignored him just now on the bridge. Was she controlling it better than he was, or did she resolve to just walk away? Perhaps the news of his collapse below didn't disturb her at all? Why was he having so much trouble pushing her out of his mind? Was it the venom from the spiders in his brain controlling something? Too many questions and not enough answers. Ah, yes, the spiders. His mind drifted towards them again, and the crunching returned. He switched his focus to Benson, and the crunching stopped. Like it or not, he had something, someone to focus on, that seemed more powerful than the spiders. For now, he would rely on his attraction for her to get through this mission. He cleared his mind as the elevator slowed.

THIRTY-ONE

A FEW HOURS after Hackett was released from the medical facility, Lieutenant Malcolm Desai investigated the poisoning.

Desai, who was from Turkey, spoke with a pronounced accent from that part of the world. He was in his 12th year serving on starships. He took it upon himself to do the full investigation on his own based on Commander Morris' recommendation. Morris was concerned that several people were involved throughout the ship, and trust was in short supply on this mission.

Desai began by talking with the doctor and nurse who treated Hackett to gather their information. He also spoke with the security guards who assisted in restraining Hackett, and finally, with Hackett himself. He was convinced it was a poison placed in his food the night before that triggered the event.

After the midday lunch, he went to the mess hall to meet with Harold Linques, the ship's head cook and the cook on duty the night before. He sat at the counter and waited a minute.

"Lieutenant, what can I get for you?" Linques asked.

"Some answers, Harold. Are you working alone today?" Desai asked while looking around the room.

"Yeah, Stout called out and said she was ill. I sent her to medical. Several others helped but had to return to their posts."

"I have to ask you about the captain."

"Oh?" Linques replied.

"Yes, I know you and the captain talk often, so it is a tough thing to ask," Desai said while looking around to see if anyone else was listening.

"We talk on occasion about various topics. What is on your mind?"

"I am investigating how poison was placed in his food last night."

Linques leaned on the counter. "Is he all right?"

"Yes, he did have a reaction that came out against a couple of crewmen. They will be okay as well." He paused a second. "I want to know how the poison got there and by whom."

"I don't know, it was busy last night. I did have some help, though."

"Who was on duty with you?"

"CPO Stout and Ensign Graves. Both women were kept quite busy all night."

"Where is Graves right now?"

"She is in the teleporter controls today until her shift ends, and then she is here after seventeen hundred."

"And Stout went to medical?" Desai asked. Somehow, he knew this name. She was a recent transfer and was on Admiral Hodges' watch list as a potential threat.

"That is where I sent her, but I have not had time to confirm that she actually went."

Linques noticed someone was still waiting for their lunch and excused himself. When he returned, Desai was gone.

Desai returned to the medical area and quizzed the nurses and doctors about CPO Stout, but no one had seen her. He then went to the teleporter controls and found Ensign Graves. He asked her a few questions and took her off his list of suspects for now.

Desai returned to his office and searched for Stout's locator. The computer searched the ship and found it in her quarters. He took two armed guards with him to her quarters. He pressed the page button, but no one answered the door. He tried again and again. There was still no response. He unlocked the doors to her quarters, and the door slid open. On the floor was CPO Stout. She was face-first on the floor with blood lightly splattered on the floor around her head.

He immediately called for a medical team while he checked for a pulse. He found one.

A few minutes later, two orderlies and a doctor arrived. They placed her on a backboard, and the doctor examined her. He waved smelling salts under her nose, and she came to.

"What, what happened?" she asked groggily.

"That is what we would like to know," Desai said.

"I must have passed out," she said, still groggy.

"Take her to medical and check her out. Do not release her until I can question her," Desai stated with a nod to the security guards.

An hour went by as Desai waited in his office. He studied the molecular readout for the poison used on his Captain. It was Inean. It certainly was no accident that it had found its way into his food. Just a few drops were enough to unleash the dormant spider venom in his body, quickly attacking his brain.

His watch beeped. He looked at the screen and pressed its face. "Go ahead, doctor," he said.

"Lieutenant," replied Doctor Alice Williams, "we have finished evaluating Stout."

"What are your findings, Doc?"

"We are waiting for some results to come back. However, she does not appear to be ill. There is a welt on the back of her head which came from a small round object, and her facial injuries, as best as we can tell, came from her impacting the floor after being knocked unconscious."

"Has she said anything while there?"

"Um, some gibberish about we are all going to die. Then she

would smile and laugh out loud. Kind of strange. I would recommend a psychiatric evaluation at this point."

"Thanks, Doc. I will be down to take her back to the brig for more questioning."

"Yes, please get her out of here. She is making the nurses uneasy. Williams out."

Desai rushed from his room, which he ensured was locked, before walking away.

A short time later, CPO Jennifer Stout was seated at an empty table, her hands shackled behind her back as well as her feet together on the floor. Her uniform was messy, with dried blood on the front of it. She was sporting two black eyes and a fractured nose from her fall to the floor. Her dark hair remained a mess, being too short to pull back into a braid or ponytail. It would remain a mess for now.

Three cameras were recording her from different angles, in addition to the one-way mirrored glass wall. On the other side of the window was Commander Morris.

Desai entered the room, carrying a folder of papers and his tablet. He sat across from her and folded his hands. He stared at her, saying nothing for some time.

Stout stared back, refusing to look away.

Finally, he spoke. "Do you know why you are here?"

"I poisoned the captain's dinner."

"You do know your rights?"

"Yes, they were read to me. There is no sense in avoiding the issue any longer. The ship is going to explode, and everyone is going to die anyway."

"Where are the bombs so we can defuse them?"

"I won't tell. The Captain has to die. Unfortunately, we all have to go with him."

"Whom are you working for?" Desai asked.

"I think you know already. I am a part of the Earth First Foundation," she said with a wide grin.

"Why destroy this ship? We are not on Earth."

"This ship represents the survival of the human race, which is responsible for destroying the Earth. We can't allow this species to find another planet to ruin."

"So you want to kill all the people. Wipe us out?"

"Oversimplified, but yes. Humanity must go. We are a virus that is ruining everything we touch," she said with a constant grin. "The only way to save Earth is to eliminate the people. Let Earth restore itself so other beings and animals can enjoy it."

"So you admit that you tried to kill the captain?"

"Yes, I admit it. My only regret is that I did not succeed. Luckily, others on this ship will finish the job."

"Who are they?" Desai asked firmly.

She laughed out loud. "Nice try. You only have 30 seconds more to ask me before I die."

"What do you mean?" Desai asked nervously, which prompted Morris to enter the room.

"There is a cyanide capsule in my nose. I just felt it pop. One thing about nasal passages is that they are good at getting chemicals into the bloodstream."

Desai went to ask her another question when she began to shake. Her breathing was labored. Her body convulsed, and she flung herself onto the floor with the chair. She continued to shake as her skin turned a pinkish color.

Morris was on his comm talking with medical, but help would not arrive in time. She stopped shaking and drooled on the floor. It was too late.

Desai bent over and checked for a pulse. He looked up at Morris and shook his head.

Morris cursed as both men looked down at the woman. Still too many questions and no answers yet. What they did know was that Hackett and the crew were in danger.

Morris was back on his comm to alert the Captain and Larson that the ship needed another complete sweep. Stem to stern, port to starboard, deck by deck. A painstakingly long and tedious effort, and it had to be done before reaching Inea.

THIRTY-TWO

SATURDAY, **September 26, 2246**

The elevator doors opened, and two guards snapped to attention. "Captain on the bridge!" one exclaimed. Hackett acknowledged the guards who made room for him to pass. This new security they were employing made life more difficult on the ship. However, it was necessary, given the threats and failed attempts to destroy the ship.

Morris exited the Captain's seat and regarded the Captain while handing him a tablet. On the tablet was the ship's readiness from all stations. Hackett immediately noticed that speed had been reduced, pushing their arrival at Inea to Tuesday. He was not pleased with what he read and handed the tablet back to Morris.

"Mr. Morris, you have the bridge. I will be in the engine room," Hackett stated with irritation.

"Aye, sir."

Morris returned to the Captain's chair as Hackett exited the bridge.

Several minutes later, he arrived in the engine room and found O'Toole with a few technicians looking over the railing towards the mix chamber. Above their heads, on the panel, were several gauges and lights. Many of the lights were not green as they should have been. Some were yellow, and others were red.

One of the technicians was waving a laser scanner along one of the pipes going into the chamber. It was for coolant, and he was manually checking the temperature.

The mix chamber is a large, round, heavily shielded chamber with many pipes going in and out. Some pipes delivered coolant to the chamber while others took the heated coolant away to the external nacelles, where it is cooled. Other pipes took the superheated plasma created from the combining of matter and antimatter and forced it to flow over the lattice matrix, which O'Toole and his engineers had reconstructed from the Kosuan Hafnium and gold platters. This lattice converted much of the energy every second into enough electricity to power a large city for a month.

The hot plasma was then piped out to the external nacelles, where it was cooled and stored for use as a propellant for the conventional engines and maneuvering thrusters.

In front of the mix chamber was the particle accelerator, which began in the primary section of the ship and shot regular matter at near-light speeds into the mix chamber. The matter would smash into the antimatter charge, where the two masses would be annihilated. The resulting explosion was enough to vaporize a small city each time if it were not contained behind an immense shield and cooled. At full power, these collisions would occur every half-second and would have to be regulated precisely. Additionally, as each charge entered the chamber, thick valves would have to close to prevent the explosion from escaping back up the accelerator or to the antimatter storage tanks.

This is why the technician was investigating the temperatures on the coolant pipes. If the chamber overheated, the valves could stick open, potentially causing the ship to be destroyed.

The chamber was surrounded by catwalks, leaving a twenty-foot space around it for a secondary blast shield to close around it if needed. Also, around the chamber was a thick glass wall coated with lead and other materials to minimize radiation exposure.

. . .

Hackett approached the group and stared at the panel above their heads. "Commander!" Hackett said firmly over the pounding of the muffled explosions taking place just feet away.

"Sir!" O'Toole yelled as he snapped to attention.

"I read your status report. What is the situation? Why the speed drop?"

O'Toole motioned for the Captain to walk with him to another room so they would not have to yell back and forth.

Once inside and the glass door closed, they could speak more easily.

"Captain, we have a temperature problem in the port side cooling system. There appears to be a restriction of sorts between the pump and the return from the reaction chamber."

"Could something be blocking the chamber?" Hackett asked.

"We think it is before the chamber. The starboard side appears to be clear. We were discussing sending in a micro-robot to take a video of the pipe to see what was there."

"What do you suspect?" Hackett asked with interest.

"I'm not sure what we will find. There are filters at the nacelles and just before the pumps, so nothing bigger than a grain of sand should be in there. So we are baffled at what it could be."

"Proceed cautiously. It could be something placed there to cause problems."

"Aye, sir. Commander Morris enlightened me about CPO Stout's threats before she died. So we are going to treat this as that threat."

"Carry on then. Keep me informed as to your progress."

Hackett turned and left the room. He paused and looked at the suspect area, and shook his head. He went back to the bridge.

THIRTY-THREE

MORRIS WENT to his quarters to check his private messages. He sat at his desk, flipped open the computer, and noticed an encrypted message from Vice Admiral Griffin. He opened it, and the video began playing.

In the center of the video was Griffin with his hands folded in front of him, and to his side was President Wakefield of the North American Union. "Commander, we have been aware of a situation on the *Saratoga* that puts the crew and the mission at stake. We have intel that clearly implicates Captain Hackett as the person who is attempting to destroy the ship. You must stop him."

Wakefield leaned into the camera's view. "We need you to eliminate him once and for all. We don't care how. Our last operative was murdered and could not carry out the task."

"Stout," Morris mumbled. "I can't kill the captain," he stated.

Griffin was back in view now. "We have had concerns about Hackett's mental state, and it appears that his torture at the hands of the Ineans has turned him. While on the surface, he appears to be as he always has been, a new video of him has surfaced, revealing a different side. Watch."

A window opened on his screen, and he watched CPO Jennifer Stout giving a log entry. She whispered and then turned the camera to view Hackett talking with a woman whose face was obscured by a pole. In the video, Hackett is heard telling her to plant the device in the starboard nacelle near the antimatter bottles. She questions him, but he reassures her she won't be on the ship when it explodes in Inean orbit. She nods and turns away, never revealing her face. Hackett looks around and leaves the room.

The window closed and returned to the image of Griffin. "We need you to kill him and Lieutenant Commander Benson, who is working with him. She has abandoned her mission and joined Hackett as he tries to start a war."

Wakefield came back into view. “In case you have reservations about your orders, here is some incentive.”

A new window opened to show a woman tied to a chair in a dark stone room. She was gagged and crying as well. Morris quickly recognized his sister as she struggled against the ropes holding her to the chair.

Wakefield's voice carried from the other open window. "Your sister's life depends on you doing your job. Kill Hackett and Benson, and she lives. Goodbye, Commander."

His screen went blank.

He ran his fingers through his hair and pounded his fist on the desk. "Son of a bitch!"

He punched his computer screen. It crackled and sparked as the screen shattered. He got up and walked about his quarters, mumbling. He was frantic. He could not kill Hackett or Benson. For all he knew, the video was a fake. He thought about the woman in the video. It was not Benson. He could not see her face. He did not need to. This woman was much shorter than Benson and had darker, shorter hair under her cap.

He sat at his desk and pondered his situation. This was a test, a deadly test. He had to save his sister, though, and he reached into his desk drawer and removed a laser pistol. He checked the charge and clipped it to his belt. Given the current state of their security, no one would question the ship's executive officer with a gun strapped to his hip.

Morris pushed away from his desk and left his room to plan Hackett's murder.

THIRTY-FOUR

SHAWN HACKETT ENTERED the conference room a few minutes late. Morris, Benson, Larson, and Channing were already there.

"Sorry, I'm late. Got a late message from Admiral Hodges." He sat at the table. In his hand was an Inean book and a thick notebook. He passed the Inean book toward Channing to look at. He opened his notebook. "When we were on Inea last time, I took the opportunity to borrow a few books with no intent to return. I got lucky and stole the right ones, apparently. The book that is going around the table concerns Inean history about a thousand years ago. In that book is a detailed account of their run-in with a race called the Ardons. That race defeated the Ineans and nearly destroyed Inea. Part of the story revolves around how the Ineans got distracted by the Ardon women. The book goes into great detail about what the Ardons looked like, and it is too human to be a coincidence."

He paused for a moment to consult his notes before continuing. "The Ineans, under the leadership of Marduk, vowed to track down these Ardons and destroy them." He looked around the table at all the faces attempting to find meaning in what their Captain was saying. "From what I have experienced and read, I believe that the Ineans think we are the Ardons."

Channing looked up at him as he passed the book to Morris. "I had heard that term from them before, but never realized what it meant."

"It does not surprise me, Ambassador. The Ineans treat that loss with great embarrassment, and with every passing day, they plot their revenge. And with every passing day, they get closer to fulfilling it, against us."

"So war with the Ineans is inevitable?" Benson asked.

"Or preferred," Morris blurted out.

Hackett glanced at Morris for a second and then continued. "No, it is not preferred, Commander. I provided you with that information so you are all aware of what we are dealing with. We are not here to start a war. However, that does not mean we bow down to the Ineans and give in to their demands. Any sign of weakness on our part will surely result in war."

Channing spoke up next. "I am aware of Marduk. He is regarded as their greatest leader and revered as a god. I am told much is written about him."

Hackett glanced at Channing. "He is more than a god. He is their purpose. The Ineans are fanatical about him, and it is written in that book that once the Ardons are found, the final great war will commence. He will return in a cloud spewing lightning and gather his fighters, past and present, to annihilate the Ardons. This would leave the galaxy open to Inean conquest."

"How do we even negotiate with people like that?" Larson asked.

"That is why we are here tonight. Ambassador Channing has many details to share with us while we are on the planet. Kind of an Inean Do and Don't list," Hackett stated. He closed his notebook and glanced at Channing. "Whenever you are ready, Ambassador."

"Thank you, Captain. With the delay because of the engine problem, it would be best if we split this into two nights."

Everyone nodded.

“Okay, let’s begin," he said, opening his tablet and finding the document he was looking for. "First up. When we land on Inea, there are some protocols we need to go over so we don't start a war before the meeting begins."

He talked well into the evening anyway.

THIRTY-FIVE

SUNDAY, **September 27, 2246**

As Woods and Perry entered the cargo hold, they noticed that the keypad to one of the primary doors had been disturbed: the face of the pad had been pulled out. Perry yanked the keypad from the wall easily, which he should not have been able to do, and inspected the wires behind it. The wires had been tampered with. He pressed the face of his watch, "Security to cargo hold one."

"Security here. What is the situation, Lieutenant Perry?"

"Someone has tampered with the keypad to the cargo hold locks."

"I'll send a couple of guards to investigate, security out."

Perry noticed the edge in the officer's voice. Since the ship was in lockdown, there had been dozens of calls regarding broken locks and tampered with equipment. Many in the crew knew this was to slow the search of the ship for other bombs. However, every call had to be investigated in the hope that whoever was behind it would make a mistake or leave a clue behind.

Several minutes later, two armed marines arrived in complete gear. They examined the keypad and took pictures. One marine scanned the device for fingerprints and skin oils from which they could pull DNA. All they found was Perry's.

One of the guards spoke up, "Have you been inside?"

"Not yet," Perry stated.

"Open it up then."

Perry typed in his code, and the doors slid open. The marine held out his hand to block Perry from entering and stepped in front of him and Woods. He began scanning the room to make sure there were no booby traps.

They entered behind the marine and surveyed the room. Perry noticed a container that was not sealed properly and pointed it out to the marine. They all walked over slowly and studied the container.

Perry scanned it. "It contains spare parts for the food processing plant."

"Open it," the marine stated, holding his scanner up to the seam.

Perry lifted the lid slowly while the marine scanned to make sure it wasn't rigged to explode. Woods helped remove the cover and set it on the deck. The marine looked in, and his scanner was displaying information.

"What is it?" Perry asked.

"I haven't seen a food processing plant that left residual radiation. Whatever was in this container is no longer here and could be quite dangerous."

The other marine looked at the scanner and said. "That's the signature of a portable nuke!"

He glanced at the other marine, who was not amused.

"Lieutenant Harris to the bridge," the marine said into his watch.

"Bridge here," Morris stated.

"Commander Morris, we are investigating a security breach in the cargo hold and suspect there is a nuke loose on the ship. The manifest says it is spare parts for the food processing plant, but obviously not."

"Are you certain?" Morris asked. He already knew the answer.

“One hundred percent, sir.”

"Lock up the hold. I'll alert the Captain. Morris out."

"All right, people, lock it up," the marine stated.

“We have orders to retrieve several containers for Commander O’Toole. He needs these containers!” Perry exclaimed.

"Commander O'Toole will have to get permission from the Captain. Until then, the only thing that leaves this hold is the four of us. Let's go."

The marines guided Perry and Woods from the hold. They assured the lock was secured with an overriding code that only security could unlock.

The yellow warning lights changed to red as they walked away from the hold. Three successive pings played over the speaker.

“This is Captain Hackett. We have had a security breach. We are going to security level five until further notice. That is all.”

There were three more pings, and the message was over.

The ship had been under security level three for days and had now escalated to level five. Five was the highest and most restrictive. Under level five, you did not leave your quarters except to perform your duty shift and eat. That was all. Anyone caught outside their quarters and not on duty would be put in the brig, period. No excuses except for the Captain and his executive officer, Morris.

THIRTY-SIX

MORRIS RETURNED to his quarters and sat at his desk momentarily to collect his thoughts. He reached up and opened his portable computer, and the screen oozed its liquid from the cracks in the screen. Morris remembered punching it earlier and slammed it back down. He opened his drawer and reached for a notepad and pen, but instead found another laser pistol. This one was low on charge; according to the display, it had been fired recently. He gripped it in his hand and studied it. It was not there earlier, and he knew someone was setting him up. It was an older, bulky, well-balanced laser pistol.

He checked the laser on his hip and noticed it was still fully charged. Not that it mattered. A 10 percent charged laser pistol was more than enough for what he was thinking. He flipped the safety off, and the laser read his fingerprint. It was programmed to his print only. For anyone else, the weapon would be useless. The display at the back of the pistol displayed the battery power and intensity setting. All weapons stored in personal quarters must be set to a minimum setting for safety. If you shot yourself by accident, it would be embarrassingly painful but not deadly. He looked at the gauge and stared at it. Then he reached with his other hand and pressed the up button. The display changed from green to yellow, to pink, and finally to red, the highest setting. The kill-with-no-hope-of-surviving setting. He looked at the weapon for a longer time, thinking. Then he placed it on his head and held his breath. He began to squeeze the trigger, which was nothing more than a spring-loaded electrical switch. He grimaced as his finger bore down on the button, sweat beaded on his forehead, and his hand began to shake. He could hear the weapon whine, building its fatal charge. "Arrrr!" he yelled, throwing the gun against the wall. He sat at his desk and sobbed. He couldn't do it. He couldn't kill Hackett or Benson, which would surely mean his sister's death. He picked up the planted gun and gripped it. The weapon recognized his prints and powered up. He was shocked. He had never seen this gun before.

He could not kill himself, or Hackett, or Benson, and there was nothing he could do to save his sister.

He spent the night at his desk and fell asleep.

A scream. "Bil-l-l-l-l!" Morris looked up as Sasha was ripped from his hands by the Ineans. They threw her to the ground and began to savagely rip her clothes from her body. They passed her body up, and it was now his sister. "Bil-l-l-l-l!" she screamed, "help me!" But he couldn't. Other Ineans held him from moving. He could only watch in horror as the Ineans savagely tortured her. He could hear bones breaking with each thud of an Inean fist. Her screams became gurgled pleas for help that would never come. Then she fell silent, and the Ineans cheered as they began to toss her limp, bloodied body around like a beach ball. A large, bony fist entered his field of view and struck him in the face. That is all he remembered until he woke up in the dingy holding cell. He was sitting in a puddle of the foulest-smelling urine, not his. He looked up, and in the cell beside him, a lizard creature was staring at him, grinning, while it urinated on him.

He woke up a short time later and sat back. He hated sleeping. Thoughts of Sasha's death came almost every night. He swore at himself for not finding a solution to the mess he was in.

Finally, he pushed away from his desk and returned to the bridge.

THIRTY-SEVEN

MONDAY, **September 28, 2246**

In the early morning hours, O'Toole woke the Captain. "Sir, a security team has found the bomb in the primary hull near a plasma storage bottle."

"Can they disarm it?" Hackett asked groggily.

"It was never assembled. They are gathering the pieces to be disposed of," O'Toole stated.

"Make sure all of the forensics are done, and it is carefully recorded in the event we find the person responsible."

"Aye, sir."

"Have you corrected the obstruction in the coolant pipe?"

"Ye-e-s-s-s." O'Toole dragged out.

"What was it?" Hackett asked, picking up on O'Toole's hesitance.

"It was a body."

"Whose?"

"We don't know who yet. Medical has taken it to perform tests. Let's just say it was well-cooked from the heat."

"How could a body get in there?"

"There is an access panel in each nacelle near the storage tanks for cleaning purposes. We are checking to see if either of them has been opened recently," O'Toole said with a yawn.

"Thank you, Commander. Have the bridge get us back on course to Inea and get some sleep."

"Aye, sir. O'Toole out."

Hackett sat at his desk for a moment and rubbed his eyes with his fists, thinking about how easy it was, or was it? The obstruction was found before the cargo hold was accessed, which likely means someone else is still trying to destroy the ship. Probably more than one person. Hackett was aware of these access ports in the nacelles, and even though the artificial gravity was weaker in those parts of the ship, it would still require more than one person to dispose of a body. He pressed the button on his desk. "Bridge."

"Bridge here, sir."

"Have Lieutenant Desai and Commander Morris meet me in conference room one in half an hour."

"Aye, sir."

"Hackett out."

Hackett pushed away from his desk and went to the head to splash water on his face and get dressed.

THIRTY-EIGHT

MONDAY, **September 28, 2246**

Ambassador's quarters.

Channing sat in front of his computer, which had a secure connection off the ship. He had been discussing the mission with Admiral Griffin and the President.

"Channing," said Wakefield. "Benson is there for one reason and one reason only. She is a gift to the Inean council. You must give her up to him, and he will sign the agreement for the scrubber technology."

"Mr. President, I cannot give up another human being for the sake of the deal. It is wrong. Plus, they will kill her."

"Small price to pay for peace, Channing. She goes, and it makes you Earth's lead council from now on. Wilcox has become too much of a liability to protect any longer."

"But, sir?"

"No buts! Benson knows her role. She agreed to take that assignment. She knows her part, Ambassador, know yours. Earth depends on it. Your future as lead Ambassador depends on it, or we could sacrifice you. Wakefield out."

Channing sat for a moment, thinking about his orders. He was to sacrifice Benson for the greater good. It would mean his dream of succeeding Wilcox would come true. However, something did not add up. Benson was against going to the surface for obvious reasons, especially with Wilcox. If she really knew about the sacrifice she was about to make, then what Wilcox had planned for her should not have mattered. He decided to go along with the president's plan. One thing he learned on this mission is that each person had their own agenda, and now he had his.

THIRTY-NINE

MONDAY, **September 28, 2246**

Midday.

Hackett, Morris, Benson, Larson, and Channing met to discuss the final details of the landing.

Channing stood by the large monitor, which displayed the layout of the meeting chambers. The table was roughly 12 feet square, surrounded by a railing, leaving a 10-foot space between the observers and four parties working on the agreement. The spectators would be seated on benches surrounding the center stage, much like a boxing arena. Enough seats for five thousand hostile Ineans to intimidate Hackett's people.

Channing pointed out the seating changes handed down by Admiral Griffin and President Wakefield. It would separate the women from the men, so that what little protection they could provide would be gone. Hackett and Channing would be seated between two Ineans, facing the Angowain ambassador and his team. Benson and Larson would be positioned to the left, between two other Ineans, and they would face the Kosuan people.

Hackett was furious and knew it was a ploy to separate the

women, forcing him and Channing to give the Ineans what they wanted in exchange for the women.

"The women cannot speak or raise a hand during this meeting. Just sit there," Channing stated.

"What if they touch us?" Larson asked.

"Just sit there. They want you to raise a hand in defiance, and with this arrangement, it would be suicide."

"That setup is suicide. There is no coming out of there in one piece with that setup, Ambassador. I, for one, have second thoughts about going down there. We may as well go down there naked with a juicy steak tied around our necks," Benson fumed.

"If you only knew what I had to do to convince command not to do that, Lieutenant Commander," Channing said. He was now getting mixed signals from Benson. He suspected Command lied to him again. It was too late now. She had to go.

"If we go down there, it is with fully charged laser pistols," Larson stated.

"I second that," Benson exclaimed.

"Mister Morris, you have been quiet," Hackett stated.

"I'm with Larson and Benson."

Hackett was typing into his tablet, and the image of Sasha Young appeared on the screen facing Channing. Hackett sprang from his seat and went to the screen. "This was our previous navigator, Lieutenant Sasha Young. Those animals ripped her from our hands the last time we came here and brutally, no, strike that, savagely ripped her apart while others prevented us from helping." Hackett turned towards Channing, who was looking away. "Take a look at her!" Hackett gripped Channing's chin and turned his head to force him to look at the screen. "Take a long look at that woman, Ambassador. We had the promise from the Ineans that there would be no trouble, and they ripped her limb from limb until she died. There was no apology, there was no investigation, there was no body to take back. I was tortured. Morris was tortured to a lesser extent. We got our agreement signed with them, but at what cost? It is also an agreement they choose to ignore. Take a long look at the loss due to Inean savagery." Then he turned Channing's face toward

Benson and Larson. "If they go down there, they will be seated between us at all times and fully clothed and armed to protect themselves. Understood?"

Hackett released Channing. No one said anything for several seconds. All were in shock.

“Captain, I will contact the admiral and request your changes.”

“Don’t ask! This is what we are going to do, Ambassador, and that is final!”

Hackett tossed his pen down on the desk. It bounced and landed on the floor. "Are there any other surprises from Command?"

"No, sir," Channing said softly. He was afraid of Hackett and knew Hackett would kill him if anything happened to his crew on this mission. He now had many questions for the admiral.

"If Benson and Larson go to the surface, they will represent Earth as an integral part of our society. As equals, you and I will live up to our historic roles to protect them. This way, the Ineans will see that our society has some morals and convictions they may find to respect. Everyone has profiles with whom we will be meeting?"

Everyone nodded.

“Good, I have an admiral I need to talk with.” With that, Hackett promptly left the room.

While Hackett reported directly to Admiral Hodges, he needed to clarify the changes with Admiral Griffin, who was working with President Wakefield and Ambassador Channing on this mission.

“Captain, secure link to Admiral Griffin established,” came the voice of Lieutenant Giovanella over the speaker in Hackett’s quarters.

“Send it down to my terminal.”

“Aye, sir, here it comes.”

The screen on Hackett’s desk displayed the fleet logo for a few seconds and then changed to the face of Admiral Griffin.

"Captain, what can we do for you?" Griffin said with a grin that said, "You lose."

“Sir, it has been brought to my attention that Lieutenant Larson and Lieutenant Commander Benson are to be separated from us on the planet and placed between two Ineans. I need not remind the admiral of what happened to Sasha Young."

"No, Captain, you don't. We don't need to remind you of the implications of returning empty-handed. Both of those women are capable of defending themselves."

"How can they defend themselves if their orders are to sit down, shut up, and don't raise a finger to the Ineans?"

"Do not raise your voice to me, Captain. The Ineans have made the request and said it would be in our best interest to follow their request. Besides, if you knew what it took to not send them down there naked, you would thank me for this." Griffin's grin got wider.

"They cannot be trusted, Admiral."

"The Inean council has given me their word that they will be safe."

"I don't trust them and won't trust them."

"You have your orders, Captain. If you can't follow them, then we need to put someone in charge of that ship who will. Griffin out."

Hackett's computer screen went back to displaying the fleet logo. He swore softly to himself and decided he needed to change the rules in their favor. There was one person on the ship whom he could trust to mix things up.

FORTY

MONDAY, **September 28, 2246**

Benson was at a table in the forward lounge with a paper notebook in front of her as well as a tall glass filled with ice. The waitress filled her glass with a bottle of 151 rum. She took a sip and felt the alcohol burn its way down her throat. She thanked the waitress, who walked away.

Hackett arrived a few minutes later with a similar paper notebook. He sat, and before he could flag the waitress down, she was there.

"Would you like a drink, sir?"

"Yes, bring me the bottle of what the Lieutenant Commander is drinking."

"Yes, sir," she replied. She was back in a moment with the bottle of 151 and a glass of ice.

"Thank you," Hackett said, and the waitress nodded and left the menus for the evening.

"Had any luck with the admiral?" Benson asked, already knowing the answer.

"None, but I have a plan."

"I figured as much," she said. "What is it?"

Benson took another sip of the rum and put the glass down. She realized it may have been a poor choice on an empty stomach.

Hackett noticed her looking at the glass after she put it down and knew they had better switch to something less potent.

"You cannot say anything to anyone."

"Okay," she replied.

"I plan on switching Morris for Channing for the landing. We will have you and Larson carry the briefcases for the meeting and force the Ineans to sit us together between Morris and me."

"Will Commander Morris go along?"

"I have already spoken with Morris. He is a go." He took a sip and placed the glass down. "I want everyone armed, and I want everyone to carry tracer tags under their skin."

"Tracer tags?"

"So I know where everyone is at all times."

"What about the ambassador?"

"He will run the show from the *Saratoga*."

"That sounds too simple."

"It is. I want you and Larson to cozy up with the Kosuan. They will respect that and remember that you and I are together. They seem to pick up on something we could use to our advantage."

"If the Ineans touch us, then the Kosuan will feel obligated to help you protect us," she stated.

"That's the plan."

"Wow, okay. Um, define cozy?" she asked, hoping not to trade one bad compromise for another.

Hackett held up his glass to her. She held hers up, and they clinked. "Cheers," he said. They both took large sips of the rum and put their glasses down. "Ahh, good. Get them drinking. Nothing bonds a Kosuan better than a good stiff drink."

"We already learned that," she stated.

The waitress returned, took their orders, and quickly departed.

Their conversation turned more personal after that, thanks to the 151 rum.

After their dinner, Hackett and Benson strolled along the corridor toward her quarters. Benson had a good buzz going and actually contemplated inviting the Captain into her room. She thought against it when they reached her room. She took her notebook from him and backed into her door.

"Good night, Captain."

"Good night." He turned and walked away.

Her door closed, and she placed the notebook on her desk. She showered and crawled into bed.

Benson was awakened by a knock on her door. Groggily, she said, "Come in." She left the light off, but the figure that walked in was Hackett. He didn't say a word as he got into bed with her. He kissed her repeatedly, and she didn't stop him. He pulled off the blankets that covered her, and she still didn't stop him. He removed his clothes and got on top of her. She slept nude and tried to say no, but couldn't form the simple word. She finally pushed him and yelled at him. He came back and hit her across the face. She went to hit him, but he caught her hand and repeatedly punched her in the face with his other hand. She tried to cry out but couldn't. He beat her into submission, and when she opened her swollen eyes, there was an Inean male above her, snarling. She cried out as he attacked her. With one hand, he folded her head back to the point of breaking her neck. She opened her eyes again, and Lieutenant Charles Rogers whom she served with on the Challenger was now attacking her.

Suddenly, there was a beeping noise, and she woke up startled. She looked down at herself and saw that she was covered with her blankets, which were now damp with sweat. She reached over, turned off her alarm, and sat in bed. She was noticeably shaken by the nightmare and couldn't get it out of her mind as she got dressed for the new day. She went for breakfast and kept to herself as she reflected on the nightmare.

Hackett seemed to be the only person who got a good night's sleep, whether it was due to the medication, the drinks, or simply exhaustion. He never stirred or dreamed the entire night. He woke up refreshed and ready for work at zero-five-hundred and was in an exceptionally good mood when he went for breakfast.

FORTY-ONE

TUESDAY, **September 29, 2246**

Benson went off duty early and proceeded to the gym. She dressed in her workout clothes and proceeded to mentally prepare for another round of abusing the punching bags. She taped up her hands and warmed up, slowly punching the bag, which moved little at first. She gradually increased the abuse as she thought about her nightmare. She envisioned the punching bag as Hackett and then Channing for literally throwing her and Larson to the wolves. She envisioned Wilcox, who wanted her for other activities. Then she pictured the punching bag as Admiral Griffin. Griffin was behind her transfer to the *Saratoga* to spy on the Captain and test him. However, her thoughts for Hackett swung wildly from hatred to liking him to the point of wanting to invite him into her room, which was against regulations, then back again to punching his imaginary face in front of her.

After some time, she stopped and placed her hands on her knees to catch her breath. After a couple of minutes, she showered and dressed.

She ate a light lunch and went to review her notes one more time. She glanced at the notebook and decided she was ready. She had the feeling of impending doom and could not shake it. Benson discarded her tray and dishes and left the mess hall.

As she walked along the corridor, she had a vision of Harrison again. He was telling her that she would be fine. She wanted to believe him, but could not. The odds were against them coming out alive, especially her and Larson. However, Harrison's voice was stronger than ever: "You will be okay. Come back and trust in Him," he kept saying.

She turned the corner and stepped onto the floating cart. She zipped off to the rear of the ship and took the elevator down to the hangar bay as she wondered what he meant by *come back and trust in Him?*

She got past security easily enough. They had been expecting her. She made her way to the transport, where Larson was inspecting their weapons and supplies. They regarded each other and went about their tasks.

Benson sat in the pilot's seat and began her preflight checklist. She programmed their destination and plotted the course from where the ship would be in orbit. Done. She checked with Larson, who was also finished. "Are you ready for this?"

"For once in my life, no."

"Me neither. Do you think we will come out of it alive?"

Larson pondered that for a moment before replying. "The Captain has a way of knowing what is going to happen before it does. It is kind of spooky, and he always finds a way of getting us out of danger."

"Is that why some people are afraid of him?"

"Could be. I know he scares Admiral Griffin," Larson replied as she double-checked her laser pistol. "Time to go to the bridge. We must be getting close to Inea."

"Yeah, let's go," Benson said.

Harrison's voice played in her head again. "You will be fine. Trust, Tamora, trust in Him."

They exited the transport, and Benson looked around. Several transports were lined up, facing the center aisle at an angle, pointing towards the large doors at the ship's rear. The elevators that brought down the fighters from the upper level were parked at the top, and she could see two rows of fighters on the upper deck below the engine room. The upper deck was no more than a steel mesh deck that allowed you to see through, with steel beams providing support. She could tell by the venting that was going on above her that the fighters were fueled and ready for action. This made her feel better knowing they had support.

They went to the bridge. Inea was very close now.

As the ship drew closer to Inea, Morris remained quiet the entire time as he plotted a way to save his sister. He couldn't kill Hackett as he had been ordered, and he couldn't kill himself like he wanted to.

Hackett remained focused on the mission, still calculating each variable. Even the unknowns that he knew were plentiful on this trip. He stayed clear of Benson, and she was doing him a favor by being with O'Toole, whether intentionally or not. Morris, for one, had backed way off and now didn't speak to the Captain unless he needed to. This disturbed Hackett. The abrupt change was not factored in, and Morris's intentions were unknown now.

The *Saratoga* was only two hours away from Inea when Hackett walked onto the bridge. The main bridge crew had already arrived to prepare their stations and were busy anticipating every possible scenario they would come across when the ship reached orbit. There were many possible outcomes for their visit to this planet, and not many meant they survived.

A nurse arrived on the bridge, and Hackett instructed her to inject a transponder under the skin of each person going to the surface. The transponder is a tiny electronic device the size of a grain of rice easily inserted just below the skin in the armpit. It emits a unique frequency that only the Alliance sensors can detect. The transponder would allow the ship to easily track people's movements on the surface.

The nurse shot Hackett first, then Morris, Larson, and finally Benson. She used a high-pressure injector that shot the device through clothing into the skin below. The sensation was similar to being stabbed with a pin.

Hackett ordered each person remaining on the ship to carry a firearm. This was a precautionary step in case the ship was boarded.

Each station reported to the Captain every detail of their readiness. The only station with an issue was engineering, and Hackett was already aware of their problems.

Hackett conferred with Benson to see if she was ready. She said she was, but he sensed there was a problem. She was short with her response, and she seemed to be preoccupied with something. He would have to find out before they went to the planet.

Benson was still deep in thought about the strange dreams she was having. It was becoming clear to her that another force was at work on this mission, and she was reluctant to admit it.

The rest of the ship was prepared by midday, and Hackett requested that Benson go with him to discuss the final details. She glanced over her shoulder at him and reluctantly followed him to the elevator. Hackett left Giovanella in charge.

Neither Hackett nor Benson spoke the entire time in the elevator and the corridor leading to Conference Room One. Once inside, she turned to him and dropped a bomb. "Captain, I don't think I can go on this mission. I've done some thinking over the past couple of days and concluded that I am the wrong person for this mission." She quickly turned away from him so he couldn't see the tears rolling down her cheeks. She wasn't afraid of dying. She was afraid of being overpowered by the Ineans, just as in her dream. Benson was one to be in control and regretted backing out of the landing. It would definitely hurt her career.

"Tamora, I understand your fear of this mission. I am also concerned that we won't make it out alive," Hackett began.

She clenched her hands into fists that remained by her side, frustrated that he wouldn't let it go. "No! That's not it at all," she said, still with her back turned.

"Then what is it? We only have minutes before we head down to the planet. You are not giving me much time to make changes," he said tensely.

“I, I had a weird dream last night, the same one over and over,” she said as she turned to him.

Hackett stared at her for a few seconds; the pause was noticeable, and he didn't care at this point. "A dream!" he exclaimed as he folded his arms in front of him. *What next?* he thought quietly. *Yes, she fits in with this crew nicely. She's nuts like everyone else.*

"Yes, you must understand that I see things, and they happen. That has been the case since I was a child. Unfortunately, it has been many years since I had a vision, but this past week it began again, and many of the old ones have returned. Many of which I had forgotten about," she said, staring at him. The tears stopped for now.

“There is nothing about this in your record. Why now?” Hackett pried.

“Because I never told anyone. It doesn’t matter right now. Something goes wrong on this mission.”

"Something goes wrong!?" he couldn't help being exasperated. "Everything has gone wrong so far!" Hackett threw his hands up and walked away, but he wasn't done yet. "We need to go down there, Tamora. Can you let me know when that time comes, so maybe we can avoid it?" Hackett asked. "Besides, this mission has gone completely wrong since we left Earth, so I don't know what to say."

“I can try, but I never did that before.”

“I need you down there. I need you focused.”

Benson looked at him. “I need to get something off my mind first.”

Hackett folded his arms again and sat back on the table's edge. "Go ahead."

"This isn't easy for me to do." She walked up to him. "My orders from the vice admiral." She stood inches from him and looked down at him, leaning on the table as he looked up at her. This made Hackett uncomfortable. "As part of approving my transfer to this ship, I was asked to evaluate you."

“Evaluate me? No kidding. I know all about that.”

“Yes, I was told to make you fall for me and see if you would compromise the mission or violate policy.”

“I see. So have I?”

"No, I have," she replied while Hackett looked puzzled. "I don't know what I feel for you, but visions of Harrison keep coming back, and I don't want to go down that road again."

"I am aware of your relationship with Cadet Harrison at the academy. I know what your plans were and how he died," Hackett stated. "But regardless of how we feel, there is still a job to do, which begins soon. I need you down there."

She took a deep breath and exhaled. “All right. I just needed to clear my conscience because what I did was wrong. You’re a good captain. You deserve to be a captain.”

“When this is over, we’ll talk about the other stuff,” Hackett replied as he started for the door. “We should be on the bridge.”

"There is nothing else. There will be nothing else. I'm not ready to go down this road again. It hurt too much the last time. It still hurts. Let's get this mission done, then, and I'll transfer to another ship when we get home."

“So that’s it? You’re just going to run from your feelings?”

“I’m not running! I’m protecting both of us,” she yelled. “Sorry, sir.” She said in a calmer tone.

"Uh-huh, we'll talk about this later," Hackett said as he continued out the door.

Benson followed him out the door and back to the bridge. She didn't say anything else to him the entire time, even though she wanted to. In her mind, different scenarios played out of how she could have done it better. She wanted to be with Hackett, but the image of Harrison, her past love who died, kept flashing in front of her, telling her not to walk away, and she couldn't shake it off.

Hackett was confused, to say the least. He knew his mental troubles were because of the poison in his brain, and he was puzzled about what her problems were. *Great!* he thought. *I finally found a woman I like, and she's crazier than I am!*

The elevator door opened, and Hackett walked out, followed by Benson. Neither of them spoke nor acknowledged the other as they returned to their posts. Giovanella saw Hackett, surrendered the chair to him, and returned to his console in time to see the incoming light flashing. He sat, and his chair slid forward and locked. He listened to the message.

Ensign Davies sized up Benson when she sat back at the Navigation console. Benson wiped her eyes and went back to work. Davies watched for a minute to make sure she was okay.

Giovanella looked over his shoulder, "Captain, we have an incoming from Inea. They want us to slow down to quantum two for the final approach to their planet. They are sending four escort ships to bring us in."

"Four of them? That's overkill. Reply to the message that it was received, and we will comply."

"Aye, sir," he replied to the Captain and answered the message.

Sensors officer Stephan Bowers watched his monitors as four dots streaked towards them. “Captain, we have four Inean warships approaching from the system ahead.”

“Thank you, Lieutenant. Miss Benson, slow us down to quantum two,” Hackett said.

"Yes, Captain, reducing speed to quantum two," Benson replied with a softness in her voice.

Hackett knew his problem with her wasn’t over yet. He was now concerned that it would spill over and compromise the landing.

Compromise the landing, he mused. It was so compromised that it had to be laughed at. No wonder alien races didn't take them seriously. All he could think was it reminded him of "The Three Stooges," black-and-whites from the twentieth century. Timeless classics, he thought. He had seen them all several times and did a historical study on them as a cadet. Oh, how their lunacy applied to this mission, only no one was laughing. This was deadly serious.

After several minutes, the Inean ships passed the *Saratoga*, turned around, and sped up to come alongside. The four ships surrounded the *Saratoga* and kept it boxed in all the way to Inea. There was no escape now. They were committed to the mission.

The Inean warships were smaller than the *Saratoga* and didn't have shields. However, they did have thick armor plating that stopped almost everything you could throw at them. The ships were shaped like ancient race cars with quantum field generators where the wheels would be. The ships also had a low bridge at the very top and skewed towards the rear. Their weapons were primarily mounted fore and aft, and they were heavily armored. The weapons consisted of multi-directional laser cannons and nuclear-tipped torpedoes. These were very dangerous ships, and the reason the Kosuan had a hard time winning the war. The Alliance also abhorred using nukes and therefore wanted to avoid war if possible. The Ineans knew everyone feared the firepower of these ships and used that to their advantage whenever possible. That is how they convinced people into slave trading. If you traded for them, you wouldn't be nuked.

The Ineans were a bigger race than humans, also much stronger. Their only downfall was their physical slowness. These people would never win a duel with a human, but could crush one easily with their hands if they could catch them.

The planet of Inea-Four was coming into view as the ships approached. Ambassador Channing entered the bridge and stood by the Captain, waiting for his turn to speak. "Captain, is everyone ready to go to the surface?" he asked.

Hackett looked up at him. It was time to inform the Ambassador about the change in plans. There would be no time for him to contact the Alliance, as it would take several hours to send and receive a message. He wondered how Channing would take it. Would he be mad? Would he accept the Captain's reasoning? Would he pull a Wilcox and try to take over the ship? Hackett didn't know, but Channing was in front of him now, so he wouldn't have to wait any longer.

"Ambassador, I regret to inform you that new information has come to light. I have decided to replace you with Commander Morris for the trip to the surface. I would like you to be available on an open channel to listen in and provide feedback. If we fail, then it will be your job to secure the peace agreement. Unfortunately, I feel your safety is in danger if you go down right now," Hackett said.

The Ambassador looked at him for a moment. "Captain, what new information did you receive?" he asked.

“It has to do with the women and the inclusion of the Kosuan in the meetings. I felt it was best to change the match-ups and include the Kosuan for a different reason,” Hackett said.

"I understand where you are going, Captain. It is a good idea. It is also a dangerous one. It has a high degree of failure associated with it," Channing said. "Where do you want me to be?"

"On the bridge. Commander O'Toole will be in charge of the ship while we are on the surface. I instructed him to allow you to monitor and participate from here."

"I will do it, Captain, but I'm pulling your team out of there at the first sign of trouble," Channing said.

Hackett thought that was too easy, but it still wasn’t done yet. “Agreed. I will tell you when I feel we are in trouble, however. Besides, there really isn’t any escaping from this point anyway.”

Channing hesitated. In the end, he wasn't going to win this battle. So he nodded yes and sat in the chair the security guard had set up for him. The planet was growing larger, and Giovanella said there was an incoming message from the lead Inean ship.

"Sir, they want us to slow down to 100 kilometers per second and assume orbit at the following coordinates," Giovanella said. He read off the coordinates, and Benson wrote them down on her console.

"Respond that we will slow to 100 kps, Mr. Giovanella. Miss Benson, make the changes and execute them," Hackett said to her with an unmistakable edge to his voice.

“Responding now, Captain,” the communications officer said, and Benson laid in the new speed and target coordinates.

"Executing changes now, Captain. Initiating low orbit above the capital city of Inea-four in 20 seconds," Benson said. She had calmed down some and responded with a more unemotional tone.

The ship slowed and rolled to port, and the thrusters fired, putting the ship in orbit. "Captain, standard, low orbit achieved," Benson reported without looking back.

“Thank you, Lieutenant Commander,” He replied.

Morris was watching the interaction between the two and noticed the tension between them. He became concerned about the mission's outcome if they couldn't control their personal issues.

“Sir, there are two Kosuan battle cruisers in orbit as well as over 30 Inean ships. I wouldn’t want to start a fight right now if I were us,” Bowers stated.

“Thank you, Lieutenant, nor would I.” Hackett turned to the Ambassador, “What happens now?” he asked.

“We wait for them to contact us for instructions on landing,” Channing replied. “The women should go and prepare, Captain.”

“They are, Ambassador. They are going in uniform,” Hackett replied.

Channing rolled his eyes and huffed slightly, but loud enough for Hackett to hear. "Captain, may I speak with you in private?"

Hackett looked at Channing, “No!”

Giovanella turned to Hackett. “Sir, I have received landing instructions. I have sent them to yours and Morris’s tablets.”

"Thank you, Lieutenant," Hackett replied with a glance at his tablet that was strapped to the arm of his chair. He read the brief instructions and took the unit in his hand. "Okay, people, it is time to go."

“Aye, sir.”

“Commander O'Toole, the bridge is yours until we return.”

“The ship will be right here when you get back, Captain,” O’Toole replied.

Benson entered the transport first and strapped into the pilot's seat. Larson entered next and buckled herself in near the weapons locker. Lastly, Hackett and Morris were the last to board the transport and sealed the hatch.

“Landing information programmed?” Hackett asked.

Benson replied, "Yes, it is, Captain."

Hackett ordered the flight deck cleared, and red lights began flashing around the hangar bay. The deck cleared rapidly. Shortly after, the bay doors slid open, exposing the flight deck to open space. Benson powered up the transport's engines and slightly slid the two throttle levers forward. The transport lifted a few inches off the deck and floated toward the hangar doors at the ship's rear. Once in open space, Benson typed in their approach, and the transport took off toward the planet.

The transport ride went without incident, which was unusual for this mission. Benson circled the compound and gently set the transport away from two Kosuan landing pods. They glanced up at the monstrous, modern-looking palace. The palace towered over one hundred floors, many of which had balconies above the square they overlooked. It was a marvel of ingenuity, being so large and constructed of glass. There were statues of what appeared to be Inean heroes surrounding the square, with one large one in the center. It was a statue of Marduk.

Benson humored herself by thinking about knocking it over with the transport, but she didn't. Hackett and Morris gathered their equipment, including a laser pistol for everyone. Morris handed each person an earbud translator that clipped onto the earlobe and fit into the ear canal. The translator was capable of translating all Earth's languages and hundreds of alien languages into English. Without it, the peace talks would not have been possible.

They slung their packs over their shoulders like children heading for school, and Morris looked to Hackett, who nodded. Morris opened the hatch.

They stepped back from the blast of heat that hit them from the outside. Inea was a hot planet with daytime highs ranging from 110 to 120 degrees Fahrenheit, and it was oppressively humid. The sun was also brighter than Earth's, and it hurt their eyes to look outside. Hackett guided the party out of the transport, followed by Benson, Larson, and Morris. They did it that way to keep the woman between them for their protection. They stopped about 10 feet from the Inean greeting team and spread out so they all faced forward. A slight breeze blowing did nothing to ease the oppressive heat and humidity.

“Welcome to a beautiful winter day on our planet,” the Inean ambassador said.

“He can’t be serious!” Larson mumbled.

He was smiling. Was he joking, or was this winter for them? The last time Hackett was here, they landed high up in the northern latitude, and it wasn't this warm. "Please come inside where it is warmer." He motioned for them to follow.

Morris saw Larson's face, and he leaned into her. "Inea doesn't have seasons. He's messing with you." Larson nodded that she understood.

As they walked toward the palace, the four officers took notice of the marketplace. Everything from fruits and meats to slaves of various races was sold there.

They walked inside, and it was slightly cooler, which made them feel better. There wasn't any breeze inside, either. Benson glanced at Hackett while he focused forward. For a moment, she thought he was ignoring her. She dismissed it quickly. She knew that look. He was calculating something in his mind as he looked around the palace.

Benson didn't like how the Ineans looked at her or Larson. She partially understood some of the rude comments coming from the gathering of people, many of whom had begun to take bets on how long they would live when the Ineans got hold of them. Many joked and laughed about it.

They spread out and walked side by side behind the Ineans. The corridors were vast and lined with people from various races, talking and making side deals before the negotiations began.

Several faces caught the Captain's interest. The Moroc Chu Nog delegation was here, which was odd because they detested the Ineans. The Angowains also had a delegation here and were supposed to remain neutral in their conflicts; of course, the Kosuan had several members present. All of them had females of their race with them, and the women were naked. The humans, it seemed, were the only species here that covered up their women, and this drew a collective loathing from all the other races.

They walked up to several large, heavy wooden doors. The

Ineans stopped before them and swung the massive doors open with an eerie creak. The guards stood to the sides and motioned for the humans to walk in. They formed a single line, just as they had when exiting the transport. They walked into the room. The Inean woman inside guided them to their seats. The room resembled a boxing arena in its layout. There had to be at least 5,000 people present already, waiting to get started. Hackett noted the guards posted along the outside walls of the room. The Inean woman walked them down a few steps to a table in the middle of the floor. The table was made up of several tables set up in a 12-foot square and surrounded by intricately detailed wooden chairs, just as Channing had said it would be.

Hackett continued to scan the room, noticing the numerous paintings hung throughout, along with many statues of leaders carved into the walls. Much of their history over the past thousand years was depicted in carvings and paintings. The detail was impressive. If you stared at them, the images of the old warriors appeared to jump from the canvas and the walls. At the table, seated to the left, was the Kosuan delegation, composed of four males. Seated to the right were the Angowains, represented by three males and one female. The seats on the far side remained vacant, awaiting the Inean delegation. The humans regarded the already seated members and proceeded to occupy their side of the table, making themselves as comfortable as possible.

"I need to switch seats with you," Hackett whispered in Benson's ear.

"Okay," she replied.

This put Benson on the outside next to the Kosuan, whom they had met on Verna-3.

Larson remained between the Captain and Morris.

FORTY-TWO

SOL SYSTEM.

On board the orbiting Solar Observatory, Specialist Sarah Hines was facing a wall of computer monitors. She studied the latest activity the Sun was about to throw toward Earth. The observatory maintained an orbit just outside that of Mercury. This put them on the front line in predicting and reporting solar activity back toward Earth. Their job had become increasingly busy in recent months as the Sun became more active. The solar storms were also becoming more violent and destructive.

Hines was jolted back to reality by a warning chime from her console. She became quickly interested in a magnetic buildup beneath the surface of the Sun. The Sun rotated, bringing the disturbance precariously close to a direct line with Earth. Hines watched the disturbance grow. Her computer models displayed on the monitors on either side of her the potential explosion's intensity. It was off the chart. This was a storm that could blast off the surface of the Sun and engulf the planet Mercury in hours. The observatory was not safe either. They maintained a position 20 degrees above the direct line between the Sun and Earth. Still, the enormity of the blast could quickly destroy their station.

She had no choice in the matter. She pressed the public address button on her console. "Commander Williams, I need you on the main deck ASAP!" She watched in horror as the Sun began to swell noticeably towards Earth. It wasn't a matter of if it would blow, but when. She glanced again at her monitors. Now they flashed red, and alarms began to sound throughout the station. They were in the danger zone with no way of escaping. The station was designed to orbit at a predetermined position. Hines stared in horror as the magnetic lines of force began to snap on the surface of the Sun. She knew Earth was going to be a direct hit. Earth had at most 48 hours to prepare.

Commander Williams entered the observation deck in a hurry. He was a commander more out of courtesy than any military training. He was a scientist with numerous discoveries to his credit, but his most significant discovery was yet to come. Williams looked the part of a scientist with his scraggly beard, extra-thick glasses, and a penchant for wearing out-of-date clothes.

Several others gathered on the deck after the alarms went off and stared bug-eyed at the monitors.

Williams raced forward and nudged Hines to the side. He worked the controls frantically, not believing what he or anyone else was seeing. The Sun was tearing itself apart. This was the worst explosion ever recorded, and it had only just begun. "Hines! Run a diagnostic. This can't be!" he screamed.

"All ready have, Commander, twice. There's nothing wrong with our equipment!" she yelled back, not out of disrespect but out of fright.

Williams banged the console in frustration. She was right. "Peredo, fire our orbital thruster. We need to get out of here! Stern and Eddy, get the escape pod ready." He looked down at the frightened intern, Sarah Hines. "Sarah, contact Earth and send them everything we have. Also, send out a distress call. We need to be evacuated from here and soon."

She looked up. "Ye…es, sir," she said nervously.

Everyone in the observatory felt the shudder through the station as Peredo fired their orbital rockets. It wouldn't help, though. The solar explosion was too large. They needed to be millions of miles away in a few hours. It wasn't to be.

Williams stared at the data and knew he needed to create a new class of solar events. This was too strong to be called a CME, too weak by far to be considered a supernova.

The static-laden, audio-only, frantic voice of Sarah Hines played into the headset of Communications Officer Ensign Edward Noble aboard the Alliance space station orbiting Earth. He immediately went to work and paged his commanding officer. "Commander, I need you over here right now, sir!" he barked over his shoulder.

Commander Foley broke off his conversation with a female officer he was hitting on and quickly made it to Nobles's station. "What is it?" he asked, annoyed at how close he came to getting a date with the woman.

"Sir, it's the Solar Observatory. The Sun has gone critical, and they are requesting immediate evac!" Nobles replied anxiously.

"Can't be…" Foley began to say, but stopped when the data flashed on the screen. "Holy crap!" He and Nobles exchanged horrified looks, and Foley jumped away from the station, beginning to yell. "Put this station on highest alert. I need this station behind the Earth in 12 hours or less. Recall all fighters and dispatch all starships immediately. This is not a drill, people." Everyone around him scrambled to their jobs as red warning lights began to flash. The automated alert began to call out, "Alert, Alert. This station is under attack. All hands to battle stations." It repeated several times throughout the station, and the PA system remained open, waiting for the Commander to bark his next batch of orders. Everyone hurried to prepare the station for the catastrophic solar explosion heading their way.

Foley looked around the command deck of the station as it buzzed with activity. He tapped Nobles on the shoulder. "Get me the vice admiral."

. . .

All Hines and the others could do was watch as the hot, fiery chunk of the Sun exploded from the surface and headed their way. The size of which would engulf a hundred Earths. It was so massive that the computers indicated it would remain intact as it cooled, while traveling well beyond Earth.

Several of their systems went down quickly, and the monitors, one by one, went to static as their sensitive sensors burned out from the overload of charged particles bombarding them. The observatory lights flickered as all the electrical systems overloaded and shut down.

The station went dark except for the warning lights. Williams looked around at all the scared faces; he was frightened too, but he was in charge and couldn't show his fear. The only sound was the growing hiss from outside. The highly charged particles flowing from the Sun at high speeds began to hit the station. Williams looked out his window, and the station was beginning to glow.

"Okay, everyone, there is nothing we can do. We must ride this out. Everyone to the escape pod now, but do not launch. You are better off with the station between us and those particles." Everyone cleared the deck in an orderly fashion and went down to the escape pod to wait out the storm.

Vice Admiral Griffin's transport docked at the space station a second before the alert was called. He raced to the command deck as fast as possible with the NAU president close to his heels.

They walked onto the deck, and everything was frantic. Foley spied him, walked briskly to Griffin, and guided him to a wall-sized monitor split into four screens displaying different information. The first corner displayed a live image of the Sun, with its huge wart protruding from its surface. The next frame showed the computer's simulation. The next showed the potential damage path on Earth: Much of Africa, from the equator down to the southern 30th parallel, was in red, and the destruction path crossed the Atlantic Ocean into South America, from Porto Alegre, Brazil, north to the equator. The red zone ended just before hitting Peru.. Wrapped around the red zone was a 500-mile-wide yellow zone. The red zone represented the most likely path of intense damage, where wildfires would typically begin and end. The computer added the most likely zone of death and displayed it on the screen as a growing purple zone within the red zone. This is where the fire from the Sun would actually touch the Earth. Millions of people lived in this zone, and there was not enough time to move them.

Another alarm went off on the command deck as the first charged particles from the Sun made it to the station. Many communications consoles shut down as the sensitive antennas could not handle the barrage. They managed to warn Earth that there would be no more communication until the charged particles passed by. Earth would have to rely on ground observations and wired communications to spread the word and get people to the shelters.

Everyone stood and watched as the wart on the Sun's face continued to grow outward toward them. It still had not detached completely, and no one was sure how much of the Sun would blow off the star.

There was a worst-case scenario that was quickly becoming a reality, but no one dared mention it, not yet.

FORTY-THREE

ALL THE INEANS in the room stood and cheered when the Inean delegation entered. The Inean Ambassador saluted his people and made approving gestures in response to their cheers.

Hackett and his people also stood and greeted the Ineans by bowing slightly as they came to the table. The Ineans were intimidatingly large, and this scared Benson. Everyone else had seen them before. Other than her visions, this was her first face-to-face, or more realistically, face-to-chest meeting. Each one had to weigh six times her weight, and their arms were the size of her legs and much tougher. Their skin was like leather and not nice leather either, more of the rough, cracked, dried-out leather.

The Ineans pulled out their seats and plopped down into them. Everyone else followed. The Inean Ambassador was seated in the middle, and he banged his gavel on a stone plate in front of him to call the meeting to order. The armed guards spread out around the room and quieted the spectators, who were reluctant to do so.

The Inean Ambassador welcomed all the guests and delegations from several planets. His voice was deep and hard to understand, even with the earbud translator each one wore. He knew this and took the time to introduce each group in their native tongues.

Hackett opened his portable computer and searched several pages of notes for something, which he eventually found. The Ambassador finally got around to the Alliance delegation, and several species in the crowd hooted and yelled obscenities when they were introduced. This wasn't going to be a friendly meeting, and Benson and Larson slid closer to the men. Any closer and Benson would have been on Hackett's lap, which, under different circumstances, he wouldn't have minded at all.

The Inean Ambassador was quick to get started. He handed each member at the table a copy of the agreement drawn up between Ambassador Wilcox and himself. Hackett and his people had been briefed in detail on what the document was to say. However, after a quick review, Hackett realized this document was completely different. It was something his people had not seen or anticipated. The Inean Ambassador was trying to pull a fast one on Hackett. He glanced at Morris, who came to the same realization. Hackett looked around the table and had no choice. He raised his hand to speak.

The Ambassador banged his gavel on the table for the room to quiet down. “The floor recognizes Captain Shawn Hackett of Earth.” Some more shouts and insulting comments from the crowd.

Hackett stood to speak to the group once the Ambassador quieted the room. "Sir, honored guests, due to circumstances on our voyage here, the person responsible for this agreement could not complete it or inform us of the many changes in its contents. I respectfully request a recess so we can view the details of this, so we understand what it contains." Hackett bowed to the Ambassador and returned to his seat.

The Ambassador looked at Hackett and was amazed at his composure. "Captain Hackett, you are looking well. I trust your previous experience here is not affecting you?"

"Not at all, Ambassador. I am in perfect health," Hackett replied. He lied, of course. He could hear the spiders crunching in his mind. The only thing that kept him from going crazy was his preoccupation with glancing at Benson, who was nearly hugging his leg.

The Inean Ambassador looked down at his notes and said, "The Earth delegation has six Earth hours to review the document. We will reconvene at that time." The Kosuan ambassador went to object, but the Inean delegation quickly vacated their seats and left the room. The Kosuan ambassador swore and stomped out of the room, followed closely by the Angowains. Hackett and his crew were guided from the room and down a long corridor to an elevator. Beings from several races hissed at them and made gestures toward the women. The elevator whisked them up several floors to a room. It was like a cheap motel room, maybe slightly nicer.

The room was round and made of glass. It had a wedge-shaped bed, a chair, and a couple of dressers. All the furniture blended into the room and the walls and was designed with humans in mind. Benson laughed at the dressers and wondered if they were ever needed, referencing the anticipated wardrobe. There was also a complete bathroom, designed for human needs. The bathroom was round with pockets for a sink with a mirror, a pocket for the toilet, and one for the shower. The towel rack was also round and contoured to the room's overall shape. The Inean woman stated that there was another room for the other couple. She bowed slightly and backed out of the room.

Morris was the first to speak. "Captain, if we stay, how do you want to pair up, men in one room and women in the other?"

"No, I want one of us with them at all times, Commander. I will stay with Benson, you and Larson can take the other room. If we stay the night, you and I will take the chairs, and the women can have the beds, Commander," Hackett replied. "I just don't trust these animals."

Morris replied, “Understood, sir.”

Hackett knelt down at the foot of the bed and winced at a brief pain in his head as he opened the portable computer and handed it to Benson, who was at his left at the side of the bed. Morris and Larson knelt on the other side.

Benson was the only one to see it and decided to not say anything yet. She would, however, keep an eye on him.

"Larson, please sweep the room for bugs," Hackett requested.

She nodded, jumped up, and wandered the room with her scanner. "We'll have to speak softly. I'm sure there's a reason this room is made of glass, and keep all notes folded." Hackett looked at Morris, who was preoccupied with watching Larson walk around the room.

Larson nodded, "Yeah, simple vibrations from speaking can be picked up in the glass."

"Did you see the way that Inean soldier was looking at me?" Larson asked while scanning the room. "I may as well have been a cheeseburger."

"Yes, I did. You stay close to me." Morris added.

"Don't have to tell me twice," she replied.

Larson had found a few bugs and destroyed them. After a few minutes, she came back to the table. "All set, Captain." Hackett regarded her and opened the proposal. It was about ten pages long, and Hackett had each person read it over and mark it up. He also scanned and transmitted a copy to the *Saratoga* for Channing to review. After they had read it over a couple of times, they all had questions.

Morris started by objecting to the women being handed over as sex slaves to seal the agreement. Hackett also objected to this and opposed the Alliance handing over technology that would aid them against the Kosuan. Benson objected to both of those, plus the establishment of a human colony here. She saw it as a means of getting more slaves. Additionally, both women objected to the Inean presence on Earth. What was missing was an essential element that they could not leave the meeting without. The technology to correct the Earth's ever-worsening climate, which had been promised.

Hackett had them write counter-proposals, which he would take back to the chamber. He then contacted Channing and asked for his opinions. Channing agreed with them and reworded the counter-proposal to sound more formal. He also doubted it would work, but added they may as well try. Worst case, it would produce a counter-proposal from the Ineans.

FORTY-FOUR

SEVERAL FLOORS BELOW, a secret meeting was taking place between the Inean Ambassador and his chief military adviser. The Ambassador was sitting behind a desk while the general stood before him.

"Didn't your people plant the device on their ship when they ran across it the other day?" the Ambassador asked harshly.

"They did, Your Excellency," General Chong-Howei replied.

The Ambassador jumped up from his chair and went nose-to-nose with his general. "Then explain why HE is here!" he screamed.

“I have no explanation, Your Excellency,” the general replied.

"You have no explanation! He is the only human to survive our torture, and you have no explanation!" The Ambassador screamed even louder.

"We scanned their vessel, our device is attached to their hull, and it is functioning," the general said as he became uneasy. "I don't know why he didn't go crazy. Nonetheless, he seems immune to everything we do."

"We must kill him. He can't leave this system alive," the Ambassador stated as he worked his way back to his seat.

“That should be easy, Your Excellency. Their ship is falling apart and probably won’t make it out of the system anyway.”

"You can do what you want with his ship and crew. I still want his brain dissected so we can prevent this from happening again," the Ambassador stated.

“Yes, Your Excellency,” General Chong-Howei said.

"Oh, and his bitch is mine. No one else can have her except for me." It was one of the few times an Inean smiled, and it had a scary look about it, especially when followed by a deep, sinister laugh.

The general nodded and backed out of the room. The Ambassador waited for him to leave before calling his next adviser in. He looked at a computer screen on his wall, and the six hours were almost up when he paged his head chef.

The chef entered the Ambassador's room and stood before him, waiting while the Ambassador finished dictating a correction into his computer. When he was done, he looked up at the chef and cleared his throat.

"That human is here. You are aware of that?" the Ambassador asked.

"Yes, Your Excellency, and we have a meal prepared especially for him. It should make his brain explode," the chef said with a booming laugh.

"I want his brain in one piece. I just want him to go crazy and start a war so we can be done with these puny humans once and for all," the Ambassador said while staring at his chef.

“Yes, Your Excellency, I can tone it down some to make sure it works properly,” the chef replied.

The Ambassador grunted as he stood, walked around his desk, and placed his large arm around the Inean chef, who was a woman, turning her to face a shelf on the wall. "I am reserving that spot on the shelf for a jar with his brain so I can admire it forever. Then I will put the head of his bitch next to it when I am done with her," he said as he squeezed his mate.

She looked at him, shaking her head, "The things you collect. I will do my best." She removed his arm and backed out the door, leaving the Ambassador staring at his shelf, which held many trophies of past negotiations. One was the head of a Kosuan ambassador, and several others were from races that had long since been conquered by the Ineans.

There was one large jar turned away from view. The Ambassador grew annoyed that he couldn't look at his latest, most prized possession. He lumbered to the shelf, turned the large jar to face him, and smiled. In it, the head of Sasha Young, Hackett's previous navigator. Her facial expression was hauntingly distorted and twisted as the head bobbed in a jar filled with preservative liquid. The expression was indicative that she may have still been alive when beheaded. The Ambassador tapped the jar, tormenting the lifeless head as her brunette hair floated about.

FORTY-FIVE

THE FEROCIOUS CME pounded into the Solar Observatory, blowing out every system. The force of the impact pushed the observatory out of its orbit and dragged it toward Earth.

In the escape pod, the occupants had buckled in. However, heads, arms, and legs still flailed about uncontrollably. Specialist Sarah Hines screamed out in fear, as did everyone else in the pod. There were no windows in the pod. A window would be a path for the deadly, high-speed particles to gain access to the people inside. The life pod was coated with lead, which enveloped a liquid solution that stopped most of the fatal rays, but not all. The occupants began to suffer from exposure to the deadly rays, more like a bad sunburn that was starting to blister.

The pod shuddered and groaned as it was torn from its mount, which was attached to the observatory. The lights inside the pod flickered slightly. The gauge that registered air quality had swung into the yellow and slowly crept towards the danger zone, or red. They had hours to survive, and they were on their own. There was no way for an Alliance ship to rescue them right now or for the next several hours.

. . .

Commander Foley had prepared their space station for the oncoming assault; they could only watch the helpless observatory being bombarded through long-range sensors.

The solar explosion reached from the Sun's surface to beyond the orbit of Mercury and the observatory when it finally broke free of the Sun's surface. It was good that Mercury was on the other side of the Sun. Some people on the command deck speculated that its orbit could have been altered if it had been hit head-on. This may have happened in the distant past, as Mercury's orbit was already noticeably elliptical.

The tail end of the solar explosion lifted off the Sun quickly, and now the race was on. Orbiting satellites broadcast the image of the tail end of the CME snapping toward the front with incredible velocity. If it caught up with the rest of the giant, million-degree gas blob at the right time, it could have crushing consequences for whoever was there, namely Earth. Earth was in danger. There was no escaping this threat as it bore down on the helpless planet.

Every country went on alert throughout the world, trying their best to move people out of harm's way, but it was a fruitless task. The damage path was too large. There was no way to move millions of people in less than two days. What if you could? Where would you put them? The sheer size of the task would overtax the limited supplies of every country, but they tried.

You could not see the blob from Earth yet, but it was there and coming. The Sun's glare masked it from sight, but death was coming.

The Alliance space station picked up the grainy, crackling video feed from the surface. The President of the Global Council declared a global emergency, activating the military of every government on Earth, not against each other for once, but against the roaring monster bearing down on them from space.

He spoke at length about the impending disaster and displayed computer animations of how the event would unfold. None of it sounded good or hopeful. Just another in the long list of disasters man must endure on this fragile, dying planet.

FORTY-SIX

HACKETT and his team had no idea about their fate. They concentrated on their mission and had their counter-proposal in hand when the Ineans came to collect them. The Ineans were not friendly towards Hackett and his team as they growled and hissed at them. The Ineans grabbed and shoved them slightly as they proceeded, just enough to raise the tension level a few notches. Once in the meeting chamber, the meeting promptly resumed. Hackett was becoming agitated at how they had been treated; despite this, he held back his displeasure for the time being. Besides, the more aggression he mustered up, the more his head hurt from fighting the venom of the spiders. He instead focused on Benson sitting beside him. It was working.

The Inean Ambassador brought the meeting underway and called upon Hackett to submit his motion. Hackett stood and acknowledged each of the members at the table. He suddenly winced at the pain in his head, which appeared without warning. It was gone as abruptly as it appeared, except for the faint crunching noise in his mind. He hesitated for a moment as he tried to block the noise. He glanced around the table at each face and finished by looking at Benson, who stared at him with wide, wild eyes. She was afraid he might lose control, and she was by his side. She also knew how violent he could become while under the influence of whatever it was. She took a chance and placed her hand on his. He cleared his throat and started with his counter-proposals.

"We had a chance... to review this document... that was prepared for us... I must say that... most of this is acceptable... but... there are four issues... at hand, we need to discuss." The pain in his head interfered with his ability to form complete sentences. He took his time and frequently paused. He looked around the room, making sure everyone was prepared. "The first item we need to... revise is the use of these... women... at this meeting... and pertaining to the final acceptance... of the agreement." The chamber quickly became unruly, and the Ambassador didn't like what Hackett was saying. However, for now, he was obligated to control the room and protect the delegates. Once the room quieted, Hackett looked at the Kosuan, and they saw Benson practically hugging his leg in fear. Hackett knew they were leaning his way.

The pain was beginning to subside. "Second, Ambassador, we are not... prepared to allow a technology... exchange... between our peoples that we foresee as destabilizing this region even further. It would also give you an unfair advantage in your existing battle with the Kosuan." The room erupted more violently this time as bottles and other projectiles flew toward the table from the crowd. Benson's head became a bull's eye and was hit by a bottle, as was the rest of Hackett's team. She actually saw stars floating around her head. The Kosuan also became targets, with many in the crowd yelling that the Alliance had sided with them.

One Inean jumped over the railing, grabbed Benson with one arm around her throat, and easily pulled her out of her chair. She tried to scream but managed only to gag as she grabbed Hackett around his waist, and he went down with her. Several guards rushed over and pulled the beast off them. Hackett landed on top of Benson and was slow to rise from the pain growing in his head.

Benson didn't need words to tell the Captain she was scared. Her facial expression said it all. She sat up once Hackett got off of her. Her hands shook as she adjusted her shirt and jacket.

Hackett knew she was scared and held her hands firmly for a few seconds. "I know," he said. "Just stay close. I don't like this either."

She nodded that she understood.

The Kosuan were very interested in the exchange between the two. The closest one could smell the attraction between them, and he mumbled something to his closest counterpart. The Ambassador ordered guards to surround the table and face the crowd to protect the delegates from further attacks. Hackett helped Benson to her feet, and they resumed their positions.

The Ambassador spoke. "I am sorry for that display, Captain. We will take steps to prevent any more outbreaks." Hackett nodded his approval and picked up his notes, which had been scattered about.

He took a deep breath and paused for a moment. "Third and fourth," he hesitated as the pain reappeared, more intense this time. He rubbed his forehead and slumped a bit before it was gone.

Everyone stared at him, especially the Inean Ambassador. There was a lot at stake here, and if he could force an impasse or, better yet, a war with the humans, he would be regarded as a hero. He knew the state of Earth and knew it wouldn't take much to finish destroying the planet. What man hadn't done on his own, their own star conspired against them in scorching the planet beyond hope.

Hackett gathered his thoughts and continued, but putting the words together was becoming increasingly difficult. "Third... and fourth,... we think it would be more beneficial... to our... mutual... cultures if we establish diplomatic ties... instead of colonies on each other's worlds at this time."

He paused momentarily as he spied a guard against the far wall with a small black box in his hand. He studied the guard for a moment until Benson tugged on his sleeve. "Captain?"

He looked down at her and winked, and then continued speaking. "This could be something... which could... be negotiated in the future after we have established a mutually agreed peace period."

Not many people yelled at that one. Besides, Hackett knew why the Ineans wanted to place their people on Earth. To him, it would provide a point of entry and exit for the slave traders, and that wasn't going to happen, not if he had any say in it. The slave trade problem was still out of control and only worsening.

Hackett sat back down and waited for the response he knew wouldn't be pleasant. The Ambassador looked over the notes his assistant had made, and they passed them among the rest of the Ineans at the table. The Ambassador stared at Hackett for a moment and knew he wasn't well. He then glanced at a security guard on the far side of the room holding a portable transmitter aimed at Hackett. Then he spoke. "Captain Hackett, we agree to wait to discuss the last two items until a future date. Regarding the first item, we are unsure why it is an issue. Also, on the second item, we are exchanging some of our technology with you to correct your planet's climate so your people can live there as well, Captain, so you are losing out by eliminating it." He sat down and looked at Hackett with a puzzled expression. Then Hackett realized why. Benson was so scared that she had her arm around him tightly, and she wasn't letting go.

Hackett turned and whispered in her ear. "Just have faith in Him, Lieutenant Commander. We will be fine." She released her grip slightly and allowed him to stand. She was confused by his use of Him. It was as if Cadet Harrison were speaking to her again.

"The floor recognizes Captain Hackett of Earth," the Ambassador said, anticipating his response. There were shouts and yells of hate from around the room, and Hackett knew he was only a few words away from being killed. Hackett heard them and ignored them as best he could, choosing his words carefully. The others cringed at the hatred spewing from the seats behind them. Morris reached into his pocket and had his hand on the communicator to muffle the voice of Ambassador Channing, yelling for them to get out of there.

Hackett had beads of sweat on his forehead that he wiped off with his sleeve. He closed his eyes, shook off the thoughts in his head, and talked. "Ambassador, on the first topic regarding our women, I should start off with an explanation of our beliefs so you can understand our position." The Ambassador nodded to proceed.

The Kosuan leaned forward with curiosity to hear what the Captain had to say. The Kosuan shared similar beliefs with humans, despite being an aggressive species. "Our culture has a strong moral and spiritual belief in the area of sexual contact within our species and outside our species. We believe in an afterlife for those who adhere to and live by the ancient doctrines and follow our God's will. An afterlife of hideous torment is in store for those who don't." He paused for everyone to digest what he said so far. "These beliefs are what have structured our society, at least in the past. As males in our society, we are bound to protect our women from forces that can harm them, and that includes what you want them for. That is why we object to that paragraph in the peace agreement. We do not approve of it, and we cannot sign this while it is present." He stood waiting for the Ambassador to respond.

The Ambassador stood up and looked at Hackett. Hackett thought he saw a glimmer of admiration. "Captain Hackett, would you die to protect her?" He pointed to Benson. She looked up at him, as did Morris and Larson.

Hackett remained focused on the Ambassador. "Yes!" The room was shocked. Shouts of "kill him" rang out around the room. Others yelled, "Kill him and feed us his bitch!" The room was ready to explode, and Morris looked at the Captain. Hackett shook his head "no" and looked back up. Because the Ineans regarded the female as a lesser part of any race, there was the possibility that they would carry out their threats. "There are several reasons for this, Ambassador. First are the moral implications I mentioned. Additionally, I am her Captain, and I am sworn to protect my crew, even if it means I have to die. Lastly," Hackett looked at the Kosuan and then at Benson. "Lastly, Ambassador, she is my mate, and I will also die to protect her for that reason." Hackett put his hand on her shoulder and waited. He noticed she was shaking, most likely from fear, because it was way too warm for it to be caused by her being cold.

He didn't have to wait long. The Kosuan ambassador stood up and spoke to the Inean Ambassador. "These people are much like us, Ambassador. We will also die to protect our females. These humans are honorable. I vote to remove the clause and to remove the weapons exchange!"

The Angowains stood up and said they sided with the Ineans on that subject but wanted the weapons exchange abolished. "I don't understand this morality thing of theirs, so take their women, but get rid of the technology swap. From what we have seen of their corrupt society with its bizarre and warped values, I don't see what the Captain says to be true. They contradict themselves every time they open their mouths. They treat their women like trash. They have gangs that prowl their cities raping and torturing. The men of their society make it a point to film these acts and sell them to the highest bidder for profit. They've burned their churches and ignore this God he claims they have. They penalize their public for being 'indecent.' Still, if there's a doknarius to be made, then the rules don't apply. Theirs is a culture in chaos. Their culture is a virus that is spreading in our galaxy and must be contained now!"

Several heated arguments broke out among the delegates as they bickered across the table from all directions, and the yelling kept getting louder. The Inean Ambassador was banging his gavel in an attempt to restore order in the room. Finally, he looked over to a guard who began firing his laser rifle over everyone's heads. The delegates took their seats, but the arguing and hatred between each other and the spectators continued.

More guards were called in to control the room. Hackett remained standing and asked to address the table again. The Inean Ambassador was reluctant to do so, yet he yielded the floor to Hackett.

"On the technology exchange, the technology that we would receive is already in development by our people and would only cut months off of acquiring it on our own. The technology we provide would significantly reduce your development time by years and decades, and cause a shift in the balance of power in this region. Therefore, the Alliance does not take sides in other races' conflicts and cannot provide the technology requested. We can assist you in many areas, but from a military standpoint, we cannot."

The room erupted in fights, and several Ineans pushed forward, crushing Hackett and his people against the table. The guards had difficulty breaking up the pile, as the Kosuan came to Benson's and Larson's aid, pulling them from the pile while several Ineans grabbed them and pulled them in the opposite direction. It became a tug-of-war, and the women became the rope between the Ineans and Kosuan. The women yelped in pain as their bodies stretched to the limits from the huge alien men trying to win them. Finally, the Kosuan won, and everyone tumbled to the floor. Several Ineans screamed that they be turned over for execution. The Kosuan protected them until Hackett and Morris could crawl from under the pile.

Hackett was shaken but unharmed. Morris was injured. His right arm dangled from its socket like it was either broken or dislocated. Larson went to him as soon as order was restored, pulled a medical scanner from her bag, and checked him out. Hackett went to Benson and helped her back to her seat. He thanked the Kosuan for doing the honorable thing, and the Kosuan growled his pleasure back at the Captain. The Kosuan dwarfed the Captain by a foot. The Kosuan also knew the size difference was an illusion and didn't want to fight this human.

The Ambassador ordered the guards to push the crowd back and control the room. This took several minutes, and a few more objects flew in their direction. Larson checked on Morris and found that his shoulder was dislocated; she attempted to pop it back into place. She succeeded, and he yelped in pain. Using his jacket, she made a makeshift sling, placed his arm carefully into it, and tied it behind his neck. She gave him a shot to kill the pain, and he was all set.

The guards turned the tables upright and found the chairs. Hackett took several more minutes to gather his notes and thoughts before continuing. The rest of the delegates looked around the room at the mess created by the riot and collected their thoughts as well.

The Ambassador eventually stood to speak, and the room hushed. "Fellow Ineans, Kosuan, Angowains, humans, and honored guests, we seem to have an impasse. We will not ratify this agreement until the humans give us the women and the technology we seek." The Inean members of the crowd shouted and cheered their leader's speech.

The Kosuan ambassador stood up and didn't wait for permission to speak. "The Kosuan government will not allow the humans to give the technology to the Inean military. This will cause a war between the Alliance and our people." He abruptly sat, and the Angowain leader shot out of his chair in response. Hackett could sense that this was unraveling and not in their favor. He leaned in on Morris, who was still in pain, for any ideas. Morris thought for a moment and whispered to the Captain.

The Angowain got his permission to speak.

"Fellow members and guests, the Angowain highest council will not allow the humans to provide arms as well, and we feel they should check this morality of theirs and do what is right to preserve peace in this quadrant." He shot Hackett a look of disgust and spat at him as he sat back down.

Hackett looked over some notes and stood up. The Ambassador gave him permission to speak. Hackett nodded, "To put the Angowains and Kosuan at ease, as far as I am concerned, there will be no weapons exchange, and no women will be exchanged either. As far as my Angowain counterpart is concerned," Hackett glared at him, "while many in our culture have fallen away, I have checked my morals and spiritual beliefs, and they stand as they always have."

The Angowain stood up and turned to Hackett. "That is unacceptable. You bring war upon your people with those words! Millions will die!" He yelled. "And! Your planet is dying. You mean to tell me you would hold your women from them and let your planet die?"

Hackett took it all in. "If war breaks out between Inea and Earth, *they* will lose. *'They'* can not afford another war. *Their* society can't absorb the huge expense of fighting the Kosuan and us. It would be suicide for them. As for the condition of Earth, like I said earlier, we are on the threshold of solving those problems on our own. We would hope the Ineans would be interested in establishing peace and negotiating on terms we can both live with. My proposal stands. Eliminate those options from the agreement, and we could provide other items, such as medical training, food, and financial assistance for the poor. We have a wide range of options that can help the *'Inean people.'* That is what we are prepared to provide." Hackett looked around the table at each face, including his own, then sat down and folded his arms, which was a sign that he was done talking.

"You are crazy, Captain! What was your government thinking when they sent you? There will be war! And the blood of millions will be on your hands!" the Angowain yelled.

"Bold words from a race that looks for others to protect them," Hackett said, pointing to the Ineans. "You're awfully eager to get them into a fight with us. Why is that, Ambassador?"

The Angowain sat back down and conversed with his counterparts, who were yelling at him to stop.

The Inean Ambassador stood and called for a recess until the next day. The delegates were free to go to their rooms and prepare for dinner in their honor. The Inean women guided them to their rooms and cursed them the entire way. One of them spat on Benson while the other Inean woman shoved Larson against the wall. Hackett and Morris intervened and kept them separated the rest of the way. However, the verbal assault continued.

FORTY-SEVEN

COMMANDER FOLEY STOOD beside Admiral Griffin and President Wakefield as they watched the space station's officers study the incoming plasma flare, which had blown off the Sun. The flare was heading directly toward Earth and would arrive in less than 12 hours. The plasma cloud was so large that it stretched from the orbit of Mercury past the orbit of Venus. It was more than a cloud. It was a million-degree chunk of the Sun that was heading their way. It was more than ionized particles. It had mass. It could wreak havoc on Earth and its inhabitants. It was a fiery blob of death heading their way.

Red warning lights flashed throughout the station while Foley's people prepared to move behind the Earth for protection. The million-degree plasma would vaporize the station in no time at all if it were exposed to it. Hiding behind the Earth would provide enough protection, at least the Alliance officers hoped.

However, Foley and Griffin had another problem. The scientists on the solar observatory had not been heard from for many hours. Foley had dispatched the battleship *Nordstrom* when the flare blew off the Sun. Still, the ship had yet to get near the observatory, with the radiation levels so high. The only hope was that the scientists made it to the escape pod in time.

The bridge of the *Nordstrom* was much larger than the *Saratoga*'s. The *Nordstrom* was an actual battleship designed to take the heat and the abuses of flying through debris and many other objects. Still, they could not take the radiation levels of the plasma cloud. They watched from several million miles away for their chance to swoop in and rescue the scientists, but the wait was painfully long.

Captain Lewis hovered over his communications officer on the bridge. At the same time, he called out for the observatory to respond, but they didn't. They couldn't.

"SOBS-two-alpha, please respond on frequency one-zero-niner," the officer kept repeating. At the same time, he and his Captain watched the bar graphs on the monitor, watching for any sign of a reply.

"Keep trying. As soon as we can confirm someone's alive in there, we can plan to go in, but I'm not going to risk this ship until then," Lewis said for all to hear on the bridge.

The communications officer just nodded as he repeated his message and tried a different frequency.

"Tactical. Do you have a fix on the observatory yet?" Lewis asked as he turned and headed for that officer's console.

"No, not yet, sir. It isn't where it is supposed to be. They said something about firing thrusters, but I would only be guessing if I knew what direction they went in," replied the officer without looking up.

"Keep looking, people, it's out there somewhere, and we can't help them if we can't find them." Lewis paced for a few seconds, walked up to the forward viewer, and stared at the immense blob of solar plasma filling the wall-sized view screen, racing by his ship several million miles away. Luckily for him, the viewer had filtered the image, as it would have been blindingly bright if not. Even so, he sensed he could feel the heat of it through the glass. He stepped away from it out of respect for what the plasma cloud could do.

"Sir! I found the station. It's 3.2 million miles directly below us, and it's drifting away. The plasma cloud seems to be dragging it along with it," The tactical officer piped up excitedly.

Lewis rushed back to view the findings. “What condition is it in?” he asked.

“I can’t tell. There is too much interference to make out much of anything clearly,” he replied.

"Comm. Focus your antenna on that area below us and try again," the Captain said as he watched the forward screen that was switched to the ventral cameras. All that was on the screen was the same fiery plasma blob flowing by. There was no sign of the solar observatory.

“Trying to raise them, sir. There’s still no reply.”

“Keep trying. Defense controls, raise shields. Helm, move us closer. Life support, go to maximum cooling.” Lewis spread his orders around the bridge.

The massive battleship descended toward the fiery blob.

Several long minutes passed before anyone said anything. "Captain, hull temperature is climbing rapidly. Radiation levels are also rising," Lewis's first officer called out from the ship's systems console next to the tactical station.

Lewis already knew it. The ship was beginning to skim the plasma cloud, and finally, they were engulfed.

“Captain, hull temp is in the yellow band and rapidly rising, sir,” the first officer responded with a slight nervousness filtering into his voice.

Lewis still did not respond.

"Captain! I'm picking up the station's distress beacon. It's on automatic. That is a good sign," Tactical stated.

Lewis turned to his sensors officer. “How much further?”

"Almost there, sir, another 20,000 miles."

“Can we latch onto the station and drag it out of here?” Lewis asked.

"Yes, but the heat will weaken the cables. It is almost 5,000 degrees out there and only going up," Commander Thomas Watkins, Lewis's first officer, said.

Lewis didn't need his first officer to tell him it was hot. The temperature on the bridge had increased noticeably over the past 10 minutes. Obviously, the ship's cooling system was not keeping up with the demand. "Very well then. Let's not waste any time in here," he said as he wiped the beads of sweat from his forehead.

The ship dropped in front of the station as the ventral cameras began to fail. They did get enough of a visual to tell that the station was melting. The fuel canisters had already blown off, as well as the backup oxygen cylinders. Most of the station was burned black, and the bulkheads showed signs of buckling.

"Mr. Watkins, lasso that station, and let's get out of here."

"Yes, sir," he said, and he went to work, targeting what he thought would be the strongest structure to grab. He finally pressed the launch button, and two long, carbon-fiber reinforced cables shot from the front of the battleship and tangled themselves around a support pole.

Lewis had his helmsman fire their engines, and the cables pulled tight. The engines groaned against the added weight that was almost double what they had been rated to pull.

The ship lifted away slowly, dragging the observatory with it through the extremely hot plasma cloud.

"Time to cloud boundary?" Lewis asked.

"One hour, ten minutes, sir," Watkins replied.

"How are our cables holding?" Lewis now turned to face Watkins.

"I'm surprised they are still holding, Captain. The heat of the plasma far exceeds their rating."

He had no sooner said it when the ship jolted. Now there was a flashing light at Watkins' terminal. "We just lost the first cable, Captain. The second can't be far behind."

Lewis pressed a button on his chair and switched the view to the forward camera. It showed the observatory spiraling behind them, much like a parachute that didn't deploy properly. He knew the drag on the second cable would snap it. He needed another plan and fast.

"Sir, I'm picking up life signs on that observatory," the sensors officer said as he looked up. "Looks like they are in the escape pod in the middle of the main hub."

"Sir, the second cable is losing its integrity."

It snapped, and Lewis and his crew could only watch as the observatory faded behind them. Back towards the fiery hell from which it was being pulled. That would be the least of their problems.

An alarm sounded. It was the proximity alarm. Something was coming close to the ship. Suddenly, there was a loud crack! More alarms sounded, and then an explosion.

The last cable hadn't snapped. A large pipe from the observatory had failed, but the forward cameras could not determine what had failed. The cable recoiled toward the ship once the tension had been removed and slammed the pipe into one of the reverse engines. Suddenly, the rescuers found themselves in a desperate situation.

FORTY-EIGHT

ONCE INSIDE THE ROOM, and as soon as the Ineans closed the door, Hackett contacted the *Saratoga*. The report could not have been worse. Several Inean battleships had closed in on the *Saratoga*. They surrounded it completely, just as they had done to the Kosuan and the Angowain ships. The pressure was on, and a battle was brewing that no one could win.

"And, Captain?" O'Toole hesitated.

"What is it, Commander?"

"Sir, Earth is warning about a serious CME brewing on the Sun. It has the potential to be the largest ever recorded. It could be a direct hit on Earth, depending on when it erupts. This one could be bad, Captain. They are already calling it a planet killer," O'Toole stated.

"I understand, Commander. What are my orders?"

"Sir, the Global Council has asked that you put the technology from the Ineans at the top of your list. We must have it at all costs," O'Toole exclaimed.

"This would change our tactics, Commander. Does Command have proof that it actually works? Because you know what they want in exchange."

"They claim it works, sir. That's the best they can give us besides emphasizing that at all costs, give them what they want," O'Toole said. "That was all we got from them before we lost contact with Earth."

"Understood, we'll have to change how we propose this. This isn't going to be easy, Commander, because we would be handing over Earth's women to them in exchange for a technology that I'm not convinced works," Hackett replied. This drew horrified looks from Benson, Larson, and Morris.

"Yes, sir. We know, and the Ambassador is at a loss for ideas right now."

"Fine, keep me posted hourly on how Earth fares, Commander. Hackett out." Hackett ended his communication with his ship and thought for a moment. He looked at the faces of his officers around him. They all heard the report O'Toole gave the Captain. Their faces told the story that they knew would someday come true. The human race was probably hours from being homeless in a very unfriendly universe. It seemed that every race they came across wanted them dead. Without Earth, it would be impossible for the species to survive.

Hackett asked his people for comments. He looked around and saw Benson sitting on the end of the bed. She had a full-blown black eye on top of the fading shiner she received from O'Toole during their boxing match. Her shirt was torn, and she appeared shaken by what had happened. Morris was still in pain. Larson was roughed up. She was holding her left elbow and flexing her arm while grimacing, and her hair was a wild mess.

Benson was the first to speak, albeit slowly, obviously upset over the news. "Sir, the Kosuan are on our side. With that said, that can change at any second. The Ineans know that the Kosuan are pivotal in this negotiation. If they can swing them to their side, then we are sunk. We need something to put them in our back pocket," she said with a grimace as she realized that her left pocket was torn, most likely by the tug-of-war that she was in the middle of. "The Angowains are useless. I wouldn't bother with them right now," she finished.

"Understood. From a military standpoint, the Angowains might not be a threat. Still, from a political standpoint, they have an enormous influence on the Ineans, and what our Angowain counterpart said was true, unfortunately," Hackett answered as he reflected back to their last visit to Earth. The headlines were not very flattering regarding human "progress." He then asked, "Any other ideas or thoughts?"

"What could we possibly give the Kosuan that would assure their loyalty?" Larson asked, and it was a good question. Hackett didn't know what to offer them as he looked at the faces surrounding him.

"Sir, I know what we can offer them. We would need to contact our government for approval." Benson said quietly, still not accustomed to being the only one with answers.

"What's on your mind, Miss Benson?" Hackett asked. "Bear in mind that we can't contact Earth right now."

"We have had several skirmishes with them over the past few years over a right-of-way to a planet we hold in their territory called Maxlar-Four. We have a mining facility there, but it is so remote, and we have found everything we need closer to... home. Why don't we give it to them? They can use it, and we don't need it."

She looked at her tablet and opened a file. She sat back down and read her notes. "Yes, we can do this. We just need Command to approve it."

"Thank you, Miss Benson," he said, choosing his words carefully while making eye contact with her. He continued, "Contact Channing and have him authorize it. Right now, he's the highest-ranking political figure at our disposal. I'll find a way to get the Kosuan alone."

She nodded and contacted the ship. While waiting for the Ambassador, she walked to the glass wall and looked upon the alien city. She could feel the heat of the day through the glass. She turned away when Channing spoke through her wrist transceiver. Hackett walked toward the door, thinking about how she may have saved them again. He was also becoming frustrated that his only solution to getting the technology was to hand her over as a slave to the

Inean Ambassador. He also needed a solution for this. He opened the door and spoke with the woman standing outside. He requested a conversation with the Kosuan who rescued his mate. She nodded and left. He re-entered the room, sat on the end of the bed, and looked at Benson. "Any luck?"

"He will make the call. He said it would be tough to persuade our people to give it up, but said there was a way."

"He better make the call," Hackett said while shaking his head. "I think the Kosuan will be here shortly. I'm going to offer it to him, pending our government's approval."

They all agreed and went back to scribbling more notes. After half an hour, the Inean woman returned with the Kosuan, and they entered the room. Hackett excused her, but she wouldn't leave. The Kosuan growled in her face, and she turned up her bony nose, hissed at him, and backed out of the room.

“You wanted to speak, Captain Hackett?” the Kosuan growled.

"Yes, first, I wanted to thank you for being an honorable Kosuan in saving our women from them."

"It was a pleasure, Captain. Is that all?" he growled, giving Benson an approving look.

"No, it isn't. The Ineans are going to try to sway you to their side against us. I am prepared to offer you a deal for your allegiance in this matter. You know what we want from them and what they want from us."

“What is your offer, Captain?” he was growing impatient.

"Maxlar-Four. You agree to side with us regarding the weapons exchange and the women. We will give you Maxlar-Four. It's that simple."

“You can do this?” he growled.

"Yes, I am waiting for approval, which is just a formality. If you help us, we will help you."

“I will have to discuss it with my people as well. You will know our answer tomorrow.” He turned and walked out the door.

Hackett went back to the others and sat on the floor. "We may need a backup plan. Keep thinking, people."

Benson went to say something and chose not to, for now. She

just looked at him, struggling to sort her thoughts. What Hackett didn't know was that Benson had a vision of these events. She was about to tell him what she had been shown. She didn't know if, by revealing to them that the events could be altered, or if they should. She knew Earth would survive, barely, and these CMEs would continue to worsen. She also realized the attraction she had for him. However, he was too preoccupied with ensuring this mission succeeded to notice her at the moment. She knew he felt the same way. He couldn't show it, especially with Morris lurking. He had taken a considerable risk earlier by publicly stating she was his mate. It was staged for the Kosuan's benefit. Still, it could be misconstrued. He would have to answer for that when the admiral read his report if they made it back. Or was it just a tactic to gain the trust of the Kosuan? She knew what it was, and she wondered if Morris had been brought up to speed.

Larson removed the medical scanner from her backpack and walked over to the Captain. She pressed a few buttons, and the scanner displayed Hackett's vital signs.

“Is that necessary, Lieutenant?” Hackett quipped.

"Sir, your heart rate is up, your BP is through the roof, and your body temp is 101 degrees right now," she said as he grabbed the scanner out of her hand to review it himself.

“I'm fine!” he said harshly, gritting his teeth.

“No! You're not. I am aware of the situation, Captain. What did the doctor give you yesterday to counteract the effects of the spiders?” Larson asked.

“We don't have time for this, Lieutenant!” Hackett yelled.

"Lieutenant, he needs this right here," Morris said as he fumbled around the medical bag. "Give him five cc's of this now and ten more before dinner."

“Yes, Commander.”

"Sorry, Captain, but we need you a hundred percent now. Billions of people need you at your best, and you know damn well the Ineans are going to pull something if they haven't already," Morris added.

"Fine! Give me the damn shot so we can move on," Hackett said as his face turned red from his anger. He was angry because he was not in complete control for the first time in his life. He was angry for being vulnerable in front of his crew. He needed to be solid and lead without question. However, his mental state was in question by everyone involved at all levels.

Benson was awfully quiet as she watched the exchange, and she wondered how bad his condition was. Her expression said it all as she saw the fire in his eyes. She was afraid of him. Not entirely because he could hurt her physically, but emotionally. Vivid memories of Harrison's death had come back. They had been buried for a long time until now. Now her attraction to the less-than-mentally-stable Hackett brought back the painful memories of losing her husband-to-be. She didn't want to go down this path again, but couldn't stop. Something was driving her, pushing her towards him. She couldn't pull back.

At the designated time, the Inean guards came to collect Hackett and his team for dinner. Hackett let Larson and Morris go ahead. He wanted to speak with Benson in private for a moment.

Once Morris and Larson were gone, Hackett turned to Benson and looked at her. "I just wanted to say that you are doing a great job and that you are holding up well, considering the circumstances." He put his hands on her shoulders and stared into her eyes. "And I still don't believe what you told me earlier." He pulled back and inspected her black eye. She didn't mind his touch. She longed for it, even though she knew it was impossible right now. He ran his fingers through her hair. "Just how well do you know these Kosuan?" he asked.

"I have gone on several missions while on the *Challenger* to several of their planets. I got to know their ways and customs well, Captain," she said, ignoring his first statement completely. She closed her eyes briefly as he continued stroking her hair. "They are an interesting race. I kind of like them in a way," she continued. "They are blunt, they don't hold anything back, and you'll know exactly where you stand with them. There is no guessing with the Kosuan."

"Anything about this dinner I should know about to gain their trust and their votes tomorrow?" Hackett asked as he pulled away slightly.

She thought for a moment. "Plenty, don't use politics. Follow my lead and take over for me when I put my head down. You'll know what to do," she said. "And make sure the Ineans stay away," she finished speaking.

"Okay, the first sign of trouble, and I'll step in," he said.

He patted her on the shoulder and said it was time to go.

Upon entering, Hackett noticed there were many thousands more people present. He was amazed they could all fit. The Ineans seated Hackett and Benson next to Morris and Larson, who sat on the right side beside the Kosuan. Hackett thought that was a tactical mistake on the Ineans' part. They switched seats to put Benson close to the Kosuan. The dinner trays came by, and there was little that looked appetizing.

Nevertheless, they sampled small amounts of each dish to be respectful, except for Hackett, who barely ate. The smell of the Inean food turned his stomach. There was no way he could eat it, much to the irritation of the head cook, who watched the guests from a side entrance to the kitchen. The dinner lasted several hours, and there were discussions about how to maintain peace. Meanwhile, several fights broke out among members of the crowd, prompting guards to be posted around the room to protect the delegates. Morris had struck up a conversation with the Inean Ambassador about how they could rectify their differences. As he suspected, the Inean was of little help. They wanted what they wanted, and that was it.

The Inean Ambassador was growing more irritated with Hackett's fickle eating habits. His food was poisoned, and he wouldn't eat it. Hackett didn't know about the poison, he just wasn't hungry, and the smell of the Inean food reminded him of a comedian saying something about eating the butt of a skunk, which is exactly what this food reminded him of, road killed-skunk. Moldy, rotten meat was what he kept thinking now. He glanced at the others, who gagged as politely as possible when sampling the food. It couldn't be food, he thought. It must have been something the cook found rotting in the sewer and decided to feed it to them.

Benson bit down on a piece of meat on a stick, grimaced, and spit it out like she had accidentally put something rotten in her mouth. He placed his hand on hers to get her attention and shook his head no. She pushed the plate away and guzzled a whole bottle of ale to kill the taste.

Morris and Larson did the same. The food was awful, rotten, and not meant to be consumed by anyone other than an Inean. No wonder their breath smelled so bad, Morris now realized.

Benson, on the other hand, started a conversation with the Kosuan and switched seats with him so she had a Kosuan on either side of her. Hackett was amused by the sight. She looked like a child dwarfed by two large adults. Morris and Larson had their heads together, discussing something about the Ineans. Hackett thought they were talking about getting the Inean drunk, but the room was noisy, and they were speaking so softly that no one else could hear. Hackett felt comfortable that his officers knew what they were doing.

The server came around with Kosuan ale and served them all. Benson and her new friend each took two from the tray. They chugged down the first one, which took her breath away for a second as she choked on the intense alcohol. The Kosuan laughed and slapped her on the back, which got Hackett's attention. She held her hand up to the others to show that she was okay, yet the handprint would last a while. The Kosuan handed her another. Kosuan ale was a cross between a hard liqueur and beer. To the unsuspecting, which Benson was not, the ale hits hard, especially when served cold, and there is no real food in the stomach to soak it up. The Kosuan always served it at room temperature, which made the ale go down much smoother.

Hackett watched as Benson got chummy with the Kosuan. He noticed that she knew an awful lot about them and had no problem matching them bottle for bottle. To Hackett's advantage, he was thankful she knew so much. She had the Kosuan laughing, which everyone in the room was aware of. Kosuan had a laugh that bellowed through the room. Hackett figured a laughing Kosuan was better than a growling one, so he let her indulge for a while.

However, Benson accepted the third drink and downed it as fast as the Kosuan did. They smashed the bottles together in the air, which sent glass flying everywhere. She said something in the primary Kosu dialect, which drew the Inean's attention to their corner. She was quickly getting drunk. However, she decided to try another. The Kosuan accepted her challenge and growled at the server to bring more ale. She drank the fourth and followed it with a fifth and a sixth. She was drinking too fast, and she was swaying slightly. Hackett saw her and laughed. He got up, approached her and the Kosuan, and slapped them both on the back. He obviously slapped the Kosuan harder. The Kosuan was also starting to get drunk. He turned to the Captain and offered him a drink. Hackett accepted and pulled up a chair between them. Benson put her head on the Captain's shoulder and threw her arms around him while he drank with the Kosuan.

The Captain and the Kosuan guzzled several drinks each. Larson and Morris got involved, and it turned into a drinking party.

The Ineans were becoming increasingly agitated by the behavior of the humans and Kosuan, and they sensed that any hope of swaying Kosuan was in trouble. The Angowains, who frequently sided with the Ineans, did so again in their dislike of the other species.

Benson downed a couple more drinks with them and passed out. Hackett wasn't far behind. The first Kosuan passed out and dropped onto the floor, and Hackett was trying to keep up with another and couldn't. He turned his glass on its side to indicate that he was done. Morris and Larson chugged away with the remaining Kosuan until it was finally interrupted by the Ineans and Angowains.

The Ineans grabbed a Kosuan who had stood up and forced him back into his seat. The Inean leader swore at them and said it would weigh heavily on their decisions the next day. The Angowains spat at the humans and cursed them. The Kosuan that remained conscious jumped up and began pushing the Ineans closest to them, swearing back at the Ineans, saying they were going to lose the war because they were so uptight (to put it in human terms). The exchange became heated, and several people in the room began to brawl.

Morris decided it was time to get out of there while they had the chance. He grabbed Benson and helped her out of the room and into the elevator. Larson helped the Captain, who could still walk, but not very well. They dragged them to the elevators and eventually into the room. Morris set Benson on the bed, and she fell over unconscious, and Larson dropped Hackett into the chair across from the bed.

There was a knock on the door. Morris opened it slowly with his laser pistol in hand. On the other side of the door was a Kosuan woman. In her hands were a dozen bottles of warm ale. She passed them to Larson, who brought the bottles into the room. She set them on a table by the large windows while the Kosuan woman regarded Morris and walked away. Larson made eye movements to the ale.

"Grab some and bring them to our room," Morris stated.

She did just that, and Morris locked the door behind them. They retired to an adjacent room for the night.

Hackett had too many drinks on top of the medication Larson shot him with, and knew he would pay for this in the morning. He stumbled to the bed and nearly fell on Benson. Benson was utterly gone. He tried to wake her, but she was so drunk it was impossible now. He pulled the blankets down and rolled her into bed. All he could do was pull the blankets back over her before falling again. He got back up and stood there for a minute, gazing at her. Every fiber of his being wanted to join her, yet he knew he couldn't. He ran his hand over her hair and kissed her on the forehead. He stripped to his underwear, grabbed a blanket, and fumbled for the chair, collapsing into it and immediately falling asleep.

In the next room, Morris swayed to the lavatory to clean up and returned in his underwear. He tossed the towel to Larson, who had a heavy head. She strolled in and took a steamy, hot shower. She emerged wrapped in the towel and sat beside Morris, sitting on the end of the bed, talking to O'Toole on the *Saratoga* with an open ale in his hand. Larson opened one, and they clinked bottles.

So far, the Ineans hadn't started anything beyond boxing the ship in earlier. O'Toole had rotated the shifts and kept everyone on alert in case the status quo changed. He reported that the matrix was wearing down, and they should break orbit in 24 hours to have a chance at getting home. He also noted that there was still no news regarding Earth. Morris reported the evening's events to O'Toole, who would then report them to Channing in the morning. He signed off and looked at Larson.

Morris was getting attached to her now. It took close contact with her to realize he was interested in her. That was a luxury he hadn't had previously. She looked at him and then at the bed. Should he join her? She got in bed, and once she was covered, she removed her towel and tossed it to him. Was that a hint? Morris wasn't sure. He knew the Captain and Benson wouldn't be doing anything inappropriate tonight. Should he?

He decided to join her. Wrong move. She told him not yet, but did allow him to lie on the outside of the blankets. He lay there, and they talked.

“I hate to keep bringing this up,” Larson began. “What are your thoughts on the captain and Benson?” Larson wondered if she should take the plunge with Morris.

"I don't know. They seem to like each other, and then, just when I think they are messing around, the Captain pulls back, or she pulls back. I don't get it," Morris replied.

“Get what?” Larson asked.

“You know, how a person can turn it on and off just like that,” Morris snapped his fingers.

"I know. He is the Captain, and I would think he would need that control," she said.

Morris just lay back and thought. *Yes, a Captain does need that sort of control. Am I cut out for the Captain's chair after all?* He was ready, just now, to put his career on the line to sleep with Larson. She was now in control. Not him, and that bothered Morris. Here he was riding the Captain for Benson, and he was having the same problem with Larson.

“Did you notice the friction between them on the bridge before we came down?” Morris asked.

“No, what happened?” Larson replied.

“I’m not sure, maybe nothing. Oh, forget it for now,” he huffed, turning to face her.

“Do you think we’ll get out of here alive?” she asked him.

"Yes, I do. The Captain has a good plan, and between you and me, he has a few more tricks up his sleeve," Morris responded. He was still lying on the bed, staring at Larson.

“You can join me.” Larson looked at him and pushed the blankets open. He looked at her and got up to turn the light off. He slid into bed with her. He knew he was violating regulations. Who would know?

Several floors below and near the elevators, the Kosuan delegates met in their spacious room. Most of the Kosuan had arrived from the dinner carrying bottles of ale. They sat around the table and began to drink more.

The one Benson tangled with was the first to speak in his naturally rough voice. "These humans know what it's like to have some fun. That woman, the Captain's mate, drank with me tonight. She did well for a puny little runt." They all laughed because they had seen Morris help her up. "These Ineans have no soul. We should just kill them off and do the galaxy a favor," he said as everyone in the room cheered. He chugged another ale.

The others egged him on. Another one spoke. This time it was the Ambassador. "I have contacted our people, and they left it up to me to make the decision tomorrow. Do we want to deal with the humans or the Ineans?" Three of the five there said 'humans,' and the two who didn't attend the dinner said 'Ineans.'

The Ambassador asked the two dissenters why they chose the Ineans. "Why did you pick them?" he asked. The others growled at them, hoping to pick a fight.

"We don't trust the humans. They think they can control us," one of them said. He grabbed an ale and guzzled it.

The other dissenter grew angry and drew his laser weapon from his holster. "These human females, like we saw tonight, are not, as the Captain says, moral. We should let the Ineans do as they want. Then we can get back to winning this war. Besides Bemock, she would have done anything for you."

Bemock is the Kosuan Benson drank with. He was angry at the comments and smashed an empty bottle over Mebihg's head. "Human females are too fragile. I would end up killing her. I would enjoy the company of a Kosuan woman. These humans are not our enemy. We have a chance to help them, and in return, we can get something we desperately need. I say we side with them and not the Ineans."

The Kosuan ambassador took it all in. Then he made up his mind. "I will side with the humans. As we saw today, they are honorable and share many of the same values. These Ineans do not. Besides, it is not the time for war with them. The human was right when he said it would be a disaster for the Ineans or us to get in another war until we are done fighting this one." He looked around the room and waited for someone to challenge him. No one did, so he held his bottle towards the middle of the circle of males. The others did the same, and all the bottles met in the air and clinked as they growled. The ale began to flow heavily now.

Several Kosuan females entered the room from the next room. They began to drink and engage in rather bizarre mating with the males. This went on for several hours.

Below, the Angowain counsel was meeting with the Ineans to discuss the possibility of the Kosuan and humans joining forces. The Angowains became outraged that this could happen, and a loud argument ensued. The Inean Ambassador tried to calm his Angowain counterpart, but it was to no avail. The Inean called in his military adviser to discuss a few ideas.

They all sat around the table, and the Inean Ambassador asked his general of the Fleet if he saw any weakness in the human's ship.

"Yes, plenty, the ship in orbit, we detected power problems with their ship. Their hull is all cracked and broken. I don't know how they managed to get this far! We could destroy it easily," the adviser said proudly.

The Ambassador wasn't done. "How about the Kosuan ships?" he asked.

"Those ships are in better shape and would be a formidable battle." The adviser influenced the Ambassador's decision.

"What do you propose?" the Ambassador asked.

"We could ambush them and destroy them before they had a chance to figure out what happened."

"So in the morning, we sign a peace agreement with them and give them the technology to save their planet, and then in the afternoon, we destroy them. Why should we bother?" the Ambassador asked.

"We could make it look like the Kosuan did it. It would be easy to do. We have the technology to make the blast marks resemble those of Kosuan lasers. We can set a trap near their space and make it appear as if they did it. We can also adjust our quantum spectrum to resemble Kosuan. That's how we won the battle of Goos'Ganna last month. We fooled them, and they went for it," the general said. "The humans would suspect the Kosuan, which could lead to a war between them."

The Angowain smiled at this. "So you force your two enemies into a confrontation and then pick them apart while they go in circles. I like it."

The Inean Ambassador gave a noticeably disturbed look toward his Angowain counterpart. The only reason the Ineans tolerated them was because of their highly proficient mining and engineering skills. The Ineans paid handsomely for the raw minerals which the Angowains provided. It was a job the Ineans could not do. It was only a matter of time before the Angowains found themselves enslaved and working for scraps of food. The sentiment had been growing for years in the Inean secret counsel, of which the Ambassador was a select member.

"These humans have disgusting habits. We must deal with them now and be done with them." The Ambassador walked across the room to a large map of the quadrant on the wall and pointed to it. "There's a nebula there. Make it happen," the Ambassador said, and his general got up, nodded to the group, and backed out of the room.

The Angowain was finally pleased with the outcome and looked forward to a lasting relationship with the Ineans. The Inean waved him off and excused himself as well from the room.

Unfortunately for the Angowains, the Ambassador caught up with his general and pulled him aside. He leaned close to his ear and whispered. "Make sure our friends from Angowa need to explain how an Earth ship was destroyed by one of theirs while on a peace mission. Our friend was right about dividing our enemies." The two leaders laughed loudly. "I have a different plan for our Kosuan adversaries. I will fill you in later."

The general growled in agreement and walked away.

The party still raged below in the main hall, but the Inean diplomats were not present. They had left in disgust. Brawls broke out every few minutes, and the security people could no longer contain them. Troops entered the room and began firing to break up the crowd. It took many shots, and eventually, the room was cleared to the square outside. Many people started attacking the Alliance transport parked in the courtyard. They couldn't inflict much damage with stones and beer bottles.

The Angowains remained and tried to work the crowd for anything they could get, being the scavengers they were. Much of their culture was based on bartering and stealing from whoever they could. This funded the false sense of protection received from the Ineans, as the Angowains didn't have a substantial military to defend themselves.

. . .

Morris and Larson continued to roll around in the bed. They gave in to their emotions and desires. Morris knew he couldn't go after the Captain any longer for what he may be doing. They continued for several hours, and when they were satisfied, they both lay on their backs, staring at the ceiling.

Morris wondered if they would be able to work together after this. They shared adjacent stations on the bridge, and he would be leaving to command his own ship in a month. How would this complicate that? Or would Alliance Command find out somehow? He was concerned and regretted what they had done, despite the enjoyment it had brought. What was Larson thinking right now?

He slid out of bed, went to the bathroom to splash water on his face, and returned several minutes later. Larson was still lying there, staring at the ceiling. "What's the matter?" He asked.

"Nothing, just thinking. I'm just trying to come up with some ideas for the Captain tomorrow in case the Kosuan pulls something."

“Do you regret what we just did?” he asked.

“Do you?” she shot back.

“No, I don’t,” he lied.

“Then I don’t either. I thought it was fabulous, Commander.”

"I'm going to sleep now." He grabbed a pillow and blanket and curled up in the chair. After several minutes, he returned to the bed. "May I sleep here?" He asked.

“Why? Is the chair not comfortable?” she asked.

“No, it isn’t.”

She looked at him and told him it was all right. He slid into bed, and they slept back to back.

FORTY-NINE

BENSON WAS BACK ON EARTH. She was much younger, more like 18, just before entering the academy. She remembered this day. It was the day the whole town got together to send her off. She glanced out the open window at the picnic put together on the church lawn for her. The day was pleasant. It was cool for mid-May. Everything was in bloom and colorful.

Her mother, the minister, stood before the congregation and read an excerpt from 2nd Peter. "The day of the Lord will come like a thief. The heavens will disappear with a roar; the elements will be destroyed by fire, and the Earth and everything in it will be destroyed by fire." This passage kept playing over and over in her mind.

In her drunken mind, she thought, *This can't be it! What of all the other visions I have had? Could what O'Toole said be happening now?*

She visualized the fireball from the Sun engulfing Earth. She saw her family's farm go up in flames, then her hometown. Then she saw cities burning. She saw people running from burning buildings only to be burned up instantly by the fire falling from the sky.

She was now high above the Earth, watching as the whole

planet glowed from the fires raging. Everything burned. Even the oceans were ablaze.

No response, no answers, just "destroyed by fire" playing in her mind. She awoke suddenly. It was still dark. She saw Hackett sleeping in the chair near the bed. All was quiet here for now.

She lay back and watched the room float around her. She cursed herself for drinking so much. The hangover from Kosuan Ale would be her penalty in the morning. She fell back to sleep. "The Earth and everything in it will be destroyed by fire."

Her flashback continued to the actual party. She is pulled aside by her father.

"Tamora, do me a favor," he said.

"What's that, Dad?"

"Be careful. This space fleet is very dangerous work, and I will worry about you every day."

"Oh, Dad, I will be fine."

"Just be careful. That's all." He hugged her as her friends dragged her away. Her friends turned into Ineans that forcibly dragged her away. Her father turned into Hackett as he struggled to reach her.

She woke again, and the morning light was starting to shine between the large buildings. With each move she made, the room floated about. She grunted and closed her eyes. Soon she was asleep again.

FIFTY

WATKINS WALKED into the reverse engine room at the front of the *Nordstrom* just as the fire control team put out the blaze. He studied the mess: one complete engine was blown apart. Luckily, they were not quantum drives like the *Saratoga*. Otherwise, he wouldn't be here to see the mess. None of them would be.

He walked up to his head engineer, who stood staring at the mess himself. "Mr. Adams," he said.

The engineer turned towards him. "What a freaking wreck. We got lucky."

"Can it be fixed?" Watkins asked seriously. "We need to grab the observatory and get out of here as soon as possible."

"We can do that with two engines left. All we have to do is shut off the fuel supply to the damaged engine, which should take about half an hour at the most."

"Get on it. The Captain wants to use the thrusters to grab the observatory before it falls too far away into the fiery abyss."

"Got it. By the time you grab the station, we'll be done here," Adams replied.

"Get on it then. I'll tell the Captain," Watkins said, leaving the engine room.

Once on the bridge, he conferred with Captain Lewis. They turned the ship and traveled towards the station again. This time, he used the last three cables the ship had left.

He launched the first cable, which tangled itself around a support beam, but Watkins wouldn't be fooled this time. He would target the next one around a more solid object. He fired. A small rocket sped away from the *Nordstrom* with the cable attached. It stretched tight and wrapped around a sturdy column much like the first, and the cable hooked around itself as the small rocket burned up.

Now, for the third and last cable, he hesitated and leaned towards his Captain. "Sir, I want to hold back on the third cable until the last second. We may need to, just in case."

Lewis looked up, nodded his approval, and returned to talking with his head engineer. After a moment, he turned to Watkins, "Main engines are a go, Commander. When you're ready, let's get out of here."

"Yes, sir. Helm, fire thrusters to take up the slack in the cables and slowly increase speed," Watkins said as he watched the tension gauge on his panel.

"Aye, sir, one-half thrusters," She replied, and the ship began to move again. After a few seconds, the ship lurched slightly as the cables tightened.

"Increase speed slowly now and get us out of here," Watkins said as he continued to monitor the cables tethering the observatory to the *Nordstrom*.

The ship moved outward and towards open space, which was still several hundred thousand miles away.

Watkins watched the gauge on the first cable rise faster than the second. It was beginning to redline. "Helm, back off our speed slightly!"

She did, but it was too late. The cable snapped and rebounded toward the *Nordstrom*. This time, Watkins was ready. He jettisoned the entire cable mount so it didn't inflict any damage when it struck the ship, but he didn't wait to make sure. He watched the other cable's gauge begin to spike upward because it carried the entire load. He dialed up his target and fired the third cable. It missed. It got tangled in the broken cable. "Son of a bitch!" he swore, which got Lewis' attention. He went back while Watkins reeled in his cable. "Cable control, clean up the mess I just pulled back in, and rearm it quickly," he said. "Helm, keep backing off our speed until the tension improves."

"Aye, sir," she replied, and she began to slow the ship nearly to a stop. It bought Watkins some time.

He had a new rocket on his cable. The old one had drifted past the ship by now and was out of the way. He wiped the sweat from his face. He aimed and fired once again. It headed outward, away from the ship, and spun itself around the lower power transfer tower. Although not the strongest structure, it would have to do. "Okay, we're hooked on. Let's go!"

The helmsman wasted no time firing the thrusters and heading outward again. "Time to exit, 23 minutes, give or take."

Watkins watched his gauges again. They continued to rise faster than the time they had. "Helm, slow us down a bit."

She did.

"Keep going. Keep going," he said as his gauges continued to rise despite what she did to reduce the drag.

The second cable snapped and hurtled toward the rear of the ship. He jettisoned this one while watching the last cable begin to come apart. "Captain, we're losing it!"

“Cut the cable now!” Lewis exclaimed as he jumped out of his chair and went to Watkins’ station. “Cut the cable and swing the ship around. We’ll have to push it from here.”

"Aye, sir, releasing the cable." With that, the ship shifted slightly.

“Helm, rotate around the observatory and nose up to it on that flat central surface there,” Lewis said while walking up to the big view screen and pointing out his target.

“Aye, sir, here we go.”

She guided the ship up to the spot he picked out, and everyone felt the impact even though it didn’t strike the observatory very hard.

“Now, full thrusters and then main engines,” Lewis stated.

"Aye, sir," and they began pushing the charred observatory out, finally making it to open space.

FIFTY-ONE

EARLIER.

Admiral Griffin's car rolled to a stop outside the main gate leading to the NAU president's residence. The residence was an ornate palace constructed on the site where the White House once stood in Washington, D.C. The residence was decorated with tall pillars and gold trim. It had domes of blue decorated with the NAU colors of red, blue, and green. The walkway leading to the main entrance was made of stone, and in the middle, it had the NAU flag. On either side were the flags of the countries comprising the NAU. The Canadian flag, the Quebec flag, and the Greenland flag were to the left of the NAU flag and set lower. To the right were the American flag, the Mexican flag, and the Newfoundland flag, also set lower than the NAU flag. Quebec and Newfoundland had broken away from Canada after the Third World War and established their own countries.

Around the perimeter were statues of historical leaders from each country. Other monuments dotted the landscape, depicting how the NAU came together.

Griffin's driver walked around the car and opened the door for the admiral to exit. Griffin slid out of the seat and grabbed his briefcase. "Wait for me. This shouldn't take long," Griffin stated.

The driver nodded.

Griffin walked past the security guards, who stepped aside and saluted the Admiral. As he made his way toward the main entrance, two other guards stepped aside to let him pass. He was such a frequent visitor to the presidential residence that the guards knew him and did not need to check his ID. Once inside, he paused momentarily and reflected on the many portraits of leaders and battles depicted on the walls of the main hallway.

President Wakefield's secretary walked forward, "Welcome, Admiral, the president is waiting for you. Come this way." She held out her hand to guide him toward the meeting room.

After a minute, she opened the door and let him in. She then went back to her desk and waited for her next order.

Griffin stepped into the room and spied the president sitting behind his desk. Before him stood the Inean Ambassador to Earth, Monq-Sai. Monq-Sai was as refined as an Inean could be. With that said, he was still very rough to deal with.

"Griffin, sit!" Wakefield stated in his usual harsh tone.

Griffin sat in the seat next to the ambassador, and he noticed the Inean leader on the view screen on the wall. He knew something was wrong, and it would most likely be his fault.

"Admiral, Captain Hackett has thrown the talks into complete chaos. I don't even think he will return with the scrubber technology we desperately require," Wakefield stated angrily.

“What has he done now?” Griffin asked, knowing that this situation was probably true and probably more the Ineans’ fault.

“He has thrown out months of work by Ambassador Wilcox and Ambassador Channing and is rewriting the entire proposal.”

“Oh, crap!” Griffin exclaimed. “Is there a plan in place to deal with this?”

"The ambassador and the Inean leader have proposed that we will receive the scrubber technology if we can eliminate Captain Hackett," Wakefield stated with a glance at the Inean ambassador, who nodded.

"By eliminate, you mean kill?" Griffin asked, already knowing the answer.

“We prefer the term sacrifice,” the Inean Ambassador stated.

“How do you plan to do this?” Griffin asked.

Wakefield painted an evil grin on his face. “Two ways. The first is to blow up the ship and be rid of him and Benson. Second, an ambush once away from Inea and destroy the ship.”

President Wakefield disliked Hackett for the way he criticized his administration. People began to take notice and started doing the same. He also loathed Benson because he despised her religion. He found her dangerous by the way she handled herself, and that she found favor with Admiral Hodges. He also did not like Admiral Hodges and would deal with him later after receiving information about the warships rumored to be hidden on a distant moon. He knew Hodges was prepping Hackett and Benson to command the lead ships in a force to take on the Ineans, should they attack Earth.

“Ambushed by whom?” Griffin asked.

"The Angowains, of course," the Inean ambassador stated in his rough voice. "That way, it does not implicate us and gives you a reason to help us get what we want from them."

“What is it you want from the Angowains?” Griffin asked.

“We want them weakened so we can subjugate them into doing our mining for us.”

“Why not just bomb them yourself?” Wakefield asked, knowing Griffin would ask it himself.

"If you bomb them to oblivion, they would willingly give in to us to save themselves. It is how they operate," the Inean said with a widening grin.

"So we get the technology to save Earth, and we get rid of a growing problem, Admiral," Wakefield stated.

“I hate to lose all those people on the ship. Can't we just get rid of Hackett and Benson on Inea?” Griffin asked.

"The problem is Commander O'Toole. He is loyal to Captain Hackett and would bomb the hell out of Inea before the Ineans could destroy the ship. It would be quite messy back here if the people were to find out. They would want war," Wakefield said. "It would be best to destroy them away from Inea and pin it on a weaker race we can beat easily, and the Ineans would benefit."

“I see, then make it happen,” Griffin stated.

"We will keep Hackett occupied here and send him away empty-handed. That should discredit him so no one will be sympathetic when he is sacrificed," the Inean leader said in an unmistakable time-delay message. Then his image went away and was replaced with the NAU logo.

The Inean ambassador rose to his feet. "My transport awaits to take me and my staff away from Earth until the solar storm passes." He turned his back on the president and the admiral and lumbered towards the door.

“We should be back on the space station as well,” Wakefield stated. Both men followed the Inean Ambassador out the door.

FIFTY-TWO

THE FOLLOWING day was difficult for the four officers. Larson and Morris crawled out of bed, each took a shower, and got dressed, albeit slowly, their heads pounding from the strong Kosuan ale. Morris asked Larson how the Kosuan drank that stuff. She didn't know. She swore that she wouldn't drink it again. They didn't speak much after that. Both thought about the previous night and what they had done. Remorse had set in. While it was enjoyable for both at the time, the reality of the rules they violated had sunk in. Morris was more concerned because if word of what happened got back to the Admiral, he would lose his chance at command. He also thought about his secret mission. It had slipped his mind for some time yesterday while they negotiated with the Ineans. Now he had time to think. What would he do about Hackett, Benson, and his sister? The torture of his predicament made his head hurt worse. He knew this mission, despite what the vice admiral stated, could not fail. The survival of Earth depended on them, and unfortunately, the lives of a few may need to be sacrificed. He only hoped his brother got his message in time to take his sister and go into hiding until this all blew over. He knew the video Admiral Griffin sent him was faked after he watched it a few times. He noticed some glaring mistakes in the cut images.

Morris cleared his mind and checked in with the ship. O'Toole was still on the bridge and relayed that everything was okay with them, including an Inean battleship slamming into a Kosuan battle cruiser, which nearly started a fight too close to the *Saratoga*. O'Toole had to inch the ship away before the *Saratoga* got caught in a crossfire. In the ship's weakened state, it would have been disastrous.

O'Toole also stated that there was no news from Earth, only static. Morris confirmed he heard him and closed the channel. He knew it might be days before they heard anything.

Larson took a steaming, hot shower and felt better after soaking in the hot spray of water until Morris mentioned an Inean breakfast, the thought of which was too much for her queasy stomach. She decided not to tempt it and opted out of breakfast. Morris checked his watch. It was past zero-seven-hundred hours, and he had yet to hear from the Captain. He decided to check on them alone. He left Larson behind in the room. He needed to get away from her for a few minutes.

Morris walked out to the hall and passed the Inean guards who watched him closely. They followed him to Hackett's door, and he knocked. There was no answer. He knocked again. Still no answer. One of the Inean guards stood behind Morris, breathing down his neck. Morris turned to glare up at him. The guard's breath was rancid, which made Morris want to vomit. Then he thought about the Captain being under the influence of the Inean spiders and all the varied foods and drinks he had had the previous evening. The fear that he could have harmed Benson or himself made him begin to panic. He banged on the door again. Still no answer. He hit the button on the side of the door, and it buzzed loudly, indicating it was locked from the inside. He banged some more, and the door finally slid open. Hackett stood in the open door in his underwear, leaning on the door frame.

"Quit banging," he mumbled, obviously hung over from the previous night.

Morris walked in and saw Benson asleep in the bed. "Sorry,

Captain, you didn't answer right away, and I got concerned," Morris said as he surveyed the room. He walked over to Benson and checked her. She was breathing and still in a deep sleep.

Larson followed in and closed the door behind her as one of the guards tried to grab her. She turned and swore as the door closed. All she could see was the guard laughing as he made a vulgar gesture toward her, which made her even angrier.

Hackett stumbled into the bathroom and stripped. He brushed his teeth three times, trying to kill the taste in his mouth, but was unsuccessful. He shaved carefully and made his way into the shower. He listened as Larson went to Benson's side and woke her. Her head hurt so badly that she could barely open her eyes. She sat up and nearly fell over, but Larson caught her.

Larson helped Benson to the bathroom, where she vomited everywhere. Hackett looked out and saw them and immediately closed the shower door and turned around. He was waking up now and was feeling better from the shower. Larson helped Benson sit up to see if she could, and she could. She was finally coming around as well.

Hackett peeked over his shoulder and saw she was sitting up. "Good morning, Miss Benson. A little too much Kosuan ale, it's tough the next day, isn't it?"

"Ugh, good morning, Captain," she said softly while smacking her lips from the taste in her mouth, eyes squinting in his direction. "That's the downside of negotiating with Kosuan, the next morning." She glanced toward Larson. "Do we have any detox pills in the medic bag?" Benson asked with a pained expression.

Larson handed her a towel. She looked at it and placed it on the counter beside her as she heaved again. She put her head in her hands and sat on the closed toilet. Larson left the room after locking the door open so she could keep an eye on her. Benson wasn't going far.

"I didn't think you liked taking pills, Miss Benson," Hackett said from the shower.

"I don't, but I will make an exception this time, Captain." She replied softly while holding her head. "I should have eaten something, but that food was awful." The thought of the Inean food made her heave up what little her stomach still had.

He shut the shower off and wrapped the towel around himself. He slowly stepped out. He walked out to the main room and found fresh clothes in their supply bag. He pulled on his underwear and discarded the towel. He pulled on his pants and glanced at Benson, who was watching him.

She went to get up and couldn't. Not yet, anyway. The urge to throw up returned with every move.

"Here, let me help you." Hackett put his arm around her and walked her to the shower. He reached down, set the water, and turned it on. She began to strip, and he turned his back to her until she got into the shower.

She tried to smile again, but it still hurt. "About what I said yesterday," she began.

Hackett hung the towel on the wall-mounted holder next to the shower. "We'll discuss that later. I need to contact our ship and get a status report," Hackett said quickly. He turned and cracked the door open again. "I still think you are full of crap."

She stood facing the shower head with the water running over her. They had known each other for a short time and had learned a lot about each other over the past few days. She felt he was on her level, and she was on his. She opened the door and peeked out. He was standing there with his back to her.

He turned around, and their eyes met. He smiled at her, and she returned the smile until she heaved and closed the door. She vomited again in the shower.

Hackett laughed at her. She knew he felt the same way she did. She was falling for her Captain.

He had Larson call the ship for a fresh uniform for him since this one was wrinkled.

Larson lifted her hand, pressed the call button on her wristwatch radio, and ordered fresh uniforms for him and Benson. She turned to him and said that it would be down shortly. He nodded.

Hackett walked back into the room and surveyed the area. "Where is Morris?"

"Oh, crap!" she exclaimed. She opened the door, but he was gone, and so were the guards. She panicked and hit her wristwatch to page him. He didn't reply. Hackett called the ship to track his transponder. They said it looked like he was several floors below. They were not entirely sure because there was heavy interference. He was moving back up towards them. After a few minutes, he rounded the corner and entered the room.

"Where were you?" Hackett asked, thinking he was abducted or worse.

“The hallway cleared, so I went down to the Kosuan’s suite and talked with their ambassador,” Morris replied as the door closed after they reentered the room. “They feel that they will accept our arrangement. They just want to see what the Ineans come back with. I think I convinced him that the Ineans wouldn’t offer anything better. Oh, and they said to hold on to Benson and Larson. The Ineans may make a move on them today.”

Larson rummaged in the package that the *Saratoga* teleported to the room, found the detox pills, and passed them out to everyone. They swallowed the pills quickly, hoping it would help them feel better faster. The detox pills countered the effects of a hangover. Unfortunately, the side effect is strong, uncontrollable intestinal gas, which should make the meeting interesting in a few hours if they are still there. Benson staggered out of the shower, and Larson brought her a fresh uniform. It took several minutes before they both emerged from the bathroom. Benson took her pill and said she was ready. An hour had passed since they woke, and it was nearly zero-nine-hundred hours. The Ineans would be coming for them shortly.

Hackett contacted the *Saratoga* for a status report. O'Toole told him the Inean ships had closed in on them and were trying to force them away from the planet. He told the Captain that they were holding their ground. He confessed that the Kosuan matrix was becoming a bigger issue. They would have to break orbit in 12 hours at the latest to make the rendezvous point he had set up with Captain Jefferson of the *Challenger*. Hackett told O'Toole to target the building they were in with high-yield torpedoes and wait for his or Morris's command. He agreed reluctantly. Hackett told him that if he got the order to fire, then they were not coming out alive anyway. He was okay with that, and Hackett pressed the off button on his wristwatch when there was a knock at the door.

Hackett told Morris to get the door, and he opened it. Four armed Ineans rushed into the room. These Ineans were larger than usual and there for one reason, which was to bully Hackett and his people. They did a good job of it. The Ineans quickly pushed Hackett and Morris around, separating them from the women. Neither of them could draw their weapons in time, and their laser pistols were swatted away. The other two threw Benson and Larson against the wall. Both of them got back up slowly. One of the Inean men grabbed Benson by the throat, picked her up off the floor, and held her to the wall. She kicked and punched him. It was useless as she gasped for air.

The Inean watching Hackett grabbed him and slammed him to the ground. He put one knee to his chest and pressed. Hackett couldn't breathe. The Inean looked at him. "Why did you contact your ship?"

"Daily check-in," Hackett forced out.

"We know you are planning something with the Kosuan. If you know what's best, Captain, make sure you make the right choices, or you will watch what we really do to human bitches" The Inean growled in his face, "To their death," and then grabbed him by the arm, pulled him off the floor and dragged him towards Benson. He nodded to the guard who held Benson to the wall.

The guard tightened his grip around her throat so she could not breathe. After a minute, she stopped kicking. Hackett tried to help her. Unfortunately, the Inean held him back, and they could only watch helplessly. He yelled at the Inean guard to stop, and the Inean only laughed. "Let her go. It's me you want. Let her go!"

The Inean holding him nodded at the other guard to release her. When he did, she collapsed to the floor, grabbing her throat, gasping for air. She curled up in the fetal position as her lungs slowly filled with air. She continued to gasp for air as tears rolled down her cheeks, and she began to sob on the floor. Her neck had the pink outline of the Inean's hand, and she was still having trouble breathing. The Inean that choked her kicked her, and she fell over. The Ineans held the others from attending to her.

Another one of the guards shoved Larson into the wall, then picked her up by her hair as she screamed. He tossed her on the bed like a rag doll and pulled her to him. She tried to kick him, but it was useless. He was too strong and overpowered her easily with one hand. In a rage, he slapped her face and tossed her to Morris' feet, but he was powerless to help her.

Morris was screaming at the guard and then at Hackett, who couldn't do anything either.

The head guard walked up to Hackett and grabbed his face, pulling Hackett to his toes. "We will be back soon to collect you disgusting animals for the meeting. Be ready. I can't wait until we can annihilate your race from the stars," he growled and released Hackett, but he wasn't done yet. He looked at Benson curled up on the floor and turned, grinning at Hackett again. "The Emperor would like to see her." With that, he laughed and punched Hackett in the stomach. The guard holding Hackett released him, and he crumpled to the ground. The guards laughed and backed out of the room, carrying Benson away with them.

Hackett slowly got to his feet. "Morris, get our weapons and cover the door."

Morris looked at the Captain and screamed, "What was that all about, sir? Why didn't they just finish us?"

Hackett turned to him. "That was intimidation, Commander. If they wanted to kill us, it would have been easy for them. It appears your Kosuan friend was right, Mr. Morris. Now we know they fear any deal we strike with the Kosuan."

"So if we deal with the Kosuan, we die," Morris said.

"We die anyway, Commander. So let's focus on the mission," Hackett blurted out as he looked around the room at his two concerned officers staring at him. He knew he had just dropped a bomb on them that they didn't expect. He needed to clear it up before the Ineans came back for them. "Okay, come here." They approached in close.

"All right, I'm sorry for being blunt. The Alliance considered this mission a failure even before we got here. The ambassador got himself arrested on purpose because he didn't want his win streak to come to an end. However, we can save this mission and get this done despite the odds. We may even live to tell about it. Our ship is surrounded and can't escape, even if we tried. If we do manage to get away, we will run out of power before reaching the rendezvous point. We have chosen a volatile ally that can't be trusted."

"Now that we have the unpleasant stuff out of the way, how do we overcome the odds against us and get out of here alive with a peace agreement?" Hackett looked at the faces in front of him, which were blank.

"Okay, we only have a few minutes before we are dragged truly into hell. Are we going to give up or dig in and fight this?" Hackett asked loudly.

Larson stepped up, and Morris passed her a laser pistol. "I plan to fight!" Larson stated as she checked her laser pistol and clipped it to her belt.

Hackett pressed the face of his wristwatch, "*Saratoga*, come in!"

No response.

"*Saratoga*, come in!" he repeated.

Still nothing.

"Morris."

Morris tapped his wristwatch. There was no response.

Larson pulled out her pocket scanner and swept it around the room. "Signals are being jammed, sir."

Hackett went to the door. It was locked from the outside. He wanted the *Saratoga* to scan for Benson's ident chip to see where she was and ensure she was alive. He turned towards Larson, "Can you scan for Benson's ident chip?"

"I've been trying. No response. I hate being blind," Larson huffed.

"What's our plan then?" Morris asked.

"Taking Benson was to distract us, so we make mistakes and concessions."

"They will kill her," Larson stated while placing the useless scanner back in her pocket.

“They'll kill her anyway. We stick to the plan. Get the deal signed. Get the scrubber technology and hope the Kosuan side with us,” Hackett stated. He banged his fist against the door in frustration.

“We cannot abandon her!” Larson huffed.

"I agree. The Ineans are playing with our emotions. We can't show weakness. We must be strong. They will respect that, and hopefully, we will get her back in one piece."

"I don't like it, Captain. What do we do now?" Morris asked with a glance at Larson, who was searching the room for anything to break the door down. She found nothing.

"We wait. Right now, the Ineans hold all the cards, Commander. Now we wait."

Hackett went to the large windows and looked down at the square below. He spied their transport. It was still intact, at least from this height. He watched the marketplace with all its hustle and bustle. "We wait," he said through gritted teeth.

FIFTY-THREE

DAYBREAK IN ZANZIBAR, Tanzania. D-day. People lined the beach and waited for the plasma cloud to smash into the Earth. Everyone looked up toward the sky as the few clouds quickly dissipated like a drop of oil in a pot of water. Yellow-orange ribbons descended and rippled across the sky like a harmless aurora normally seen at night. People screamed in fear as the sky was filled with thunder all around them. The cloud began to turn bright red and orange as it fell from the sky toward the ground. The thunder became deafening as it got closer: a million degrees of plasma burning and pushing the atmosphere aside at tremendous speed. Soon, the entire sky was bright red, swirling and flowing east to west beyond the horizon.

The sheer intensity of the storm had overloaded Earth's magnetic field, causing it to collapse and then snap back to life, with devastating consequences for any animal with ears. Each time the field snapped, the sky was filled with horrendous thunder. Unfortunately, the animals that relied on Earth's magnetic field to navigate were lost. Birds flew frantically in circles, crashing into buildings, people, and almost everything possible. Many animals had disappeared; however, somehow, they knew what was coming and ran for higher ground.

Suddenly, giant lightning bolts crashed down upon the ocean and moved towards land as Earth's magnetic field continued to collapse and spring back through the plasma cloud, crashing into the Earth. Mega-bolts slammed into the water with such force that water was pulled hundreds of feet into the air. The lightning bolts were so strong that the sandy beach turned to glass-coated craters where each bolt struck, from heat greater than the surface of the Sun. People ran screaming for cover, but there was no place to hide as the Earth rotated into the solar storm at nearly a thousand miles per hour. The fiery storm swept across the ocean toward the beach with incredible speed, sending the helpless people scattering like ants.

Zanzibar had become a tourist trap in the twenty-third century with large hotels and imported sandy beaches. The country had gone from one of the poorest in Africa to one of the richest since the last global war. The country was enjoying another booming season.

People (tourists and locals) were knocked to the ground. They turned and froze as they stared in horror as another mega-bolt of lightning crashed down from the sky into the Radisson Hotel. It exploded, leaving nothing of its existence except the remaining crater. It had been totally vaporized beyond what any human bomb could do. Nothing was left except for a mushroom-shaped cloud of smoke slowly rolling into the sky.

People got to their feet and ran frantically from the other buildings, looking over their shoulders toward the coastline. Many were barely clothed as they had awoken to the commotion coming ashore. They had no time to gather any belongings. The ocean was ablaze with fire as the plasma cloud touched Earth and began to sweep across the planet as it rotated into the fire. The cloud was so dense it blotted out the Sun, and the new day actually turned darker, much like twilight.

People watched as the wall of fire swept up onto the land and engulfed the high-rise buildings. It swept inland across the countryside, burning everything and everyone in its path. It tore a path clear across Africa, into the Atlantic, and into South America.

Griffin and Wakefield returned to the space station and joined Foley as they watched the nightmare unfold. Earth was being burned, millions were dying, and there was nothing any of them could do. The number of dead and missing today would be incomprehensible compared to other "natural" disasters in man's brief but ugly time on Earth.

However, none of them were safe on the space station either, and Foley stepped away to confer with his people as the station began to drift. The station's maneuvering engines had failed, and now a fear swept across the command deck of the station. The magnetic lines kept breaking and crashing through the station, charging all of their systems, millions and millions of volts cascading through every electrical circuit. Fires broke out around the station. The people were busy keeping the station alive and behind Earth, out of the path of the million-degree plasma cloud that would destroy the station in minutes. If the station were destroyed, it would take all of Earth's defenses against the Kosuan and Ineans with it. It would open up the door for invasion.

The station went black. Everyone watched the show from the large windows. The Earth glowed from the dark side. The auroras wrapped around both poles, extending from the equator to the poles and back again. The colors were vivid; if so many people were not in trouble, it would be a show to sit back and enjoy.

This storm would last for many hours and trek thousands of miles across three continents and an ocean before it was done.

Behind them, the fire extended outward into a funnel. Clear space was a shrinking black dot in the distance, growing smaller and smaller with each passing second. The storm would be past them in a few long hours.

. . .

The volcanic island of La Palma in the Canary Islands began to shake, causing the local inhabitants to be hurled from their beds. Their homes began to rattle and disintegrate as the earthquake grew stronger and stronger. People crawled to their windows and looked towards Cumbre Vieja, the island's unpredictable volcano. To the wonder of the occupants, smoke began to flow from its crater. A few puffs at first, and then stronger, more dense smoke began to escape from the mouth of the beast.

The ground settled some, but not completely, and the locals hurried to escape. They knew this volcano and didn't have much time as the Earth trembled again. People turned instinctively as a reddish flash lit up the countryside. Then all hell broke loose. The mountain exploded towards the sky. There was another earthquake, stronger than the first. The ground began to split slightly, then it grew wider as the island lifted and bulged as the pent-up magma pushed towards the surface with renewed vengeance.

People clawed at doors that were jammed shut while the roofs collapsed upon their heads. The ground cracked further and further as it rumbled. Cumbre Vieja woke from its brief 70-year sleep.

On the island's western side, scientists ran for their Alliance-issued transport craft as the rocky slope began to crumble. They made it into the transport, and as it lifted off, the entire western flank of the island fell away. Millions of tons of rock were dropped into the ocean, followed by a river of lava.

The scientists had been watching this volcano for weeks as it suddenly awoke from its long period of dormancy. Nonetheless, tonight's eruption still caught them off guard. They watched as more than half of the island (an area the size of the Isle of Man) fell away and disappeared into the cold Atlantic Ocean, more than enough material to force the sea outward from La Palma at tremendous speeds towards England and North America. It was a mere ripple as it crossed the vast ocean, but that would change as it was driven upward toward land.

Unfortunately, all the space-based early-warning systems were either destroyed or not functioning due to the solar storm sweeping past the planet.

FIFTY-FOUR

THE DOOR SWUNG OPEN, and four Inean soldiers rushed in. Hackett, Morris, and Larson jumped up to meet them. "Where the hell is my officer!" Hackett yelled at the Inean closest to him.

The Inean growled at him. "The meeting awaits you."

"We will not go until you bring me to check on my officer to ensure she has not been harmed!"

"You will get her back after the agreement is signed," the Inean stated while grasping Hackett's arm harshly.

"No!" Hackett struggled uselessly against the large alien's grip. "Bring me to her now. My government will not accept this turn of events."

The Inean laughed while tugging on Hackett's arm.

"Do you understand the consequences of taking her hostage during a diplomatic mission? Do you understand the consequences of not allowing us to contact our ship? Do you understand the consequ..."

"Enough!" the Inean screamed, which made the windows rattle. "You will come with me then!" The Inean dragged Hackett out of the room.

“Morris, if I'm not back in 20, kill as many as you can,” he yelled over his shoulder.

The other Ineans laughed as they backed out of the room. The door slammed and locked from the outside.

The Ineans dragged Hackett into the elevator. They kept him surrounded as the elevator went up and up. Their smell made him nauseous.

Hackett knew where they were going. There was only one being in this building that would be this far up. The Inean Emperor resided at the very top of this building, enjoying a 360-degree view of the city and the countryside. Much like his predecessors of old, this Emperor lived a lavish lifestyle.

The elevator doors opened, and the Inean guards shoved Hackett off the elevator. Two new guards grabbed Hackett and dragged him to face the Emperor.

"Greetings, Captain Hackett. I overheard your conversation with my elite guards," the Emperor snarled. He was dressed in a white robe with gold trimming and gold cuffs on his sleeves. He was well-groomed for an Inean.

“Good. It will save me from repeating myself!” Hackett exclaimed while struggling against the grip of the two large guards.

“I won’t bore you with the details, Captain. Your ship is safe, and your female officer is unharmed, for now,” the Inean smiled, “however, I cannot allow you to speak with your ship right now.”

“Why not?” Hackett asked.

"You will learn why soon," the Emperor stated. He got up, walked over to the large windows, and gazed upon his glass and steel city. "Bring him and leave us alone."

The guards looked at each other and brought Hackett to the Emperor. They released him and walked away. Just far enough not to overhear, but close enough to intervene if their leader needed them.

Hackett stared at the Emperor and waited for him to speak.

The Inean continued to stare out the large windows. "A long time ago, a leader called Sankar stood in a room similar to this one.

It was high above the city, like we are now. He was the most powerful leader of all time. He had the universe in his grasp and made a fatal mistake." He turned to face Hackett. "That mistake was a lust for your fragile Ardon females. He became obsessed with them, as did many of our military leaders. I won't repeat that mistake. We need to remove the temptation once and for all. That is why your race cannot survive. Do you understand?"

“We are not the Ardons.”

"Yes, you are!" He growled. "You have to be, but if you insist on denying it, your race fits every detail of them. We have pictures of the Ardons of old. You are identical to them in every detail." He grabbed Hackett and forced him to look out at the vast city. "I have noticed the same intoxicating lust in many of my council members and, yes, even myself. I have sampled Ardon women, or if you prefer, human, female flesh, and you must all die to save our race. We will inherit the universe, which is rightfully ours. Just a thousand years late."

The Emperor walked back towards his desk and glanced at a view screen that Hackett could not see. He pressed a button and motioned for the guards to come forward. "Take the puzzled captain to his female."

“Wait! What happens now? We won’t allow you to just kill us and destroy our planet. We will fight,” Hackett stated.

"We won't destroy Earth, Captain. However, we do look forward to the fight. What Sankar failed to do so long ago, I will accomplish. Now go, collect your bitch, and take this warning to your people. We are coming for you!" He waved the guards off.

"Then why give us the technology to fix the Earth?" Hackett asked.

"I thought you were smarter than that, Captain. You, of all people, should know the answer to that question."

"I do, Emperor. I just want to hear you say it."

The Emperor smiled and bared his pointed teeth. "Tell me what you think, Captain, and I'll tell you if you are correct."

"Alright, we take the technology and fix the Earth, saving you the trouble of having to do it. We waste our resources doing your dirty work."

"I stand corrected, Captain. You are smarter than I gave you credit for. You are correct." The Emperor waved the guards forward again.

"Good day, Captain. Oh, and you would make a good Inean warrior," he smiled again.

Hackett looked at him briefly and turned for the door.

The guards took Hackett into the elevator and descended dozens of floors to the ambassador's chambers.

The doors opened, and he was pushed out into the crowded corridor. There were no windows here; instead, paintings of previous leaders hung on the walls. There was a common theme to all of the paintings: blood and death. All the paintings portrayed leaders conquering by the sword and the newer ones by the gun.

He was escorted to another room, accompanied by armed guards on either side of the door. They stepped aside and opened the door. Hackett was pushed in, and the door slammed shut.

Hackett surveyed the room quickly. Behind the desk was the Inean ambassador. Against the wall were shelves with large jars. In the jars were the heads of his conquests. He noticed an empty jar on a table near the shelves. There was also a bloodied knife beside the jar. On a chair facing the ambassador, he spied Benson's leg over the arm of the oversized chair. Several strands of blond hair were draped over the other arm of the chair. He could not see the rest of her, but knew she was unconscious or dead. On the opposite wall were shelf after shelf of books.

He fought back his rage for the moment. He could hear the crunch of the Inean spiders in his mind returning. This was their plan. Make him lose control and then start a war.

The ambassador looked up. He grinned at Hackett. "Your bitch was so fragile. It is too bad she did not last long enough for all of my guards to enjoy!" he laughed.

Hackett struggled against the grip of the two guards. It was useless. "What have you done?" he yelled. "If it's war you want, I will be happy to give it to you!"

“Calm down, Captain. You won’t make it out of here alive to start it,” the Inean stated while pushing out of his chair. He walked around to face Hackett. “Release him.”

The guards complied.

Hackett went to shove the ambassador, but it had no effect. He stared at the giant alien, who weighed three times as much as Hackett. "You bastard."

"Good, now we understand each other. Take your bitch and gather the other two. The meeting begins in one of your hours." The Inean shoved Hackett, and he fell over. The ambassador and his guards laughed and left the room.

Hackett got to his feet and quickly went to Benson. She was unconscious, and he checked for a pulse. He found one. Her clothes were torn, but in a way to give the impression she was abused. He reached into his pocket for smelling salts and pulled out a small packet. He broke it and held it under her nose. Benson shook her head wildly for a second and opened her eyes. She saw Hackett's face and threw her arms around his neck. She sobbed for a few seconds and composed herself. She pushed away and checked her clothes.

He grasped her hand and helped her to her feet. "Are you okay?"

“I think so. How long was I out?”

Hackett wiped a tear from her eye. "I don't know. How did you end up like that?"

"They shoved me around and ripped my jacket and shirt. Then they choked me with their hairy paws. Next thing I know, you are here, and they are gone." She glanced around the room and spied the jar on the table. "Was that meant for me?" she asked while glancing at the heads suspended in dozens of jars on the shelf. Some were human, some were Kosuan, some were Angowain, and others were from races they had not met. Perhaps they no longer existed.

He looked her over and noticed the bruises on her neck, each a perfect match for an Inean finger that had choked her earlier. He saw a fresh bruise on her face, in addition to one she had received earlier in the week. He noticed bruises on her wrists, which were mostly covered by her shirt and jacket.

“I don't think so. This was Inean intimidation at its ugliest. I thought you were dead at first.”

He squeezed her hand. She turned to look at him, and their eyes met. She kissed him. "Thanks for saving me."

She pulled away and walked over to the bookshelf. Some of the books had been pulled out enough to get her attention. She pulled one off the shelf and looked at it. It was old. Had to have been a few hundred years old. She held onto it and spied another one. She pulled it off the shelf. She noticed the name Marduk written in Inean on the cover.

"I just met with the Inean Emperor," Hackett stated.

"Oh really?" she said while flipping through an old book. "Care to tell me?"

"Not here, but later we can talk about what he said."

"Over a good bottle of wine and some real food?" She asked.

"Sounds like a plan."

Hackett watched her for a second and went to the ambassador's desk. He had left his PDA behind, along with a folder. Hackett grabbed them and walked over to the wall where the jars with heads were. He spied one that had floated around in the jar. He knew it was Sasha Young. He flashed back to her, laughing at the nav-con. Others around her were laughing, and he knew she had blasted off another of her off-color jokes.

“Captain? Captain?” Benson asked as she watched him pause. “What is it?”

“Oh, uh. Nothing. I was just thinking. Let's get out of here.”

They stuffed their stolen treasures into their jacket pockets as best they could and exited the room. The guards had gone, and Hackett knew they were being let go.

"Who did that head belong to?" she asked him as they approached the elevator.

“I don't know.”

"Sorry, Captain, but you do," she said, reaching for his hand.

She found it, and they intertwined their fingers. "That was Sasha, wasn't it?"

“Yes.”

“Do you...”

“No. Let's get back to the room and check on Morris and Larson. The meeting begins soon.”

They did not speak the rest of the way up to the room. Hackett did not want to talk about it.

FIFTY-FIVE

HACKETT TOLD the Inean guard to open the door and ensure it stayed unlocked. The guard growled at him and spat on Benson. She wiped the slime from her face and flung it back at the Inean, who laughed at them.

The Inean unlocked the door, and Hackett pushed it open. He and Benson walked in as Morris and Larson turned to see them.

The door slammed behind them. They all turned to take notice.

“We need to prepare for the final meeting,” Hackett stated.

Morris had another idea. “What the hell happened to her?” he yelled.

"Be careful, Commander," Hackett said calmly as he watched Larson's expression. She was not surprised, and he knew this was planned.

“Be careful? What is wrong with you?” Morris yelled.

Benson went to step between them until Larson pulled her away.

Hackett grabbed Morris by the collar and quickly shoved him against the wall. “I wouldn't go there, Commander.”

Morris shoved him back and fixed his jacket. “How could you

let them take her? Who knows what they did to her or could have done while you did nothing!"

"I won't get drawn into this with you, Morris. Clear your head and get ready."

"No, you will answer for her right now. I see the looks. I know what is going on, and yet you sacrifice her just like Sasha."

Morris never saw it coming.

Hackett spun around so fast and planted his fist into Morris's face that he had no time to react. Hackett connected solidly, and Morris's head snapped back into the wall behind him.

His knees buckled, and he slid down the wall. Morris shook off the hit and lifted himself. He spat out blood and looked at Hackett and then at Benson and Larson, who were shocked.

Hackett unclenched his fist and stared at Morris. "Sasha died under the flag of diplomacy by animals that have no regard for us," he said while fighting back the urge to kill Morris. "You, of all people, are the last one to lecture me on what I do regarding women."

Morris looked puzzled.

"I know about you and Sasha. I know she was pregnant with your child when she died. I am also aware of your orders regarding Benson and myself. I also know about your sister."

The puzzled look on Morris's face was replaced with one of shock as blood trickled from the corner of his mouth.

Hackett continued. "Your sister is safe. Do you still wish to carry out your orders?"

Hackett stood back with his arms outstretched. "Come, carry out your orders, Commander."

"Captain, I..."

"I said, do what you were ordered, Commander!" Hackett yelled as he tossed a laser pistol at him. "Do it!"

"Sir, I'm sorry."

"You are not fit for command." Hackett brought his arms in. "It is time for you to get your head out of your ass and grow some balls, Commander." Hackett turned away and then back. "Tougher orders are coming, Commander, and you are not ready. You need to get your priorities in order."

"S-sir," Morris stuttered as he searched for words, but he had no idea what to say. He was now afraid of Hackett because he knew way too much.

Hackett walked towards the bed and picked up their notes. "Right now, we need to get this agreement by the means we discussed. And when we thoroughly piss off the Ineans, I need everyone on the same page so we get out of here in one piece." He tossed the folder onto the bed. "That means no distractions, or we die. Understand?"

Hackett looked at each face.

Morris nodded, followed by Larson and Benson.

There was a knock at the door.

"Here we go," Hackett stated as the door flew open.

"There's one last thing, Commander," Hackett said, returning his attention to Morris. "You chose your devil without thinking about the ones closest to you. There is no way you will succeed, so you better become part of OUR team." And he abruptly turned away before he could reply.

Morris knew Hackett was on to him. Until then, he had no idea of the depth of Hackett's knowledge or how he had acquired it. Morris was beginning to fear Hackett. He was powerful and had powerful connections. Connections that knew intricate details of secret Alliance negotiations, secret plans only a handful of high-ranking people are privy to, and Hackett was not high enough on the food chain to know.

FIFTY-SIX

"KEEP THEM BETWEEN US, COMMANDER," Hackett told Morris. "And keep your finger on the emergency button."

Morris nodded and opened the door. The Inean women had come to collect them for the meeting.

They walked down the hallway to the elevator, and Hackett looked at Benson's neck, which still had the Inean's handprint around her throat. He touched her neck and moved her hair so he could take a closer look. She looked up at him. "Is something wrong, Captain?" she asked.

"Are you okay?" Hackett replied.

She looked forward again. She couldn't look him in the eyes on this one because she was having second thoughts about signing up for this mission. In her heart, she was ready, but in her head, she was not. This mission had subjected her to many of her fears. She never feared nudity until now, but now she feared rape, and these Ineans did worse than rape. She also feared getting attached to someone and losing him again. "Captain, my neck hurts, but not bad."

"Is that all?"

“For now, sir.”

"Unfortunately, I can't promise that I can protect you from worse today. I personally know what it's like to be tortured by these people, so take the pill if you find yourself in that situation." He paused a moment and continued, "You do know that I care for you and wouldn't tell you to do that if I didn't think it was for the best?"

She continued to stare ahead. "Yes, Captain, I know and appreciate that you care so much." She reached and squeezed his hand. She then mumbled a prayer for the crew to hear.

They all responded with an "Amen."

The Ineans turned to stare at her. Wondering what that was all about. Hackett patted her back, Morris followed, and Larson rubbed her shoulder. Benson relaxed, now knowing it was out of her hands. She looked around and knew the others did too.

They entered the room and were bombarded by shouts and yells. Several bottles flew by them, but they didn't flinch. The Kosuan were seated already. However, only a few of the Angowains were present. The Inean women led them to their seats and walked away. Hackett watched as they approached the guards. Benson's prayer must have gotten to them because Hackett could tell that's what they were talking about. Eventually, the Inean women moved away. The guards kept an eye on Hackett and his people. The Kosuan regarded them in a positive fashion for once. It was several minutes before anyone else showed up.

Morris struck up a conversation with the Angowain ambassador. Hackett watched as the Ambassador kept nodding yes at what Morris was saying. Hackett knew he was getting somewhere; he just didn't know where. After several minutes, they broke off the talk. The Angowain leaned to the female of his species, and she began to speak to someone on their ship. Hackett wondered if Morris had succeeded.

Morris tried to tell the Captain but couldn't over the commotion of the Inean delegation entering the room. The roar went up from the thousands of Ineans present. Everyone stood as the Ineans approached the table and sat in their seats. The Inean Ambassador called the room to order before they began.

"Does anyone have anything they want to say before we get started?" the Ambassador asked.

Hackett cleared his throat and raised his hand.

The Inean stared at him in disbelief. *What now,* he wondered as he sized up the Captain's mental state. "The floor recognizes Captain Hackett," the Ambassador stated finally.

Hackett stood and looked at each member seated beside them. "Fellow members, I just wanted to say that it has been a pleasure working with each of you since we arrived. I know it has been challenging to have our four races at the same table for two days in a row, and I expect we can finalize this agreement and work toward a more lasting relationship. I, however, have one request to make." He looked at the Inean Ambassador. "There have been obvious threats against us since we have been here. I request that the security personnel go around the room and remove any objects that the crowd can use as projectiles, and form a wall between them and us to protect everyone at this table. Everyone here knows the implications that could result if some of us don't make it back. I would like to conclude by thanking the Ineans for taking the initiative in planning and hosting this meeting. Thank you." He sat back in his chair, and everyone at the table clapped and made other gestures to show the Captain they accepted what he said. The crowd was unusually quiet.

Hackett didn't believe what he had just said. He detested the Ineans. He wanted to kill them for what they had done to him, Sasha Young, and many others he did not know. Regardless of what they say here, he knew peace would never happen. He knew the slave trading would not stop. The Ineans also knew how he felt. He was sure his facial expression gave away his true feelings. His primary goal was the safety of his people and escaping this planet in one piece. That was foremost on his mind and, of course, his lovely new navigator clinging to his side, his other problem.

The Inean Ambassador motioned for a security guard to approach. Hackett recognized him as one of the four who had attacked them earlier. The guard was highly perturbed at what he was asked to do, and he shot Hackett a glare that said to Hackett, "I'm going to kill you." He turned while staring at Hackett and went back to his post. He talked to several others, who dispersed throughout the room and began collecting weapons from the crowd. The people gave up their possessions reluctantly and without incident. Several more guards came in, surrounded the table, and faced outward toward the testy crowd.

The Inean Ambassador stood and looked around the room. "The Alliance captain has a point. We are here to secure peace. Not to escalate the conflict beyond the current one. Everyone in this room will remain seated and refrain from attacking the delegates. Anyone who does will be severely punished."

The room remained eerily quiet as beings from a dozen systems just watched. The Ambassador scanned the room and continued when he felt it was secure. "We have devised a counterproposal for the Alliance representatives to consider. My assistant will distribute the proposal for all parties to review." One of the Inean women walked up to the Ambassador and received the pages. She backed away and proceeded to distribute the documents around the table. All that was passed out were the corrections in each species' native language. The bulk of the document was not included. Hackett received his and promptly read it, as did the rest of his team.

Once everyone had a copy, the Ambassador continued. "The first item has to do with trading human women. We will remove this clause if the Alliance agrees to provide us with the technology we seek. On the other items, we will hold the colony clauses for a future date. Captain Hackett, do you have anything to add?"

Hackett looked at it, and he didn't like what he saw. He stood up and asked to speak. "Unfortunately, Ambassador, we cannot provide you with weapons or technology that would aid in your battles. It directly violates the Alliance's most important values, which state that we cannot aid an alien or foreign government in their internal affairs, including the ability to wage or win a war. I must remain firm on that principle."

The Ambassador remained standing and faced Hackett. "So

what do you propose, Captain?" he asked, subduing his growing anger for Hackett.

Hackett looked around the table at each face that looked at him. "I think the table should vote on this and allow a majority rule, Ambassador."

The Inean leader looked around and knew the Kosuan and Angowains did not favor this at all, and he knew it wouldn't pass. "Captain, let's tie it to the women, then. If you agree to that clause, we will let the other drop?"

Hackett reviewed his notes and the proposal, and an idea occurred to him. "After we leave here, ambassador, I will agree that any human female who comes to your planet will have to adhere to your laws, but they must come here of their own free will, which does not include diplomatic missions."

The Ineans in the crowd cheered. Many jumped up, screaming at the Ambassador to take it.

The Ambassador sat back down and huddled with his people. Benson glanced up at Hackett with a horrified look. She grabbed him and yanked him down to his seat.

"Are you insane? What are you doing?" Benson whispered harshly.

"Maybe. It only applies to women who come here of their own free will. We have to make sure that doesn't happen," he whispered in her ear, so only she heard it.

The Inean Ambassador stood up and faced Hackett. "So you would allow any woman who comes here of their own free will to be subject to our laws and traditions?" Hackett nodded. The Ambassador continued, "What happened to your morality concerns, Captain?"

Hackett replied. "Any woman who comes here of her own free will would most likely come here for what you want anyway, and we can't stop that. While our culture has strict morals, there are some who do not follow them. There is nothing we can do about that because we are a free society, and our people are free to choose how they conduct their lives."

The Ambassador looked at him and wondered what he was going to pull. Then he spoke. "We agree to those terms. I will have the doctrines written and ready to be signed shortly."

Hackett wasn't done. "Sir, I respectfully would like to discuss the slave trade issue as it could be tied to this." The Ambassador nodded and remained standing. "I request there be a clause prohibiting the trading of human slaves, and slaves don't have free will under this agreement."

The Ambassador spoke up. "The slave trade industry was abolished months ago and therefore is not binding here, Captain."

"I am aware that it was abolished on paper. However, it still continues. The situation needs to be policed better, and the traders need to be caught, prosecuted, and punished under your laws," Hackett stated loudly as the room became unruly.

"I am not aware of any problem there, Captain. We are finished with that." The Ambassador was getting angry. "Now, you mentioned that you had other items of interest we could swap. I think we would be interested in medical supplies, nurses, and training."

"Any nurses that come to this planet would not be subject to free will because they are acting on a diplomatic assistance policy, Ambassador," Hackett tried to shoot it down as fast as he could.

"Yes, I suppose you are right, Captain," he said with a widening smile.

The Kosuan ambassador stood up and growled at the Inean, "How does this help our war effort with you?"

The Inean Ambassador was taken aback by the hostile Kosuan. "You and the Alliance have struck some sort of deal before coming down here. Tell me what it is."

"There is no deal with these weaklings!" The Kosuan growled.

"I also request that the humans and Kosuan do not enter into a peace agreement together while we are at war," the Inean Ambassador said.

An Angowain stood up, seconded that motion, and looked at Morris. "The Kosuan and humans are not at war, but neither are they at peace. If they remain that way, Kosuan forces will be needed to counter the human threat between their boundaries, giving the Ineans and our people a fighting chance against a powerful aggressor."

Hackett stood up, needing to end the discussion quickly, as it undermined what had been accomplished. "The Alliance and Kosuan are not at war. We consider our relations with them cautious yet peaceful. The Kosuan have not allocated many resources to patrolling our mutual border. So the fight you have in front of you will not be affected in any way by the Alliance negotiating deeper peace with the Kosuan government." Hackett looked at the Inean Ambassador. "No one will benefit by adding that clause to our peace agreement."

The Ambassador said it was a good idea and expressed that he would not add it. Hackett had more ammunition to use. "If that is the case, Ambassador, then you will put in that clause that you will not seek an alliance with the government of Moroc Chu Nog. Such an alliance would give you an advantage over the Kosuan, which is what you are trying to prevent here." Hackett moved his hand between the Kosuan and himself.

"We don't plan on including the Moroc in our war," the Ambassador said.

“Then you won’t have any problem writing it in then?” Hackett replied.

"I am not doing that, Captain. A Kosuan Earth alliance is more threatening to us than adding the Moroc to ours," the Ambassador replied.

"Then we need to sit down and discuss the issues further because we made a concession on a sticky issue," Hackett said. He watched the process unravel before him, and he didn't know what to do.

The Ambassador looked at Hackett and smiled at him. Hackett stared back and said *Here it comes* to himself. "Captain, the agreement will stay as I had mentioned before. You can freely work with the Kosuan, and we can choose our alliances as we wish. In exchange for this, there is only one thing I want."

Hackett knew what he wanted, and he had to ask formally. "What would that be, Ambassador?"

"Let me have your bitch for one of your hours, and I'll call it a deal," he said, looking at Benson now.

"You know I can't do that, and you know why, Ambassador," Hackett stated.

"Captain, you are in no position to argue with me. I'll take her and have her, and if she lives through it, then you can have what is left, which won't be much. Plus, you go home with no deal," the Inean said.

Hackett stared him down. "We are prepared to die if that is the case, Ambassador."

"Then you will die, all of you!" The Ambassador motioned to the guards to turn and grab them.

The guards turned around and pulled Benson and the others out of their chairs. They held on tight to their arms with a crushing grip that made them wince in pain. They struggled against their captors, which was useless. The Ineans were too strong.

The Kosuan stood up, and their Ambassador looked at Hackett. "Is our agreement in place, Captain?" he asked.

“Yes, it is, Ambassador,” Hackett replied to the Kosuan.

“Then we will fight with you to defend the honor of your woman,” he growled. He glared at the Inean.

More guards turned to grab the Kosuan until the Angowain stood up and said, “Stop!” Everyone turned to look.

The Angowain looked at the Ineans. “This is not in your best interest, Ambassador Sharoock. The humans have made it clear what they will and will not do. Besides, you can’t win a war with them at this time.”

“It doesn’t matter because none of you will live long enough to see us fall,” another Inean at the table spoke up.

That was one statement that could end up being true as the room quickly spiraled out of control, and Hackett needed something to quell the situation quickly. He cleared his throat. "Mr.

Ambassador, no one wants to see your planet fall or lose a war." He struggled against the tight grip of the huge Inean holding him. "Our interest here is peace and protecting our people, that is all." Shouts and bloodthirsty yelling intensified to a deafening roar as Hackett continued. "The Kosuan are interested in peace because war is expensive and drains valuable resources from their society and yours! The Angowains are not a hostile race, but will fight if needed. Let's take a step back from this and put the deal together as we have agreed. We will continue our negotiations with the Kosuan on our time, and you are free to talk to whatever races you choose."

Hackett stared at the Ambassador, and when he blinked, he continued. "We will supply medical assistance to your people. In exchange, you will provide the technology to help us cool the Earth. There will be no exchange of the women for anything except those who come here of their own free will. Lastly, we expect safe passage from your territory into ours when this meeting is finished."

Everyone in the room quieted, waiting for their leader's response. Hackett and the Inean Ambassador stared at one another. Neither one was backing down. It was like a gunfight; the crowd was waiting for someone to twitch, which would start the shootout.

Benson jolted as an Inean began tearing off her jacket. Then another grabbed Larson's jacket and began to pull it off her. They managed to turn her slightly and tear the jacket off her.

The Ambassador stood and watched for a few seconds, then called them off. The guards let them go. Both women were shaken because they knew what the Ineans could easily do to them.

All four groups stood and stared at each other for several seconds before the Inean Ambassador spoke. "We will agree to those terms." He was cornered, and Hackett knew it. They were not out of trouble yet. "We will reconvene tomorrow afternoon to finish this up."

Hackett wondered what the delay was. So he spoke up. "Sir, I was informed that we need to report back to Earth. There is an emergency that requires our attention. We need to leave orbit in less than ten hours to make it on time. Is there any way we can wrap this up today? It is not a lot to revise."

"Fine, Captain! Fine! This will reconvene in six hours. You will get off our planet right after that. I will have ships escort you out of our territory," he said, fuming now.

Hackett nodded and sat back down. The Kosuan and Angowains did the same. They all looked at one another with caution as they gathered their papers. Everyone knew you don't normally piss off an Inean and live to tell about it. For the moment, that is what just happened. For now, they lived.

The Inean guards that had harassed them before escorted Hackett and his crew from the conference room to their room several floors up. The guards pushed and shoved, taunting them the whole way. One guard grabbed the jacket away from Benson as she walked. They tormented her by grabbing at her, then shoving and pulling at her hair. They even started on Larson by tearing at her shirt. Both women were nervous. The men were kept from them as they walked and couldn't do anything to help. They tugged and pulled at them. Finally, as they got to the door, one of the guards pulled Benson toward him and started tearing at her shirt. Hackett lunged forward and pushed her into the room ahead of him as another Inean guard tried to grab her by the hair. He missed, and they all fell into the room. Hackett leaned up with his laser in hand as the door slammed shut.

FIFTY-SEVEN

MORRIS COULD HEAR the Ineans laughing outside. Hackett looked at Benson and helped her up off the floor while she pulled her shirt together. Morris helped Larson up, and everyone stood for a moment.

Hackett pulled out his wristwatch communicator, which was in his pocket, and contacted his ship. "*Saratoga.* Come in?"

"*Saratoga* here, O'Toole speaking. Go ahead, Captain." O'Toole sounded stressed.

"Is everything okay up there, Commander?" Hackett asked, knowing darn well it wasn't.

"No, Captain. The Ineans rammed into us a few minutes ago. Our primary energizer is offline. We are making repairs. I assume it is getting rough down there as well?" he asked.

"You could say that, Commander. We should be signing the agreement in six hours. I can't help wondering what curveballs will be thrown at us next, so be ready to get us out of here. Also, do you have a lock on our transport?"

"Yes, sir, the transport is still where you parked it," O'Toole said.

"Good, lock a torpedo on it in case we need to destroy it." Hackett now waited for O'Toole to respond. "Also, Lieutenant

Commander Benson and Lieutenant Larson need new uniforms. Can you teleport them to these coordinates?"

"Got it all, Captain. Uniforms will be on their way in a few minutes. *Saratoga* out." O'Toole closed the comm link.

"Thoughts?" Hackett asked.

Benson spoke first. "All I can add is that the Ineans are probably tearing into the Angowains right now, so we must be ready for a shift. I don't think the Kosuan will switch. They are acting on honor right now and will die doing so. So, at least we have the stronger of the two on our side."

Benson sat on the end of the bed.

There was a flash of light a few feet away from the group, and a box appeared on the floor.

Larson walked over to the box, which was clearly marked with the *Saratoga* logo, and opened it. She proceeded to distribute the uniforms and food packets. Hackett asked Morris to take Larson to the other room for a while so he could think.

He grabbed his food and hurried out the door. Larson followed right behind him with her laser in one hand and a fresh uniform in the other. Hackett and Benson remained behind. She was on the edge of the bed, pondering the latest events and wondering why they still lived. She stared at the vacuum-sealed turkey sandwich, which she eventually discarded without taking a bite. The thought of eating made her nauseous; no doubt, the effects of the hangover still turned her stomach. Hackett sat beside her and patted her knee. She slid closer and pulled him into her with one arm tightly around his waist. They sat there for several minutes, looking out the glass wall. They watched as a soft rain slowly splattered against the glass walls, without speaking. Hackett lay back on the bed and was joined by Benson, and they continued watching the rain fall.

Benson looked at him as he began to snore. She rested her head on his shoulder and covered them both with the blanket, and she fell asleep as well.

. . .

Several hours later, Hackett awoke to the chirping of his wristwatch. He was still half asleep when he answered it. "This is Hackett. Go ahead," he said, holding his wrist to his mouth.

Commander O'Toole was on the other side. "Sir, the Ineans just attacked a Kosuan ship in orbit. They inflicted heavy damage, and the Kosuan are fighting back. Other ships are closing in on their position. It looks like it is escalating up here, Sir."

Hackett woke up quickly now, while Benson continued snoring on his shoulder, so he stayed on the bed. "What is the ship's status, Commander? Can you put up a fight if needed?"

"Yes, Captain, the energizer has been repaired and is functioning. The matrix issue is something we are still contending with. We may win a fight, but unfortunately, we won't be able to leave the sector under our own power." There was a crash, and the warning sirens sounded over the tinny-sounding communicator.

"What happened, Commander?" Hackett asked as he left the bed and walked towards the glass wall. The rain was falling heavier now, almost pouring. Lightning crashed down to the ground not too far away, followed by wall-shaking thunder. Hackett was mesmerized by the droplets of water splattering against the glass with greater intensity.

“Sir, we’ve been hit by a particle weapon. We sustained minor damage. Unfortunately, I had to charge the shields,” O’Toole reported.

“Target the ship that fired on you and then contact them and tell them they don’t want to do this, Commander,” Hackett instructed.

Hackett could hear O'Toole talking to Giovanella and then to the Inean commander. O'Toole came back on the Captain's communicator. "Sir, they are moving off."

“Keep weapons locked on all ships. What time is it, anyway?” Hackett asked.

"Sir, it's 1615. Roughly four hours since you contacted us last," the commander clarified.

"Good, less than two hours until we get this signed. Can you get a message off to headquarters, or are we being jammed?" Hackett asked.

"No, Sir. They are not jamming us, but we have had no communication with Earth."

Hackett thought a moment. *Why would they? The Ineans must know by now that the Earth is in the midst of a colossal solar storm.* "Tell them the deal is to be done shortly, but we may not make it back. Give them a 'heads up' on your situation and tell them we did the deal with the Kosuan." Hackett instructed calmly.

"Yes, Captain, it may be all over by the time they get this," he said. "If they even get this," he added.

"I know, Commander; let's hope they get the message. Hackett out," Hackett signed off and paged Morris.

"Morris here," he said.

"Commander, it's nearly showtime. Could you and Larson wrap it up and come in here so we can plan our escape?" Hackett said.

"Yes, Sir, and I'm sorry for blowing up at you earlier, Captain. It won't happen again," Morris replied.

"That's okay, Commander. Stress does ugly things to a person. See you in a minute." Hackett ended the connection and lowered his hand. He sat back down on the bed, and Benson was still sleeping. She must have been exhausted. He lay down beside her and looked at her. Her neck still had the Ineans handprint wrapped around it. He ran his hand over her hair and kissed her on the forehead. She grinned in her sleep and curled up more. He didn't want to wake her, but he had to. He shook her lightly.

"Lieutenant Commander, wake up." She groaned, still not opening her eyes. "Lieutenant Commander, Tamora, wake up." She opened her eyes and looked at him. She sat up and yawned.

"How long was I out for?" she asked, fighting the sleep.

"Four hours. O'Toole woke me up. The Ineans attacked a Kosuan ship, and they took another shot at ours," Hackett said, looking at her. "The *Saratoga* sustained minor damage. The ship is okay for now."

She got up, grabbed her new uniform, and proceeded to the bathroom to clean up.

There was a knock at the main door, and Hackett drew his laser pistol and opened the door. It was Morris and Larson.

Larson looked around. "Where is Lieutenant Commander Benson?" she asked.

"In the head, getting ready," he replied, turning to Morris. "Have you any ideas how we can do this, Commander?"

"I do, but it's risky, sir," and the two men walked off to the corner of the room to discuss it privately. Larson wondered why she wasn't included, so she walked to the bathroom door and knocked.

"Hey, Benson, you all right?" she asked.

"Yeah, I'm fine, just taking a quick shower. I needed to wake up," Benson said through the door.

"Okay, just checking," she said, and went to the food packs in their backpacks, pulling out a drink for herself.

After several minutes, there was a hard knock at the door. Hackett and Morris drew their weapons and aimed while Larson opened the door and stepped aside. The Inean guards began to rush into the room and stopped. They looked at Larson and spat at her. Inean spit was thick and pungent, like the foulest breath you could ever imagine. Wiping it off did nothing to remove the odor or the putrid green color, which stained whatever was spit upon. Benson walked out of the head, fixing her hairpin in time for them to spit at her. She punched the first one in the mouth as hard as possible, and he reeled back.

"Idiot!" she yelled. "I've only had a clean jacket on for two minutes, and you have to dirty it with your spit," she yelled at him. Blood trickled down his face, and he wiped it with his sleeve. She sat on the edge of the bed and pulled on her boots. Then she picked up her laser pistol and strapped it to her belt. She stood up and tugged her jacket so it fit perfectly. Hackett and Morris looked at Benson and then at each other. They walked over, stripped the Ineans of their weapons, threw them under the bed, and pushed them out the door.

"Now it's our turn to take you for a walk," Benson growled. She stepped back and lunged feet first into the back of the guard, who grabbed her throat in the morning. She hit him square in the back of his knees, and he fell over, taking the others down with him like bowling pins.

They slowly got up and stared at her, and she cocked her gun.

"Lieutenant Commander, I know you want to get even, but now is NOT a good time," Hackett said.

She looked at him and smiled. "I'm just having some fun, Captain. Maybe we could keep them as slaves, and they can experience what that kind of life is like." She nailed another one in the back of the knees, and he buckled under his own weight and fell to the floor.

"That's ENOUGH, Lieutenant Commander," Hackett said firmly.

She backed off and joined the rest of them. "I never had a pet before. Well, other than the ones that moo, at least."

Larson was envious that she had the guts to do that. "You're tough. Teach me some of that later," Larson said, and Benson nodded.

They piled into the elevator and went down to the main floor. The Ineans exited first, then Hackett, Morris, Larson, and Benson. One of the Ineans Benson beat up was limping, drawing the attention of the Kosuan, who exited from another elevator. They all walked to the main hall. The Kosuan sized up the women and approved.

The Ineans left them at the door, and they lumbered off. Hackett led his party to the table and took their seats. The Kosuan came in behind them and took their seats. The Ineans entered the room and took their seats. The Inean Ambassador stood up and apologized that the Angowains could not complete the meeting because they had to leave on urgent business.

Hackett and Morris looked at each other with the *yeah, right* look. The Kosuan didn't buy it either. They wanted to see how the meeting went. A buzz went around the chamber, and the Ambassador had to bang his gavel to bring the room to order.

The Ambassador stood up. "Fellow delegates and honored guests. We have come to the end of this meeting and are distributing the final version of the agreement for everyone to review and sign."

The Inean women spread the papers around and shoved Benson and Larson harshly into the table.

Everyone flipped through it, and Hackett and the rest of his team were satisfied. The Kosuan nodded that it was acceptable. The Ineans noted the nods of approval and began signing documents. The papers were passed from person to person around the table until everyone had signed off and received a complete copy in their language.

The Inean Ambassador abruptly stood and thanked the Kosuan for coming and participating, and he wished it was the beginning of the peace process between them. The Kosuan growled at him and started for the door.

The Inean Ambassador then looked at Hackett. "It was an interesting negotiation, Captain Hackett. We look forward to growing ties between our cultures."

"Thank you, Ambassador. I look forward to that as well as do the rest of our people," Hackett stated as he recalled his brief conversation with the Inean emperor. He knew long-lasting ties would not happen. They would be lucky if they lasted long enough to escape the Inean system.

The Inean leaned in toward Hackett. "Are you sure I couldn't have her for just half of one of your hours?" the Ambassador asked, keeping his eyes on Benson, making her uncomfortable.

"No, sir," Hackett replied quickly.

"Very well then," he said while looking at the others regarding them. "I trust you found what you came for in my office?" He turned back to Hackett, "It would be in your best interest to get to your transport and get off the planet quickly before someone changes their mind." He paused for a moment. "We have two ships that will escort you out of our solar system in one of your hours."

"Is that necessary?" Hackett asked.

"Some of our military people have a habit of acting independently and have vowed to destroy your ship. So don't delay. I won't have those ships available for long." The Ambassador reached into the case beside him and handed Hackett a large folder. "Here are the plans for the machines you will build on Earth to correct its climate. Based on the size of your planet, you will need to build 20 of these over the next five years, and they must be fully functional in that time. Your planet is at a dangerous point and will soon be beyond our technology."

Hackett nodded and turned away. He was concerned about the threat because he knew it was all too real. His ship was in no condition for a fight, and he suspected the Ineans knew it as well. Without haste, he heeded the Inean's words and quickly ushered his people out the door.

Several Inean guards surrounded them and walked with them until everyone was outside the building. The guards stood by the entrance while Hackett and his people entered the square. The day's heat held them back for a moment as they adjusted to the change. Steam rose from the brick courtyard as the rain fell heavily again. The steam created a thick haze that made Hackett's people uncomfortable. It was also challenging to see the transport through the mist. To Hackett, it was like wearing a scuba suit to a sauna.

There were still hundreds of angry Ineans outside between them and the transport. Hackett could tell a riot was brewing. Many shouted obscenities and death threats their way. Others threw anything they could find, rocks, bottles, discharged weapon power cylinders, and so on. Morris had to duck as a rock, the size of a baseball, buzzed by his head.

Hackett unlocked the transport and stepped aside while the hatch opened. Benson jumped in, sat in the pilot's chair, and powered up the engines. While she waited for the engines, she tossed her backpack under her seat. Larson was next and sat at the tactical station, checking the transport's weapons. Morris checked the shields and the fuel. Hackett tossed the folder the Ambassador gave him to Larson, who locked it away.

As Hackett began to enter the transport, several Ineans reached in and grabbed him. They succeeded in dragging him out of the transport and back towards the compound. Morris reached for his laser pistol and went for the door. He was greeted by a pair of Inean guards, and they slammed him back into the transport. His pistol flew back against the wall, and he scrambled to pick it up.

Benson fired thrusters and turned towards the direction from which the Captain was being dragged. The Ineans beat and kicked him as they dragged him across the square. She flew low, knocking people over with the hot exhaust of the transport as she closed in. Several guards fired hand lasers at the transport, and many bursts entered the open door.

Morris regained his laser pistol, staggered back to the door, and returned fire into the crowd. The transport flew low and dragged on the ground, creating a shower of sparks behind it as Morris and Larson were both shooting out the door, clearing a path around their Captain.

The guards dropped him. Morris noticed them putting something down the back of his jacket, and they ran off.

"Benson! Drop us here!" Morris yelled as the adrenaline rush took over.

Benson dropped the transport and looked over her shoulder. "Here they come, Commander!"

"We'll be just a second!" he yelled as he and Larson jumped out of the transport.

Hackett stumbled to his feet. He noticed a woman, a human woman, naked and tied to a post like a horse to a hitching post. The Ineans were almost on him as he lunged toward the woman. He got to her in a split second. She had been beaten badly and had many open wounds caked with mud and dirt, but she was still alive. Her face was covered with dried, cracked blood. He looked at her as her eyes went big. He fumbled with the rope around her neck. Her neck was raw from the coarse rope cutting into it. He cut her loose, and Morris caught up with him. He shoved the woman to Larson, and she gave Hackett her laser pistol. They began shooting at the feet of the Ineans to make them back off. Some did, and most didn't. They continued to press forward.

One of the Ineans clubbed Hackett from behind. He never saw them coming. He collapsed to the ground while tossing the laser to Larson. Larson made it back with the woman and pushed her into the transport. She then turned around and ran out of the transport again with Morris.

Benson cursed. The mob was almost on top of them as they ran.

They ran several feet to Hackett, who was unconscious on the ground, as a handful of Ineans stepped away from him. Morris grabbed him while Larson fired several shots at the closing mob to hold them off. It didn't work. They still advanced.

Morris dragged Hackett back to the transport while Larson continued to fire round after round toward the advancing Ineans. Her laser was getting hot from the constant use, and she had to keep switching hands. She finally locked the laser in overload mode and threw the gun as she followed Morris into the transport.

"Benson, get us out of here!" Morris yelled as the laser pistol overloaded and exploded in the crowd.

Rocks and bottles pummeled the transport as the mob outside grew increasingly unruly. Larson charged the outside of the transport and shocked the crowd near the transport, forcing them to fall back.

Morris tried to contact the *Saratoga*, but there was no response from the starship to his pages. Morris paged them again and again, but still no response.

"Morris, scan for our ship," Hackett said groggily.

"Captain, are you all right?"

Hackett just nodded.

Morris continued, "Yes, sir, scanning," he said. After a minute, he responded, "Sir, I found our ship. I'm sending the coordinates to Benson. I also know why we can't communicate, Sir."

"Why is that, Commander?" Hackett asked.

"We are being jammed again, Sir. I'm scanning for traffic overhead." Morris dove back into the viewer. "There are several Inean ships overhead, and they have the *Saratoga* surrounded, Captain."

"Get me the Inean ambassador," Hackett ordered. He was getting angry.

"One minute, sir," Morris said, "they are finding him, Captain."

"This is Ambassador Sharoock," came the gruff voice over the speaker.

"Ambassador, this is Captain Hackett. Your people are jamming our transmissions to our ship, and your ships have converged on our starship, so we cannot dock. Why is that?"

"We are doing it for your protection, Captain. The Angowains told us about your plan with the Kosuan, and they are hunting for you. You will stay between our ships all the way to yours. Once you are close enough, we will drop our jamming so you can land on your ship. I would suggest you take off now while you have a chance." The screen went blank.

"Any validity to what they say, Commander?" Hackett asked.

"I doubt after what just happened. The way the ships are lining up could indicate what he said, but I can't be a hundred percent positive," Morris said.

"We'll have to take our chances then. Tamora, set course, and let's get the hell out of here."

Morris noticed he called her by her first name. Hackett never addressed someone by their first name. This was something new, and Morris felt he needed to find out why. To ensure Hackett was all right. It wasn't like him to deviate from his character.

"Yes, Sir, gladly. Course plotted and laid in, starting engines," Benson said, and the ship rumbled to life. "Taking off, Captain." The ship slowly lifted off, rolled to port, and accelerated as it sped toward *Saratoga*.

Hackett looked at their unexpected passenger huddled in the corner, shaking from fear. She was crying. Hackett got up and staggered towards her and held out his hand. He guided her to a seat and buckled her in. She was still naked, but she didn't seem to care. Morris came over with a blanket and wrapped her in it.

"What's your name?" Hackett asked.

"My...my name is..." she sputtered. She looked up at him, and tears rolled down her cheeks. "My children... I... I need to find my children." She was shaking uncontrollably now.

"Where are you from?" Hackett asked, knowing full well the woman was in shock. He was also horrified at the prospect that there could be human children on Inea.

She stared at him, then at Morris. "Colony S... S... Saco three."

"Saco Three! That was raided weeks ago. You've been here that long? Are there others?" Morris said, unbelieving.

"Yes, too many. The ships... just kept... coming and bringing us. Ship after ship. Bringing hundreds of us," she cried. "No one to protect us!" She wiped her eyes on the blanket. "They beat us and tortured us, and beat us again while laughing at us. So many dead. Why, why do they hate us?"

"I, I don't know, but we are trying to stop it," Hackett said, wishing he could believe what he just said. *Trying to stop it, ha! You tried to stop it, and it only got worse!* He said to himself. *You failed, Hackett.*

Benson guided the transport out of the atmosphere and between the Inean ships toward the *Saratoga*. One ship swung out of position, and Benson had to maneuver quickly and then again. They closed on the *Saratoga*. Hackett tried to contact the ship, but with no luck.

Hackett squirmed in his chair, which got the attention of Morris.

"Sir, are you all right?" Morris asked.

"Something? Ahhh!" he yelped as he jumped out of his chair. He frantically ripped off the top of his jacket, and several palm-sized spiders fell to the floor. One of them hissed at Hackett, and Morris saw the venom dripping from its fangs. Hackett went nuts as he stomped them to death on the floor. He grabbed a laser pistol from his belt and began firing at the floor of the transport, which punctured several holes through the metal plating and into the control systems of the transport. As the craft rocked hard from the damage he caused, he fell on top of Benson while she tried to control the transport. He continued to fire the laser pistol until Morris and Larson subdued him. A loud snap and a blue beam of light sizzled by Larson's head as a laser pulse singed her hair as it went by into the ceiling. Morris removed the weapon and held him to the floor.

Larson grabbed a medical kit and ripped it open while Morris fought to hold Hackett on the floor. She snapped a tube of liquid onto a gun-shaped device, held it to his neck, and shot the substance into his body with a pop and hiss of the medical injection gun. The sedative worked quickly, and Morris was able to release him after a minute.

Benson had the transport under control and returned to their previous course. However, several red lights were flashing brightly on her panel.

Benson looked over her shoulder towards Morris. "Commander?" she asked as her voice broke from the vibrations running through the transport.

Morris looked up and saw the blood rolling down her cheek from her ear. "What is it, Miss Benson?"

"What's wrong with him?" she asked as she looked down at Hackett.

"I can't say, Lieutenant Commander, but it isn't good," Morris replied.

"Screw this 'it's classified' bullshit and tell me what is going on!" she screamed.

Morris looked at her and decided to tell her, but not all of it, just enough to satisfy her curiosity. "Fine! The last time we were here, he was taken from us and tortured by the Ineans. They used specially-trained spiders to attack him while he was tied down to a table. They bit him all over, injecting his body with a venom that attacks the brain. It is supposed to make you go insane and kill everything you come in contact with, including yourself. Only it didn't quite work as they had planned. He is the only human to fight it. Most of the time, he wins. Other times he doesn't." She went to say something. Morris cut her off before she could say it. He knew what her question was. "No, there is no cure, only time. He is getting better, very slowly."

Benson struggled with their craft. "What happened to your last navigator?"

Morris couldn't talk about her. Larson saw him fight for the words and answered for him. "She's dead."

Benson spied a tear in Morris's eye. "I know that already."

"Yes, she," Larson replied. "Her name was Sasha Young. She and Morris were..."

"Stop! Enough!" Morris yelled.

Sasha Young. The attractive third-year navigator was the woman Morris had walked away from. The memory of her was too much for him. If he had only acted on his feelings when he had the chance, she would still be alive, and he would be happy. The pain hurt more now since Hackett revealed she had been pregnant with his child. He looked at Larson. He didn't love her. With her, it was just sex and nothing else.

Hackett began to stir, slowly got up, and leaned on the back of the chair. He swayed side to side as Benson fought to keep the transport in a straight line. He looked at Morris and then Larson. He was concerned that his career was over now.

"Captain?" Larson queried.

"Lieutenant?" Hackett replied as he wiped the sweat from his forehead.

"What happened to you?" she asked him.

"Those things, the Ineans planted them on me. They knew what would happen once I knew they were there. Is everyone all right?" he asked as he looked around.

"Everyone is fine, Captain. We are closing in on our ship," Morris replied.

Hackett sat back in his seat. He watched Benson while she piloted the transport, but she would not look at him. He saw the streaks under her eyes as she stared out the window. He knew there was no hope of a relationship with her now, so he also looked out.

Morris and Larson took their seats and buckled up. No one said anything for several minutes as the transport left the atmosphere.

They were now less than 5,000 kilometers and closing. The *Saratoga* didn't appear to know they were coming up behind them. Benson had to swerve again to avoid an erratic Inean ship. She was wondering if they actually piloted badly or were getting in the way on purpose.

FIFTY-EIGHT

SARAH HINES REMAINED strapped in her seat in the life pod and wept as the heat inside the pod rose beyond the unbearable point. The heat was oppressive inside, and breathing became difficult. The six scientists from the observatory were being cooked slowly. She glanced at the thermometer on the wall, which was inching beyond 130 degrees. She glanced at Commander Williams, who had already stripped off his shirt and t-shirt. His skin was soaked with perspiration. She unzipped her shirt and began to fan herself as best she could. She didn't care anymore. The rest of her team had already passed out or probably died. In either case, they stopped moving a while ago.

She could hear the voice of someone calling them over the speaker. It was another ship, but she was too weak and lethargic to reach the blinking transmit button on the control panel inches from her.

The observatory jolted hard and then again. After a minute, it felt like they were moving. A few minutes later, she was snapped back in her seat, and then it began to spin. The sensation was too much, and she vomited all over herself. She looked over to Williams. He was awake again and looking at her. Blood began to trickle from his nose, and he vomited as well. "Too... ho...t," he mumbled, and he slumped back down again.

Some time had passed, she wasn't sure how long, but it seemed like forever. Her eyes glazed over, and she could no longer focus on anything. It was all just a blur. There was the sensation of moving again.

The lights on the life pod flickered and finally went black. There was a croaking noise from the control panel, and a red light flickered and went out after a minute. Suddenly, everything went out. Their power cell had vaporized off the pod. Hines knew it would only be minutes before the temperature skyrocketed and cooked her. She also knew she would be dead before then.

After a few minutes, she checked the temperature gauge on the wall, which had dropped below 130. It was cooling down! She tried to tell Williams, but her throat was so dry she couldn't speak. She looked up again; it was now only 120, then 115. She began to cry again. It was over.

Outside the fried observatory, two crewmen in spacesuits from the *Nordstrom* banged on the life pod with a wrench. Outside, in the vacuum of space, there was no noise, but inside, it rang through the life pod. Williams was awake again. He was counting the clangs on the hull of the pod. Morse code! He knew this! Someone was telling him something. For the life of him, he could not remember all the letters.

One of the *Nordstrom* officers lifted a handheld scanner to the pod and watched the display. It showed five weak life signs inside. He then gave his partner the thumbs up and attached the last cable to the pod. He pressed a button on his sleeve. "*Nordstrom*, this is Ramerez. The cable is wrapped around the pod. There are five weak life signs inside. You can begin pulling it to the ship. Their life support is off, and they have no power. We can't read the air quality. I can bet it ain't good in there."

Lewis listened to the report from the bridge. "Got it, Ramerez.

We are pulling it in now. Once we get it close enough, we can cut it free from the rest of the station and pull just the pod in."

"Got it, Captain. Morse and Bollins are waiting with the cutting lasers," Ramerez said, and he could see the *Nordstrom* getting bigger as the observatory was reeled in.

After a few minutes, the observatory was within feet of the *Nordstrom*'s lower bomber doors, which had been opened to space. Morse and Bollins began cutting the three pins holding the life pod to the observatory. Why the explosive bolts didn't go off is anyone's guess, but they didn't, and they were also difficult to cut. They cut and cut —one pass, then another, and another. Eventually, the pod broke away from the observatory.

The four officers grabbed the nearly 20-foot round pod and pushed it into the lower bomber hold with their rocket packs. Once inside, Ramerez pressed another button on his sleeve, and the large double doors swung shut with a bang. His men pushed the pod against the doors, and he pressed another button that activated the gravity plating. The pod settled on the doors. He watched the gauge on the wall display the air pressure in the hold. It was rising slowly. After a minute, maybe two, a green light flashed on. His was the first helmet to come off, revealing a soaked man inside.

Considering the environment, it was a hazardous procedure, but it was ultimately successful.

Morse and Bollins found what was left of the hatch. It had been melted into the frame, and there was no way to open it. Both men lined up the cutting lasers and began to burn through the hatch casing.

Inside, Hines and Williams felt gravity return. They knew they were inside another ship, and now the wait was on for the hatch to open. They looked at their friends and fellow scientists. None of them had stirred yet. At least they saw them breathing. That was a good sign. After the pod settled they heard the cutting lasers working on the hatch. They unbuckled, stumbled away, and waited.

FIFTY-NINE

ON THE BRIDGE of the *Saratoga*, Stephan Bowers was at his sensors station, monitoring an object coming up behind them. He called over to O'Toole.

O'Toole looked over, "What do you have, Lieutenant?"

"I think it's our transport, but they are coming at a vector and speed that is inconsistent with a normal transport approach," he replied.

"Son-of-a-bitch!" O'Toole cursed. "Battle stations, charge the shields. Target that transport, but DO NOT fire. Giovanella, try to contact that transport."

"Yes, sir, trying. Those Inean ships are jamming us," Giovanella said.

"Boost the gain. Try and cut through it!" O'Toole yelled.

"Yes, sir, trying focused beam, 100 gigawatts... transport four, this is *Saratoga* Respond?" Giovanella said.

"Sir, the target is within our security perimeter," Bowers turned to tell O'Toole.

"Understood, Mr. Giovanella." O'Toole was getting nervous. If they couldn't raise the transport, they would have to fire upon it.

. . .

Back on the transport, Morris was frantically pressing buttons on his console. "Sir, the *Saratoga* has a laser lock on us. We're entering their security perimeter." He cocked his head to listen to the radio. "I think I've gotten something from them. It's Giovanella. Hold on a minute. I know what they did." He pressed several more buttons and turned the frequency knobs to dial it up. "*Saratoga*, this is transport four. We are OK. It's us, don't fire. Open the bay doors!" He repeated it.

Larson was at her station. "Commander, they didn't get it. They are powering lasers!"

"Mr. Morris, try again; Miss Benson, all stop," Hackett commanded.

Morris repeated his message.

On the *Saratoga,* Giovanella was straining to hear anything over the interference. He shook his head at O'Toole, who had only one option left. "Target the transport and fire."

"Aye, sir, firing..." said Larson's replacement.

"Wait, wait!" Yelled Giovanella.

"Hold that order. Don't fire!" O'Toole yelled.

"What is it, Mr. Giovanella?" asked O'Toole.

"It's Commander Morris. They're on the transport. He says they're OK. Open the doors. Protocol one-five-two-nine-morris," Giovanella said with a sigh of relief.

"Lower aft shields and power down the lasers. Hangar bay control, open the doors," O'Toole said as he wiped his forehead. "Mr. Giovanella, that was too close."

"Yes, sir," he replied, slumping slightly in his chair.

In the hangar bay, the huge, damaged doors chattered and growled their way open just enough to accept the transport. Benson ignited the thrusters to move toward the open doors. The inside of the hangar bay was crowded with several transports lined up ten deep on each side of the bay and all angled toward the door for quick departure. The hangar bay was almost two hundred feet deep, but was quite packed for its size. Benson would have to be careful flying the transport at the angle and speed they were moving so she wouldn't crash. As the transport approached, an Inean ship broke formation and closed on the transport.

On the bridge, Bowers watched as the Inean ship approached. His sensors began to flash, indicating a power surge in the Inean warship, and the transport rolled to starboard, dove, and then came back up as a bright red bolt of light nearly ripped the transport apart.

O'Toole ordered the lasers locked on the Inean ship and to fire if they came any closer.

"Time until the transport is inside?" O'Toole asked.

"Two minutes, Commander," replied Bowers. "The Inean ship is making another run at the transport, sir."

"Lock lasers on the Inean ship, Ensign," O'Toole said.

"Sir, they are locking weapons. They are building to fire," Bowers replied nervously.

"Fire, Ensign!" O'Toole said.

Blue bolts of light erupted from the aft laser cannons just under the hangar bay and barely streaked over the transport and burned into the Inean ship as it was getting ready to fire on the transport. The ship lurched to its side violently and broke off its attack.

Another Inean ship moved in and fired into the hangar bay, which erupted into flames as one of the parked shuttles exploded. Due to the vacuum of space, the fire extinguished itself quickly, leaving the landing bay severely damaged. They fired another shot at the transport, which Benson was unable to avoid altogether. It struck their starboard thruster, sending the transport into a spin. Benson fought the controls and manually steered the craft straight again as warning buzzers sounded throughout.

Blue bolts of light left the aft laser cannons of the *Saratoga* and blasted a hole into the Inean ship. The *Saratoga* continued by firing several torpedoes that struck and destroyed the Inean ship in a mammoth explosion that pelted the transport and the aft section of the *Saratoga* with shrapnel.

“Everyone! Buckle up quickly!” Hackett ordered as the transport was still not under complete control.

Benson dumped the remainder of their fuel and ignited it as they hit the landing bay. There was a bright flash of light as the transport hit the edge of the landing bay and began to tumble. Dumping the fuel and igniting it gave the impression that they had blown up. It also avoided that scenario once inside the ship, which could have destroyed the *Saratoga.* The transport tumbled rapidly out of control and slammed into other transports before coming to rest on its side against the far wall below the hanger control room. The bay doors began to close before they had come to rest.

The control room could see that a fire had broken out inside the craft. Unfortunately, they had to wait for the bay to pressurize before sending people to help them. It would take three minutes for the bay to be pressurized enough, assuming the bay doors closed.

On the bridge, O'Toole had his hands full. Several Inean ships had broken formation and were now following the *Saratoga.* O'Toole knew he had to run but had no idea how far they would get. As he sat back in the captain's chair, a red flash of light appeared on the floor before them. An object took form on the floor, and O'Toole expected the worst.

He slammed the button on the chair before the object finished building on the floor. "Aux-com, take control now! Clear the bridge. Clear the bridge! Mr. Bowers, place a force field around that object." O'Toole was out of his chair, grabbed the navigator by the collar, and threw him towards the elevator doors. Everyone cleared out, and Bowers set a force field around the object before leaving the bridge.

In the elevator, O'Toole caught his breath. He thought to himself that he was getting too old for this. "Aux-com, set course and get us out of here, maximum speed."

“Sir, there’s an Inean ship in the way! We can’t move,” the Lieutenant on duty said.

"Lock lasers and torpedoes on that ship. We'll be there in a minute," O'Toole said.

The aux-com was located several decks below the bridge, somewhat forward of the main bridge. It was designed to take control of the ship in the event of an incident that rendered the bridge unreliable.

The elevator doors opened, and O'Toole ran out and down the corridor. The rest of the bridge crew followed him. Something rocked the ship hard, causing much of the crew to spill against the wall and onto the floor. O'Toole knew they were under fire. They quickly jumped to their feet and continued their run to the auxiliary control room while the lights in the corridor flickered and sparked. Once in aux-com, O'Toole relieved the Lieutenant on duty and took over. The rest of his team settled in and got to work immediately.

O'Toole assessed the situation and had them fire lasers at the Inean ship blocking them. The Ineans returned fire, draining the shields. The *Saratoga* banked to port and fired again, striking the Inean ship in its bridge. O'Toole then ordered a spread of torpedoes that shot out of the *Saratoga* and hit their mark. The Inean ship exploded into a blinding fireball. A shock wave erupted from the blast, peppering the *Saratoga* with bits of the destroyed ship. Davies turned the *Saratoga* into the wave. Once it was beyond the ship, she engaged the quantum drive.

The space in front of the *Saratoga* twisted into a funnel in space. The ship fired its main thrusters and disappeared through the fiery mess of the Inean warship into the wormhole. The ship accelerated to quantum three, then four, and leveled off at quantum five. Some of the Inean ships were capable of going that fast and were in pursuit. O'Toole ordered more speed, and the ship began to shudder as it passed quantum six. At least they began to inch away.

"Engine room! I need a status report, " O'Toole yelled into the comm.

"Hafnium composite matrix is down to 20 percent, sir. We have about six hours of power remaining at this speed. The integrity of our hull is dangerously low. We have many supports and reinforcing ribs that are damaged. You can't go any faster, Commander, not without flying apart."

O'Toole pressed another button. "Hangar bay, what is the status of the transport?" O'Toole asked.

"The transport is on fire, sir. We are trying to put it out now. An Inean laser hit it as they dumped their fuel when they entered the hangar bay," the operator said excitedly.

"Any survivors?" O'Toole asked, feeling the lump in his throat.

"We don't know yet. It will be a few minutes before we can confirm," the operator replied.

"Understood. Security, this is O'Toole. Meet me on the bridge. We need to investigate the package we received," O'Toole said. He was calming down some. He was concerned about what was teleported to the bridge as they left and by whom. Was it a bomb? *Probably* he thought, *and if so, when was it set to go off?* He was also concerned about the captain and the others on the transport. Were they dead?

He got out of his chair and left control of the ship to Giovanella. He met the security team at the elevator to the bridge. The elevator shuddered and groaned its way to the top, stopping with a thud. The doors slid open, and the security team cautiously entered the bridge. O'Toole looked forward at the view screen with the twisted space spiraling in front of them, chasing the elusive black dot that never seemed to get closer. Two guards had handheld scanners and swept over the box on the floor.

"It isn't a bomb, sir. It's high-grade Hafnium platters," one of the guards determined.

O'Toole lifted his arm and spoke into his communicator, "Auxcom, you can release the force field on the bridge."

"Yes, Commander. Done!" Bowers said.

He slowly approached the wooden box once the blue rippling energy field disappeared. O'Toole pried off the lid with his fingertips and tossed it aside. He looked inside. He rummaged through some packing dust and pulled out a half-dozen shiny synthetic silver platters. They were Kosuan, and they had been cut nearly to Alliance specs. It would be enough to get them home. The challenge now was that they would have to stop and power down long enough to install them, and the Inean ships remained hot on their tail.

Over the ship-wide speaker, O'Toole heard the page, "medics to the transport bay, stat." He knew that it couldn't be good. He immediately had the security officers take the box and contents to the engine room.

SIXTY

MORSE AND BOLLINS finished cutting into the melted hatch of the life pod they had rescued. Several others, including Ramerez, stepped up with pry bars and wedged them in the small space created by the cutting lasers. They began to put pressure on the pry bars as the medical team ran onto the deck with all their equipment.

"One, two, three, push!" Ramerez yelled as the melted steel hatch groaned away from the opening. "Next team, step in and grab it at a different point."

Four others stepped in, wedged their pry bars into the opening, and pushed while the others pulled out. The hatch began to release.

"Step back. Don't let it fall on you!" Ramerez barked.

The four crewmen leaned to the side and pried harder, and the hatch fell away and landed on the deck with a crash. Ramerez was first in to help the occupants out. He spied Hines and unbuckled her and guided her out. She was dizzy and soaked with sweat. Then he assisted Williams out of his seat and to the opening, where the medical staff received him. He then went to the next person, who was not moving, Peredo. Ramerez felt for a pulse, but there wasn't any. He unbuckled him and dragged him to the opening. He continued until he had evacuated all the scientists from the pod. He remarked afterward about the smell. It was the smell of sweat and death. It was true, however. The only survivors were Hines and Williams. Everyone else had died in the pod, literally cooked to death.

Hines and Williams spent the next few days in the ship's hospital as the giant battleship lumbered back to Earth on only two burned engines.

Both scientists struggled to cope with the loss of their friends. Both decided to do their research closer to Earth from now on. It should be safer, or so they thought.

SIXTY-ONE

ONCE THE BRIDGE had been secured, O'Toole hurried aft to the hangar bay. He walked onto the deck and saw the charred remains of the transport smashed up against the wall. The supports holding the upper deck had been damaged, and the deck above had buckled. Techs were standing on top of the overturned transport, struggling to open the hatch. It was hot and smoking. They managed to pry it away, and they jumped in. After a minute, they lifted the captain out of the transport, placed him on a stretcher, and lowered him to the medical team that waited below. They laid him on the floor, hooked up their equipment, and began evaluating his condition. They started feeding him oxygen and performed CPR on him. Next up were Larson and Morris. More medics entered the hangar bay and set up a triage unit. O'Toole knew it was serious, or they would have taken them directly to the sick bay.

Next, they passed up the woman whom they had rescued. Her blanket hung uselessly from her and eventually dropped to the floor. They covered her once she was down and performed CPR on her.

"Where is Lieutenant Commander Benson?" O'Toole asked as he felt the lump rise in his throat, as the tech at the hatch had a grimace on his face. Another minute passed, and finally, her lifeless body was passed out of the transport and set on the floor. The medics hurried to her and set up their equipment.

Hackett was awake, as was Morris. Larson was still unconscious but alive. Hackett struggled to his feet against the doctor's requests, as usual, and went over to Benson. He was coughing through the oxygen mask he wore.

The medic pulled out a set of paddles, stepped back, and put them to Benson's chest. Her body jumped up and then back down. Hackett looked at the monitor on the floor. It was flat-lined. He stumbled back, sat down, and watched them frantically work on her. They used the paddles repeatedly. The doctor pounded on her chest, and there was a beep, then another, then she flat-lined again. He pulled out a needle and a bottle. He stabbed the needle into the bottle, sucked some clear liquid into the syringe, and tossed the bottle back down. He ripped open her shirt and felt for a spot between her breasts, stuck the needle in, and injected the liquid directly into her heart.

Hackett crawled over and picked up her hand, holding it tightly. Her skin was cold and damp to the touch. He closed his eyes, put his head down, and mumbled something. The medics watched for a second in disbelief, and then they zapped her again with the paddles. The monitor began to beep again and again. Slow at first, but it became faster and stronger within several seconds. The medics looked at Hackett in amazement and then administered their IVs to her. After a few minutes, she stabilized enough to be moved. They placed her on a backboard and strapped her to a stretcher for the trip to the ship's medical ward. They attached the monitors to the shelf under the stretcher and hung the IVs on the pole above her head.

Morris had gone back to check on Larson. She was awake and coughing badly. The medics prepped her for the ride up to medical as well. Morris walked over to Hackett, who remained kneeling on the floor, looking down.

"Captain," Morris coughed.

Hackett looked up at him. He wiped a tear from his cheek and stood up. He removed the oxygen mask and cleared his throat.

"Commander," he said hoarsely. Partly because of the smoke and in part because of the way he felt about Benson.

"Lieutenant Larson is going to be OK, sir," Morris said.

Hackett nodded. "We're not sure about Benson. Who's in charge right now?" Hackett asked.

O'Toole walked up beside him. "Lieutenant Commander Giovanella, sir. We are currently set up in aux-com and about to reestablish on the bridge. We are at quantum six point two and putting some distance between us and Ineans."

"Thank God. I've had enough of that hellhole for one career," Hackett stated, throwing his oxygen mask to the floor in anger. He glanced at the woman they rescued. "How is she doing?"

The medic looked up. "What happened to her, Captain?" Doctor Williams asked with sincere concern for the woman's condition.

Hackett looked down and saw the woman they had rescued in a new light. She was bloodied from head to toe and dirty like she had been dragged through the mud. Her hair was caked with dirt as if it hadn't been washed in months. "She was a prisoner of the Ineans. Will she live?" he asked with a glance toward the medics finishing their work on Benson.

"I think so. We need to take her to the medical facility and run some tests. At least she is alive," The doctor replied as she gingerly inspected the unconscious woman for any broken bones before she slid the backboard under her.

Hackett glanced one more time toward Benson and nodded that he understood. He turned away and headed for the door. Hackett needed to clear her out of his mind and think of his ship and crew. He knew before O'Toole gave him the report that they were not yet out of danger. "Walk with me, Commander, and update me on our situation."

"Yes, sir, where are we going?" O'Toole asked. He sensed the captain wasn't quite up to par and wasn't sure why. Morris wasn't forthcoming at all as to what was wrong, either.

"The bridge," he replied. The officers left the commotion of the hangar bay behind to the medical staff and clean-up crews and strolled forward to the bridge. O'Toole went into great detail on the condition of the ship and the more alarming problem of Earth. They still had not heard what had transpired back home, except for a few sketchy details from other ships trying to contact the planet for assistance. The ship was battered and still space-worthy, barely. They now had enough fuel and gold-plated Hafnium platters to get home. However, with each passing hour without communication from Earth, they began to fear the worst had happened. They began to wonder if the scientists were correct in their prediction about the fate of Earth. Hackett generally shrugged off the experts' concerns as fear-mongering. They wondered if a hostile race, like the Kosuan or any of the dozen others within striking distance, would take advantage of a bad situation. Hackett thought back to how easy it had been to negotiate with the Kosuan on the planet of Inea-Four. He quickly shook it from his mind. He knew Earth was still there and that they would receive news soon.

Hackett was exhausted and looked it. He and Morris were covered in soot and smelled like burnt plastic and electronics from the transport. The side of Hackett's jacket was burned and still smoldered as he walked.

Once O'Toole finished his report to the captain and the first officer, he excused himself and went to the engine room to retrofit the new Kosuan Materials. He knew it would take some time to execute the retrofit. The bridge crew had returned and resumed standard control of their ship.

Hackett pulled Morris aside once O'Toole was gone and told him to get cleaned up, take some time for himself, and then relieve him so he could do the same.

Morris agreed, left the bridge, and went to his quarters. Hackett remained on the bridge and spent the time updating his logs, a task that took some time. It kept his mind off Benson until Morris could return. It also gave him time to unwind from the demanding mission they had completed.

The bridge was quiet as Hackett closed the terminal on the arm of his chair. He had finally finished his log entries, for now. He sat and stared out the main viewer, watching the spiraling wormhole tunnel before him as he reflected on the mission they had just finished. Bowers turned to Hackett and brought him back to the present with his report that the Inean ships had fallen beyond the sensor's range, but at last check, they were still in pursuit.

Hackett acknowledged Bowers and sent another message to Alliance headquarters, including his logs, which confirmed that the mission was a success. He didn't believe it, though. He also added a footnote questioning how the treaty would be enforced, since they had to blast their way out of Inean orbit. He closed the connection and wondered if Earth could receive it or not. He sat back in his chair, his hand resting on his chin as he stared out at the main viewer and returned to reflecting on the day.

Morris returned as planned and relieved the captain. Hackett got up slowly because every bone in his body ached from being tossed around by the Ineans and in the transport when it crashed. The venom from the spiders also inflamed his joints, which also ailed the captain. Hackett surveyed the bridge and headed for the elevator. The captain went to his quarters, took a hot shower, and changed into a fresh uniform. He noticed that it was his last one. A glance toward his duffel bag revealed it was overflowing. He picked it up when he left and took it to the laundry room. He didn't want to raise suspicions about his feelings for Benson, but the need to know her condition was concerning him. The fact that there was no information from the doctors did not bode well for her. He decided to take a chance and went to the medical deck to check on her. She was still unconscious and breathing with the help of a respirator. The doctors looked at him and pulled him aside. They told him she would not survive the night. There was little brain activity, and they were concerned about the amount of time she spent without oxygen to her brain. They feared she would be a vegetable if she lived, even though all her other vitals appeared good. The doctor told him that her proxy had instructed him to unplug in this instance, and her mother's name was on the proxy.

Hackett stared at the doctor, then back at Benson lying in bed with all the equipment hooked up to her. He looked at the readings on the monitors above the bed. He followed the many wires and small hoses down to her limp body.

"I can make the call, Captain, if you want," the doctor said as he studied Hackett.

"No, I will do it." He looked back at her. "It's my job. I have to do it. Let me have the folder."

Hackett walked over and sat with her for a minute, holding her hand and praying over her. He was unaccustomed to it and knew he was doing it wrong. He looked at her face, and it seemed so void of life. After a few minutes, he patted her on the shoulder and left. What else could he do? He went to the engine room at the rear of the ship to check on their progress, and it was going smoother this time. He left and roamed around the ship, eventually winding up in the officers' lounge. He sat at the bar, ordered a drink, and relaxed for a few minutes, thinking about how close they came to pulling it off. He thrived on these kinds of missions, but not this one. He was losing someone he had just met, and she had affected him like no other woman before. In the mirror, he spied the four gold captain's bars on his shoulder, and for the first time in his career, he began to think about quitting. He was starting to wonder what it was he was fighting for and why.

He thought back through his life at other women that he had liked, some more than others, and one in particular, he even considered marrying for a brief moment. This was before he went into the academy. Since then, it had been only one or two dates, and they were gone. Either he was called away, or they were. He decided he had been alone for the most part far too long, almost 20 years since he considered marriage to Allison. He ordered another drink and pondered the What ifs." *What was she doing right now?* He wondered. *Was she even still alive? What if he never went into space? Would all of the missions he went on have turned out all right? Would it be better? Maybe his greatest mistake WAS going into space. Maybe by some strange twist of fate, he chose the wrong path, and now the universe was out of sync*. He chuckled to himself at the thought that he, Shawn Hackett, could cause the universe to be out of sync. What would have happened if he decided to stay at Inea and nuke the daylights out of every city there? Now then, he could have really left his mark on history, or would that have mattered in the bigger picture? He had no idea. He decided that his own importance was just that, self-importance. Outside of his own sphere of influence, he didn't matter. If he disappeared right now, the universe would go on without him just fine.

He looked back up into the mirror. H*ow did I arrive at that answer, thinking about my past?* He wondered some more and ordered another drink. "Rum and Coke, hold the Coke," he told Harold, the bartender. Harold gave Hackett a grin, more out of politeness than actually finding Hackett's humor funny, mainly because he ordered the drink the same way every time.

The bartender, Harold Linques, watched the captain and chose not to talk to him. He knew Hackett would have to sort this out on his own. It was something that would take time. Hackett knew it as well. Time, it appeared, was something they had plenty of right now.

After an hour, O'Toole paged Hackett. "Captain, this is O'Toole. We are ready to fit the new Hafnium Carbide into the grid, sir."

"Hold on, Commander, bridge..." Hackett called.

"Yes, Captain?" Morris replied.

"O'Toole is ready to swap the matrix. What is our status, and are there any other ships in the area we need to know about?" Hackett asked.

"We are all right for the moment, sir, and Mr. O'Toole should be able to take his time," Morris replied.

"Very well, Mr. Morris. Shut down the drive and let it cool, Mr. O'Toole, when you are ready. Hackett out."

"Yes, Captain," they both said before the channel closed.

Hackett pushed his drink away, sat back with his eyes closed for a few more minutes, and thought more about Allison until Ambassador Channing brought him back to the present.

"Captain? Captain?" Channing asked while hanging over him like a vulture.

"Yes, Ambassador?" Hackett said groggily. Channing noticed he had dozed off and felt bad for waking him.

"Captain, I just wanted to say that you did a good job down there the past few days. I don't think this mission would have succeeded any other way, sir," Channing said as he sat beside him.

Hackett looked at him, dumbfounded. "What do you mean? We got a peace deal signed with the Ineans, and they proceeded in trying to kill us as we left. I'm unsure what we accomplished besides getting beaten up and our two women officers being humiliated down there. One of them is in sick bay, barely alive. Please explain how you rate this as a success?" Hackett was upset.

"Captain, I know you don't see it now." He paused a moment before continuing. "I am trained in this area and know this will make a difference over time. The Ineans are difficult to reason with."

Hackett thought about that last statement and nearly laughed out loud at the "difficult to reason with" comment. If he had his way, he would have leveled the planet once and for all.

Channing was still speaking. "Add to that the Kosuan and Angowains, and you have a recipe for trouble. But you and your team got through all of that and secured a deal for us. Now the hard part is for all parties to enforce it." Channing sat on a bar stool next to Hackett and stared at him for a minute. He knew Hackett didn't buy it, but it was true. "Captain, this will go in my full report to the president, and it will all be positive. I will also put in a recommendation to promote Lieutenant Commander Benson to Commander. She is ready to move up, and with Commander Morris leaving when we get back, you will need a first officer."

Hackett nodded. For once, he agreed with the Ambassador. "I was planning on doing the same thing, Ambassador, so that would look good for her if it comes from you as well."

"I was also putting in for you as well, Captain. You should move up, sir." Now Channing was in dangerous territory.

Hackett thought for a moment. As he considered what Channing said, the prospect of quitting exited his mind for good. Hackett knew it would be a mistake to let his emotions of the moment dictate his life decisions. He knew where he belonged, thanks to Channing. Channing knew what Hackett had been thinking about.

He did make a difference. Humanity survived another day because of what he and his crew did. "I'm sorry, Ambassador, I belong out here. I was having doubts until now." He chugged his drink, and Linques refilled it without hesitation. "This is where I belong. I'm too young to be sitting behind a desk. Thank you anyway, sir," Hackett said as he took a sip of his drink and pushed it away.

"I appreciate that, Captain, and I have to concur with you. I will still tell them what they have." He slid off the stool and saluted Hackett, which he didn't have to do. Hackett stood up and returned the salute. He couldn't bring himself to tell Channing that Benson's condition was poor, and the doctors felt she wouldn't make it.

Hackett watched Channing leave the room. He looked around, adjusted his jacket with a tug to ensure it was perfectly straight, and proceeded out of the lounge. He walked around the ship, studying the beams and walls. He looked at the control panels and felt the rumbling of the engines powering down through the walls as he patted them. He also looked at the people under his command. He saw their faces and their confidence, and he continued walking.

SIXTY-TWO

THE CITY of Boston was still awake as the clock approached midnight. People sat by the reconstructed Hatch Shell on the Esplanade while the Boston Symphony Orchestra finished its concert, the last of the season, before moving indoors for the harsh winter. A light coating of frost had settled on the grass during this rather cold early October evening. Several hundred spectators huddled in groups and began clapping as the orchestra finished its performance.

People marveled and pointed at the strong northern lights flashing and rippling overhead. They watched as the ribbons of light swayed in the sky until there was a thunderous boom. The ground shook as spectacular lightning bolts crackled across the sky. Not a cloud in sight, but this was no ordinary lightning. This was lightning caused by the collapsing magnetic field, which was starting to affect the entire globe.

Musicians and people began to run for cover as the sky lit up brighter than daylight, and then back to darkness once again. The ground shook more violently this time, and the Hatch Shell cracked, with bits of the shell falling on the abandoned instruments below. Lights had gone out across the city, plunging it into a moonless darkness. A blackness so dark you couldn't see the person next to you. Then it was so bright you still couldn't see.

People stopped and looked up in awe as the plasma cloud swept past their planet and out into deep space. Then their attention was drawn towards a thundering sound from the ocean, which was getting stronger, and they ran away screaming. It was too late. A wall of water roared over their heads and crashed down upon them. The scene was the same from Newfoundland to the tip of Florida.

Water swept inland for miles, smashing buildings, vehicles, and everything else in its path, and then it began to recede, taking nearly everything it touched back out to sea.

The larger towers fared well, while the smaller and older buildings didn't. The wave swept back out to sea, bringing with it tens of thousands of people all along the coast who would never be seen again.

Foley and his team struggled with the station's rockets, but finally got them working as the station came within 10,000 miles of being torn apart by the plasma cloud.

He still had one concern: the scientists on the observatory. He had not heard from them in hours, and there was little hope for them now.

SIXTY-THREE

THERE WAS BLACKNESS EVERYWHERE. An intense white light began to shine in the distance. Benson lay on the floor in the fetal position. Her eyes fluttered open. Slowly rising to her feet, she stared at the light. She looked down and saw she was wearing a sheer white robe, nothing else. She was standing barefoot on a floor that was neither hot nor cold. She pondered whether a floor was beneath her. She patted herself down and found no injuries. She reflected on the images of people in similar clothes from her visions and wondered where she was. Benson took a few steps and still needed to figure out if a solid surface was beneath her. She looked about and finally turned towards the light. She held her hand up to shield her eyes from its blinding intensity. There was no pain. There was no warmth or cold. A feeling of contentment washed over her, and she was compelled to move toward the light. She placed one foot in front of the other and walked slowly forward. Again, there was no floor, just the perception of forward motion with each step. It was like walking on air. She stopped at a familiar voice.

"Tamora, it is not time yet for you to come here," the voice stated softly and calmly.

"I don't want to go back," she said without emotion as she thought back to the Hell she had just come from.

"You have done much in your life. There is, however, much more to do, and I need you to go back," the firm voice stated.

An image appeared in the nothingness. It was her lifeless body on the flight deck, with her clothes all burnt and soot all over her face. She saw her shirt ripped open and the medics working on her. They placed the paddles on her, and her body jumped. She saw the monitor flat-line. She was dead.

"Am I dead?" she asked. Then she thought back to her vision earlier. "This isn't right." She said as she watched Hackett take her hand. He leaned over her, mumbling. She watched from above as the medics continued to work on her. "What is the captain doing?"

"He is praying for you." The voice stated. "You need to go back. There are tasks you need to do in preparation for the end."

She collapsed to her knees and bowed her head to the light. Her skin tingled from the words spoken. It was the first physical sensation she had experienced since waking. She had become speechless. In awe of her surroundings, she began thinking about the last mission. She knew she had done many things wrong, many things unworthy of passage to where she was now, many things she didn't take the time or care to take the time to atone for. But yet, she hadn't been cast into her mind's vision of Hell. A small tear rolled down her cheek as she watched him holding her. "I am sorry for what I have done," she prayed. "Please forgive me. I haven't been good, or, um, I'm sorry. I haven't been a good servant."

"Get up!" He said firmly. She looked up at the image before her while getting up onto her feet. The light had manifested itself into the shape of a human. The man glowed in a white light, and He spoke again. "He," the image said as he pointed to the scene on the flight deck, "needs your help. The two of you will work together. There is much work to be done in preparation. The people of Earth don't know me anymore and the time has come to fulfill what has been written," the voice said.

"I, I don't understand," she was puzzled by what he said to her.

The face looked so much like Harrison's that she found herself fighting emotions she had fought to repress over the years.

"You will when the time is right," the voice said softly. "The visions I sent you when you were young are just the beginning. There will be many more to come, each will carry its own meaning, and you will know what to do."

"I am just an ordinary person. I'm a screw-up. Why me? I am not worthy of the task. Until recently, I didn't consider myself a believer anymore," she said, not believing in her importance to history.

"You have come back because I brought you back."

"But why can't you do that with everyone else?" she asked.

"They don't listen. To them, I am an inconvenience, a noise to be drowned out with the cares and worries of life. People have chosen their way."

"I see," she said.

"You will have great difficulty. Listen closely. I will be a whisper in the back of your mind. Do what is right, and you will understand. There are others you will discover, and together you will bring many home." He paused as she looked up at him, "Now you must go and prepare the way."

"It is your will. I will go back to do your work," she said. Deep down, she had no idea how to pull it off.

The light went away in a brilliant flash.

In the medical bay, the monitors above her head beeped, indicating brain activity, where there had been none just a few seconds before. Benson could hear a beeping sound.

"Doctor, Doctor, she's coming to, sir!" The nurse exclaimed.

Benson's eyes fluttered open to the fuzzy image of a nurse over her. She moved aside, and the doctor took her place.

"Lieutenant Commander Benson, can you hear me? Can you hear me? Tamora?" She just looked at him for a moment. She remembered meeting with God, and a chill went up her spine. Now she was back here. "Can you hear me, Lieutenant Commander?"

"Yes, I hear you, doctor. I'm all right." She said in a hoarse voice. She couldn't believe it. She coughed a few times. One second she was, was where? Heaven? It couldn't be. It was too dark. It had to be, though. Now she is back on the *Saratoga*, light years from Earth. How could she do his work to save Earth way out here? It couldn't have been him. It must be the medication wreaking havoc on her mind. That must be it. After all, there was nothing during this mission that she was proud of. She knew she had done many things wrong, but still, it explained a lot.

The doctor looked over the monitors attached to her. He looked at the nurse, who looked back at him. "It's a miracle, Doctor."

He studied the monitors for a few more seconds as the flat lines scrolled off the screen to only show active brain patterns. "Everything is normal again. Brain wave activity, pulse, heart rate, blood pressure, everything. I don't understand."

They looked at her, and she smiled back. "I can explain it, but you won't believe me. I'm not sure if I really do. May I see the captain?"

"Um, yes, certainly. Let me find him for you," said the doctor. He walked away, dragging the nurse with him. "She should be a vegetable, if not dead," he said.

"Yes, I know, doctor, but did you see the look on her face? She saw God," the nurse said.

"Oh, please, nurse, there must be a reasonable explanation for this. I want to run some tests on her," the doctor said. He didn't want to believe.

"I'm telling you, doctor. I've seen this before. She was sent back for some reason," the nurse said.

The doctor looked at her in disbelief. "It's called a near-death experience or NDE. It's a scientific term used to describe what you say. There is no God involved here, nurse."

"You are wrong, Doctor, and the proof is in bed five." The nurse was becoming angry and had to walk away toward the comm pad on the wall and pressed the page button. She tried to hold her excitement. "Captain Hackett, please report to medical, Captain Hackett, to medical."

A moment passed, "On my way," he said, almost scared at what he was being called for.

. . .

Hackett walked along the corridor and prepared himself for the worst. Why was he so upset, he wondered. He had previously lost people under his command, which didn't affect him like this. What was his problem? He turned the corner, stopped before the door, and collected himself. The door opened, and he walked in, greeted by the nurse.

"There is someone who wants to see you, sir," the nurse said.

Hackett's first thought was the woman they rescued from Inea-Four. She must have woken up and wanted to thank him for saving her. *Yeah, that must be it,* he thought.

The nurse guided him around the corner and past the sleeping woman, Jane Doe, for now. All she had gone on about were her children, but she couldn't say her name. Why? Why couldn't she tell anyone her name?

The nurse guided him to bed five and pulled back the curtain. Benson sat up slowly and smiled at him. "Good morning, Captain."

Hackett stood in shock. He was supposed to call her mother hours ago for permission to "pull the plug." Luckily, there was still no contact with Earth, and now she sat grinning at him. He stepped towards her and threw his arms around her, and she returned the embrace. They held each other for nearly a minute. Then he pushed her back and wiped the tear away. "You're all right!"

"Yes, I am fine. I now know what I am here to do, Captain."

The doctor and nurse watched. The nurse wiped a tear away. The doctor threw up her hands. "Everyone has just gone nuts around here." Everyone looked at the doctor for a second with expressions of concern, then looked back.

"I see, and does that include me?" Hackett asked Benson in response to what she said, hoping it was true.

"Yes, it does," she said.

"Get some rest. We'll talk in the morning." He patted her shoulder and started to walk away. The nurse stopped him and gave him a tissue. He wiped his eyes. He tossed it into a waste basket nearby.

“Oh, captain. Can you do something for me?”

“What is it, Miss Benson?" he replied, turning back to her.

“In the top drawer of my dresser is a small box. Can you bring my gold cross to me?"

“Yes. I will be back soon with it.”

"Thank you." She replied as she lay back on the hospital bed.

He glanced at the woman they had rescued, sleeping in the bed on the opposite side of the room. “How is she doing?”

“Those Inean animals tore her up badly. She won’t have children ever again,” the nurse replied.

"She has children. That's all she would say. I need her name so we can track them down as soon as possible," Hackett said urgently.

"I'll work on it, sir, but she is in shock from what has happened to her."

“The Ineans have that effect on people. Do your best with her, thanks,” Hackett said as the door hissed open.

Once outside, he leaned against the wall and looked up at the light in the ceiling. It was brighter than expected. "Thank you," he said, then looked around to make sure no one heard him. He collected himself again and went back to the bridge.

One look from Morris told the story. “Captain,” he said, “you look beat, take the rest of the night off and rest, sir.”

“I’m fine, Commander,” Hackett replied.

“I know you are, sir, but we have this under control.”

"Very well, Commander, the ship is yours. See you later. Oh, and Lieutenant Commander Benson is fine," Hackett said. "Call me if anything happens," and he left the bridge.

“Thank you, Captain,” Morris replied.

The captain wandered along deck five and found Benson's quarters. He typed in his code, and the door slid open with a slight chatter. He walked in and looked around. Spartan was his first thought. He turned and opened the top dresser drawer, finding the small box. He popped it open and spied the sparkling gold cross and gold chain. He lifted it and studied it. He turned it over and read the inscription: "John 3:16." He looked at it again and knew she was special in some way. He put the box back in the drawer and closed it. He held the cross in his hand and returned to medical.

The nurse guided him back to where Benson was, and he sat beside her. Her eyes opened, and she smiled at him.

"I brought your cross." He said.

"Oh, good." She sat up and reached for it, but he placed it around her neck and reattached the clasp. She fixed her hair and let it fall against her neck as she lay back down. "I have been away far too long."

"I think I understand," Hackett said as he studied her lying in bed. Her face was bruised and cut from her fights with O'Toole and the Ineans. Plus, her crash into the flight deck a short time ago. "Get some sleep."

Aye, aye, captain." She saluted with a grin.

Hackett patted her on the shoulder and left the room.

Some time had gone by, and Lieutenant Bowers had a perplexed look on his face as he was taking readings from inside the ship. "Commander? Come look at this," Stephan Bowers said with a concerned tone.

"What is it, Lieutenant?" Morris asked, which he followed with a yawn.

"A strange energy surge in medical about fifteen minutes ago. It was only there for an instant. I have searched our database, and there is no record of anything like it, sir." Bowers was baffled by it.

"Is it still there, Lieutenant?" Morris asked.

"No, it's gone. There was a similar surge on the flight deck almost four hours ago, the same intensity as the other one." Bowers replied.

"What are the exact times, and do you have any theories?" Morris asked.

"Twenty-two minutes ago and at four-twenty-six this morning," Bowers answered.

Morris hit the comm pad. "Medical?"

“Dr. Natachi here,” the doctor replied.

"Doc. What time was Commander Benson resuscitated on the flight deck, and did something happen down there just recently?" Morris asked.

"Um... let me see," the doctor said as he flipped through the stack of papers on his desk. "The official report from the medic was that they got a heartbeat at four twenty-eight this morning and, yes, something bizarre happened about twenty minutes ago." The doctor left Morris hanging.

“What was it, Doctor?” Morris was eager.

"Yes, one minute. Nurse," he said, carrying two conversations at once. "About twenty minutes ago, Lieutenant Commander Benson had no brain wave activity to speak of. A minute later, she was sitting up and joking with us like nothing was wrong," the doctor replied.

“I see,” said Morris.

"You don't understand, Commander. She was dead, cold when they pulled her out of the transport. Her brain was dead. She was kept alive by a machine. Next minute, she was perfectly fine!" the doctor exclaimed.

"Thank you, Doctor, the information was helpful." Morris turned off the communication and looked at his arms. He had goosebumps all over him.

Morris looked at Bowers. “Lieutenant, between you and me, we just witnessed the hand of God working a miracle.”

"Yes, sir, I know, sir." Bowers stumbled at what his sensors witnessed. They both stared at the monitor, which displayed the two graphs with the apparent spike. The lower half of the screen displayed the analysis of the energy spike. It still had yet to find a match in the vast Alliance database.

"Mr. Bowers, you have the bridge. I'm going to medical," Morris said.

“Yes, Commander, good idea,” Bowers replied as he continued to study the graphs playing on his monitor, yet still no match. An energy surge of unknown type, unknown origin, and an energy surge with a profound effect on at least one member of the crew.

Morris headed for the elevator. He walked into the ship's hospital and stopped in front of the nurse. She brought him over to Benson. She was lying on the bed, fully awake. She sat up and saluted Morris. Morris was in shock. He stood there and just stared at her with his jaw open.

“Commander, quit looking at me like you’ve just seen a ghost.”

"I, um, ah, I don't know what to say," he said. He knelt down beside her and took her hand.

“Commander, you are freaking me out here.”

“Miss Benson, I was never a true believer until now. You being here is a miracle. I’m sorry. I just never witnessed an act of God before.”

“What are you talking about?” she asked nervously. Was Morris going to blurt it out? Was her secret blown already? Maybe this was it. It wasn’t to be a secret. Her presence would bring the few remaining “home” once the word got out.

The nurse stood a few steps back and watched. A chill went up her spine as Morris spoke. It added credibility to what she had said to the doctor.

"Our internal sensor logs recorded a power surge when you were brought back to life on the flight deck and again about half an hour ago when you woke up here."

“So you know about that then,” she said, looking at him.

Morris stood up and let go of her hand. He looked at her and then at the monitoring equipment by her bed. "Unbelievable. Who are you?" he mumbled. "Get some rest, Miss Benson."

“Y-yes, Commander,” she replied hesitantly.

Morris turned to walk out and stopped. He turned to her and walked back. He leaned over and hugged her. He stood up, saluted her, and walked away. Once outside, he stopped and took a deep breath. He walked to the elevator and went down to deck seven. He exited the elevator and walked to the ship's chapel. He entered, sat in one of the pews, looked at the statue of Christ, and broke down in tears as he began to reflect on his life and all the mistakes he had made, which were numerous, especially lately. Among the latest were his orders to destroy Hackett's career and then his orders to kill him and Benson. He admitted to the empty room how he plotted to carry out those orders. Luckily, he didn't get his chance.

It was more than an hour later before he could collect himself. He wiped his eyes on his sleeve. He left the pew, walked forward, knelt at the railing, and prayed. He wasn't sure what he was doing, but it sounded right to him. He hadn't been in a church since he was a child, and he only knew a few of the words. He became upset with himself for his lack of knowledge.

Morris had never set foot in the ship's chapel before. He only thought he believed until tonight. He made a promise to God to do his best from now on. He asked for a way to save his brother and sister from the vice admiral's hit squad. He finally finished and left the chapel. For the first time, he felt like a weight had been lifted from him. He felt good. He felt alive. He went to the head, splashed water on his face, and wiped it off. Morris returned to the bridge and took the captain's chair back from Bowers. He sat there with renewed purpose.

In the 23rd century, most people had given up hope. After centuries of war and the Earth dying, people abandoned religions and tore down the churches in favor of barrooms and strip clubs. Human society had become so dismal that people lived for the moment because there may not be a tomorrow. Murder, rape, and sexual assault became so commonplace that there was no way to police it anymore. The morality Hackett spoke about on Inea was from another time, not the present time—a more Utopian view held onto by just a few people now.

“O'Toole to bridge,” came the page from engineering.

Morris jumped. He looked around. Good, no one saw that. He pressed a button on the captain's chair. "Morris here, go ahead."

"Sir, we are ready to bring the quantum drive back online."

"Go ahead, Commander, let's go home."

There was a shudder and a slow, rhythmic, pulsing rumble through the ship that grew faster and faster over the next few minutes. "All systems nominal, bridge, you can engage the engines at will," O'Toole stated with excitement.

"Thank you, Commander. Helm, set course for Earth, maximum sustainable speed," Morris said.

"Setting coordinates, quantum six, aye, sir," the night shift helmsman said. The ship turned slightly to port and jumped to star speed. The engines stabilized, and the ship smoothed out.

Everyone on the bridge let out a sigh of relief. They knew they were finally going home from a difficult mission. Morris finished his log entries and left the bridge to Bowers.

COMING DECEMBER 2025

Book 2 of the Inean Debacle series.

Eye of the Storm

Captain Hackett's troubles are just beginning as he and his crew are rescued from a frozen wasteland. Corrupt leaders working with dangerous aliens discover that Hackett holds crucial information that will expose the treacherous ties between them and the malevolent Ineans.

Hackett is pulled into a one-sided court case with no way out. His chances of surviving are slim, loyalties are tested, and the line between friend and foe is blurred.

As the bizarre court drama unfolds, one person dares to risk life and career to help him.

www.ingramcontent.com/pod-product-compliance
Lightning Source LLC
Chambersburg PA
CBHW020253120726
47904CB00001B/187

* 9 7 8 0 9 8 5 2 6 1 7 7 1 *